I0818332

DANGEROUS WAYS

THE BOOKS OF WINTER:
BOOK ONE

R.R. VIRDI

Dangerous Ways
The Books of Winter: Book One
R.R. Virdi

Acknowledgements

Oooh boy, this is going to be a long one. First, as always, my wonderful and patient editor, Michelle Dunbar. My lovely cover artist, Sarah Anderson, for putting up with me. Lacey Sutton for her wizardry. Cayleigh Stickler, an amazing editor to work with and help slap on the final polish. My fan club for all their love and support. Thudsquad and Austin Lee Blanton for giving me a certain surprise. Thanks to my betas for doing your best. And lastly, to my mentor and best friend, Jim Hurd, for always being there for me and being a great role model.

Also by RR Virdi

The Grave Report

GRAVE BEGINNINGS

GRAVE MEASURES

Short Stories

"CHANCE FORTUNES"—THE LONGEST NIGHT WATCH ANTHOLOGY

"A BAG FULL OF STARS"—ALWAYS STARDUST ANTHOLOGY

"CHANCE DEALINGS"—THE LONGEST NIGHT WATCH ANTHOLOGY, VOLUME 2

"CHEATERS AND FORTUNES"—THE LONGEST NIGHT WATCH ANTHOLOGY, VOLUME 2

What reviewers are saying about Grave Beginnings:

"I believe R.R. Virdi belongs with other Urban Fantasy greats like Jim Butcher. The Grave Report is sure to go far and only pick up more fans with each successful novel. I can't wait to see where R.R. Virdi will take us next."—A Drop Of Ink Reviews

"Fast paced, humorous, with action and drama on every page and paragraph, this paranormal thriller is reminiscent of one of my all-time favorite authors. This is like Jim Butcher's The Dresden Files but with a flavor all its own. RR Virdi is fame-bound with this series. If you like Jim Butcher, you'll enjoy this one. Highly Recommend."
—CD Coffelt—Author of The Wilder Mage

"A fast paced story with great characters, I loved the story and fell even more in love with the future possibilities… Virdi maintains both the suspense of the case at hand, and the character's past and current transformation, making us feel both for the victim and the investigator. He excels at action scenes - I have rarely read books with such well-described yet fluid action scenes."—Shadow and Clay Reviews

DANGEROUS WAYS

Chapter One

When I stood here well over a hundred years ago, Longacre Square was the center of New York's carriage industry. Today, Times Square was a colored pinwheel caught in a blizzard. A neon-washed blur of flashing screens and scrolling marquees. The streets thronged with endless crowds, everyone bundled tight against the snow.

As good a place as any for my sentencing.

There would be an inquisition first. There always was. Old people loved tradition, even when it carried little meaning. It would be a formality—nothing more.

I turned up the collar of my gray trench coat against the buffeting December winds and ice. An occasional flurry of snow made its way through, causing the muscles in my throat to stiffen. I rubbed a hand across my neck, realizing that if I didn't figure something out, I could kiss it goodbye.

I wasn't too fond of that outcome. I'm rather attached to my neck.

A gentle throb filled my shoulder as someone jostled to move past me. The side of my coat brushed aside. The person's fingers moved with deft purpose.

At one point in time, this place was known as Thieves' Lair.

I shifted my weight, bringing my hand up and clamping it around his wrist. I twisted; he stumbled forward—empty-handed.

He gawked at me, off balance. The kid was mid-teens—red hoodie, jeans, remarkably plain-faced.

I waved an admonishing finger, and he took off. It wasn't worth pursuing. The wallet was empty. I'd learned long ago to stow my valuables somewhere harder to reach. My hair plastered against my skull as the storm built. I ran my fingers through the dark locks, shaking my hand free of excess water from the snowfall.

People bustled by, making it difficult to navigate and, more importantly, clear my head.

Inquisitions weigh heavily on a man's mind.

A sickly sweet smell tickled my nostrils. I stopped abruptly, causing an agitated huff of breath from the person trailing me. They swore as they stepped by, casting a glare over their shoulder. I ignored them. Instead I focused on the disheveled man sitting with his back against the aged concrete.

His skin was dark and weathered like old leather, covered in a mat of wiry, coarse hair of steely gray. Thin strands, like fishing wire, hung from beneath his woolen hat, a patchwork of red and yellow yarn. He spread his mouth upon seeing me. Yellowed teeth—some of which were missing, others crooked and chipped—greeted me. He held out a dry, cracked hand. The fingernails were overgrown and caked in grime. His canvas coat, several sizes larger than him, rustled as he moved.

And he reeked of the smell you'd expect to find in a candy store.

I didn't expect to see his kind sitting on the street, begging, with his legs buried beneath layers of tattered blankets. I reached into my coat, dipping my fingers into the breast pocket. Removing my real wallet, I flipped it open. Something jingled.

The old man's earthy eyes sparked with a hungry gleam.

I pulled out several small bills as I fished for something else. The greenbacks did nothing for him. He didn't spare them a look. Copper coins fell into my palm as I upturned the wallet. He jerked, restraining the impulse to lunge forward. I spread the pennies between my thumb and forefinger, making sure they were in his view. Bowing my head, I held them out for him to take. His hand darted out with surprising speed, but I pulled mine back in time. "I want your ears to the ground; you hear of any trouble from the other side, let me know? I'm in enough of it as it is."

He nodded, his eyes never leaving the coins.

I smiled and dropped them into his palm.

A McDonald's cup appeared out of nowhere. It might as well have been magic, but I've seen enough of that to know it wasn't. The cup was near the point of overflowing with coins, copper ones.

Old people aren't the only ones bound by tradition. Some creatures are just as stubborn in breaking habits.

I touched my first and middle finger to my forehead and gave him a mild salute.

He returned a wide smile.

A strong chill racked my body, and I pulled my coat tighter. The bottom of my jeans pulled tight against my ankle when I took a step. I looked back over my shoulder. The old man nodded to one side. I followed his gaze.

Coming down the street towards me were two figures wrapped in more layers than the weather warranted. The muscles in my back stiffened. I kept my eyes on the approaching duo. If the smell of sweets wasn't strong before, it was overpowering now.

The sides of their parka hoods were drawn shut, obscuring their faces. One wore blue, the other black. They were built with the proportions of competitive bodybuilders. I kept my eyes trained on them, making the effort to keep my lips from moving as much as possible. "Friends of yours?" I chanced a look at the old man from the corner of my eyes.

He offered a hapless shrug, rubbing his fingers together in a symbol that couldn't be misconstrued for anything else.

I exhaled through my nose and fished out a handful of pennies, tossing them to him without looking. "Advice?" I wasn't sure if he heard me through my tight-pressed lips.

"Run." His voice was like thick smoke.

My hand brushed against a flat sliver of metal in my coat. I clenched a fist around it and thought again. I was already in trouble. Starting a fight on the streets of New York would ensure a one-way outcome in my sentencing, even if it was self-defense. I heeded the homeless man's words.

I turned on my heels and ran—

—and felt something impact my chest, sending me reeling. The newcomer fell to the ground, scrambling to avoid passersby who shot the pair of us odd looks as they walked on. The hood of their oversized, gray sweatshirt managed to stay up. A pristine white bandana hid most of their face. Truth be told, I paid little attention to strangers on the street. I'd seen too many thousands over the century.

I offered the fallen stranger a hand, casting a quick look over my shoulder. The pair following me hadn't made any hasty moves. They strolled towards me at a casual pace. A perfume of cotton candy spread over the area, noticeable by the crowd who covered their mouths and noses as they went about. Clothing rustled as the hoodie-clad person righted himself. He brushed a caking of frost from his jeans.

"Sorry." I took a step towards him, offering an apologetic smile.

He tilted his head to the side, staring past me.

I followed his look.

He went rigid when his gaze fell on the parka-clad pair advancing towards us. The pair stopped. Even beneath the heavy jackets and layers, it was obvious when they tensed. Their posture shifted in the subtle manner of a predator spotting prey. Both men hunched, setting their massive shoulders, glaring past me.

I turned back to look at the person I had bumped into. It was a moment's stare. The kind when a deer sees the pack of wolves hunting it.

And that's when I was thrown to the wolves.

The gray-hooded-figure lunged, using all of his weight as he crashed into me. Both palms slammed against my chest. I stumbled back as he tore off. Arctic needles pricked my hands as I landed against the freezing sidewalk.

The burly pair of men burst into action, moving in long strides that should've been limited by their restrictive clothing.

I scrambled to my feet, tensing for a fight.

An arm built like a large log struck my shoulder,

pushing me aside. The second of the pair rushed by, shoving me the other way. I tumbled to the ground.

There was something else under the pervading odor of sweetness they oozed. I fought not to retch against the undercurrent of raw sewage, badly preserved fish, and rancid meat.

I knew that smell. And I knew well enough to stay out of the way of monsters.

Stubble tickled my palm as I rubbed my hand across my face and I spat. "I don't need this, not today." I righted myself and watched the pair chase after the bandana-wearing person. The trio made quite the scene through the crowds. The figure in the hood slipped between people with practiced deftness and skill. The mountainous duo didn't bother with subtlety.

I flexed my fingers, pumping a fist several times. *Don't do anything stupid. You can't afford any more slip-ups. Don't get involved.*

"Damn it." I took off after them, taking the same approach as the pursuers. "Move!" My forearm slammed into a man's back as I rammed him to the side. I didn't turn back to see his reaction. I didn't need to; I could hear the string of obscenities.

Pursuits aren't about being fast, being agile, or even being smart. They rely on keeping your quarry in sight. As long as you have an eye on them you can track them, wear them down, or come up with a multitude of ways to catch them. If you can see them.

It wasn't easy in the crowds of Times Square. The longer the chase went on, the higher the chance of losing them.

I maintained a line of sight on the one wearing the blue parka. My throat dried and ached the more I inhaled the winter air. The mass of people swirled together like watercolors. I pushed the crowd from my mind, homing in on the dark hues of the parka. I leapt, twisting my profile to slide through a gap between people. I landed hard. A jolt radiated through my shins as I almost slipped on the frosty sidewalks.

The blue coat vanished into the crowd.

"No!" I picked up my pace, barreling through the masses and eliciting angry shouts and threatening gestures. A flash of dark blue turned down an alley. I sped up, pumping my arms for what good they would do. I approached and took the turn too fast. I suffered for it. A fist-sized pulse flared within my shoulder as I ricocheted off the brick wall. I grimaced, rubbing the spot. There would be a sizeable bruise.

"Nowhere to run now," a voice called from the shadows. It was guttural, awkward. I imagined a bullfrog learning to speak English.

I squinted, trying to peer through the evening light and darkened length of the alleyway. The dark blue figure advanced towards something unseen. The person in the gray hood, I wagered.

"Mine," grumbled another voice. A second later, the figure I had dubbed "Blue Hood" stumbled into my vision. He snarled and hunched, taking an aggressive stance.

Blue Hood grumbled. The air around him bowed and waved. Even the snow avoided the area around his body. The noise intensified and, for the briefest of moments, I felt it as a gentle pressure against my skin.

I regretted my involvement.

Blue Hood took a step toward their hidden cohort. "Not yours. Mine!"

His pal answered back. "Boss don't care. Just wants 'em gone. Mine. I'm older."

The blue hooded one bristled. "I'm bigger." They took a step into the dark. If things got out of hand, whoever was in the gray hoodie could get seriously injured—or worse. Two sets of basso rumbles echoed down the alley.

That settled it. I set my jaw and walked towards them, trying to close the distance as best I could. When I was close enough to be heard, but still out of arm's reach, I barked, "Hey!"

The deep rumbling ceased. I couldn't see a thing, but

felt their eyes. The pair of them stared at me. I raised my hands above my head, hoping to appear as non-threatening as possible.

"Hey," I repeated, trying to keep their attention on me.

"Who are you?" asked Blue Hood.

"Hrmm, leave," ordered his pal.

I was sorely tempted to heed the advice. Getting involved was my problem. One that had landed me in an inquisition. Some people never learn.

I took several more steps, praying they would take no hostile action. "I just want to know what's going on. When two people follow a third down an alleyway, it raises questions."

The cavernous grumbles echoed again, but I pressed on.

"Go away—"

"—or you next," cut in the second voice.

"Next for what?" I was close enough to make out the pair now, their outlines at least.

Another rumble left their throats. I could see the vague shape of the third figure, huddled against the brick wall at the end of the alley. He shuddered, arms wrapped tight around himself. I had a feeling it had nothing to do with the cold.

I let an edge of heat into my voice. "Next for what?"

I sucked in a breath as my feet left the ground. Two fists clenched the collar of my coat, holding me with ease. The hood of the black parka fell back to reveal the face of gruesome man. It was too solid and layered in generous mass. There was no grunt of effort as he shifted his body. The world sailed by.

Pain blossomed across my left shoulder blade, making its way to my right as I hit the ground, rolling through the snow. I blinked. The muscles in my throat fought for air as my lungs pumped in futility. Lying there was not an option, and doing something—anything—was beyond my ability. The gray-hooded figure was within arm's reach. My head lolled to the side. The man in the black parka approached.

He cracked his neck. The air around him shimmered,

and his features changed. There was no subtle transition. His head and face increased in mass, becoming inhumanly thick and flabby. The creature's skin was a pale, unhealthy gray with a wet sheen. Purplish lips, missing a chunk of flesh, pulled away from his mouth. A handful of teeth remained, chipped into sharp edges. Bits of rotting meat wedged between them.

The putrid odor increased.

Fabric tore as the monster took its true form. It towered well over eight feet, built of ropey muscles engorged to grotesque proportions. The creature's body was bare save for a haphazard assortment of clothes tied together in a makeshift girdle. Its hands dwarfed my skull, and, if things continued the way they were, those hands would crush my head.

"Trolls." I coughed and spat. "It had to be trolls."

The advancing creature was missing a fair bit of his left ear. It looked as if it had been gnawed on. It pointed to me. "Mine." The troll jabbed a finger at the shivering figure behind me. "Yours."

Blue Hood chortled and followed his companion's example. He dropped the illusion. Shreds of clothing fell to the ground.

The bitter winds and having been tossed by the troll left my fingers hesitant to move.

"This is bad," someone whispered behind me.

I grunted, trying to dig into my coat.

"I'm sorry for this," said the man in the gray hoodie.

"For what?" I turned to look at him, and for the first time that day, my loss of breath had nothing to do with physical reasons.

His hand slashed diagonally through the air. Silver light burst into existence; a tear in the space before me.

A Way. The stranger had opened a Way.

My collar constricted against my throat as he hauled on my coat. "Come on!"

Both trolls let out defiant snarls and lunged. I kicked, bringing myself to my feet without proper balance. I tumbled back. My newfound friend held onto me.

We fell through the tear.

Chapter Two

Times Square was dense, thickly populated, and sported a symphony of colors. Old, with an air made up of chemicals and smog. The kind that clings to skin. We had clearly left that behind. One color dominated the scenery around us: green. Unmarred, lush, vibrant green. The air was as thick as the city's, but richer, more alive—fresher.

Trees and plant life grew to heights unattainable in the mortal world. Lengths of shrubbery, standing well over seven feet, raced ahead to form intricate paths. This was a place untouched by man. It was enough for me to know where we were. Enough for me to regret getting involved.

There was a groan at my feet. I looked down at the source and sucked in a breath.

The hood must have fallen back during our tumble through the Way. Her hair was a shade of red that could have only come from a bottle. It hung past her ears in a layered bob cut. She reached up with a slender hand to remove the bandana obscuring most of her face.

I froze.

Her eyes were the color of fire opals, prismatic reds and oranges flecked with hints of green. They glimmered under the bronzed light falling upon us. The light within them intensified when she rose to her feet, brushing herself off.

"What's wrong with you, dude? Are you crazy?"

"I'm starting to think so." I kept my voice neutral as I offered her a hand.

She ignored it, removing her baggy sweatshirt to reveal a rumpled gray shirt. On it was a figure clad in black, armored like a strange samurai. Underneath it in bold white lettering: *We Have Cookies.* The shirt had seen better days. Its seam around the collar was frayed, and much of it was covered in dust.

She let the hoodie fall to the grass, wrapping her arms around herself as she rubbed them. Even at my age, I could appreciate her figure. It was the sort that could give younger men ideas and issues concentrating. She was a hair shy of five-foot-seven, lean and well proportioned. Her mouth moved to say something, but she cut herself short when she noticed our surroundings. Her eyes widened as she looked from side-to-side, ignoring my presence.

I gave her a moment to come to grips with our situation.

She spoke in hushed tones. "Where are we?"

"You...don't know?" I fixed her with an oblique stare. One didn't open a Way and not know where they were going. Something was wrong or she was lying. "You brought us here."

"Listen, jerkoff, I don't know if you've noticed, but my life is out of control at the moment. I have no idea what's going on, where we are, *or* why it's happening." Her voice cracked near the end.

I watched her eyes take on a hollow look. She stood in place, quivering. Bits of grime, sweat and tear stains dulled her fair complexion. Her white and black sneakers were heavily scuffed. Her close-fitting jeans were tattered near the bottom. The knees were torn and stained in a manner indicating they weren't done for fashion. She had been on the run for quite a while now.

"The only thing I know is...that you shouldn't have gotten wrapped up in this."

I silently agreed, but what was done was done. I'd gotten involved. No matter what I did, I was going to face the consequences. I decided it best to follow through. "We're in the Neravene," I said.

A blank expression went over her face. "That's part of the Shire, right?" She gave me a weak smile.

Weariness took hold and I rubbed my eyes with my thumb and forefinger, taking a moment to massage my forehead as well.

"Just...stay away from me, man. You wouldn't believe what's happening, or the things chasing me."

"Chasing?" I realized the stupidity of the question after I said it.

She glared at me. "Yes..." Her tone that suggested she believed me to be mentally deficient. "Like what happened in New York. Big guys that turned out not to be guys. Things trying to corner me in an alley."

"Right."

"They were monsters—"

"Trolls," I said.

"Right, trolls, of course. What else would they be?" she spat. "Monsters are chasing me. I don't know why, or why you stepped into this. I don't know what to do or where we are!"

"Me either. Because I'm an idiot. We can figure this out. And the Neravene."

She blinked before she looked to the side and muttered something I managed to hear: "Smartass."

I ignored the comment, deciding it best to explain what I could, learn what I could and, if possible, find a way out. "The Neravene is the world beside ours."

She turned to regard me, listening intently.

"It's the world of many worlds—theoretically, infinite worlds. It's the home of monsters and magic. Myths and legends. Creatures from stories you heard as a child, and some—if you're fortunate—that you haven't. Faeries, gods, dark and forgotten things, all of them have a place here. Some have managed to carve out entire dominions, kingdoms, and have considerable influence. This is a place with rules beyond any on the normal side. Time moves of its own accord here. Manners and knowledge can be more useful than any mortal weapon."

"My life's become *Once Upon a Time*...in a world of magical bullshit," she mumbled.

"Most people would have a hard time believing any of this."

She rolled her eyes. "I've been chased by monsters and

fallen through openings in the air that have me popping out all over the world—worlds apparently. One time I ended up in France."

I shrugged. "Not a bad place to be."

"If you speak French."

She had a good point.

"So what now?"

"You open another Way and take us someplace safe," I suggested. A gentle breeze stirred the wall of leaves and brambles ahead of us.

"I don't know how..." The girl looked at the ground as she kicked a tall patch of grass. She hugged herself tighter than before, shutting her eyes and rubbing her palms against them. "It happens by itself sometimes, normally when I'm scared, or stressed, angry."

"So what happened back there? I saw you open the Way by what looked like your own will."

"I was freaked out is what happened. I pictured a garden, and wanted to be far away—" She broke off. "I like gardens." There was something in her voice that made me not press the issue.

"Fair enough. Then we keep things simple. We, at the very least, move from here and keep moving until we find a way out by other sources, or you manage to open another Way."

She took several steps back, and her body tensed. "Uh, hold up there. You think I'm going to go with you? Look, we just met. Yeah, you tried to save me, and no offense, but you did a shitty job. I don't even know your name."

A spasm shot up from my back to the base of my neck. Sharing one's name in the supernatural world was a dangerous thing. Names are important. But I did it anyways. "John. Jonathan Hawthorne." I extended a hand.

She wiggled her fingers, debating whether she would take my hand. I remained still, trying not to startle her. Her hand balled into a fist, one she flexed several times, before she forced a smile and mirrored my gesture.

"Cassidy Winters." The first part of her name came out

clipped, forced.

I shook her hand, giving her a reassuring smile. "Is Cassidy your real name?"

She bristled under the question, releasing her grip on my hand. Cassidy turned her head and eyed me askance.

"If you want my help, I'd appreciate some honesty."

"Who says I need it? I've held out fine over the month."

A month. This young girl had been on the run, with no one else, no support or guidance—from monsters—for a month. Shutting my eyes, I breathed slow and heavy, trying to see if I could shut this away.

Three days. That was what I had, at best, to solve this problem. Three days hence, I would be on trial. Missing that date would lead to two things: hunting me down, and separating my head from my shoulders. There was the option to leave her. One I refused to consider. Three days...Christ.

"Think about it." I tried to keep my voice level. "You've been running for a long time, Cassidy." She flinched when I said her name. "I know about this world. I've been a part of it for a long time. A very long time."

"How long?" She continued looking at me out of the corners of her eyes.

"I lost track after a hundred years. If I had to guess, I would say I'm around one hundred and eighty."

Silence.

A hint of her tongue slipped between her lips before she bit down on it and stopped any reply. Cassidy folded her lips, wetting them as she dealt with what I said. "You don't look over thirty."

"Technically speaking, I'm not."

"Say what?"

"This is going to be hard for you to believe, Cassidy—"

"Funny, I could've sworn I used that line on you."

I suppressed a smile. She had attitude. Good. That would help her—us—with whatever lay ahead. "I'm one of the Timeless."

"Oh, word? Cool. Last time I checked that was a

nineties album."

I didn't know how to respond. I'm not well versed in popular culture. "The Timeless are men and women who stand outside of time. They're removed from the passage of it. We stand by and watch, record, observe, and are forbidden to get involved in the affairs of the world—mortal or otherwise." I waved an arm to everything around us.

"Uh...huh. How's the 'not getting involved' part working out for ya?"

"It would be better if you trusted me a bit more."

"Give me more reasons."

"I risked my neck to help you."

"I noticed. Great job." She clapped her hands in an exaggerated, slow manner.

"This isn't my first time getting involved. For someone like me, there are consequences if we do it too many times."

"How many times?"

"Three."

"How many times is this?"

"The third." Another gust of wind rolled by.

She put on an animated and ominous voice, making dramatic gestures with her hands. "What happens if you dick around in the world of mortals too many times?"

I dragged my index finger across my neckline.

"Oh. Thanks."

I nodded.

"So, you're in the penalty box, and I'm guessing this is going to make things worse. Death row?"

I nodded again.

Her voice came out rough. "Cassie. My friends—when I had them—called me Cassie."

I took note of how she said it. It came naturally to her, authentic. The name she really went by. That honest exchange meant a great deal, even if she didn't know it.

"Okay, Cassie, there's a lot going on in both our lives. I know a lot about both worlds, and I promise I'll get you out of here and see if I can get you some help."

"How?"

"There are members of the Timeless far older than I. Someone might know something to help you."

"Wait, aren't these the assholes that are going to Benihana you?"

I stared at her.

She extended her fingers and arm, stiffening them like a weapon. With a turn, she chopped the air. "You know, *shink*, *glurk*, good-bye rough, rugged, and handsome mug?"

"I'm too old for you."

She blinked. "Was that a joke? First off, I'm twenty-one. I'm old enough to do whatever. Drink, drive, and make bad decisions on my own. But props for the wit, Antiques Roadshow."

This was going to be a long trip.

I stumbled to the side, swinging my arms to fight for balance as the ground trembled. Cassie fell to her rump, wincing when she landed.

"The hell was that?"

A deep, resonating groan emanated from below, and around us at the same time.

"Uh..." Cassie got back to her feet, looking in every direction. She took a few steps towards me. The ground shuddered again. A deep and irritated bellow echoed. The groans continued, each one accentuated by another tremor. "I've seen enough *Jurassic Park* to know this is bad."

I tuned her out, listening, watching. The ends of the shrub-like pathway stirred. The wind wasn't blowing.

There are many places within the Neravene. Some of them are pathways, old ones—important ones. They often lead to places of power, or the domains of lords, or worse.

We were in one of them. The Long Gardens. A place far worse than the name suggested. It represented nature in its entirety. Pure nature, untouched by man. A place tied to the old world powers of the Earth. And it had a temper.

Bark creaked. Trees standing higher than any skyscrapers shivered, showering us with leaves. Branches twisted and furled like decrepit fingers stretching from a long rest. A strip of ground rose. The earth protested, and a root thicker than a python burst out.

Soil rained down, and I grabbed Cassie by the shoulder. I shoved her ahead of me. "Run!"

"Yeah." She took one last look at the tree fighting to uproot itself.

"Move!" I shoved her forwards, pointing to the passageway ahead.

Walls of flora surrounded us, and thunder echoed behind. The tree scuttled across the ground, its many roots moving like the limbs of an octopus. It wasn't fast, but it didn't need to be. Leaves peppered us as an invisible force stripped them from their branches. A series of lengthy, slender shadows danced across the ground, closing in on us.

"Duck!" We sank, struggling to move as the tree's clawed limbs raked the air above us. A sizeable chunk of plant life was gouged out of the wall to our left, only to grow back in seconds. I gave Cassie a quick look. "Are you okay?"

She huffed out an irritated breath. "If I wanted to run, I would've taken track in high school!"

"Why didn't you?"

"Netflix!"

"Can it help you now?" I pushed ahead, unable to see her reaction. Given her attitude, I imagined a fiery glare.

The greenery bristled, and my gut sank. Our surroundings burst into life with hostile intent. Thin, reed-like strands arced between the walls to form a thorny web.

"Watch out!" I tucked my head, pulling myself into the safety of my thick coat. Making my profile as large as possible without exposing any vulnerabilities, I tore through the sharpened blockage.

Cassie leaped through. A rogue vine lashed her cheek. She winced but didn't falter. "Which way?"

"What?"

She pointed ahead. "Look!"

I turned to find the path forked into four paths. Truth be told, I wasn't fond of any of them. The enraged tree bellowed again, as if frustrated it hadn't killed us yet. All light within the shrub maze dimmed as a shadow spread over it. The tree fell.

"Left!" I barked.

"There's two lefts. Which one?"

I let out a low growl then swallowed it. "Far left."

She nodded.

We hit the corner hard, but not fast enough. I turned and a sharp lance of pain sliced up my thigh. I gritted through it. My fingers closed around Cassie's shirt and I pulled. She collided with me, and I wrapped my arms around her as we tumbled.

A hellish symphony of cracking wood, breaking brambles, and quaking earth sounded off. The tree crashed. Dust, dirt, pollen, and white petals flew into the air, forming a cloud around us.

I blinked, staring at the gnarled branch that had landed a mere foot from us. Had the tree taken another step, it would've accomplished its goal. A gentle weight pushed against me. "Are you all right?"

Cassie coughed, clearing her throat. "You're a clingy guy, you know that?" She planted a palm against my chest and pushed herself off.

"It's been a long time since I've held a woman in my arms." I gave her a light smile.

She snorted. "Yeah? You'll have to keep waiting, buddy."

Whatever magic compelled the plants to come to life had ended. The shrubbery lost its color, fading to brown as it rotted. Soon, we were no longer walled in, but stood in a field of plain grass. Trees surrounded the outermost edges. We watched the scene unfold in silence.

"So...that just happened."

"Yes." I nodded.

"That was bullshit."

"How so?

"I oughta kick Tolkien's teeth in. Helpful trees, my ass!"

A gentle fire filled my gut, and I had to wrap my arms

around my torso as I rolled over. My laughter filled the field. The muscles in my stomach ached as I laughed harder.

"First reference you got. Ten points to Grandpa."

When I was under control and my laughter died, I said, "I told you, I'm technically thirty."

She rolled her eyes.

"Tolkien would have appreciated the joke."

Cassie did a double-take. "You knew Tolkien?"

"We talked, had tea. Nice guy, good listener."

She arched an eyebrow, silently prompting me to continue.

"I may have told him quite a bit about the supernatural, creatures of myth, and magic."

She blinked several times, putting it together. "Dude, I hope you've got a fat bank account packed with royalties."

"Yes, to the first. No, to the second. Hundred-plus years of income and interest is a wonderful thing."

"Don't suppose you could buy our way out of here?"

I shook my head. My palms were raw, and I had to shut my eyes to help me bear the pain as I pushed off the ground. I offered Cassie my hand. She took it without hesitation. A good sign. She trusted me.

After hauling her to her feet, I reached out to brush the leaves and debris from the back of her shirt. "Come on, we should keep moving."

"To where?"

"All paths lead somewhere. We just need to stay on this one long enough."

"Yeah, or like the fortune cookie you just quoted, we get eaten by something."

"You're pessimistic."

"For as long as I can be, but how long will that last?"

I fought to restrain another bout of laughter. "Touché."

With the walls gone, it felt harder to navigate my way out. The paths offered us some forced direction. Without them, we had nothing. As far as I could see, what lay ahead of us was endless green: plains and small, rolling hills. None of which gave any indication of how to leave the Neravene, except for my original idea—walking.

Adrenaline had run its course, leaving weariness behind. My posture sank, and I stuffed my hands into my pockets, bearing down on them to support myself.

"Hey."

I didn't stop moving. Time wasn't something we could afford.

"John."

I stopped. She had said my name perfectly, reminiscent of a tone mirroring one person's alone: my mother's. I suppressed a shudder. A mother's tone can always send a tingle down a man's spine.

"Yes?"

"Look, I know things just got crazy, being chased by Giving Tree back there...but, can we stop?"

I looked at her, giving her a silent response.

"Please? I don't get much time for rest or breaks with what's been going on. Especially with people, someone to talk to, someone who—you know—*knows* things about monsters and magic and all of this."

"Sure, we can stop. One thing, however: stay vigilant. We're not out of the woods yet."

Cassie arched an eyebrow, regarding me with a mixture of surprise and appraisal. "I don't know if you're being literal or a smartass."

"Yes."

Her body shook. She managed to hold out for several seconds before she lost control and burst into a fit of laughter. After a minute, she pulled herself together, coming to rest cross-legged on the ground. Her hands settled on her ankles as she leaned forward, getting comfortable.

I chose to remain standing.

"So," she said.

"So?"

As she exhaled, Cassie moved her arms back and used them to brace herself as she straightened and leaned back. "What else can you tell me about this place? I'd like to know more about not-so-Wonderland, since I've bounced in and out of here before, now that I think about it."

I didn't answer. Instead, I raised an eyebrow.

"Hey, I didn't stay long. Like I said, I don't have great control over this. It just happens. Sometimes I've popped into places that look like they're out of books or movies, then poof"—she clapped her hands—"I'm back in the normal world...just millions of miles away. The first time it happened, I was in my backyard. I don't know where I ended up, only that when I got back, I had been missing for eight hours."

"Time moves at a different rate in the Neravene. Worse, there's no accurate way to gauge the variances in its passage. Minutes can become hours...hours, days or longer. There are stories of people crossing over and losing years, Cassie."

She shuddered.

"Do you mind if I ask a question now?"

Cassie stared. Her breathing quieted. "Yeah, sure, I guess."

"Why are you alone? Where are your parents?" I would have gotten more of a response had I dropped a bucket of ice on her.

She looked at me, unmoving, unblinking, then her stare passed through me. "Mom's back home, in Baltimore." She cut herself off, turning to look off in the distance. "It's not exactly easy to go, 'Hey, Mom, guess what? I'm falling through weird portals into different places, and even worlds; my life's crazy.' I couldn't bring her into this." Cassie gripped herself tight, looking at her knees.

I dropped my voice to a soft and reassuring tone. "No, no you couldn't. But I'm sure after this is all said and done, she would love to see you again."

There wasn't a single tear on her face, but she sniffled. "Yeah," she said, her voice dry. "Then there's my dad." She broke off again; I didn't press it. "He walked out on me and my mom a long time ago. I think I was five."

"I'm sorry."

"Yeah." Her voice was still rough, and the apology passed over her.

"Are...are they both mortal?"

She looked at me like I was speaking gibberish. "No, they're frickin' faeries. Duh, they're normal. Kind of why I'm losing my shit with all of this."

"Right, sorry."

Cassie's mouth moved, but she didn't respond.

"Do you mind if I ask one more thing?"

She nodded.

"How do you do it? If you're mortal, in truth, you shouldn't be able to open a Way like that. You shouldn't be able to open one at all."

Cassie shrugged.

"Is there anything you can tell me? You said it happens when you're scared. Do you see anything? Feel something? Smell?"

A light breath left her lungs. She blinked several times and swallowed. "Honestly, it's a lot. It's kind of like an overload of everything."

I pursed my lips. That didn't sound right. From everything I knew about the Ways, opening one consisted of focus, control. There was intent behind opening one, knowing exactly where you wanted to go. It was never random, and there were limits to where one could go, regardless of power. Navigating the Ways was no different than driving on roads. You had to know the streets and where they lead. Without that, you couldn't access the roads necessary to reach your destination.

Cassidy Winters didn't seem to have that issue. Passing through and into places she had never laid eyes on, into worlds she knew nothing about.

She was powerful. And dangerous. More than she realized. Both reasons warranted her being hunted.

"What can you tell me? Choose an incident, any of them."

Her nose twitched, and she ran her tongue over her lips. "Um, when I ended up in France. I panicked. I was being followed by something. It was night. Whoever—whatever—they were, they weren't big and dumb like the trolls. They were shorter than me, wearing—I swear to God—a cloak. I started running and they followed. Don't ask me how, but they went urban ninja and were bouncing on the rooftops, watching me from up there. I just wanted to be away, anywhere.

"I've thought about France a lot. I wanted to go there once for a summer break. I kept running, and I just knew what to do. It was like hitting your head, a flash of colors, not just the reds you imagine. Red, flashes of lighting, white and blue, green and yellow. Between it all, I saw images of France I'd seen before. Posters, brochures, the occasional travel ad. I remembered a piece of a television show I saw once. I imagined what the beaches would smell like, the streets, and the food. I thought about how Paris would sound with all the people, traffic, and noise."

"And then?"

"And then I just wanted to be gone. I wanted to tear away everything in front of me and be somewhere else. I wished I could pull the air in front of me away, replace it with another place...and I did."

All of what she said sounded difficult and, to many a being, it was. Creatures with years of experience in navigating the Ways would struggle to do what she had. And she had done it with more ease than she knew. The Neravene had more rules than I could recount off-hand. Cassidy Winters had broken many of them. You cannot simply tear a Way to a place you've never been before. That's not how it works.

You have to know. Knowing—knowledge—it's power in this world. A person or creature has to have been to a place before, or have the knowledge of how to get there at least. They cannot simply open a Way and hope for the best. Yet Cassie was doing that on instinct.

One hundred and eighty years and, in all that time, I had never heard of something—someone—like this. The grass below my feet bowed to the side as a breeze flitted through. Nothing seemed out of sorts, but a solid lump formed in my stomach. I cleared my throat. "We should go."

"What's wrong?"

"Probably nothing. Just a feeling."

"Yeah, I can roll with that. A month of playing Carmen Sandiego with monsters makes you trust those feelings." I offered a hand, which she ignored. Cassie got to her feet without aid. She brushed her shirt with a few quick movements and patted her backside. Minute cracks rang out as she torqued her neck to the side. "Alrighty then, where to?"

"Anywhere but here." I took several steps, using my long strides to carry me a few feet away from Cassie. A faint glow of pale tangerine hung on the horizon. It seemed like as good a place as any to walk towards.

"Yeah, good point, but it would be nice if anywhere had an address."

"Addresses are irrelevant. Wherever you go, there you are."

"I think I heard that once in the school of No Shit, Sherlock."

"Buckaroo Banzai," I informed her.

"Well, sure, I guess there's bound to be some pretty wise strippers out there."

I breathed through my nose, fighting not to sigh.

The wind increased. Leaves danced, carried within a stream of air rushing by us. Debris from the earlier tree crash mingled with the gust of wind swirling past. Twigs, leaves and earth spun in a small storm. The wreckage whirled like a child's mobile.

"Okay, that's a ten on the weirdness meter."

"And what did the giant tree score?" I asked.

"Shut up."

The debris grew closer. Odd bits clung together, taking form. Grass rose to dwarf me, bending and widening like a curtain. Within seconds, the earthy material took shape: a bipedal figure. Its visage was masked behind a cloak of grass that spread over its face, as well as the rest of its body. The entirety of the mass was shrouded from sight, save for what I presumed were its eyes.

Pulsating orbs were visible from behind the grassy cowl. They shifted in size and hue. In truth, it looked like they changed material. One moment they were clods of dirt, the next, dancing blades of irradiant grass. I saw every imaginable color and style of gemstone pass by, the color and look of bark, and the orbs continued to morph.

A basso burble formed in its throat. The ground shook. It spoke and I felt pressure, like the world was tightening around me. My body grew weary, and my legs quaked, struggling to hold me upright. I glanced at Cassie. Her body was doubled over. She braced herself on her thighs.

"You are trespassing." There was no malice or harshness in its voice, only weight.

I worked to clear the invisible blockage in my throat. Spreading my fingers, I raised my hands in the universal gesture of calm and placation.

"You are trespassing. Leave now and no harm will come to you."

I took a chance and spoke. "Apologies, but we cannot. We stumbled into your domain by chance. We have no ill intent; we are trying to leave—"

"Immaterial. Leave now. This domain will not tolerate the touch of man. *I*...will not tolerate it," the being rumbled.

I didn't know much of the Long Gardens, but I had an inkling of whose domain they belonged to. I wasn't sure, but it was enough to prompt me to take another risk.

"Cassie," I whispered.

Her voice rose several octaves, coming out in a near squeak. "Uh...huh..."

"I need you to imagine something for me. Can you do that?"

"Uh...huh..."

The ground trembled. Finger-like cracks spread through the earth. It was like watching glass develop cracks only to have them worsen. Fissures formed around us.

"You are not welcome here. Leave now!"

"Cassie, picture a two-story building. It's made of brick, something that's endured for decades and it shows. A green sign with white, flowing lettering. I want you to smell cinnamon, sugar, and baking sweets. Imagine your favorite confectionaries as a child. Two large windows filled with cakes and stacks of brownies."

"I don't want to die hungry, John."

"Just do it," I hissed. "There's a yellow fire hydrant just outside, and a payphone."

"Okay, now what?"

"Be gone!" roared the entity. The ground erupted. Roots leapt from where its arms should have been, twisted and sharp.

"Cassie, I want you to be there, not here. I want you to pull the air away. I want you to be there!"

She trembled. Her face was a tight mask of concentration, but she did as I asked. Cassie swept at the air and it parted. The Way was different than before, a wide maw of the purest glowing white.

I sprinted towards her, praying I'd make it before we were impaled. The roots hissed by as I grabbed Cassie. "Rargh!" My leg faltered as heat enveloped my shin. I kept hold of Cassie and pushed through.

Chapter Three

Entering one of the Ways, in the best of circumstances, can be disorienting. What followed served to redefine the word. A sea of green melted into a cyclone of colors. Blaring lights, snow, and the shades of the mortal world. The transition happened in a flash.

I landed hard. Equal parts fire and ice arced through my leg. Finding my balance was a task. Cassie slipped under my arm, helping support me. Grunting took effort, but it was the only sound I could make.

"Oh my God!" Cassie let go of me and I stumbled. She grabbed my collar and reeled me back. A car horn sounded as a red and black cab swerved to avoid us.

"Asshole!" the cabbie called. His car slowed to halt a few feet from us and he leaned out. His face could absorb no more black. A cotton cap clung tightly to his skull. "Get your hooker out of the street!"

Cassie bristled, taking a step towards him. "Aw, hell naw."

The driver ignored her, turning back to mutter something under his breath as he eased his car down the icy road.

She stood there seething until I decided to redirect her attention. I coughed, nodding to my torn jeans.

"Oh, crap, you're bleeding!"

"There." I pointed to the building ahead. It was an exact representation of what I had described earlier. A small brick building, something that had endured close to a century. No one smell could describe the aromas wafting from it. Only one word to sum it all up: wonderful.

"Help me?"

"Yeah, duh." Cassie took my arm again, helping me

hobble through the street as we crossed onto the sidewalk. "What now? Looks like they're closed."

"She's never closed. Not for me."

"Ooooh, girlfriend or something?"

"She's too young for me." I winced. The muscles in my leg spasmed, tightening like an electric current passed through them. "I live here." The step up to the sidewalk caused a little whimper to leave my mouth. The winter climate did nothing to dull the pain.

"Now what?"

"This." I rapped the forest green door with my knuckles. Nothing happened.

"You're lucky I have a policy about kicking crippled old men."

"I'm not old," I groaned. My fingers curled into a fist, and I pounded on the door.

Metal slid against metal. Something clinked against the door. It was barely audible. A chain. The door juddered from the impact. "Ta-ti-a-na!" Each syllable was punctuated with another bang of my fist. A louder, more solid click sounded behind the door. I let out an agitated huff of breath as she took her time unlocking the deadbolt. The knob twisted, *finally*. Being over a hundred years old did not mean I'd mastered patience. Snow rushed in to fill the gap as the door opened, flowing into the store.

There was a fleshy impact. A rolling pin struck her palm, hitting it several times as she stared at me.

I forced a cheery smile. "Tatiana."

Her eyes were beautiful, the color of faded dollar bills with inner rings of pale gold. They hardened for a brief moment.

"Jonathan Hawthorne." Another wooden *smack* accompanied my last name. "Do you know what time it is?"

"No, no I don't. But since when have I been concerned with time?"

She arched an eyebrow. It was the same color as her champagne hair, which was pulled into a neat and out-of-the way ponytail. Tatiana was the embodiment of Nordic beauty. Taller than the average man, built with the lean, flat muscle of athletes without compromising her chest or lower half. If I didn't know any better, I would have said she'd cheated to attain the physique. But I did know better, and learned long ago to be wary near women toting rolling pins.

"I'd like to enter my home now. It's cold and we've had a long day."

Tatiana's eyebrow rose higher as she regarded Cassidy. "You brought a guest. A young woman. Here?"

I could feel her stare become telescopic. "It's not what you think."

She blew out through her nose. It was near enough to a snort, without becoming one, to be impressive. Tatiana pressed the wooden pin to her hip as her hands came to rest there. With a simple shift of balance, she stood at an angle and regarded me in silence.

"What does she think it is?" asked Cassie.

"Nothing. Tatiana, move. Please."

Her eyes widened before she finished her appraisal, finally taking notice of my leg. "You're hurt."

"Yes."

She flung her arms into the air and I flinched for fear of the wooden tool going airborne and striking me. "Of course." She scowled. "Don't track any blood on my carpets. I just cleaned them." She waved the pin at my face as a warning.

"I'm bleeding. I can't avoid that. Plus, you're the one keeping me out while letting the snow in."

The corner of her mouth twitched. A dangerous gleam filled her eyes, but she stepped aside, beckoning us to enter.

I placed a hand on the doorframe as Cassie helped me lumber in. The warmth of candles filled the place that was part-bakery and part-home. Tatiana preferred candlelight to illuminate her home during the later hours of the night, especially after closing.

Old stone and polished wood made up most of the bakery. A fireplace, set in mottled stone, housed a crackling fire in the corner. Everything from the counters, walls and shelves, was made from well-cared-for dark wood. The paneling on the sides of the refrigerated displays had been replaced with a burnished walnut, carved with images from Scandinavian mythos and legends. The place was colored in rich greens and earth browns like a forest.

Most of the products on display were various versions of sweet breads. One piece was a rainbow-colored knot of dough sprinkled with powdered sugar. Saliva built in my mouth as I stared at it. The blood loss was making me hungry.

Tatiana caught my stare, moving over to pluck a piece from the display. She lobbed it to me without looking. It was an effort to catch it with one hand. I fumbled the treat a few times, nearly dropping it altogether.

"Get him downstairs, girl," said Tatiana.

I could feel Cassie's body tighten. She didn't like being called "girl" or being ordered about. I remained silent. Groaning, I nodded to a pair of heavy-set ebony doors festooned in Nordic art ahead.

Cassie paused before the doors. "What's back there, the bat cave?"

"The pantry. Please stop talking." The pain searing my shin and calf doubled. The muscle shook of its own accord. "Tatiana," I rasped.

"I know!" Tatiana said. "You don't have to remind me. I'll get him."

"Thank you." I placed a hand on one of the doors and leaned into it. Cassie helped open the other. The smell of raspberries tinged the cool air as we passed into the back. Endless rows of jars lined racks, stuffed to the brim with fruit in the process of becoming preserves. I love raspberries.

Cassie's voice was dry and unimpressed. "Don't tell me you live back here, with the ingredients..."

I grunted. I limped past the racks, cupboards and equipment to a series of plastic flaps hanging over a doorway. Cassie followed along, holding me upright. "Through here."

She led the way through. We entered a metal cage set into a stone wall. "You sleep in a cage?"

It was like something out of fantastical Victorian novel. An elevator made of soft metals, polished bronze and brass. A beautiful thing, highly impractical, and in need of constant maintenance. I liked it.

Everything around me dimmed. My hand flailed around before I found the wire gate. I swung my arm, sending the gate crashing shut. "Lock it." My voice came out gruff, the moisture gone from my throat. I slumped against the wall as Cassie stopped supporting me. There was a *click, thud* as she locked the gate. "Lever," I croaked.

Breathing was difficult. My temperature rose and I was sweating. Poison.

"Found it."

I pushed off the wall, coming to stand in the center of the cage. My balance wavered. "Pull it." Metal moaned, gears ground, and the cage shivered to life.

"This has got to be the most rickety-looking elevator I've ever seen."

I didn't respond. I sank to my knees, focusing on slowing my breathing. Calm, deep breaths, which hopefully lowered my heart rate. Whatever the poison was, I didn't need my heart pumping it through my bloodstream any faster. Through my blinks, I was able to make out the aged stone walls as we descended. An itch developed between my ears, one I had no hope of scratching. Everything shook.

"Crap, this thing's going to fall apart. I'm going to die in an elevator with someone older than Dumbledore."

It took me a moment to rack up enough moisture in my throat to respond. "I'm. Not. Old." The elevator came to an aggressive stop that rattled the metal bars.

"Worst. Ride. Ever," muttered Cassidy. "Come on, Gramps." She knelt beside me, easing my arm around her. "Don't die. You're supposed to be helping me, not the other way around."

An indiscernible noise was my only response. Dull lights made up most of my limited view. A mess comprised of varied antiquities blurred by. "Chair."

"You know, this single syllable crap is annoying. What chair?"

"Red chair."

"Bravo." I could picture her scowl. "Two syllables. You're moving up. All right, here, let's get you down slowly."

My support vanished for a second. I fell an inch before Cassie's arms wrapped tight under mine, cinching around my torso. She lowered me into my favored seat, an ancient couch I had found at a yard sale in the seventies. It was the same shade of red as a child's fire engine, covered in velvet that somehow managed to remain perfect, and stuffed with clouds if I had to guess.

"Hot."

"This isn't the time to be hitting on me. Plus, I'm not into old guys." Her voice wavered as she made the quip.

Humor is a great thing to calm one's nerves. It deflects tension and heals wounds.

My coat stretched and pulled against me as she removed it. "Better?"

I lolled my head instead of making an effort to nod.

"Hey." She patted my cheek. "You okay? Hey! Say something all Buddha-like."

"It's good...to be...home." I struggled for breath after finishing.

She snorted. It was adorable to see a girl her age making such an indelicate sound. "Good enough. Crap, your leg's a mess."

"He's always a mess," came a tight, discontent, gravelly voice. "Aiyah, what did you do?"

"Who are you?" asked Cassie.

"The doctor, hsst!" Strong, thin fingers, calloused and wrinkled from age and work, cradled my leg.

"Shush me again and I'll break your little finger," Cassidy mumbled.

He ignored her, eyeing the wound I imagined. "Tch, bad. What did you do?"

"Got...involved."

"Yaaaaah, stupid is as stupid does."

I didn't argue. He had a point.

A quick burst of breath left his mouth, making its way across my exposed skin. "Can't do anything like this. Help me get his pants off."

"Say what?"

"Pants, girl. Help me get them off. You want him to keep bleeding or let the poison to kill him?"

"Poison?"

"Aiyah, yes. Hurry."

"So not how I planned my day." Her hands came to my waist. I could feel her breath as she undid my belt. "Stuck here with two geezers, trying to get one of their pants off. Ugh, this is how pornos happen. It is so not happening here. Not happening."

Honestly, I found her rant amusing. It helped with the pain, and there was lots of that.

Gasoline ignited within the wound and the surrounding area as the waistline of my jeans rubbed the skin. The only sound I could make was a sharp, pained wheeze. My stomach roiled like an ocean storm. Every inch of my body spiked in temperature. The only bit spared was my leg, which grew colder by the second.

"Alcohol. The good stuff; where is it?"

"Don't you have medical stuff to clean it?"

"Don't argue, child. Find it."

Consciousness was a task to cling to. I pictured Cassidy's reaction to being called a child. It helped. Maybe she would go as far as to hit the doctor for me. He deserved it on occasion.

"Man, this place is a mess."

If I could've spoken, I would've rebutted with a quote from Einstein about cluttered spaces and minds. It may have been a mess, but it was my mess.

"Here, is this any good? It looks expensive. I mean the bottle does."

When your vision dulls, your other senses compensate.

More than a century of living also helps in honing them. I heard the liquid slosh, the top being undone.

"Here, sniff." The doctor held the whiskey below my nose. I blinked, jarred by its strength. I smelled the dry aldehydes of hay, a hint of pinewood, and the sweetness of caramel. He clasped down a hair's breadth above the wound. "This is gonna hurt."

The smells dissipated when the bottle was pulled away. I could hear the liquor slosh around. My eyes were already shut, but I went as far as wincing. I set my jaw and tensed in anticipation of the burn.

Liquid left the bottle, but nothing happened. A dry rasp followed by a fit of coughs. "Ackh, tsch." Another bout of coughs. "The good stuff always burns."

"What about him?" said a scandalized Cassie.

"Need to steady my hands. Here." More whiskey sloshed.

"Yeah sure, what the hell? Monsters, magic, trees, and bullshit." I heard her take a swig. She let out a harsher fit of coughs. "Ugh, it's like someone splashed vanilla into paint thinner."

"Settles the hands and nerves."

I wanted to protest about giving her the expensive eighty-year-old liquor. At her age, I didn't think she had much experience with the harder spirits.

Cassie cleared her throat. "So does wine, but what do I know? My stuff comes out of a box by the gallon."

The doctor's hand shook. His grasp loosened as he chuckled. "Okay, hold onto your panties." His fingers were rods of iron, applying enough pressure that I thought he would do more damage.

My body shook as it was enveloped in a cold that made winter seem like a cool autumn's night. The limb went numb. Then came the other extreme, like my muscles were being grilled. The torn skin moved on its own. It felt like paper stretching too thin as my flesh folded, knitting itself together.

"Hey, old timer?" The doctor was taking a page from

Cassidy's book. Great.

"Will he...?" Her voice sounded like it was coming from further away. The weight in my skull increased and my couch seemed all the more inviting.

"Probably. He's a tough old coot."

I needed to keep Cassidy away from the doctor.

"He's stubborn, too stubborn, but that can be a good thing here. And he's survived worse. He'll be hungry—"

The doctor was right.

"Thirsty—"

I was.

"And sleepy."

It seemed like a good idea. Always heed the advice of your doctor.

***

The stiffness left my body when I woke. My muscles felt stringy, and my eyes protested against my decision to open them. A low groan escaped my mouth as I rocked my head from side to side, cracking my neck. My face snapped to the side as something flat struck my cheek. "Mmrgh!" I squirmed, placing a hand to my stinging cheek.

"He's up," said the soon-to-be-deceased doctor.

A face lined with eight decades of age greeted me. He had a complexion common in the Orient with all the features to match: narrow, intelligent brown eyes; thinned hair that had long ago turned white. If I were able to stand, the man wouldn't reach my chest. Cassie was likely taller than him.

A small domed cap, too small for any practical use, sat atop his head. He dressed in a black turtleneck and blue pajamas depicting a British police box. Unlike most doctors, he didn't carry any medical paraphernalia. His hands were coated in dried blood, and he wasn't perturbed by that.

"Yeah, I'm up, George." Every word pulled at the lining of my throat. "Why the slap?"

"Why not?"

I blinked, unable to refute that logic.

The pile of books resting on the floor tumbled over as

something rustled. Cassie rose from her crumpled sleeping position. She placed a palm to one of her eyes, grinding it there. Her arms went up as she stretched and arched her back. She let out a light yawn, smacking her lips as she did. "Sup, Sleeping Beauty, feeling better?"

"I'm not sure. I had a horrible dream; I came across a young girl with a big mouth and an even bigger problem. She was falling between worlds. Trolls were chasing her, and I signed my death sentence by helping her. Did all of that really happen?"

She looked down to the hardwood flooring. "Yeah, yeah, it did."

"Then I'm doing fine." I leaned forward, giving her a smile. "What happened?" I pressed a palm to my temple, twisting it back and forth, hoping to assuage the drumming.

"You were poisoned," said George.

"I gathered that much. By what?"

He shrugged. "Whatever it was, it was a pain to heal."

George held up his hands. Blood coated them to the knuckles and crusted his nails. That wasn't what caught my attention. Through the dark red veneer, his veins bulged like they had been replaced by steel cords. He gave me a knowing look. Something rippled below his skin, like a wave undulating through his veins. It rolled from his hand to his elbow before disappearing.

"Are you going to be fine?"

George exhaled, his voice coming out a bit drier than usual. "Probably. Going to be taking this though." He held up my whiskey. Half the bottle remained. "Good stuff."

"I know. It's worth a small fortune."

He gave me a lopsided, toothy smile. "That's my fee." His head fell back as he tipped the bottle. After a quick swig, he capped the bottle, sighing in pleasure. "Let me know if he has any problems, eh?" he said to Cassie.

She gave him a thumbs up before releasing another groan. George waved his hand in a lazy salute and turned to leave. Cassie groaned again.

"What's wrong with you?"

"Ugh, your booze is hardcore."

"You shouldn't have drunk it, regardless of what George said."

"Yeah, old people are taking advantage of me lately, it seems."

It was my turn to groan. She refused to let up with the old man comments. I'd lived for over a century. Physically, I was thirty.

"I don't suppose you have a magical hangover cure down here?"

"If I did, I'd be rich selling it—richer."

"Yeah, for real. What's with this place? It's like the Batcave—a really nerdy, less gothic, Batcave. Without his car and all the—you know—cool stuff."

My home was one large room. The size could dwarf many a cathedral. Bookshelves reserved for the oldest libraries and universities ran along the walls without a break. Each one overflowed with books, loose pages, and random objects plucked over the decades. A warm glow of yellow spread across the place, coming from the lighting above.

My place was a mess. Random tables made of varying woods in different hues littered the place. An ebony piano—never played—covered with more books. There were maps of the mortal world and beyond. Antiques and magical items were in whichever spot I believed best upon returning home with them. And there was plenty of "cool" stuff. A point I vocalized.

"There is no end to *cool* stuff in my home."

She laughed, throwing her hands over her mouth to stifle it.

I pushed my way out of the chair, teetering on my heels for a moment, before I tapped her skull with my knuckles.

"Ow, oh my God. Aagh," She cradled her head. "You're such a dick."

"Don't drink and criticize."

She mumbled something incoherent under her breath. After she had finished massaging her head, she pointed to George, who was stepping into the lift. "So, what was that about?"

"He healed me."

"Yeah, I got that. He put his hands on you and, boom, your leg pulled itself together. I almost upchucked, no joke."

"Glad you didn't."

She stared, waiting for an answer. When I gave none, she pressed for one. "So, he a paladin or something? I mean my whole life's gone D&D anyways."

"No. If you want to know more about him, ask him." There was a loud clunk as the elevator came to life, pulling up and away.

"And Tatiana?"

"Ask her."

"Mysterious characters are so uncool."

I shrugged.

"Come on. Something?"

"They earn their keep," I said.

"Wait. What? I thought you lived under her bakery?"

"I live here." I waved a hand at everything in sight. "This is my building, all three stories and beyond. They're my tenants, and they pay well."

She arched an eyebrow.

"Tatiana's bakery does well, but that's not why I let her operate here. And George is an acupuncturist. A good one."

"Funny, I didn't see him sticking any needles into you."

"Which is exactly why he doesn't pay rent in cash. They're good friends. I've known them a long time."

"Yeah, well, it's all relative isn't it?" She smirked.

I snorted. "Yes."

"So how long is long?"

"Long."

"Tatiana doesn't seem that much older than me."

I didn't comment on that. "No? But she's a good bouncer."

Cassidy clutched her stomach and broke into laughter. I kept silent. If Tatiana heard I laughed about her, she would give me an enema with that rolling pin.

"Ohhh." She stopped, blinking several times. "Seriously,

what was in that stuff?"

"Whiskey. Really old whiskey."

"Ugh. I'm done drinking."

"Good." I placed my chin on my palm. "Now we can focus on the monsters chasing you, the why, and what to do about it."

"Maybe I could use another drink. Forgetting this is happening would be awesome."

"It's an option. Sorry to say it won't do much apart from cause another headache."

"Yeah, I know." Cassie looked away, staring into a faraway place that only she could see. Several minutes passed before she got to her feet. The young woman took another look around my home before walking over to a cream-colored love seat. She plopped onto it. Her legs dangled over the arm-rest, kicking occasionally. Cassie buried her eyes in the bend of her arm. "So, we're safe here right?"

I saw no point in lying to her. "I'm not sure. My home is safe, to an extent."

She inched her arm away just enough to peer through it. But she chose to remain silent.

"Tatiana won't let just anyone or anything through. Members of the Timeless are exempt from that. The ones who know where I live, that is."

"And how many is that?"

"Two."

"Yeah, but your...crew aren't the ones looking for me."

"Until I know for a fact who is and why, everyone is suspect."

"But I thought you guys weren't allowed to get involved with this kind of stuff." She made a series of random motions with her hand.

I cleared my throat.

"Right, so, how many of them are rebels like you?"

"I don't know. I'm the only one stupid enough to get caught."

"Yeah, how?"

I sighed and stood up, pacing around the couch as I thought. I had no bearings on this, no idea of what to do, or where to go. Cassie was a unique problem. A human being with no magical background, possessing the ability to pass in and out of the Neravene without any knowledge of it. Technically, what she was doing was impossible.

The supernatural world held little regard for that word. My thoughts quieted enough for me to hear a steady tick. I turned to the miniature replica of a clock tower, which stood against the nearest wall, wedged between another bookshelf and a weapons rack fashioned out of ebony. The tower was something I had commissioned after the Blitz. The face was functional. I had a little over two days left before I would be called to inquiry.

Forty-eight hours to come up with a strong enough defense to justify my offenses. Two problems; two days. Either problem could get me killed. The clock ticked on. I might have stood outside it, but time waits for no man.

"John?"

The clock ticked on. Little shapes resembling odd creatures—some winged, some with exaggerated mouths—spread over bits of the replica. The gargoyles were a nice touch.

"John? What did you do?"

The clock ticked on. Time slipped by and I had an idea. "Another time."

"What? Why? We've got a breather right now. Can't we chill for a bit? Tell me some more crap about this other world."

"I'm sorry, but I know what to do. Where to go."

"Oh?"

"Yeah. We need to pay a visit to the Grand Marquis."

Chapter Four

"Uh, we're going to visit a crappy car?"

"Not *a* Grand Marquis. *The* Grand Marquis."

"Oh, thanks for clearing that up." Cassie rolled her eyes. "You think they can help us with this mess?"

I can hope. "I believe so."

With a twist of her hips, she flung her legs off the seat and bounded to her feet. She teetered, spreading her arms out wide as she tried to balance herself. "Woah, okay, I'm good." She took a few deep breaths. "Alright, let's go."

I nodded for her to follow me as I walked to the furthest end of the main room. A single door made of honest iron, not steel, blocked the way.

"What's back there?"

"A lot but, for now, you're going to want the first door on the left. When you're done, go to the next door down. That's it."

She crossed her arms, giving me an oblique stare. "What's down there?"

I opened the door, giving it a gentle push. An endless hall of cobbled stone stretched before us. A never-ending number of doors were set into it. A single, curved metal rod hung on the side of every door, adorned with a single bulb emanating pure white light. The carpet was the style of those used in Hollywood events, reserved for silver screen stars. It was a hall that had no end in sight. The only visible thing was a carpet disappearing into darkness.

"Woah. It's bigger on the inside than the outside." She looked up at me, staring. "You're how old again? Please tell me you've got a screwdriver in your pockets."

I snorted. "You need to be clean when we visit. Old world, old rules. Traditions and appearances are important with the supernatural. A tip to remember."

"Noted." She hooked a thumb to the door I advised her to enter. "So, where's that lead?"

"A shower."

"Marry me," she mumbled. "It's been so long since I've had a long, hot, good one."

I stared at her.

"You know what I meant." She shook her head and huffed. "Perv!"

I adopted respectful silence.

She all but pounced at the door, leaping forward and swinging it open.

"Towels are inside."

"What, you keep your bathroom stocked and prepared for guests or something?"

"Every room is stocked and prepared, always, forever."

Her eyes widened and she turned to look back down the hall, staring for a long moment. "How many rooms are there?"

"If we survive this, I'll show you. Go shower. Next room is a closet. Pick out something clean. A dress would be..." I trailed off when I felt her stare.

"Dress? Yeah, not happening. Nice try, though. You're adorable." She stepped into the bathroom, hooking her foot around the door and pulling with it. The door slammed shut.

Some creatures are partial to dresses, fine clothing, and regalia.

Shaking my head, I left the hall, making sure the door remained wide open. I did not need it to shut while she was behind it. *Research. I need to do research.* I leaned over to place my hand on a nearby table. I may have gotten a brief reprieve with my nap, but it wasn't enough.

My leg spasmed.

I winced as the dull ache rolled through the limb. The clock ticked, and I debated throwing something at it. Being immune to time's effects does not make one a fan of being pressed by it. Patience does not develop with years. In fact, it leads to an increase in stubbornness.

It was going to be my death.

My finger trailed over the edge of the table, running its way to the end and brushing against the siding of a bookshelf. I paused, pursing my lips as I looked at the rows of books. A single shelf fitted a hundred novels wide. The shelves went to the ceiling.

I'm fond of books. I shouldn't have to defend myself. There is no knowledge that is not power, more so in the paranormal world.

My eyes felt dry and compressed. I knuckled them for a few seconds, hoping the pressure would alleviate some of my fatigue. It didn't help. I stifled a yawn and searched for a certain book. In my library, that was a task.

Ten minutes passed before I found a large tome wrapped in a blue cloth. I thumbed it open, flipping through the various mythos within. Fifty pages or so passed before I found what I was looking for. My lip curled as I took it all in. A heavy knock pulled me from the book.

Cassie stood in the doorway, a plush white towel pressed to her head as she rubbed her hair. She wore a tight red shirt featuring a white puppy head winking, with its tongue out. A cowboy hat rested on its head and crossed revolvers sat below. Dark blue jeans, slim-fitting and in far better condition than her previous ones, hung from her hips. It would be a lie to deny that they looked appealing on her. She had replaced her sneakers with a bright turquoise pair bulkier in size than the last.

"Where did you find those?"

"In the closet. Your place is dope. It's like Hogwarts with electricity, minus the moving staircases."

I stared at her.

"Wait, you don't have those do you?"

I snapped the book shut, nodding to the wall where my clock rested. "Come on." Cassie fell in step as I walked her over to a rack sporting a variety of dangerous and unique implements.

"Oh, my God, you're a psycho serial killer and you've

lured me into your torture dungeon of doom!" Her voice morphed into something cartoonishly ominous as she waved her hands in an animated manner. "But, seriously, what's with all the weapons?" Cassie's finger moved from side-to-side through the air as she went over the rack.

"Things I've collected over the years. They're going to be handy."

She arched an eyebrow. "You think we're going to need these where we're going?"

I looked back at her, mimicking her expression.

"Yeah, right." She sighed. "Stupid question."

"No comment."

A fist snapped out.

I groaned and rubbed my arm, glaring at her. It was a good punch. I hid my smile. If she was that feisty, we would be fine. The supernatural world was not nice. It didn't care for the innocent or the ignorant. Venturing into it was certainly not for the faint-hearted.

I picked up a braided thong of cord wrapped in leather. Eight feet in length, the handle was simple smooth wood, polished and unadorned. The tip of the weapon ended in a thin barb no thicker than my pinky finger. I pushed it towards her.

She held up her hands, taking a step back. "Uh...a little inappropriate right now, isn't it?"

"Do you know how to use one?"

Cassie shifted her weight, resting one hand on her hip. She shot me a look like I had said something incredibly stupid. "I can be as kinky as the next girl if the situation calls for it but, no, I don't crack that whip."

I couldn't suppress the laugh. "Hold onto it anyway. Trust me, it can come in handy."

"Where exactly are you taking me?" She looked a bit hesitant but took the whip from me.

"It's light, versatile—"

"And leather is always in."

I gave her a look.

"Sorry." She gave me a weak smile.

"Its length will be handy in keeping things backs, and the end is iron-tipped."

"And that's important because?"

"Next lesson. Pure iron is a substance of man's world; it belongs on our side. It's a tool used to craft our weapons, shape our world. Outdated, sure, but even steel needs iron. It's everywhere here and nowhere in the Neravene. To many creatures from that side, iron is poison; it's their bane. Think of it as radioactive material. Iron can cause many creatures to fall ill or worse. It can kill them." I let the last words sink in.

Her fingers flexed, tightening around the whip. "Oh. But wouldn't steel be more practical? I mean knives and swords are steel. Heck, what about brass? Please tell me you've got some guns around here." She extended her first two fingers as well as her thumb, tilting her hand sideways. "We could cap some trolls."

"Bullets are brass, and, no, we're not...*capping* some trolls."

She wasn't enthusiastic about that.

"Steel works, though not on all creatures." I reached back without looking, wrapping my hand around a slender handle. It pulled free with a *snickt.* I flipped it over in my grip, pinching the curved, polished blade, as I handed it to her.

"Woah." Cassie took the dagger in hand, holding it up in the light to examine it. Its handle was gleaming black, inlaid with gold filigree. The blade was slender and sharpened to the finest of edges. "This, I can work with."

I smiled. "Here." I handed her a dark, aged-leather belt with a series of loops hanging from it.

She took it without a word, slipping it through the waistband of her jeans. The whip hung from her side, tied in place. Its dark iron point absorbed the nearby light. With a bit of effort, she managed to get the dagger into the sheath dangling on the opposite side of the belt.

"Thanks, always wanted to get my G.I Jane on."

I blinked, not sure what to make of that statement.

Instead, I knelt, taking hold of a black metal toolbox resting beside the rack. With a snap of my thumbs, I flipped the latches and lifted the top. I fished through it.

"Seriously, dude, some people collect stamps. You've got sharp and pointy things. You ever think about stamps? They're small, portable, cheap, safe. And hey, some come with pretty nifty artwork."

I snorted and wrapped my hand around a piece of metal a tad thicker than my thumb. The switchblade tumbled through my fingers as I played with it for a moment. "Stamps can't do this." I depressed the button and the blade flicked out. I locked it back in place, rolling it through my fingers before passing it to her. "An extra knife never hurts. Hide it. Tie it to yourself somewhere discreet." I held up a thin length of fabric.

Her fingers closed around the knife and piece of cloth. She pulled up the cuff of her jeans, holding the blade against her calf as she tied it in place. Pushing the pants back down, she looked to me. "What about you? I mean, if I'm going all Tomb Raider, this place isn't going to be friendly. What are you taking?"

Between the rack and bookshelf was an empty space large enough to shove a broom inside. Well, not so empty. The saber was a little over three feet long, slightly curved and well-aged. The handle had held up well over the century. The guard was gilded.

"You steal that from the History Channel?"

"First man I killed." My words fell with a great deal of weight. Silence.

Cassie licked her lips, eyeing the saber, then me for close to a minute. "Who was it? When?"

My mouth twitched. Killing someone is never easy. It's not like killing monsters. It isn't. Some people can be as close to monsters as possible—terribly evil—but most aren't. Most people are misguided, prone to giving into their darker nature. That doesn't make them bad. It makes them something else. I don't know what and, believe me, I've thought about it for a long time. But you never forget the first life you take. You don't let yourself forget.

I cleared my throat. "America was at war then."

"With who?"

"Ourselves."

"Oh, so you *are* old."

"Yes."

"Which side did you fight for?"

"Home," I said, shutting my eyes.

"And that's...?"

"Here. New York." I hefted the sword, examining it. My mind flashed back to bright skies without clouds, and thunder cracking throughout the day. "He didn't need it anymore." I didn't know what had happened to the sheath; in a hundred years, I had lost a lot of things. I fastened it to my coat, wedging it under the jacket's belt.

"That's it? An old sword?"

"I'm already carrying all I need."

She looked at me for an answer.

I tapped my temple. "Knowledge is the best weapon there is." I didn't mention what else I was carrying.

"Yeah, well, can you kill those trolls with your mind? Didn't think so, Vader."

Youth today have developed a variant of English that I really needed to learn.

I ignored the comment and cinched my coat. "Let's go." I nodded towards the iron door.

Cassie followed without making a sound. I could feel her stiffen as we entered the hall. "No lie, this place is *trés* creepy."

"Want to know something, Cassie?"

"What?"

"This place still scares me."

"How's that?"

I walked over to the second door on the left, opening it. Long coats, a variety of boots, simple shirts, and well-made suits filled the closet. I looked back to Cassie, whose mouth hung open.

"When I came in here, the room was decked out like I'd

won a shopping spree and raided the mall. Now it's all changed. How?"

"It's a mystery," I said, my voice not quite convincing her of the lie.

"Mysteries are bullshit," she muttered.

"I'll tell you another time. Come on." I shut the door, walking off.

Cassie sidled up beside me, keeping pace, refusing to let me out of her sight.

I stumbled a bit, placing my hand on the wall as Cassie sidestepped and bumped me with her hip. I eyed her.

She gave me a similar look.

I pinched my forefinger and thumb together, dragging them across my lips. "It's a secret."

"I've got two knives and a whip," she said.

I felt it wiser not to say anything further. We moved past a dozen doors before I came to the one I was looking for. It looked like all the rest.

Don't ask me how I can tell them apart. It comes with living in the place.

I opened the door and Cassie sucked in a breath. The room had that effect on people. I had found it when I first came across the property seventy years ago. It was one of the reasons I bought it.

It was like standing above a sea of storm clouds that stretched out as far as the eye could see. They sank and rose, expanding like they were breathing. Roiling through an infinite expanse, tendrils of electricity arced and crackled along.

Cassie stared ahead, lost—mesmerized by it all.

It got me too. It always did.

"Oh my God." She let out a heavy breath.

"Look up." I put my index finger below her chin and pushed with a gentle amount of pressure.

"Oh..."

Gaseous clouds of purple, pink, and red blurred together into a heavenly scene, all woven into a tapestry of galactic black. Innumerable balls of tiny white light pulsed and flickered at an unreachable distance. One such orb floated closer than the others, noticeably so. Another rolled by on our right. Twin moons.

"Where are we?"

"Right now, we're in my home."

"And this is?"

"The Way to where we're going."

She turned her head, looking at me while not quite taking her attention off the scene before us. Her body shuddered and she grabbed her shoulders, rubbing her arms. "It feels weird. It's cool, like a nice breeze."

I felt nothing. I kept that to myself.

"I'm creeped out, John. I feel something here." She pointed to her stomach. "Like in my navel. Like there's a hook in it and I'm being pulled. And there's an invisible rope around my waist, helping that hook. What is it?"

"A Way."

"What?"

"That's what this place is, a natural Way. They exist in the world on their own, hidden. Most of them are buried or snatched up by and into the domains of powerful creatures. Not everyone and everything can open a Way of their own accord. I certainly can't. It takes a combination of skill, power, and knowledge. In that regard, I have none. But, that doesn't mean I can't find my own path into the Neravene. It's why I paid an exorbitant sum for this place."

"Because there's a Way here?"

I shook my head. "No." I backpedaled from the door without looking away. My fingers clasped around another doorknob. I twisted and flung it open. The space behind me inhaled, pulling a rush of air past us.

Cassie turned to look at the newly revealed room and Way. Her eyes widened and took on a special light like two glimmering pools of fiery opal. The color in her face paled a shade. Her mouth moved but no sound came out.

I shut the door and gestured around me. "I bought this place because of *them*."

She nodded and swallowed. "Yeah, makes sense."

I placed a hand on her shoulder, turning her back the other way. "Come on." I walked back to the other door with her. Fingers of white lightning streaked through the space above us, impacting the clouds. It dispersed seconds later. Lingering static occasionally spurted from random clouds.

"Now what?"

"We go through." I patted her back in a reassuring manner.

"Through that?"

"Yes. Close your eyes." I pushed her into the Way.

She screamed.

I'm not a terrible person for shoving her through.

I dove in after her.

Chapter Five

There is no one single experience or sensation that can define going through one of the Ways. Each is different, and leads to equally different places.

My body tightened in response to the sensation of freefalling. Hairs stood on end, and air buffeted me. A light tingle coursed over the entirety of my skin. And then the currents of air were gone. A soft jolt rolled up my legs, stopping at the knees. I blinked. We were on the ground. "Cassie, are you okay?"

She panted, doubled over, hands resting on her thighs. "You...douche biscuit!" Straightening up with startling speed, she lunged at me, flailing her arms.

I clapped my hands toward her face, causing her to blink and stumble in surprise. My body shifted as she staggered by. One of her hands clipped my arm.

"Are you okay?"

"No, I'm not okay!" She was still breathing heavy. "You pushed me through a..." She trailed off when she saw what I had.

We stood in a field of purple grass, blades high enough to brush our knees. Even in the dark, their color was visible and vibrant, catching the pale moonlight from above.

"Where are we?"

"The outermost domain of The Grand Marquis." I nodded ahead to a massive stonework.

"How do we get back?"

I looked at her.

"Me? Why can't you, you know?" She pointed at a spot behind us, waving her arms. "Open another one? Open that one back up?"

"It's one Way. That's how it works. It leads out, not

back. It's how I've traveled the world on occasion. Normally I resort to mortal methods to travel back. Other times, when I'm on Timeless business or invited to a realm or holding, the hosts open a Way back to the mortal world. If I could open Ways at will, I would have saved us back in the Long Gardens."

"Well, that sucks."

"It does. Come on. I don't know how much time will pass while we're here. Remember, I have other engagements."

"Oh, right." Cassie mimed tying a noose around her neck before raising her hand into the air and jerking it in a single sharp motion. "Krrksht!" She accentuated the sound of my neck cracking.

"Yes, thank you."

"Sorry."

"It's fine. Let's hope it stays an act and nothing more. Let's go. Time's wasting." I walked off.

"Oh, irony!" she called, throwing a hand into the air with theatrical effect. "How cruel art thou? Time slips by for the Timeless man!"

I sighed.

There is something gravely wrong with the youth of today. It must be the food they eat. Or the music. Television could play a role as well.

I felt it safest to blame all three.

Cassie marched beside me and nudged me with her elbow. I turned to look. "So, we've got a bit of a walk."

"Yes."

"Mind if I ask you some questions?"

I shrugged.

"How exactly does someone become a Timeless? How did you?"

I faltered for a step. I shouldn't have; the question was to be expected.

How do you answer that?

Honestly, I told myself.

The sky was gorgeous, a gem-infused blanket of black

slowly passing over us. We kept an even, comfortable pace as we plowed through the grass. Several minutes went by before I spoke. "I don't know, not all of it."

Cassie was silent, but I could feel her watching.

"As far as I know, Timeless are made—chosen from people who do get involved and make a bad habit out of it. It's sort of a way to bring balance I guess. To get us to serve another purpose, to watch, learn, and preserve important information. And share it on occasion."

"Share it with who?"

The muscles along my back knotted as I thought about the answer. "Trouble. Dangerous men and women."

"How so?"

"Leave it alone." Something in my tone must've got to her because she didn't push it any further. A hint of guilt racked me, so I addressed her previous questions. "Most of the Timeless are plucked from wars. I was."

"That one?" She jabbed a finger towards my saber.

I nodded.

"What happened?"

"I died. Well, almost. I remember the air rushing out of me. My chest felt like it was broken and I was thrown to the ground. It felt like all the warmth was leaving my body to be on the outside, spreading over my skin. I was vaguely aware that I had been shot. The blood and pain made it obvious. I thought I was going to die. If the wound didn't kill me, someone else would finish the job."

"Then what?"

"I don't remember most of it. Someone dragged me from the battle, tended to my injuries, made sure I survived. When I woke up, we were hundreds of miles away from where I fell. There was a small fire going, and we were in the middle of the woods. It was serene. Part of me wanted to lay there forever. After being in a battle, seeing the things you do, there's something tempting and peaceful about being in nature."

"And, what? You woke up and no longer had to worry about buying Oil of Olay?"

I blinked. "No. I woke up feeling like I had been shot. Lost in the woods with a stranger who offered me a choice."

She tilted her head to the side.

"To drop me back off home. Or to tell me about a world—worlds—I had never imagined. A perspective that would profoundly change my life and, if I did my job, change the lives of a great many others. Told me about fantasies, tales of magic and creatures I couldn't believe in and, the chance to see them. All I had to do was make a deal. Swear a pact."

"Hope you got it in writing."

I chuckled. "Not exactly. I agreed. I was young, eager to travel and see the world, even if I didn't believe his mysteries and magic speech. That's when he took to me to see the Ageless court."

"Sounds like a collection of plastic surgery bimbos," she muttered.

I resolved to keep a straight face. It was beneath a wizened member of the Timeless to laugh at something like that. A light huff of breath escaped my lips. It wasn't a laugh and I would maintain that.

I'm not as wizened as I should be.

"What did they do?"

"Apart from terrifying me to utter speechlessness? Shattering my conceptions about the world, life, God and more?"

"Uh, yeah. Crap, didn't think about that. Um, apart from that."

"They gave me the opportunity to become one of them, to bless me with the ability to remain my current age. To walk through countless ages so long as I don't suffer severe mortal harm."

"So you can die?"

"Yes, just not from old age."

"That's a deal I'd kill for."

I gave her a knowing look. "It's not all it's cracked up to be."

"How so?" She arched a brow.

"Imagine living forever, watching the people you grew up with, cared for, loved—and will love—pass. Watching the world fall into several dark moments, knowing you have the knowledge and skills to make a difference—"

"But you can't? Or aren't allowed?"

I nodded.

"Well, not for nothin'. Thanks for getting involved this time." Cassie's arms wrapped tight around me in a hug. It felt good. We were walking through a dangerous part of the Neravene into a potentially more dangerous part, and I felt fine.

Hugs are a force of their own in the universe. They're ingrained in us humans. From the moment we are born, we're inundated with and in hugs. Wrapped in the arms of parents, cradled, and sung to. When we wake from a nightmare and cry out in terror. When we go through heartbreak or experience immense joy. Seeing someone for the first time, or after a long time. It's one of the simplest mortal actions that carries one of the most magical forces in the world.

Compassion. The reason I had gotten involved in so many mortal affairs.

Compassion was an emotion that many paranormal creatures thought a weakness. Some said it would be the cause of my death. Looking around at where we were, the mess I was stuck in, they were probably right. I looked to Cassie and realized those people had no idea what they were talking about.

I threw an arm around her and hugged her back. "I'm glad I got involved. No regrets."

"You might change your mind when they *glurck* you," she said, placing her hands on her neck in a mock gesture of wringing it.

I stopped. My breath stilled. "Maybe sooner." I nodded to the immaculate courtyard of stone ahead.

The tiles were near-black in the absence of sunlight. Gargantuan pillars reached into the sky, casting lengthy shadows that looked to sway. No ceiling was mounted atop them. It created quite the view.

"Well, that's not spooky."

"You can always go back."

Cassie glared, making it clear that wasn't an option.

"You could, though. You can open a Way at any moment. You could go back to my place. You'd be safe. You're welcome as long as you like. You don't have to do this."

"But if I don't, I'll never really be safe, will I?"

I shook my head. "No, I don't believe so. Mind if I ask you something?"

"Shoot."

"Why are you sticking with me? Trusting me? I haven't been as forthcoming as I could be; we both know it. You could travel to any point in the world. Be in another country in a blink."

"I trust you."

Three words. There's magic in the number three, and that magic infects words as well. Not to say that words aren't magic. They most assuredly are. But some of the most powerful words come in threes. *I love you. I miss you. I trust you.* And many more. Those three have an effect.

"Thank you."

"I mean, at first I didn't. Maybe part of me still doesn't, but I want to. You saved me. You didn't have to. You're trying to help me and you don't need to. You're right here with me in"—she stopped, looking to the violet blades of grass—"where singing and dancing dinosaurs go to die. Off to the purple pastures they go."

I didn't know what she was saying, but I understood the message.

"Plus, you're teaching me a lot, and I know you've got loads more to show me."

I grinned. "I do. Stick around, kid, and I'll show you the ropes." Another nudge to my ribs, and I winced.

"And I've got something to teach you, old timer. Stop callin' me kid. You'll live longer." She gave me a feral smile.

"I can do that." We crossed the remaining bit of the

field, a literal footstep away from the stone tiling. I placed my shoe onto the first tile. Nothing happened. My heart raced nonetheless. We were on the grounds of the Marquis' personal residence. He wasn't the sort who took kindly to intruders.

"So where exactly is this in the Marquis' domain?"

"His home," I said. "And not the front entrance."

Her opalescent eyes glimmered with an inner light. "We're trespassing?"

"Only if we're caught."

She snorted. "Good point, but couldn't you have done what you did back in the Long Gardens? Walk me through imagining his home? I could've dropped us into his living room. No worries, no travel, no issues."

I froze. Cassie had said it with such ease, like with a snap of her fingers she could take us into the private domain of a powerful lord of the Neravene. And the terrifying part was she could. *And that's why she's being hunted, you idiot!*

Cassidy Winters was a doorway to anywhere, regardless of the rules and protection governing a place. She was a weapon or the next best thing to one. A living, breathing skeleton key. Cassie needed to know.

I couldn't have picked a worse spot to stop. We had cleared a good deal of the courtyard and stood in an area packed with more columns. The space gave the illusion of being open, but it was a tight enclosure. A semi-circle of pillars sat on either side, leaving only one path—forward. Walking back was an option. One I was afraid would trigger the guards. Hunched figures carved out of stone sat at the foot of every column.

Their faces looked long and reptilian with broad snouts that doubtless held rows of sharpened teeth. Serpent-like eyes gave the impression they were watching us. They had the bodies of men, large and muscular, with hands ending in elongated and sharpened digits. Muscular legs that would shame professional bodybuilders joined the creatures at the waist, ending in raptor-like feet with formidable claws. A powerful tail as thick as an alligator's sprouted from behind.

"Gargoyles." I let out a breath and swallowed. "Don't make eye contact."

Gargoyles are magical watchdogs the size of grizzly bears. Stone sentries that are shaped to the creator's desires and imbued with a spark of will. They hit like trucks and have the disposition of an angry pit bull. They can be animated and used to carry out simple orders. Orders like kill.

"Whoops."

My heart lurched and I eyed Cassie. "What do you mean whoops?"

"Like, whoops I think I looked at one of them."

Something sounded like chips of pottery cracking. My body turned like rusted gears to look at the source of the noise. I regretted doing so.

I looked four gargoyles in the eyes before finding where the noise came from. A gargoyle far off to the side of where we had entered had lines crisscrossing its body. I prayed they were defects in its craftsmanship. That theory went out as more lines formed, spreading like ever-growing veins. I figured the construction and shape of our surroundings were behind the echoing cracks. I was wrong.

"Uh..." Cassie shuffled towards me, placing her body against mine. Her fingers fumbled against the loop on her belt. "This seems like a whip it moment?" She undid the clasp and held the rolled weapon in both hands, uncertainty showing on her face.

The stone veneer of every gargoyle was cracking. I counted twelve in total. Twelve monstrous, strong, fast, and furious killing machines.

"I've heard of cracking yourself up before, but this is ridiculous," muttered Cassie.

I groaned. "Please don't, not now."

"Can't help it. I deflect terrible and deadly scenarios with misplaced humor. It's part of my irresistible charm." She let out a weak laugh.

The cracking came to a horrible crescendo. It was an earth-splitting sound as tons of stone shattered. Shards burst forth like shrapnel, hurtling towards us.

"Cassie!" I pulled her close, sinking my weight as I brought her to a crouch with me, folding my coat around us. The leather was thick, doubly so since I had it altered. A good coat can be like a second skin. I pulled the mantle over my head, hoping the turtle-like action would spare my face.

The chips of stone struck home. It sounded like pelting rain, each strike ringing with a unique tone. It felt like taking on a pitching machine with my body. And the machine was winning.

A stone struck the back of my hand with a sharp, fleshy crack that sent ripples of agony into my fingers. I would be riddled with bruises. George was not going to be happy. I grimaced.

"Ow!" Cassie's voice wasn't a pained yelp but a low guttural growl. "That one hurt."

The barrage stopped.

Groaning, I took a moment to shrug and loosen my body, which had stiffened in response to the rocky hailstorm. I peeled the coat back and had a moment of wishing I could forever remain inside it.

Twelve beasts, now made of skin—not stone—stood in a semi-circle before us. They blocked the path out. The only way was ahead, into the court of the Grand Marquis. All of the creatures flicked their—for lack of a better term—ears. Large, fan-like things. A series of splayed fingers with thin membranes spread between them. There was a wet slurping sound and I remembered something else about gargoyles.

Their wings. They spurted out of their backs in a single swift motion. Bat-like in shape, covered in a milky mucus. They looked too fragile to carry their weight. But where monsters were involved, the rules of conventional physics were often tossed aside.

One of them decided to prove that point to me. It beat its wings, sending fluid spraying off the limbs. Cassie ducked behind me as I was covered in the ichor.

"Hell no, I just showered!" she shouted from behind me.

I blinked and wiped a hand against both my eyes, flicking the mucus to the ground. The creature leapt into the air, spiraling as it rose several dozen feet above us.

"Move!" I shoved Cassie towards the path ahead. I dove out of the way as the tiling ruptured from the creature's weight. The impact rattled half the bones in my body. I looked back to the small crater formed by the gargoyle's dive-bomb. "There." I pointed to the narrow way ahead, lined with pillars on both sides. "Cassie, go. Use the columns for cover!"

She bobbed her head in understanding and bolted.

That move galvanized the rest of the gargoyles into action. A dozen monsters rushed me. Over a century of living and combat experience led to one outcome.

Running.

My feet scrabbled against the ground. The bare point of my saber scratched stone as I scampered forward. I saw Cassie enter the pathway and duck behind one of the stone structures. The flat of my blade slapped against my legs as I pumped my muscles harder. An ache developed deep within my chest. I could hear the gargoyles behind me.

Some took to the air. The rest pursued me on all fours, their claws gouging and crushing bits of the tiles. Not a trait I liked in my monsters.

My fingers fumbled with my belt, working to free my sword. "Come on, come on." I managed to draw the saber. Running with it was awkward, however. There was a series of crashes, louder than the rest, from close behind me. I turned without looking and sent the blade into a wide arc.

The gargoyle reeled, losing its momentum as it pawed at the gash in its snout. Its eyes adjusted from the shock and narrowed. Not a good moment for me. I spat a curse and took off again, barreling towards the columns ahead.

The creatures were gaining on me. I came into the passage with a leap, landing hard and tucking into a roll. On instinct, I sunk to my knees. A loud crash from above caused me to flinch as bits of powdered stone rained on me.

I looked up as I scuttled around the pillar. The gargoyle

had torn a chunk of rock out of the column that was the size of my head. I swallowed the imaginary obstruction in my throat. The monster rounded on me, watching as I edged around the stone post.

A *snap-crack* filled my ears and I took a double step back. The gargoyle howled, stopping in its tracks as it clutched its arm. A finger-length wound hissed spitefully as smoke poured from it.

I leaned to the side. Cassie stood next to the opposite pillar, eyes wide in surprise as she held the whip. The iron barb had clipped the creature's bicep and clearly had an effect.

"Holy crap, I didn't think I'd hit it." She wound the whip between her hands, coiling it for another strike.

The gargoyle didn't care much for that. Its attention left me completely, as if I no longer existed. It hunched, muscles coiling. The adopted posture spelled danger to all. Except Cassidy Winters.

She bristled, thrusting her chest forwards and arms back in defiance. Her lips peeled back. "Come at me!" She swung the whip in a circular motion, the barb glanced off the nearby rock and faltered.

The creature swooped towards her, arms out wide to grab her and God only knew what next. I wasn't going to give it the chance. A primal scream left my lungs as I flipped my grip on the saber, chasing after it. I sent the point sinking into its flesh.

The blade drove through the creature's thick back. I wrenched, twisting the weapon side to side. The monster's wings flapped and beat against me with near-concussive force. I held on. I let out another scream and pulled the sword free, holding it up for the killing blow.

A truck collided with my waist, taking me to the ground. The world shook and blurred around the edges. I blinked several times to make sure I was seeing what I thought I was.

The rest of the gargoyles piled into the tight area. The one atop me clasped its hands above its head. I squirmed every way I could to avoid those hands. I wasn't looking to have my skull pulped.

Another tight, elastic *crack!* Black cord snared the monster's throat, tightening to the point where the gargoyle's eyes bulged. The iron tip bit into the flesh of its chest. It served as a hook as Cassie pulled, causing the creature enough pain that it had to lean back to alleviate the pressure.

I wormed an arm free of its pin-hold and swung the sword. A section of its throat parted and violet blood sprayed. I freed myself and rushed to Cassie's side. The other gargoyles took positions around us, nearly leaving us trapped. Nearly.

"Use the columns." I jerked a thumb over my back.

Cassie nodded and reeled her whip back before taking off.

I used my lengthier gait to pull up beside her. "Nice cast back there. Getting it to wind around something's neck is difficult."

"Lucky—oh, crap!" She stumbled and weaved behind and out another pillar as one the gargoyles broke from the pack to single her out. The monster bounded after her on all fours, leaping on occasion to close the distance.

I veered towards Cassie, hoping to cross paths with her as she skirted around and through the columns. The rest of gargoyles took issue with my plan. Two moved in perfect unison, landing before me.

"Cassie—oomph." A tail met my chest, drawing the breath from my lungs. I tumbled back, rolling over the ground, struggling to keep my grip on the sword. "Argh," I grunted as I pushed myself halfway up and to the side to avoid another lash of a tail. The second gargoyle advanced with its taloned digits. I was finished having my back against the wall.

Some creatures in the supernatural world have specific ways to kill them. They require certain materials, techniques, and even timing to be destroyed. Many creatures can't tolerate salt or iron. Gargoyles, on the other hand, are wonderfully susceptible to a great many things. Iron hurts them more than other weapons, but they are essentially like any creature in the mortal world.

I moved towards the blow in a crescent-like arc, feinted, and countered. A thrust of my palm pushed the gargoyle's arm aside. I kept moving around the creature as I followed with another strike.

The aged blade parted hand from wrist with ease. The gargoyle's serpentine tongue peeked from its mouth, flailing as it let out a high-pitched cry. More purplish-blue blood spouted from the limb.

His pack mate took umbrage with the maiming of his friend. He released an odd, off-key songlike sound. It was like chimes amidst a xylophone.

And my bravado was gone. I waved the sword at its face to keep it at bay. When it didn't advance, I spun and sprinted off. "Cassie?"

"Yo!" She appeared in the corner of my vision, still being chased by the single fiend that had set off after her. "Jeez," Cassie called over her shoulder to her pursuer. "No means no! Take a hint!" She zigzagged and pulled ahead, dipping behind another pillar. Cassie popped back out and around the other end snapping the whip again. "Back, back, hiyah! Crap." She didn't bother bringing the weapon back, leaving it to trail behind her as she ran. "Crapcrapcrapcrap! John—I hate you!"

At that moment, I shared her sentiment. My body arched and quivered as the air behind me pushed against my skull. Something parted bits of straggling hair from my head. That was too close for my liking. This was going to end badly.

Chases never end in the favor of the chased. Not in situations like this. That was something reserved for television shows and movies. There's a reason predators hunt in packs. It's more effective. They can cover more ground, maneuver more freely, and control how and where the prey is herded.

That was exactly what was happening.

The columns ahead grew tighter, limiting our space. We were being corralled. Our odds weren't looking good.

"Hey." Cassie came next to me, breathing hard and fast. She was losing steam. "You suck."

"No argument here. Keep going."

She grunted.

"They're pushing us somewhere."

"What?"

"They're herding us, like dogs do for hunters."

"Where?"

"I've got a good idea."

"So far, man, I've hated your ideas."

She had good reason to. I didn't think my legs and body would be able to handle what lay ahead of us. It was a staircase built for a Tibetan monastery secluded atop a Himalayan mountaintop. Wide, solid stairs, an uncountable number of steps to climb.

Normally, high ground offers an advantage. Not so much when you have to expend energy climbing, and your adversaries can fly.

I leapt up to the first step, bouncing up to the second as soon as I made contact with the stairs. "Come on, Cassie, faster."

She didn't respond, not with words at least.

I felt a heated glower that could have melted stone.

There was a weighted crunch as one of the steps in front of me shattered. A plume of dust and crushed stone obscured my sight. I set my jaw and shoulder, plowing forward, and connected with one of the gargoyles.

I drove up a step, making it fight for balance. It snapped at me with its jaws. I sank, grabbing one of its arms in one hand, and one of its wings in the other. I fell back.

The sudden shift in momentum and loss of balance caused the creature to tumble with me. I tucked my knees and kicked out. The monster sailed over me as the edge of one of the steps ground against my spine. It landed with a soft thud before rolling down several steps.

"That hurt," I muttered as I picked myself up and

covered the ground I had lost.

Cassie was a good way ahead of me, twenty or more steps. More of the gargoyles took to the air.

I'm in good shape; decades of travel, walking, running and climbing do that to you. However, I'm still mortal. I don't have supernatural stamina, and I was near the end of mine.

Denial is a great or terrible thing. It all depends on how you use it. You deny horrible facts and situations, like ours, up until the moment they kill you. Or, you can trick your mind and body into believing whatever you want. It works.

I am not tired. I run up mountainous staircases all the time. And I'm being chased by gargoyles. I can run harder and faster than this. And I did.

Each footstep was light and quick. The second I touched down on a step, I was back in the air, hopping to the next. My lungs burned, feeling dry and stretched. My legs ached. Molten liquid coursed through the muscles, searing them. I didn't care. I was driven by a cold fear that numbed me to bodily discomfort.

More and more of the creatures were focusing on Cassie. All of them took to the sky. I pumped my legs harder, closing the distance between Cassie and me.

"This isn't looking good."

She was right.

"They're trying to force us into a corner."

"And what's in that corner?"

I had an idea. It wasn't as bad as it seemed, unless the gargoyles decided to kill once they cornered us. It was always an option. I hoped they were on a tighter leash than it looked like they were.

"How do we stop these things?" Cassie panted.

"Two ways—" I broke off as I stopped and ran sideways, avoiding a swooping gargoyle. I lashed out with the sword. My strike didn't do much aside from leaving a small notch in the monster's wing. Superficial damage. "Sunlight reverts them back to stone."

"Not an option."

"Or we kill them."

She furrowed her brows and scowled. "Not an option, it looks like then!" Cassie's pace slowed. Sweat beaded her face, plastering lengths of hair to her skin.

Things were growing worse by the second. This was a numbers game, and we were losing. We had managed to injure some and had taken one out of commission, but the odds were still in the gargoyles' favor. We were running low on energy, and the creatures seemed to have no end to theirs.

"Cassie, look at the top of the stairs. Can you do it?"

She glanced up, squinting as she kept climbing. "Think so, but I'm tired."

"Tired beats dead, kid."

She stared daggers at me.

I had promised not to call her kid anymore, but it worked wonders in riling her up, which was exactly what we needed.

Somehow, she managed to keep her balance and progress up the stairs as she shut her eyes tight. She stuck her tongue out and bit down in concentration.

I slowed down, running over to her. The air shimmered as if a thin dusting of powdered glass hung suspended through it, catching the moon and starlight from above.

Cassie moved both hands upwards in an almost graceful manner. The space in front of us parted. Her momentum carried her into and through it.

I dove too, hurtling through the Way and appearing hundreds of stairs up. I blinked, realizing I was in the air. I fell. My chest hit the unforgiving stone.

Cassie landed on all fours in a cat-like crouch.

I groaned and rolled over, sitting up to glower at her. "Why did you open it that far above ground?"

"Deal with it...kid." A smug smile spread across her face. Shrill shrieks pierced the night, pulling her smile away. The gargoyles came together in a tight-knit aerial grouping. "Well, it's been not so nice knowing ya."

I gave a slight nod of my head over my shoulder.

Cassie followed it, her eyes widened in response.

To be honest, so did mine.

Imagine the cleanest, most polished mirror you can think of. Now imagine it being made by finer hands than any found in the mortal world. Made of liquid diamonds, shining and reflecting in perfect clarity. Its height could have matched a small skyscraper, as could its width. Two figures regarded us from within the shining surface.

I hadn't seen my eyes in a while. They looked weary. The usual amber-brown appeared dull. Little branches of red crept over the whites. I looked like shit.

Cassie's reflection didn't look any better, a point I decided not to vocalize. Her eyes of tonal reds, oranges, and yellows burned bright in the mirror.

"It's a shiny dead end. What are we supposed to do?"

"Go through it."

"You're joking."

I waved a hand to the group of gargoyles about to reenact a kamikaze.

"Good point." She took a step back and leapt towards her reflection.

I followed her through the diamond wall.

Chapter Six

Dropping into the domain of one of the freestanding lords of the Neravene is never a good idea. In fact, it's a dangerous one. It's something that should not be done. But, if it cannot be helped, falling in uninvited during a meal is the worst timing imaginable.

We interrupted one, it seemed.

The hall of the Grand Marquis looked to be made from dark cobalt. It was a grim cathedral in which everything was a shade like late-night skies. A gradient ranging from near-black to navy. The color of space and blue moons.

The floor was a single piece of similarly colored stone. A few long cracks stood out. On either side of the courtroom were four statues that dwarfed the trolls from earlier. They stood sixteen feet in height with faces like bats, armored in intricate metalwork and hefting halberds. Their shields alone could flatten us, given the chance. Fortunately, unlike the last pieces of stonework we'd come across, they were completely immobile.

The room was lit solely by the efforts of three circular windows with metal bars running between them, giving each window the look of a Victorian clock face. Blue light tinged with white illuminated the small and utterly pointless set of stairs in the center, near the back of the room. Carpeted in shimmering white with gold dust sprinkled over the material, it went up the length of steps to the foot of the throne atop. Another set of stairs continued past the throne, devoid of carpeting, running up to a singular set of double doors.

I gave the doors little attention. That was held by the figure sitting on the throne, watching us in amusement.

"Well, well," he said in a crisp, eloquent tone that was almost musical. His slender, almost fragile-looking hands, gripped the armrests at the side of his throne. He rose to his feet. At first glance, his height would have appeared a trick given his position atop the stairs. It was no trick.

He stood at seven feet, fair skinned, and dressed in a one-piece robe of black hemmed with gold. The Grand Marquis' features were lean and angular. It would be fair to say he was more beautiful than handsome.

His eyes were sharp discs of green agate, gleaming with equal parts intelligence and cunning. Threads of pure silver fell to his waist unbound. His ears were long and tapered.

"It has been a long time since these halls have entertained one of the Timeless. Particularly you, Jonathan Hawthorne." He made the slightest of bows while plucking a piece of papaya from a bowl near the throne.

"Holy Legolas," breathed Cassie.

I gave her a quick look before mirroring the Grand Marquis' bow. "Thank you, and a pleasure as always, my host." I placed particular emphasis on the last word.

He arched an eyebrow, watching me out of the corners of his eyes as he turned to take a bite of the fruit. "Host? Curious. Am I your host? Interesting choice of words for one trespassing in my domain."

Technically, he was right. But elves were tricky, masters of wordplay, and appreciated cleverness. "I believe your exact words were, 'entertained one of the Timeless,' Grand Marquis."

He blinked, then repeated the action, even pausing from taking another bite of the fruit. "I did say that, didn't I?"

I nodded, but didn't say anything further. I had used a technicality in a slip up and capitalized on it. All of it was fine as far as a race like the elves were concerned, save for one point. I had implied the Marquis made a mistake. And he was aware of it. He wasn't the kind to let something like that go.

His voice dropped from melodious to flat. "You also maimed several of my sentries."

"They didn't leave us much choice. They're alive."

His eyes flashed before returning to softer greens.

"They protect my domain. I believe they were performing their duties, but I am grateful you managed to impose upon my meal without killing my gargoyles."

He cradled his forehead in one hand in a gesture I suspected was more dramatic than necessary. With his other hand, he returned the half-eaten fruit to the bowl, and scooped up a goblet fashioned out of moonbeams. That was the only way to describe it—pure white, glistening and solid.

He took a long, draining sip. Whatever it the contents, it caused his eyelids to flutter. A pleased moan escaped his lips as he placed the goblet down. "Well, it seems I have guests to entertain." In a blur of motion, he clapped once. It was a gentle tone that, nevertheless, managed to ring throughout the hall. "Will you join me for bite?"

Cassie leaned in, cupping a hand to her mouth and whispered, "Elves don't eat people, right?"

I tried to move my mouth as little as possible. "No, they don't."

She exhaled in relief. "Whew. Heck, yeah. I'm down to eat."

The Grand Marquis turned to regard Cassie seeming like he had just noticed her. He gazed at her for a moment, and I could tell he was taking in every detail, calculating and filing it away. I hoped his observations ended at the physical. If he came to realize what she was capable of, things could turn in an instant.

Elves seemed to step out of the shadows, coming to form a neat row on either side of us. It was baffling trying to discern one elf from another. Their appearances were so similar. The fact they wore the same red flowing cloaks did not help.

Both rows of elves converged in on us a step at a time, moving with more grace in each step than some dancers performed in an entire routine. It was eerie seeing that many elves move towards us at such a leisured pace.

"They will see to your needs—baths and clothing."

Cassie's eyes went wide with pleasure and hunger.

I raised an eyebrow. "With all due respect, Grand

Marquis, baths? Clothing? We did so before coming here and are sufficiently clothed, as you can see." I pulled the collar of my coat.

His lips spread into a thin smile. "Indeed. But what sort of host would I be if I didn't tend to my guests to the best of my capacity?" The smile grew.

Tricky bastard. Yes, the bath and clothes sounded nice. It was also a chance for his retainers to strip search us and remove our weapons, as well as the other objects we carried.

"Thank you for the offer, kind host. If the members of your court would be so kind as to show us to where we can bathe, we will handle the rest."

"Nonsense." A maniacal light filled his eyes. "I would appear a poor host. Word would spread, and we can't have that."

No, we couldn't. He was right. Shunning the offer of a freestanding lord, or worse, a larger and more powerful one, could have terrible repercussions. Least of which would be the offense of refusing a gracious offer. It's a stain on their name.

Respect is important to the beings of the Neravene. To its lords and ladies, it's the foundation upon which their domains are built. As well as power and fear. Being liked is optional.

The elves stood a step from me, taking my arms in their hands as they ushered me away. They led Cassie in another direction. I put my foot down. "No, wait."

"Hey, I don't know about you, but I could use another bath. I just got these threads"—she tugged the collar of her t-shirt—"and they're already covered in sweat. Keeping the shoes though." She kicked the floor. The sole of the shoe skidded with an audible squeak.

"I would appreciate it if our host did not separate us, even for bathing."

The corner of the Marquis' lip quirked. "Oh?"

Cassie voiced her thoughts a bit louder. "Wow, things are moving so fast. We met on a snowy night and fell through a Way together. You saved my life. I saved yours.

Now we're showering together." She fanned herself with a hand, "Things are getting intense. I don't know if I'm ready for them."

I almost growled, but instead, my spine turned to brittle ice. I hoped her comment about our tumble through the Ways went unnoticed by the Grand Marquis. I had figured out why she was being hunted. I didn't need others knowing, especially a lord of the Neravene, no matter how small he was.

He was intelligent, cunning, and could be treacherous. Not a good combination for us. But I needed him, or rather, his knowledge. He had many ears in many places. Elves were wonderful scouts and sleuths.

"She's coming with me, at least somewhere close enough to keep an eye on, and definitely within earshot."

"It almost sounds like you do not trust me, or my word, Hawthorne." There was a dangerous undertone in that statement.

I had good reason not to trust him. But necessity outweighed my comfort and faith in his word. He had accepted his role as host. That limited any hostile action he could take against us. With elves, loopholes were everywhere, waiting to be taken advantage of.

I stared at him without blinking. He relented.

His features sank in disappointment, an act if I ever saw one. He didn't care in the slightest. Separating us wasn't his primary concern.

"Very well. Together then." He waved a dismissive hand.

The elves escorting Cassie turned on their heels in an almost mechanical fashion. They marched her over to me, and together, both groups of elves led us down a rather bleak corridor. Our escorts took us past a set of curtains woven out of strands of starlight. We came into a room larger than most taverns. The floor was made of a low-cut purple grass. At either corner of the room was a recessed pit walled in stone. Steam billowed from it.

Cassie released a light, excited moan. "Elvish hot tubs?

Nice."

The groups split, leading me to the bath on the right, pulling Cassie to the left. Two elven women took hold of my clothes, wrestling to remove my jacket. Most men wouldn't have resisted. Elven beauty was legendary, and these women lived up to it. But we had also dropped unceremoniously into the domain of a lord of the Neravene while armed.

That's an action that can lead to swift execution in some domains. In others, notably the Marquis', that's death after lengthy torture.

So I resisted their efforts to strip me, shooing them away and opting to remove my own clothes. Before leaving, the women waved their hands horizontally in unison. A curtain of glistening, white thread appeared. An illusion, I wagered. A good one. At least I had some privacy.

Cassie had been afforded a similar treatment. A curtain was drawn around the area of her bath, leaving only shadows.

I shrugged out of my jacket, letting it fall to the floor with everything I carried inside. My shirt didn't want to leave my body. It clung to my skin from the sweat. I slipped out of it, breaking two of the buttons in the process, and threw it towards my coat. My jeans and boots landed atop them, along with my saber. I used my foot to nudge them nearer to the piping hot water.

I wasn't paranoid, but the closer my saber and coat remained to me—in arm's reach preferably—the better. But, when dealing with elves, paranoia was a useful trait to have.

"Hey!" Cassie's shadow flailed as several elves fought to restrain her.

My hand shot out to yank the curtain and rush to her aid.

She kicked out, trying to hit a shadow walking away with her folded clothes. "Not the shoes!"

I stopped, shaking my head and turning back. The bath was a welcoming thing. Two issues prevented me from being completely at ease: I was in a small, enclosed place, and stripped bare. Not ideal if I had to defend myself.

Maybe I am overly paranoid. I could use the bath.

Heat came off in waves, washing over me and easing my aches. A bath had never seemed so tempting. I fell into it, and the promise of relief was delivered. A low, long groan left my throat as every muscle loosened. The warmth felt like it was sloughing away my fatigue and problems.

A *whisking* sound drew my attention and I turned to its source. The curtain peeled back and an elven woman stood there in a robe that clung to her in all the right places. It left little to the imagination.

"I'm fine, thank you." I turned my head, dipping my hands into the water and cupping them. I brought a handful of water to my face and scrubbed.

Petals fell into the pool, and my heart rate sped up. They hit the water, spreading across the surface. A sweet, fruit-like aroma hit my nose.

"Thank you." I made my voice lower and harsher, hoping she would get the message.

"My lord expressed his desire to see you tended to." Her voice was like listening to a symphony of wind instruments. It was a light and airy thing, soothing to hear. A voice that promised many things.

I knew why she had come. Red flashed, flying past my vision as her robe joined my clothes. I sucked in a breath. She was every bit as pleasant to look at as her robe had promised. I shut my eyes and held my breath.

I am a member of the Timeless. I'm better than this. I'm supposed to be better than this.

I rattled off numbers in my head, counting by odds only, focusing solely on that task. *You're only human*, countered another voice inside my skull. I wanted to shut the voice down, but it was right. Long life aside, I was mortal, and the Grand Marquis knew it.

Something disturbed the water and I had a good idea what. The temperature increased. Maybe not in reality, but it might as well have. I felt a gentle touch along my chin and jaw.

When I opened my eyes, I found her thumb pressed against my jaw as her index finger stroked my chin. My heart beat like a fist-sized drum lodged in the side of my throat. Her lips turned up at the corners, giving me a smile that promised something far more wicked and satisfying than sharing a warm bath.

"Leave." My voice came out lower and rougher than I intended.

It did nothing to deter her. She cradled my chin between her fingers.

I folded my hand over hers, intending to push her away, but something kept me from following through. "Leave."

Elves had issues understanding English at times. It was evident when she pushed her body against me, entwining her leg around mine. She leaned closer and whispered into my ear, "But you don't want me to."

My body didn't. My mind knew better. I pushed her hand from my chin. My voice took a sharpened edge. "No, but you're going to anyway."

"Why?"

"Because, I'm mortal. I'm tempted."

Her eyes smoldered.

"But I'm not stupid."

The fire in her eyes died, and the smile followed.

"Temptation is like a knife, and a knife cuts best when you don't see it coming. When you're looking into their eyes, watching them smile, holding you close, they're looking for the soft spot in your back. That's when they drive the blade home. I don't want you slipping a knife into my back." I gave her a thin smile.

She made no response, becoming a frozen statue. An attractive, nude, unblinking statue. The earlier heat in her eyes was replaced with a cold, electric look.

My imagined temperature spike plummeted.

"My lord gave you his word of safe conduct."

"Actually, he didn't. He acknowledged his role as host and the duties pertaining to it." I made sure to point to Cassie's shadow, now standing alone behind her curtain.

"However, I don't recall the Grand Marquis saying that he offered us safe conduct, did you? One does not equal the other, especially in the Neravene."

Her eyes narrowed to slits, and I did my best to not visibly tense. She turned in one swift motion, leaving without bothering to grab her robe. Her hips swayed as she walked, giving me a great view of her backside. A gesture to make sure I knew what I was missing, no doubt.

Watching her go, I had to agree. My body was missing out. The muscles along my spine tightened for a moment, but my regrets vanished with the sensation.

Sex is never worth a knife in the back. Not even elven sex.

When she left the room, I faced Cassie's shadow. "How much did you see? Hear?"

She said nothing for a half a minute. "All of it. Kind of hard not to." Cassie made a choking sound like she had cut her self off from speaking. After another pause, she asked, "So why didn't you?"

"Weren't you listening?"

"Yeah, of course. Still, most guys in your position would have bow-chicka-wow-wowed all over that."

I was certain she couldn't see or feel my stare from behind two sets of curtains. I tried to make sure she could anyway. "I'm fairly certain bow-chicka-wow-wowed is not a set of words or a verb."

"Pssh. Is now."

I ignored the comment. "You heard my reasons. I don't trust any of them."

"You brought us here."

"For information, yes, but that was borne out of necessity. We need information. We do not need *that*."

"Everybody could use some of *that* every now and again. I know it's been a while since I've—"

"I can do without knowing that."

"You're such a child for someone so old."

My teeth ground against each other.

"But yeah, I'm not arguing, just giving you a hard

time...like she did."

The pressure in my jaw grew.

"Good choice, though. I'd high five ya if I were there. Ourselves before elves. Duty before booty."

I wondered if the entirety of my long life was an extended form of punishment destined to culminate in these final, excruciating moments. "Please, stop."

She feigned an irritated scoff, but stopped with the terrible humor. "Okay, serious time now. You really think they're going to backstab us?"

"It's possible. Next lesson in the supernatural: elves are famed for their deception, being too clever for their own good, as well as ours. They're cunning. They're not all the benevolent beings portrayed in novels. Some are; some aren't. The Marquis and his kind are most certainly untrustworthy, but they're knowledgeable and that's useful. In this world, Cassidy, knowledge is power. The more you know, the more you can use and do to protect yourself and hurt the supernatural if necessary. Remember that."

She gave no verbal reply, but her shadow nodded in understanding.

"I don't want to taint your view of this world, but..."

"I've been chased by trolls, gargoyles, plants, and now I'm surrounded by sneaky elves. I'd say my view's pretty tainted."

"There are still many wonderful and amazing things to see and be a part of in this world, Cassie. If we figure all of this out, I promise to show you some of them."

"That sounds nicer than what I've seen so far. But for the here and now, we've got to get out there and deal with this situation. We can't sit in here forever."

"A part of me would like to. It's nice."

"Yeah," she said. "I just want to find out why this is happening to me. If this guy can tell me, then fine. I'll play along."

The temperature dipped in my tub. Cassie was ten feet from me, wanting answers, ones that I had. I didn't have a chance to share them with her when the gargoyles came after us, but I did now. And there was no reason not to share them. Except for the fact that I had no idea how she would react. She was scared, and for good reason.

Just because people say they want to know things, it doesn't mean deep down they want to hear the words and reasons. Just because they say they can handle it, doesn't mean they can. Just because you know a terrible truth, doesn't mean you should share it.

But she did deserve it. So I told her.

"I don't know all of it, Cassie. I wish I did, but I've pieced some of it together. Do you want to hear it?"

Her figure went still behind the curtain. "Yes, and no. I mean, yeah, I'd love to know why I've got a bull's-eye painted on my back. I just don't know if I'm going to like the answer." Her voice was soft and weak.

"You won't." I could almost hear her breathing deepen. "Think of the networks of roads connecting a country—America, for example. They intersect, weave together to form something greater. There are so many of them, all individual yet crossing each other's paths, leading to new places. All of them have their own set of rules, different speed limits, lanes and more. The Neravene is like that in many regards, except you can't break its rules and make it up later. There are no accidents or tickets. The laws are like the laws of the universe, of science—resolute—unbreakable. You don't break the rules of the Neravene, Cassie. You *can't*."

"I'm sensing a but..."

"But *you* can. You shouldn't be able to, but you can. *You* can. And I don't know why or how, but I understand the importance behind it and the danger."

"Danger?"

"Cassie, think about it. The Neravene is a network of paths leading to the domains of powerful creatures, kingdoms, empires, and who knows what else. Things forgotten by time, and some things I wish were forgotten. Cassie, there are gods out there, and I'm rather glad that I have not and cannot come across them." I stopped and took a breath.

"But you can." I stared in her direction.

"Those places have their own protection to stop people and other beings from plopping in at will. Those Ways have to be opened by someone who knows how, has access, or is invited. It's a safety thing. In a world of worlds that is technically always at war—some part always is with another—imagine how dangerous your ability can be. There are small lords and ladies fighting for power and dominion over one another. Information being taken. Power being taken. Beings come and go. But to do all of that, any of that, you have to get into their domains in the first place. That's far easier said than done. It's close to impossible with armies, and takes decades upon decades, Cassie. You can do it in an instant."

There was a sharp inhale of air and her breathing stopped.

"The only way I managed to get us here is because of my personal history with the Marquis and a natural occurrence in the Ways that I capitalized on. That was within the rules. In the short time I've known you, you've opened Ways with no regard for the limits, unhampered by them. Think what that means for the beings in the Neravene."

She didn't make a sound, but I could hear imaginary gears clicking into place. She was putting it together.

I dropped the final bomb and felt like my insides were being gnawed for doing so. "Cassie, you are a living gateway to and through the Ways. One with free will and choice. You're not bound by the rules of the endless number of courts and domains that so many of the creatures have to abide by. You could turn the tide of a battle in favor of any being in the Neravene. You're the most valuable asset for power that any of them could have. Imagine being able to open a Way into the heart of your enemy's domain. To waltz in with your forces and take whatever you wanted. Better, with training, you could open a Way into the personal space of any creature. You could appear a millimeter behind them and be gone in an instant."

Her shadow was still before, now it had become something else. I'd come across pieces of art that looked like they moved more than her silhouette did at that moment. "Cassie?"

"Yeah?" Her voice was distant, removed.

I felt stupid for asking this. "Are you okay?"

"No." One single word, yet so much weight behind it.

"But you will be." I made sure my tone was unwavering, doing the best I could to make her believe me.

"Yeah." Her voice wavered. It was stronger than before, though. Good.

"Let's get dressed and see what we can get out of the Marquis."

"What if he's one of the people after me?"

I kept moving, making it look like the question didn't give me pause. It did. The possibility never crossed my mind, but it should have. I may as well have been bathing in a pool of ice water. I stepped out, scooping up a folded towel the elves left behind.

Whatever material it was made from, it felt like warm currents of air being pressed against my skin. The water dried within seconds of contact with the towel. I dressed myself, fastening my saber to my jacket, and peeled back the curtain.

Cassie's shadow gave me hints to her movements. She picked up a folded bundle. Even though I couldn't see her, I averted my gaze. It felt wrong. After what I told her, she could use as much privacy as she could get.

It's not an easy thing being told you are essentially a tool for conquest, nothing more. The paranormal world does strange things to you. It's a terrifying immersion. Being a part of this world is like being submerged under water and held there—a new and distorted world.

In a world of myths and magic, with Cassie slipping between worlds, she needed a reminder that she was human. She needed a lifeline. I hoped I could be it.

"Cassie?"

Her curtain eased back, and she stepped out.

I sucked in a breath.

She wore a kimono that looked like the night sky had been folded and shaped to fit her form perfectly. It was a rich—almost liquid black—shimmering with what looked like sequined motes of light. I narrowed my eyes and realized they weren't sequins, but small weavings of magic that caught and reflected the incoming light. Under a full moon, I imagined it would give off a beautiful pale glow. Now clean, and wearing that outfit, it was difficult not to admit how attractive she was.

"So, whaddya think?"

"You look great, Cassie."

She smiled when I said it. She spun in place, and I saw a flash of bright turquoise.

"Are you...still wearing the sneakers?"

"Heck, yeah. You think I'm letting someone take my kicks?" Cassie slid her foot back, brushing the heel against the stone floor, eliciting a rubbery squeak. "Plus, they took my old clothes. I'm not letting them take these."

There was something in the way she said it that tugged at my chest. She had lost a lot over such a short time—her place in the world, her home. At this point—even clothes meant a lot to her.

"We'll get you new ones that are just as flashy, over the top, and ostentatious." I grinned, and she returned it.

"I figured another reason to hang on to them would be in case we need to bolt. I'm not a fan of running in these." She held up a pair of traditional Geta, Japanese sandals.

"Good idea." I held out my hand. "So, Cassidy Winters, are you ready to be formally introduced to the Grand Marquis?"

She took my hand, intertwining her fingers with mine.

I pulled her a step closer, and we locked arms at the elbow.

"Yeah, I am, and hopefully we'll get some more answers."

"Then let's go to dinner."

"So long as we're not on the menu," she muttered.

Chapter Seven

The throne room was a different scene altogether. Before, we had interrupted a solitary meal. Now, we were to be entertained.

A table of polished, white quartz filled much of the place, festooned with bowls and platters of varying foods in equally differing colors. Fruits and vegetables, really. Not a shred of meat in sight. Yet.

All elves love fruits and veggies, but not all elves are vegetarian. An important distinction to remember.

I led Cassie to the far corner of the table, seating her away from and to the side of the Marquis' view. I sat beside her, directly opposite the lord elf, ensuring his view would be focused on me. If Cassie was right about the possibility that he was after her, I wanted to hold as much of his attention as I could and keep it off of her.

The Marquis wasn't a fool. A paper-thin smile spread over his lips as he noticed my positioning.

"My, my." He spoke without turning his head or eyes, keeping them fixed on me. "Young woman, you look ravishing—for a mortal." His near skeletal smile widened. He stood, brushing aside part of his lengthy robe, bowed his head, and shut his eyes. "I am the Grand Marquis, elven lord of the Amaranthine Veil. Lord of the Runners of the Night, one of the freestanding lords of the Neravene."

A small lord of the Neravene with an over-inflated sense of self-importance more like. But if he could tell us who was after Cassie, then I could put up with him.

"And you, young lady, are...?"

My hand couldn't have moved any faster to fall on Cassie's, nearly slamming it into the table. She gave me a quizzical look to which I shook my head. An action that did not go unnoticed by the Marquis. "Her name is Alexis—"

"Summers!" she chimed in. "Really? It sounds like a stripper name."

I didn't comment.

The Marquis' smile faltered. "I understand your reluctance, but honestly, we have worked together, Hawthorne. Would a small measure of trust be too much to ask?"

"The last time we worked together, it wasn't to everyone's benefit. Only yours."

A genuine smile crossed his face, made all the more disturbing by the hungry light in his eyes. "Indeed. We worked well together. You had some fun; I claimed all that I now hold dominion over. It was a good partnership."

He skewered a pair of cherries with a fork, plopping them into his mouth. Red syrup oozed past his lips. He licked it off with his tongue, but not fast enough. The simple stream of red against his fair flesh was an unsettling image.

He waved a genial hand to the food before us. "Please, enjoy, it's rather good."

Cassie wasn't dumb. She glanced at me out of the corners of her eyes, waiting for a discreet answer.

I gave her one, plucking a triangular piece of pineapple and lobbing it into my mouth.

Her eyes became saucers, and she lunged, grabbing fruit in a manner that went completely against the dignified nature of her outfit.

The Marquis' eyes grew as wide as Cassie's, but in confusion. He watched with horrified fascination as she raided the plates nearby.

I tried to restrain myself, but it was beyond me. I burst into a fit of laughter.

"You mortals are the oddest things I have ever come across." The Marquis' mouth quirked into an odd smile as Cassie devoured fruit after fruit, sparing the vegetables a horrible death.

"So, Hawthorne..."

Something about the way he said my name caused my

joints to lock in place. It was an effort to grab another piece of pineapple and make it look like nothing was bothering me.

"What brings you to my domain, unannounced for that matter?"

"We seek an audience...and information, if the latter is possible?" I phrased it to sound like I held a shred of doubt about the Marquis' knowledge and ability to procure it. He would take that as an insult or a challenge, possibly both. Either way, there was a chance he would find out something useful to share with us.

Elves cannot stand disrespect. They may not react immediately or violently, but they never forget. They hold long grudges, bide their time, and exact a slow revenge.

The Marquis paused, adopting a stillness that could be used to coach statues. "Indeed. That explanation doesn't answer the second part of my question, however."

"We were being chased. No time to knock on the front door or ring the bell." Cassie saved me the trouble of having to lie, and she did it well.

It technically wasn't a lie. We entered his domain through my home, but we were chased at one point.

The best lies harbored a shred of truth.

"Oh." The Marquis raised an eyebrow. "By what? Whom?"

"Big, ugly, cotton candy smelling—"

"Trolls," I said. The word fell like a hammer blow in the silent room.

The Marquis' mouth parted, revealing long, sharpened canines as he hissed. His eyes flashed. The pale green morphed into the yellow of feline eyes. The fairness of his skin was replaced by an ashen gray, one that made its way to his hair, ridding the locks of their silvery sheen.

Cassie's jaw dropped as she watched the transformation. "Woah, evil elven kitty."

The Grand Marquis composed himself the second he noticed Cassie gawking. His features warped back under the illusion of his subtle magic. Everyone was still for a moment that seemed to stretch out to be eternally long and painful.

The Marquis cradled a goblet between three fingers and gave it a light swirl. He took a sip, clicking his tongue in pleasure. "Apologies, I reacted poorly."

"Catty's more like it," Cassie muttered under her breath.

The Marquis' ears twitched. He tilted his head to regard her.

I leaned over, cupping a hand to her ear. "Elves have excellent hearing."

"Duly noted." Cassie turned to the Marquis and bobbed her head. "Sorry."

The Marquis ignored the apology, fixing his gaze on me. "Trolls." He rolled the word around his tongue as if it were foreign and distasteful. "You're sure?"

I gave him a level look. "Hard to mistake them for anything else."

He took another sip of his drink. "Yes, of course," he said more to himself. "Trolls." His face twisted in revulsion.

Cassie brushed a sneaker against my shin, and I turned my head a fraction. "I'm guessing trolls and elves don't exchange Christmas cards?"

"Have they made Christmas cards that explode?" I asked.

"Yeesh, that bad?"

"Worse." Elves and trolls had a list of problems that even I'd have trouble recounting.

A flash of sharpened white glistened as the Marquis bared his teeth. "Trolls are uncouth, savage, tools."

He wasn't wrong.

"What reason would trolls have for pursuing either of you?"

"Have you seen me? I'm adorable." Cassie batted her lashes as her lips quirked in amusement.

The Marquis looked to her, then gave me a confused look.

I shrugged. "Mortal humor."

He opened his mouth, "Ah," passed over Cassie and returned to his drink. The Marquis traced a finger over the lip of his goblet. A soft, rhythmic humming noise came from it. "The trolls—what marks did they have? Independent? A tribe?" The humming stopped as he broke off, looking at the ceiling then back to the goblet. "A court?" His voice was stone.

I shuddered, unable to hide it. My hand shook as I reached for a drink. A citrus cocktail rolled over my tongue and down my throat. Hints of pineapple and mango stood out.

I exhaled. "I certainly hope not. If the courts are involved, we have a problem."

"Yes. Three of them." The Marquis stared at me, unblinking, ensuring I got the message.

I did. The two of us would go down together if the courts were coming after Cassie and, by proxy, me.

"Anything to identify them?" His gaze passed from me to Cassie.

I blew through my nose, shutting my eyes as I thought back to the alley.

Cassie filled him in. "They wore parkas to cover their whole nasty selves. They didn't stick out much."

"Which is more caution than most show. They were smart," I added.

The Grand Marquis nodded. "Meaning they put some thought into this, or...were told what to do."

"Right." I scratched my chin, thinking harder. "Gray colored. I'm not the best authority on trolls, but that could help narrow it down. Different breeds, different colors?" I rolled my shoulders and looked to the Marquis for affirmation.

He bowed his head. "Yes, gray, but this doesn't seem like a tribal matter. If it were, they would have sent more than... How many did they send?"

"Two, and they blended in pretty well for a bunch of butt-ugly freaks. Their English could use some work though." Cassie tossed a cherry into her mouth.

"A pair then. Not enough. If it were serious, they would have sent more."

"Wouldn't that, like, reveal the existence of trolls? I mean monsters can't just walk around in big groups in the middle of cities...can they?" Cassie looked to me for an answer, then the Marquis.

I told her the ugly truth. "They do all the time—" I cut myself off. I had almost said her name.

The Marquis watched me out of the corner of his eyes but said nothing.

"You've seen how many creatures can mask their appearance." I refrained from nodding towards our host. She didn't need to know the truth about the Marquis, at least not in his presence.

"Well, yeah, but what about when they"—she hunched her shoulders and made a series of stretching and monstrous motions—"you know, rawr and burst forth with the hideous? People would notice that!"

"You'd be surprised what people are willing to ignore. Humans are great at ignoring and justifying things they can't believe, and with the strangest explanations they can come up with. Sometimes the real answer is the ugly one right before us, but that's not the answer people want, so...they make one up they like more. People hold to that, and eventually, it's not even an issue. It's something buried in the back of their mind, something they barely think of.

"That's what would happen if they saw those trolls. Someone was filming a monster movie. Those two had a skin condition, tumors, or it was a horrible prank."

Cassie's face sank as I spoke. I could see the realization dawn on her. She knew I was right, and it was disheartening for her.

Guilt gnawed its way from the front of my stomach, through muscle and my spine. Cassie shouldn't have to hear and know these things. She was in her twenties. She was supposed to be in college, being blissfully lost, and making mistakes she'd regret or laugh about later in life. Cassidy Winters didn't need to be sitting at the table of an elven lord, eating his food, discussing the monsters chasing her. She wasn't supposed to be breaking the rules—falling in and out—of a world she shouldn't have been aware of. She should have been with her mother, in her home.

Aches filled the tissue beneath my fingernails. I clenched the crystal table hard enough that my nails turned white. I let go and took a deep breath.

"I'm sorry, but even so, we don't need the help of the mortal side. We can figure this out. We will." I left no hint of doubt in my tone.

One corner of her lips turned up, the beginning of a smile. She tried to hide it, but it took her over. "Thank you."

"Of course."

"So, we cannot be certain for whom these trolls are working." The Marquis rolled his hand, speaking as if the exchange between Cassie and me hadn't occurred. "We can only eliminate a tribal decision. That does not preclude one of the courts sending them, or...an independent party."

"An unknown party...which presents a problem in and of itself." I rubbed a hand over my face, willing away the fatigue plaguing my eyes.

"Yes, and there is the possibility that this could be for personal gain, that these trolls are acting of their own accord. Although that begs the question: what gain?" The Marquis took another sip. "Why is it they are after you? What are you worth? What do you know? What can you do?" He leaned forward, a hungry look in those pale green eyes.

I couldn't tell if my skin paled, but it felt like it.

Cassie, to her credit, didn't miss a beat. She seized the moment and answered without fail. "Pssh." She snapped her fingers through the air in the shape of a Z. "What can't I do?"

"A great deal, I'm sure. Mortals are rather limited." The Marquis didn't look at her when he spoke. Instead, he toyed with a piece of white radish. Cassie's face twisted into a scowl the Marquis failed to notice. "For the moment, child"—I winced as he said it—"humor me. Pretend I have no knowledge of why they are after you."

"I'm pretty?"

The Marquis and I sighed in unison. I tried to direct the conversation away from Cassie's ability. "Does it matter? Whatever these trolls think she can do is irrelevant." It wasn't. It was the reason they were after her. But I didn't need to know the why any longer. I needed to know the who.

"I believe it is of the utmost relevance, Hawthorne. If I knew why they were after her, I could discern what party was behind this." He gave both of us a predatory smile.

"If I knew that, my host, I would assuredly tell you. I don't. So for the moment, let's move past that and onto other avenues of figuring out who sent the trolls."

"Would you? Tell me, that is?" The Marquis propped his elbow on the table, resting his chin on a balled fist as he regarded me.

"If I believed it to be in our best interest, yes." I stared back, refusing to blink. This coy game wasn't going to last long. Either he would relent and try to help us or, lose his patience, and I couldn't predict what would follow then.

I won the exchange.

With a heavy sigh, he lowered his head and rolled his hands in an exaggerated motion of defeat. "Very well. Moving on then. Based on what you have told me, it's most logical to assume these trolls are working for a private party. Their tribe is not involved nor are the courts, as evidenced by the lack of other beings and retainers pursuing you. Two trolls still seems a rather a poor choice of employee to apprehend a member of the Timeless and a young woman. There are far better choices of hunters." He smiled, the tips of his fangs showing.

My chair felt uncomfortable and rigid.

A single elf walked into the room, moving so fluidly it looked like they were gliding across the floor. It took me a moment to identify him as a male. His long, platinum hair fell to his hips. The slender, purple-robed elf came to stand by his lord, bowing at the waist.

The Marquis acknowledged his presence without turning to look, waving a lazy hand for him to speak. His retainer leaned over and whispered into the Marquis' ear. I couldn't hear what he was saying, but I didn't have to. The Marquis' eyes narrowed. They shifted towards me, then Cassie, where they stopped. His lips went thin.

A knotted rope of ice formed in my throat, falling to the pit of my stomach. I pushed away from the table and took one of Cassie's hands within mine. "Thank you for your time and hospitality, my host. I'll be sure to tell of your generosity to the other members of the Timeless and Ageless court. If you'll excuse us, I remembered that I have other pressing issues to attend to. Time sensitive ones." Which was true. I had no idea how much time had passed. I was due for an inquisition.

The Marquis clucked his tongue, a sharp echoing sound. "Of course. One thing, however." He snapped his fingers. The attendant bowed and stepped out of the room, never once turning around. "One of my questions *has* been answered. Just one." There was an unsettling undertone when he said it.

I helped Cassie to her feet, pulling her close. "Oh, my host?"

He gave the pair of us a wolfish smile, fangs bared, "Indeed. But I have a problem."

A colony of ants crawled over my skin as I felt endless pairs of eyes watching us. From within the shadows at the far edges of the courtroom, yellow orbs followed us. I could have sworn I saw a gleam of something that resembled elven teeth.

I backed away, not bothering to feign discretion. "We'll take our leave now."

"But another of my questions remains unanswered." He leaned forward, his posture hunched like a big cat about to pounce. The Marquis' glamour faded. His hair took on whiter sheen, skin fading to an ashy gray. Yellow eyes sparkled and turned to Cassie. "So, Cassidy Winters, what can you do?"

The frozen cord running through my body shattered, filling every inch of me with chilling barbs. Rows of yellow eyes closed in on us. Out of the shadows marched well over a dozen elves. Like the Marquis, their glamour faded. They were dressed in matching sets of dark, loose-fitting leathers.

"You gave us your word!" I spat. "You're our host. You're breaking your word of safe conduct."

His grin widened. "I did, but they"—he broke off to gesture to the elves surrounding us—"made no such promise. I'm certain they shall be punished for their transgressions. Punished as I see fit." His smile told me his retainers wouldn't suffer much.

Damn, caught in a loophole. I shouldn't have tried to best an elf in a game of words and manipulation. I'd lost. And now Cassie was going to pay the price.

"Cassie, get back." I brushed her waist, nudging her gently behind me.

The Grand Marquis waved a hand. "Take them."

Chapter Eight

Cassie bristled. "Curse your sudden but inevitable betrayal!" She brushed aside part of the kimono, revealing a bare thigh. A leather whip was coiled around it. With a few quick tugs, she loosened it enough to pull it free.

I followed her example, drawing my saber, brandishing it before me. "Stay back."

The Marquis looked bemused. "Honestly?" He gestured to the dozens of elves around us. He rose from the table, standing straight and turning to look at a spot only he could see, almost as if he was ignoring the scene. "No need to kill them. The Timeless would frown upon that. Take Hawthorne and throw him across the veil. Bring the young woman to me, unharmed...if possible." The lord of the Night Runners moved past his subjects, heading up the stairs.

More than a dozen highly trained, semi-immortal Night Runners against us. Hollywood is famed for portraying underdogs winning against the odds. Reality doesn't work like that, which is why we root for the underdogs, because they're not supposed to win. They can't.

I had over a century of combat experience. The elves surrounding us had far more.

"The smart move would be to surrender. We can't take them all, Cassie. The odds aren't in our favor."

"Never tell me the odds, kid." She quirked a smile and gave me a defiant look. "I'm not going down without a fight. Screw that. I've been running for too long. I'm sick of it. No more." Her jaw hardened and a light kindled in her eyes—twin orbs of dancing fire.

Cassidy Winters had been pushed into corners, chased, and forced into a rough life at the hands of monsters. But when backed into a corner, she snapped and fought back. Cassie had had enough.

If she wanted to stand and fight, I could do that. The odds were against us, but sometimes it pays to play the odds. So I did.

I bared my teeth and bellowed, storming forward. The Night Runners rushed to meet us. The first came at me, casting a scimitar into a tumble that whizzed past my ear. Cassie's whip cracked, and an elf bobbed out of the way. Another took its spot, charging Cassie.

I spun and swung the sword blindly. There was a feline hiss as I grazed the attacker's shoulder. The elf fell back, clutching its arm. Two elves pressed me, swinging their curved blades. I got an awful close look as the weapons tore the lining of my coat, nearly slicing the meat of my chest. They were fashioned from a metal too bright and polished to be found in the mortal world—if diamonds could be shaped into a blade. They sang as they arced towards me.

A whirling sound caused me to look back. I dropped to my knees as the iron barb of the whip almost took my eye. Cassie sent the whip into a spiraled, dizzying pattern. It was smart using its length to keep the elves at a distance. I wished she had warned me first. Every elf leapt back in synchrony, forming a perimeter around us as they watched the iron point hiss spitefully through the air.

I smiled. "Keep that going as long as you can. Pure iron wreaks havoc on Night Runners."

"On what?"

"Them!" I jabbed a finger to one of the dark-gray elves.

She nodded, putting more energy into her whip strikes. The elves tracked its tip, their bodies perfectly still as their eyes watched it. They were timing it. The second they felt confident, some of them would charge. Or worse, all of them. Cassie couldn't fend them all off. I reached for the ace up my sleeve.

The saber clattered to the floor, and I dug into my coat. My fingers brushed against a worn handle of wood. I whipped the out pistol, sighted on the injured elf, and squeezed. A small crack of thunder roared out. My hand bucked and the elf jerked, sprawling to the ground.

The elf's breathing died down a second before his body spasmed. A violent hiss emanated from the wound. He roiled in agony, pawing at his arm as the tissue broke down in necrosis. His screams looked like they were curdling the blood of the other elves. They hadn't expected that.

I gave the Night Runners a feral grin. "Never bring a sword to a gun fight." I fixed the Mauser on another elf and my smile grew, showing my teeth. "Iron tipped rounds, custom made, saved for an occasion like this."

"Hell yeah," Cassie cheered, breaking her windmill-like action. She singled out an elf of her own, lashing the whip. The elf darted deeper into the group, taking cover behind another. The whip would've missed had an elf not stumbled into its path.

Elves didn't make a habit of being clumsy. No honor among thieves, or Night Runners. It was a wonderful way to settle any personal issues in the midst of battle. The iron barb bit into the creature's leather armor. The elf hissed, grabbing the whip and tearing it free. A thin wisp of smoke leaked from the hole. The elf swatted its chest with a free hand, its face twitching as it did. She'd landed a decent blow.

A voice boomed above the commotion. "You bring iron into my domain? Into my home?" It was a resonant and bone shaking thing.

The Marquis didn't move down the stairs with blinding speed; it was something else. He was near the top at one moment. The next, his body blurred and he crossed the last two steps onto the stone floor. A slender, double-edged blade appeared too fast for me to register. It was a pale and luminescent metal, the sort that looked like it would have no trouble parting my head from my shoulders.

Another snap-crack of thunder. I dropped an elf; Cassie struck another. It was a violent orchestra of snaps, whips, and bullets.

The Marquis let out a sound somewhere between a howl and a snarl, throwing himself past his retainers and into the fray. He leapt, swinging his gleaming blade toward my head, looking to bisect me.

I dropped, rolled, and fumbled for my fallen saber. I grazed it with my fingertips, causing it to spin in place. His blade sank into the stone like it was soft earth. My hand beat a frantic dance as I reached for my sword without looking. I trained the Mauser on the Marquis.

Bad decision.

Spittle left the elf lord's mouth as he realized what I was doing. His arm snaked out, the back of his hand smacking the pistol as I squeezed. The force was jarring enough to cause the bones in my wrist to grind. My aim went wide, but I held onto the pistol as it kicked.

Another anguished howl. The Marquis' eyes shook in their sockets, a wild light inside them. He looked crazed.

"Kill them! Kill them both! I want to feel his heart give out in my hands!" roared the Marquis. His hair whipped around in his fury, making him look all the more deranged.

"Woah." Cassie leapt back and sent the lengthy weapon flailing. "Overkill much, dude?"

The Marquis may have held an elegant sword, but he wielded it like a cudgel, trying to bludgeon me to death. He swung it with both hands at my waist. Swords clanged as I met him with my saber, struggling with my single-handed grip. His blade pulled back and circled overhead before coming back down. I intercepted again, the muscles in my arm begging for relief.

What is his sword made from?

Each blow threatened to shatter my sword. I could feel the aged steel quake in my grip after meeting every strike. I was giving ground too quickly.

"Cassie!"

"What?" Another crack.

"This would be a good time to—oomph." The wind left my body as the Marquis' foot struck my stomach. I tumbled back, holding tight to my weapons as my brain and vision spun. I came to a stop, my right arm jerking as an electric jolt went through my elbow from where it struck stone.

"Cassie, somewhere, anywhere!"

"I don't know where. I'm a bit too busy to think!" The Night Runners crept forward, bobbing past the iron barb and working their way closer. The Marquis looked from me to Cassie, his face tight in confusion.

I fired another round. The Marquis moved with serpentine speed before I squeezed another shot off. The tip of his sword hurtled towards my face.

I went limp. The blade sailed over the tip of my nose, close enough to tickle my skin. My foot connected with the back of his knee, causing the elven lord to stumble forward. I pressed my advantage and swatted him with the flat part of my sword. He batted it aside with a contemptuous strike of his blade.

I held on as the muscles in my arm stretched and panged. The Marquis flipped the sword in his grip, point down, and sank to his knees, sending its tip plunging towards me. I rolled. The blade pierced stone.

I got to my knees and ran to Cassie. "Think, Cassie!" I didn't bother aiming when I fired again.

There was a horrible scream. A high wail that morphed into a deep, basso roar. Cassie's body visibly spasmed upon hearing it. She panicked and motioned with her hand. A thread of white light parted the air.

"Go, go. Cassie, go!"

She twirled the whip to force everyone back, and beckoned me with her free hand. I ran. She leapt into the Way, and I ran after her.

Something crashed into my back. I spun from the impact. A snarling elf's fangs flashed before my face.

As I fell back, I got a good look at the Marquis. His hand covered a cheek. Thin, black lines spread over his skin. It looked to be crackling.

I had grazed one of the freestanding lords of the Neravene with iron. If he survived, he would be permanently disfigured. An elf would take that personally.

The momentum of the Night Runner's tackle pushed me through the Way. Everything faded from sight.

I had just started a war.

Red brick and falling snow came into view as I tumbled out of the Way. The broad of my back took most of the impact as I hit the wall. Snow slipped into the openings in my clothes, making contact with my skin. I shivered and flailed as the elf struggled atop me.

Shit.

I panicked, taking hold of one of his wrists, pinning it to my side. He pulled back a closed fist, sending it towards my face. I sank the fingers of my free hand into his hair, pulling tight as I rolled my hips. His punch struck my shoulder.

We twisted; he fell to his side, and I rode the momentum to position myself atop him. He squirmed, trying to free himself from the pin hold. My legs squeezed tight around his torso and I leaned forward, using my weight and height to keep his arms pinned.

Contrary to many fantasy stories and myths over the years, elves are not some slender yet stronger race. They are nimble, light, tall—many are fair—and they are supremely skilled in archery and stealth. They can live forever unless they suffer a mortal wound. But they are not stronger than man. In terms of physical, hand to hand combat, they are rather limited.

I was taller than the Night Runner and weighed more. I pressed my advantage. I let go of his arms and drove an elbow into his chest. My balled fist connected with the underside of his chin next.

"John!"

I tuned out Cassie's shout, watching the elf's head snap to the side from the blow. A dull throb filled my fist as I knocked the creature's head the other way. The elf opened his mouth, showing me his fangs. I punched him in the mouth. A sickening crack rang out as one of his teeth broke. Blood welled from the spot, some of it coating my knuckles.

"Cassie, dagger!"

She looked at me wide-eyed, eyebrows raised. She was scared.

"Dagger!" I barked.

Cassie pulled it from the sheath and handed it to me.

The elf bucked, trying to shake me loose. I centered my weight over it and kept it in place. I flipped the blade and sank it into its throat, twisting and jerking it across. Tissue tore, and it wasn't clean. Blood spurted and pooled from the wound, some of it making its way up and out of the elf's mouth. He died with a macabre smile on his face.

"Oh my God." Cassie threw her hands to her mouth. Her skin paled and it had nothing to do with the winter winds and snow.

I looked at my hands, soaked in the creature's lifeblood, and to the red-tinged snow.

"I never...I mean..." she broke off.

"I know, Cassie." I kept my voice soft.

She had fought when she needed to, but running from trolls and fighting gargoyles was one thing. Back in the Grand Marquis' hall, she'd fought in self-defense, but even there, she hadn't taken a life. She had just watched me murder an elf. One that would have killed both of us if given the chance, but murder nonetheless.

I don't pretend to be a good person. I've taken lives over the decades, mortal and not. Cassie never did, never had to. Seeing what she just did—it was hard.

"I'm sorry you had to see that, but he would have killed me if he could. Maybe even killed you. Or worse, he would have dealt with me, and dragged you back to the Marquis. I had to do it."

She didn't respond. Cassie stared at the lifeless body on the ground.

"Cassie, are you okay?"

"I need a minute." Her voice came out a shade higher than a whisper, and she turned to look away.

I gave her the space and time she needed. I knelt and ran my hands through the ever-piling snow on the ground, wiping them as clean as possible. The dagger stained the inside of my coat from where I rubbed it dry. I looked at the body, lying slumped and losing color. I placed the dagger on the ground and shoveled as much snow over the body as I could. Content with my work, I stood and scooped up the dagger before walking over to Cassie.

I placed a gentle hand on her shoulder, giving her a soft, reassuring squeeze. "Here." I slipped out of my jacket, placing it around her. It was several sizes too big, and a tad too long, but I wasn't going to let her run around New York in winter in just a kimono.

"Thank you." She squeezed my hand and pulled the coat tighter around herself. "John...that was brutal. You're right; I know you are. That thing would have wasted both of us, but that was intense."

"I know. I'm sorry."

We stood there for several minutes. Snow pelted me, but I never moved from Cassie's side, my hand resting still on her shoulder.

She looked down and out the alley, her gaze focused on an imaginary spot only she could see. "Okay, I'm good now."

"Really?"

She shrugged. "As good as I can be. I'm not gonna forget this, but, I mean, we have bigger issues, don't we?"

"Yes, yes we do." I turned around and looked down the alley. It was a dead end with several fire escapes hanging from the walls. A lone metal door stood several feet behind us. A single stone step led up to it. "Why this alley?"

"Hmm?"

"Of all the places you've visited, you could recall, why here? What's so special about it?"

"Come on," she said, walking forward.

I followed her, and we stepped onto a little street. I had trouble recognizing it at first, having to resort to glancing to the end of the block. I blinked. "Part of Brooklyn. Been a while."

Cassie sniffed and nodded to our right. We stood next to a small diner. It was unremarkable in construction and appearance. A single, eight-foot-long and rectangular window sat recessed into the brick wall. One bar counter, that was once a brilliant shade of white, worn dull over years of use. A handful of tables between rigid, red vinyl seats.

I eyed Cassie, waiting for an explanation.

She stared into the diner before looking at me. "I came here one time. God, it feels like so long ago now. I hadn't eaten a real meal in a couple of days. I was tired and collapsed in the alley. I remember being so, so tired. I think I cried myself to sleep." She wrapped herself in her arms and squeezed.

"There's a door back there in the alley. It goes to the diner. It opened in the middle of the night. A woman who worked there—she came out with some trash. She saw me. I didn't say anything. I sort of panicked and backed up against the wall. She shut the door and went back inside. I thought she was going to call the police."

Something inside my chest broke. It felt like I had been nursing an old clock, ticking on, gears wearing until the moment they decided to give out. The clock face shattered at the same time.

"She didn't call the cops. I still don't believe it. I mean, I was on the run. I looked like crap, and I was a stranger. But she came out and helped me up. She pulled me inside. The place was pretty much closed, just one guy sleeping at one of the tables.

"They had some food left over—sausages, bacon, an egg sandwich—and she got me some iced tea. I didn't complain. After days of living off scraps and stuff I stole...it tasted like heaven. She showed me to the back and told me I could sleep there." Cassie sniffed again. It could've been the cold; it could have been something else. "She even threw her apron in the microwave, let it sit there for a couple minutes, and then pulled it out. It was warm and nice to sleep under."

I remained silent. Breathing in the cold made my throat hoarse.

"You wanna know the weirdest part?"

I nodded.

"She apologized...to me. She told me she was sorry they ran out of pie earlier that day and didn't have any to give to me." A trickle of moisture formed under one of her eyes.

"She did all that for me and said sorry. That's why I remember the alley. I remember what she did. Sometimes when I panic or feel scared, I remember this place. I still don't know why she did it. Why?"

"I've lived a long time, Cassie. I've seen a lot of terrible things done by the supernatural—horrible, horrible things. I've seen worse things perpetrated by man. And over all those years, I am still—to this day—surprised by the kindness people can show one another. No matter the atrocities committed by people, there are just as many, if not more, good people out there willing to balance the scales. Never forget that.

"She did that because she could, because she was a good person and because you are too. She did it because you deserved to have that happen. I can't promise to know if that was destiny or a random act of kindness. But I do know good things happen and, when they do, you don't question them." I smiled. She returned it.

Cassie took one last look at the diner before turning away. "We should keep moving, right?"

"What's the rush? They're open right now. Who knows? They might have that pie you were promised."

She gave me the largest smile to date. Her eyes ballooned. "Seriously?"

"Sure, why not? I can't speak on your behalf, but I'm still hungry. Fruits and vegetables don't do much for me," I flashed her a grin. "Plus, it's cold. I wouldn't mind warming up. You?"

"Oh, hell yeah. I'm down."

I opened the door and gestured inside with a polite bow. As Cassie entered, I let go of the door, letting it close. I snapped out with my foot, halting the door and peering outside.

Something had moved in the alleyway across the street. I could have sworn it. I stood there, watching for any sign of movement. The alleyway was still. Nothing moved, no sounds.

In my experience, that didn't mean it was empty.

Something could have followed us through. Unlikely, but possible.

My shirt pulled against my arm.

When I failed to acknowledge her, Cassie tugged again. "What's up?"

I gave the alley one last look. Nothing. "Thought I saw something."

She leaned past me, sticking her head out the window. "Saw what?" Cassie gave me a quick look then went back to peering down the alley.

"Don't know. Could be nothing; could be something."

"Wow, way to be cryptic. Think something followed us?"

"It's possible."

"I would've seen it. I came out first."

She had a point.

"You're right. I'm being paranoid. Old habits and everything." I gave her a curt nod, gesturing in the direction of one of the empty tables as I shut the door.

We took our seats near the window. Cassie and I exchanged a quick look as we sank into the comfortable cushioned seats. She knew why I chose to sit by the window. It was a double-edged sword. I could keep an eye out for anything that might mean us harm, but windows weren't great for protection. If there was a threat out there, a window wouldn't stop it from bursting through.

Cassie followed my glance. "You still think something's out there, don't you?"

"Just a feeling. I want to say no, but I can't shake it."

"Get these feelings a lot?"

I titled my head, arching an eyebrow as I gave her a knowing look. "When you're over a hundred years old and, fought in some wars, you learn to trust those weird feelings when you get them. I don't know what's wrong, just that something is."

"Does that mean we're gonna sit here and not eat?"

I snorted. "No, we're going to eat. Plus, this is a public place. If anything wants to start trouble, this is a bad place to do it."

"Didn't stop that elf from playing tagalong and following us through. I thought monsters like that would want to stay hidden. What's to stop something from going all 'Here's Johnny!' and busting through the door?"

"As a rule, the supernatural try and avoid the mortal world—in a sense at least."

"In a sense?"

"They don't want to make a scene and attract attention, but, at the end of the day, they're not people."

"Gee, I didn't notice..." Her tone could have dried my snow-soaked hair.

"There are creatures out there that feed on people. Many of the dark, terrifying monsters from stories exist. Know that. You've seen trolls, they're some of the sort that would, and do take people. You don't hear about monsters on the news, but you see and hear about their signs. People going missing. Odd things and circumstances surrounding those disappearances. Like I said before, humans are great at forcing themselves to believe things that are easier than accepting the truth. A ridiculous but comforting belief is better than a harsh and scary truth."

"So what about the elf back there? Someone's going to find his body. How is that going to be explained?"

I opened my mouth to speak when the waitress came into view. She had black hair tied back in a simple and out-of-the-way ponytail. Eyes the color of rich, wet earth. A cupid's bow mouth and button nose. She couldn't have been much older than Cassie. Her gray t-shirt was a bit rumpled, probably from bussing around. It was likely the same reason for the light splotch on the apron tied around her waist.

"Hey," she said as her pen clicked, "what can I getchya?"

"Coffee and a menu, please," I said.

She didn't respond verbally, just a half nod and scribbled on her pad.

"And you?" She didn't look at Cassie, instead giving a small thrust of her chin in Cassie's direction.

"No coffee, that's a definite. Please tell me you've got something warm and bad for me."

The waitress let out a little sound, too delicate to be a snort, but close. "Yeah, we've got plenty of stuff like that. You got a preference? Want to take a peek at the menu with your boyfriend or take a chance on one of the specials?"

I realized what the waitress said a second later. "I'm not her—"

"What the hell, gimme the special. I mean, he's buying. I can always get something else." She flashed the waitress a quick smile.

The waitress returned the smile with what looked like a reflex, clicked her pen, and tucked her booklet into a pouch in her apron. "Be back with that coffee." She gave me a polite bob of the head as she turned.

I leaned to the side, making an effort to catch a glimpse of her nametag as she moved away. *Anna May*. I committed it to memory. It could be another lesson for Cassie. The instant I felt comfortable the waitress was out of earshot, I picked up where our conversation left off.

"About the elven body. If anyone finds it, I don't know how they'll react. They'll most likely call the police. From there, it will go up the chain until it reaches important people. The paranormal has a hold at that point believe it or not."

"They've got peeps in the government?"

I nodded. "It's likely, but more likely they have people on the payroll. Remember, many look like normal humans. Many can take that form, whether through shape shifting or glamour."

Cassie raised an eyebrow.

"Glamour is a type of illusion magic employed by many creatures, normally the faeries and those under their dominion. Elves, as well as trickster spirits. And glamour is only one way to accomplish that task, a very specific way."

She nodded in understanding.

"Things like an elven body get swept under the rug for any number of reasons. Normally because they're paid to be dismissed. It could be a freak of nature, a mutation. Who knows?" I rubbed my thumb and first two fingers together. "But at the end of the day, many of the supernatural have a mind-boggling amount of money and resources. They spend it without thought to remain hidden. That makes them dangerous."

"I'm noticing. Okay, next question might be stupid."

I shook my head side to side. "For someone new to this world, there is no such thing as a stupid question. Ask away and learn. Knowledge is power, Cassie. The more you learn about the world, the better armed and prepared you'll be."

"Got it. Know stuff, kick ass. Alright, so I'm a bit of a geek." I didn't comment as she said it. "And I've read and watched stuff with elves in it you know..."

"And you're wondering why the Marquis and his ilk looked the way they did? Why they looked different than the tales say they do, when they dropped their glamour?"

"Yeah, what's up with that?"

"They're not the only elves out there. The Grand Marquis and his kind are Night Runners."

"Oh, yeah, duh, of course. Uh, so let's imagine I have no idea what that means. Break it down for me?"

"There are too many kinds of elves out there for me to go into, but Night Runners are the bastard little brothers of the Svartals."

Cassie looked at me like I was speaking in tongues.

"Black elves, dark elves."

"Those are real?"

I eyed her.

"Right, of course they are. Duh." She smacked a palm to her forehead.

"Night Runners are an offshoot of those elves. A different branch far down on the family tree, if you will. They are the more rowdy, uncivilized brothers. They're nocturnal and their domain is a land of eternal night. The light they live by and worship is moonlight."

Cassie parted her mouth in a silent, "Ah."

"They're hunters; they love combat, challenges and

especially word games. Elves—all elves—are fans of cleverness. They act through cat's paws if they can, manipulation, getting others to do their work, and outwitting their opponents."

"Except for what happened back there. He straight up broke rules."

"Technically, he outwitted me. He used a loophole. A good one. He welcomed us to his home, offered us his protection, something his attendants didn't. Clever."

"Douchey," Cassie commented.

"That too. Ah." I motioned with a slight gesture of my finger to the approaching waitress. I could smell the coffee from several feet away, which meant it was good stuff.

I always appreciate a great, strong cup of coffee.

Anna May lowered herself as she placed the coffee on the table. "Here you go. One coffee. Special will be ready soon." She gave Cassie a quick look and bustled off.

I let out a pleasurable sigh as I leaned over the coffee and inhaled. "Ah." I blinked several times as I let the aroma waft through my nose, helping me ward off fatigue.

Sugar doesn't harm members of the Timeless. We're not affected by the vast majority of human health concerns. Another perk of the job.

I held the container over the cup for a good bit, watching as several teaspoons of sugar granules tumbled into the coffee. I gave it a lazy stir with one of the spoons lying nearby. "So..."

"So?" Cassie shrugged within the coat. "What do we do now?"

"Aside from keeping our heads down? I don't know. The Marquis was my best idea. He knows an endless number of things, though clearly nothing of why you were wanted or by whom."

"He knew my name; he knew you." The words had an effect. Cassie may as well have thrown my mug through the glass window. My world went quiet.

"Yes, he did. Yes, he does." I didn't elaborate.

Cassie reached over the table and cupped my mug in

both her hands. She pulled it close and took a sip, looking over its lip to me.

I sighed. "This isn't something you're going to let go, is it?"

She said nothing, still staring as she put my coffee down. I pulled my mug back, taking a small swig. I took a deep breath as the coffee rolled over my tongue. It was a good blend for a no-name diner. Cassie stared at me, waiting.

"I don't have to talk about this, you know?" I stared at my mug.

"You led me there. Technically, you pushed me. Not cool. You bring a girl into danger, you owe her an explanation and definitely an apology. Just saying."

I exhaled through my nose. She had a fair point. "I warned you: the Grand Marquis has a great deal of resources. There was always the risk that he would find out your name."

"That's not what I want to know." She held her stare.

I had known that before I spoke. It wasn't something I wanted to talk about, but Cassie deserved to know. "I worked with the Marquis at one point." I broke the stare and looked into the black liquid, trying to get lost in it. "I, along with some of the other Timeless, are the reason the Grand Marquis has his title, his place in the Neravene."

"You helped that nut job?"

I nodded. "Not by choice. I told you how strict our lives can be, the rules we live by. We cannot interfere in the world of mortals. Normally, because of what we know, we're told not to intervene in supernatural affairs either."

"Told, not forbidden," Cassie said, her voice dry as she caught the distinction.

"Yes. It was a risk. There were benefits to aiding the Marquis, though, ones the Ageless court felt outweighed the risks."

Cassie yanked the coffee back, taking a sip.

"The Night Runners have always had a noticeable presence in the Neravene, but noticeable is not influential or beneficial. Many of the Timeless shared sensitive information with The Grand Marquis—information that helped him dispose of rivals. Some of us lent him something more than knowledge." I stopped, reaching over to grab the coffee. I lifted it to my lips and paused, wondering if I could stare into the liquid forever and never finish my story.

"John? What did you give him?"

"Our bodies." My voice cracked. "We fought with him—I fought with him. Night Runners are...were notoriously territorial for the longest time. At one point, there were tens of dozens of warring clans, each vying for supremacy. We helped facilitate that."

"You mean you helped him take over." There was no heat or accusation in her voice, just a simple statement of fact.

"Yes."

"Why?" She looked me in the eyes when she said it. That singular word can dismantle many an argument, thought, and justification.

"Honestly, Cassie? I don't know anymore. I believed differently then. I was younger. I wanted to see and do more. I was like you. It was my first time meeting elves. A faction of them at least. When I learned what was going on and the options were presented to me, I wanted to help. I believed that a united dominion of Night Runners could be useful, that the Neravene needed it. That—" I bit my tongue as I heard the gentle impact of shoes striking the tiled floor.

The waitress came carrying a large plate. I could see the pale yellow of eggs threatening to spill over the edge. She held a glass in the other hand.

"Here you go." She plunked the plate and cup down before Cassie. "And you?" She brushed bits of her hair aside and gave me a smile that reached her eyes.

"Nothing now. Maybe the pie when we're done?"

"Got it. Enjoy." She took a step before I cleared my throat. She stopped and glanced at me, brows furrowed and eyes unsteady. "Yes?"

"You have a beautiful name." I gave her a small grin.

"How do you say it?"

"Oh." She looked away for a second, her cheeks coloring a bit. "Anna May. Or if you're my mother, 'Anna May,' all southern like." A hint of Louisiana snuck into her voice when she said it the second time.

"Southerner?"

"Yeah, came out to New York for school. Still here. Love the place."

"You lost your accent, Anna."

She shrugged. "Yeah, happened early on when I got up here. Is...there anything else? Sorry, but I get off soon. I have studying to do."

I shook my head. "Just the pie. Pecan caramel."

She bobbed her head in acknowledgement and sped off without a word.

"What was that all about?" Cassie's tone carried a light, but noticeable edge.

"What?"

"I'm young and I'm a woman. I'm not stupid. The little flirt session."

"I was getting her to pronounce her name. I wanted to hear how she said it."

"Why's that?"

"I'll show you in a couple of minutes." I drained my coffee. It had cooled down, but not enough for me to find it disgusting. In all my years of life, I'd never once found it acceptable—or tasteful—to drink cold or iced coffee.

"I want to—well not honestly—explain why I helped the Grand Marquis." I grabbed the container of sugar and slid it in front of me. The salt shaker and the pepper, followed. "Think of these"—I gestured to the three containers—"as different kingdoms, domains, courts and the like in the Neravene. Each powerful, yet varying in power and influence. When you have a few, three for example, power resides in a small and concentrated dominion. That can be dangerous. By helping unite the Night Runners under the Grand Marquis, we introduced another player into the fold. A small player, but one who accumulated and solidified power in a chunk of the Neravene. Do you get it?"

She nodded.

"I thought it was the right thing at the time."

"And now, John?"

I sighed and shook my head. "He broke a truce he was obligated to uphold as host. He did that over you. So, no, I don't think it was a good idea, not anymore. Cassie, do you know what happened back there?"

"Yeah, he went apeshit on us."

"Not just that. He may have broken his word, but I struck him with iron. You don't do that to elves. It's like poison to them. I shot the Grand Marquis. I grazed him, sure, but he will be forever disfigured. If he survives."

"Good," she muttered. "Punk ass."

"Cassie, I started a war."

She let out a low whistle and seemed to shrink, pulling herself deeper into the trench coat.

"No matter how small a lord he may be, I maimed him in full view of his court. That's going to spread. Cassie, I'm marked now, same as you. Perhaps not to the same degree, but there's a bounty on my head. A large one."

"I'm sorry," she squeaked.

"Don't be. I'm not. I've wanted to do something like that to him for a long time. I never had the chance or courage before. I blame you." I refrained from laughing, but my lips spilt into a large and stupid grin.

Cassie chuckled and dug into her meal: a substantial amount of scrambled eggs, bacon, tater tots, and a few lean strips of chicken. It looked good. It smelled better. Or maybe it was the other way around. I hadn't had a meal like that in days. My stomach was a knotted mess, however.

I was responsible for a war, and I still had my inquisition. Food would cause me to vomit. I resisted the temptation to lean over and snake some of her well-deserved meal.

"So," Cassie managed to say between mouthfuls of food, "I got another question about—" She stopped, her features tightening into a stressed mask.

I leaned over and nudged the cup of orange liquid closer. "Drink. Don't talk. Chew your food, kid." I kept my lips pressed tight after saying it, trying hard not to smile.

Despite being on the verge of choking, Cassie managed to narrow her eyes and shoot me a venomous look. She threw her head back and swallowed a quarter of the orange juice in a single go.

I could see her throat constrict as the food gave way to the liquid.

"Gah," she gasped. "First betrayed by an elf, now by eggs. What's next?"

I buried my face in my hands. There was no dignified response to what she said. Silence was the best course.

Cassie shoveled another spoonful of eggs, peppered with bits of bacon, into her mouth. I noticed she chewed slower. She swallowed and gave me a look.

"John." Her voice was soft. "Back in the Marquis' court, when we were eating...he said my name. When he did, something happened." She pulled her arms out from underneath the coat, rubbing her hands over them. "It felt odd, like someone poured cold pudding over me or something. I felt like I was being drowned in frozen syrup—"

"Like all the warmth was suddenly pulled from your insides?"

She blinked. "Yeah, how'd you know?"

"Names have that power, Cassie, especially when uttered by those with ill intent. There's a reason I shared mine with you when we first met. It's the same reason I wanted to know yours. Names can form powerful bonds between people. They connect us, identify us."

"They're that important?"

"More so." Cassie glanced past me as I said it, but I didn't follow her gaze. "Watch and pay attention."

Anna May came into the corner of my vision, setting down two plates a tad larger than my open palm. A small wisp of steam danced through the air above each dish. Two slices of warm, golden brown pieces of pecan pie. "Thank you, Anna May." My voice carried a hint of southern inflection, mimicking the tone the waitress used earlier.

Her cheeks colored and a smile appeared on her face, the sort that made her eyes gleam.

"No problem. Anything else I can do for you two?"

I waved a hand and shook my head.

"Alright. Well, enjoy."

"We plan to. Thank you."

Anna May left, her posture a bit more buoyant. Every step was light and nearly a bounce.

I arched an eyebrow at Cassie and jerked my head over my shoulder to the waitress. "See what happened there? All I did was say her name the way her mother did. The girl is practically floating. That tells me a lot. She was close to her mother, loved her—still does. Saying her name that way reminds her of that, makes her feel the way her mother makes her feel.

"That's the power of names. True names. Not necessarily the names we're born with, but the ones we identify with. It's one of the oldest rules of the world—both worlds. The Principle of Identity. Every person, every creature has a name that makes them who or what they are. Every time that name is said, every action you take, thought you think—compound and mold to that name. They mold *you*."

Cassie's eyes remained still as I explained, but I could see the attentive shine within them. She was absorbing every word. Good.

I sliced into the tip of the pie, bringing it to my mouth and huffing out a few gentle breaths. I dropped the piece into my mouth and shut my eyes as brown sugar, flaky crust, caramel, and pecans rolled over my tongue.

No matter how much the world turns to shit around us, never underestimate the simple pleasures in life and their capacity to make you appreciate what you have. Food is one of those things.

"You should try it while it's hot, Cassie." I pointed at

the piece.

She took my advice and dug into the pie, showing less restraint than I had. I couldn't blame her. She'd been waiting for it long enough. Her eyes fluttered as she chewed the pie and took in a deep, relaxing breath.

"Good?"

"Orghmygod!"

I laughed, but it was cut short. Something stirred in the alley across the street. A gleam of silver cut through the darkness. A flash that winked out of sight the instant it appeared. *A Way?*

"Wuh-oh, I know that look," Cassie said through another bite of pie. "What's wrong?"

"I swear I saw a thin silver light in the alley." I didn't look away from the alley as I spoke.

Cassie stopped chewing.

"Could have been anything. A camera flash, the backlight of a cell phone—anything."

"Or a Way," she said, her voice flat.

"Yes."

Cassie faced the window and watched for a handful of seconds before looking down to her pie with longing. She let out a sigh. "I hate the supernatural. No regard for a woman and her pie."

"Finish it." I slid my plate over to her. "You can have mine too." I pushed myself from the table.

A flicker of a smirk appeared on her face. "You know, I can't tell if you're being sweet by giving me this pie...or if you're trying to make up for the fiasco with the Grand Marquis."

I blinked. "I'm going to go stand by the entrance and watch. If anything happens, I want you to run."

"But—"

"Promise me." My voice was harder than the brick around us. "Don't act like you know me. Don't come to my aid. Just run, Cassie. Understand?"

She swallowed and nodded, cutting off a larger piece of pie and almost inhaling it. I understood why. She wanted to say something more, but at the same time she knew I was right. The pie prevented that, and it was delicious.

"In my jacket, take my wallet and pay. Leave a great tip. I don't want... if anything happens, Anna May is not involved in this. I want to keep it that way. If I can't, just leave a big tip, Cassie."

She nodded and I moved away from the table without giving her a second look. I made every effort to give the appearance that our meal and shared seating was nothing more than coincidence as I left. The glass pane of the door was cool against my palm as I rested it there, debating stepping out and giving whatever lurked out there a clear target.

Better you than the girl.

I pushed the door open and walked out. Snowflakes flitted past, many clinging to my lashes and hair. The cold stung my eyes a bit, but I shut them tight for a few seconds. When I opened them, I saw a lone figure bundled in too many layers of clothing advancing towards me.

They wore a mottled gray and white parka, colors that blended easily under the flurries, but it didn't mask their bulk. I looked over my shoulder to see if another figure was following. There was no one.

I turned and took off at a brisk walk, hoping that I would be followed and Cassie would be overlooked. I made it to the end of the block before I cast a glance behind me. The figure was advancing, noticeably closing the distance. But they had left the diner behind. That was all I wanted.

I rounded the corner and picked up my pace as I vanished from their sight, for however short a moment. A spine-tingling and primal fear took over my body. I broke into a run and tore down the street. My lungs and the back of my throat ached, going dry from the winter air and exertion.

I looked back. The figure wasn't in sight. I slowed my pace, coming to halt before another alley, doubling over and resting my hands on my knees.

A bouquet of sugary sweets tickled my nose. Both sides

of my shirt went tight around my throat and chest. I was hauled into the air. The world spun. Bright pain, an electric flair of red and white, flashed through my eyes and body. My back was jarred, as were the bones throughout my upper body as I impacted the alley wall.

"Orgh," I groaned. My head lolled like the bones in my neck were jelly.

A meaty hand—too wide to be human—palmed my face. My neck twisted as the hand forced my head back, grinding the back of my skull into the brick. A few strands of hair tore free. The pressure was great enough to be excruciating, but not enough to break my neck or skull. The troll knew what it was doing.

"Where?" it grunted, its face masked behind the parka's oversized hood.

"Hrgh," I gasped, batting at its arm.

"The girl, where?" The hand tightened around my face.

My teeth felt like they were going to fall from my gums. Another grind against the brick. The back of my head cried out as I felt the rough stone line my scalp with micro cuts.

"Where? You know!"

The cold was getting to me. My muscles grew numb and distant. I had little to no control over my body. I fumbled for my weapons on instinct, realizing too late that I'd left my coat with Cassie.

At least she'll be safer with it.

A flash of white struck the troll's hood, deteriorating on impact into countless particulates of snowy dust. A bit of the snowball slipped through the troll's fingers and peppered my face. I sank to the ground as it released me. I landed in a crumpled heap, breathing hard against the wall.

Another snowball hit the troll, making its way through the open face of the hood. I was surprised to see the troll reel from the strike. A snowball couldn't have hurt a troll. The creature made a sound like an old diesel truck starting up.

Cassie reached into my coat and drew my Mauser, doing her best to level it at the troll. The gun quaked in her grip, her hands quivering in a manner that had nothing to do with the cold. "Freeze, ugly, or I'll cap you." Her voice shook as much as the gun.

"Cassie..." A fit of pained coughs interrupted my cry. "Leave, please. Open a Way. Leave!" I coughed again. My head spun from the violent exhalation of air.

Even with a hood obscuring its face, I could picture the frog-like grin the troll was wearing underneath. It had found who it was looking for. It lumbered towards her, an arm outstretched.

All Cassie had to do was squeeze the trigger. The iron-tipped round would devastate the troll and bring us to the attention of law enforcement.

A sharp whistle pierced my ears. The troll, Cassie, and I turned to regard its source. I sucked in a sharp breath. My insides burned from doing so.

If the troll's coat was well camouflaged for the snowfall, the new stranger's coat was the snow itself. A shifting, almost living blend of smoke and all its colors. Endless shades of gray swarmed in swatches of white. Their cowl was raised high and over their head. The stranger couldn't have been more than a couple inches over five foot. A Japanese-style sword hung at their side.

The troll snarled. I could feel the hate in it. It lunged at the stranger. That was its last mistake.

The stranger took two measured steps forward, moving with perfect grace. The flash of metal was so fast it looked like it didn't disturb the fall of a single snowflake. Flesh parted with ease as the sword sang its way through the troll's neck.

The beast's momentum carried it forward. A split second later and the troll's head, still hidden within the hood, tumbled from atop its body.

Cassie shifted her hips, pointing the gun towards the newcomer.

"Don't!" I warned.

The sword and its wielder moved again. They were before Cassie in an instant, flicking their wrist and sending the flat edge of their sword crashing against the gun. It was knocked from her grip. Cassie reached into my coat, going near her thigh for the whip. Another movement of the stranger's hand and the blade was reversed, its chisel-tip pressed against the soft flesh of my throat.

"Do not move." The voice was sharp, heavily accented English.

I didn't dare breathe. I knew who was under the hood. A single false move, and my throat would be pierced.

A slender hand appeared from a loose sleeve of the white cloak. The skin was thin and crinkled as it moved towards their cowl. The hood fell to reveal a face lined with nearly a century's worth of living. In fact, the man was far older than that.

His hair was as white as the snow falling around us, bound into a topknot with a single, shimmering piece of black silk. His beard fell to the bottom of his neck, just as white as his hair, save for a small area around his lips and chin, which managed to retain some iron gray. His cognac eyes held a sharpness that equaled his katana.

Cassie moved. I didn't have the chance to tell her not to, or the ability. A single movement and I'd die.

The same hand that had lowered his hood, snapped out in a flash. A kaiken appeared in his grip like a magic trick. He held it against Cassie's ribs. She froze, her eyes going wide like an owl's. All that moved was her nose in a small twitch.

I went out on a limb and took a risk. "Toshiro." I moved my mouth and throat as little as possible. I wasn't sure if he had heard me.

He stood still, like a fixture of the alley, a diminutive statue that had us pinned in place with a dagger and sword.

"Toshiro," I rasped, "leave her alone. Please."

The man didn't blink, but an imperceptible millisecond later, the blade was gone from Cassie's side.

"Thank you." Toshiro made no acknowledgement of having heard me.

"Jonathan Hawthorne." His gaze was still fixed on

Cassie as he spoke. Hearing him say my name in that tight, clipped manner made my body shudder. "You are called before the Ageless court to stand trial to answer for your transgressions." He pulled the tip of the blade back an inch, enough to allow me to breathe and talk comfortably, yet close enough to skewer me should he choose to.

Ever the pragmatist.

"Transgressions? Is that what we're calling them now?" I balled a fist, releasing it before Toshiro took note. My jaw clenched just enough without tensing the muscles in my neck. "You know every time I became involved in mortal affairs it was for a damn good reason!"

Toshiro's gaze narrowed. "The duty of the Timeless is to observe. Acting without emotional investment or attachment, and for balance is the duty of *my* order. You know this. You swore to abide by the laws of both orders when you were inducted into the Timeless, hai?"

"People were dying, Toshiro. Have a heart. Innocent people—young men, women, and children, dammit!"

"First defiance: October, the year of 1914. Interfering in the first world war."

Cassie let out a low whistle as Toshiro rattled off the charge in an almost mechanical manner. She ogled me out of the corner of her eyes without turning her head. "You fought in that?"

I lowered my head a fraction in a silent yes. Anything further and Toshiro might have run me through. He wasn't the sort to take chances. He was near fanatical in his duties and loyalties, which was why I trusted him. I didn't like the man, but he was honest, incorruptible, and an asshole.

"The second offense: March, 1940, France. You involved yourself in the second world war. Stubborn boy, you didn't learn the first time?"

I went rigid when he called me "boy" and understood Cassie's aversion to being treated like a child.

Cassie scoffed. "Really? Once wasn't enough for you? What is it with boys and fighting?"

I gave her a hapless shrug. "I don't like bullies. I'm sure

you can appreciate the sentiment with everything going on in your life at the moment."

She returned the shrug and muttered, "Touché. Didn't we get involved in that one later though?"

"I really hate bullies," I murmured.

"Hai, and look at the trouble it has brought you. You should have long ago learned your place in the grand scale of things. You are to observe and record. Nothing more. It is not your place to choose what happens or to act against the events of the world.

"Third offense: three days past, you involved yourself with her." He made an almost unnoticeable upturn of his head, a micro nod towards Cassie.

I froze when I realized what he had said. *Three days.* The Ageless court met at sunrise. It was the night of the third day. I had lost more time than I imagined in the Neravene. I was technically a runaway and would be prosecuted as such. "I'm not on trial, am I, Toshiro?"

He ignored the question. "You came to the aid of one Cassidy Winters, and in her company, you ventured through the Neravene uninvited into domains you should not have. In doing so, you committed your fourth offense—"

"What?" Cassie and I shouted in unison.

"Trespassing in the domain of the Grand Marquis. You broke the laws of hospitality and assaulted your guest. He is asking for your return to his lands to face judgment or risk war between the Runners of the Night and the Timeless. You will come with me." There was no emotion in his tone. It was as cold and iron as the weather and his sword.

We would be coming with him, no questions, no point in resisting.

"Toshiro, fine, I will come with you. You know me. I hold to my word. I'll stand before the court; that was never in question. I intended to anyway. But, please, leave her out of this. I don't want her—"

"Bullshit, he's not taking you anywhere," she growled. It was an odd sound coming from her.

"Cassie, don't. Please."

She didn't seem mollified by what I said, but she backed off.

"Toshiro, how long have we known each other? You owe me the truth at least. If the trial wasn't a farce before, it sure is now, isn't it?"

"Hai."

"You know what's going to happen, don't you?"

He nodded, his face a grim mask.

"Yeah." My voice was raw. "I thought as much."

"Wait." Cassie risked taking a step closer to me. "What's going to happen to you, John?"

Toshiro answered her question and broke my skin with a practiced motion. A trickle of blood licked the tip of his blade. "Death."

Chapter Nine

A great many words carried a finality with them, none more so than that one. One hundred and eighty years, give or take, and it was coming to an end. It had been a good run.

"That's bullshit! He can't. You can't, John." Cassie's face twisted into a mixture of grief and rage.

I couldn't blame her. I had promised to help her figure everything out. It appeared I was going to have to break that promise.

"I won't." Toshiro's voice cut through the air like his sword. "The court will. Come." Metal slid against wood as he sheathed his sword in a fluid, practiced motion. He held out his hand, making no other motions.

I grunted and slapped my hand against his forearm. His fingers dug into my arm with wooden strength. Five sets of dull pressure throbbed in the muscle. He hauled me to my feet with a simple tug.

"Thank you, Toshiro." I inclined my head slightly, which he returned without a word.

He sent a hand fishing into his robe and retrieved an almost delicate looking chain of silver. Two equally thin hoops sat at either end, but it was what lined the hoops that caused me a moment's discomfort. Needle-like barbs ran around the entirety of their edges, waiting to bite into whatever passed through the hoops. Toshiro eyed me, waiting.

I sighed. "Bastard," I mumbled as I held up my hands.

"You can't be serious." Cassie pulled up beside me, putting her shoulder against mine and working to shove me away from Toshiro.

"Do not interfere." Toshiro might as well have a

cracked a whip. Cassie went rigid when he spoke.

"Leave the girl alone, Toshi." I smirked.

His eyes turned to slits. Toshiro lived by a steel strict code of honor, a man that followed rules and never crossed the line. One of those things he held to was respect. He wasn't fond of someone butchering his name, but he also wasn't the sort to retaliate with needless violence. He didn't need to. He hurt me a different way.

"You have a bad habit of adopting strays, Jonathan. And a worse one for leaving them dead." Toshiro's face was flat.

My breathing intensified.

"Will you try to make her one of the Timeless as well? How long before her body is found broken and—"

A primal snarl fled my mouth, echoing through the alley and into the streets. The front of Toshiro's cloak bunched in my fists as I charged. It was a shame Toshiro was no longer in it. A lightning-quick flash of electric blue and red filled my vision as the katana's kashira crashed into the back of my skull.

As I mentioned, Toshiro was an ass.

There was a *snikt* of metal sliding, and I felt a cool touch of something across my neck. The edge of the blade rested against my carotid. If Toshiro sneezed, the Ageless court wouldn't have to bother with the trial and execution. They would love that. It would save them time. They were a practical sort.

"John!"

I could see Cassie out of the eye that wasn't pressed against the brick wall. She rushed Toshiro, pulling the dagger out from beneath my coat and her kimono.

"Cassie, no," I warned.

Toshiro held up an open hand. I couldn't see anything else, but something in the way he looked must have stopped Cassie in her tracks. "One pound of pressure—that is all it takes to break the skin. All I need to do is shift my weight...like this." He moved. Heat enveloped the area where the sword rested.

"No!" Cassie's scream was bound to draw attention.

A voice with perfect Oxford-accented English cut off all sound. "Leave the kids alone, will you?"

Toshiro stopped, somehow managing to cut me on a level so small I didn't know how to measure it. I didn't think it was possible for him to do that without severing the artery, but he did. I gained a new appreciation for his level of swordsmanship.

Cassie didn't put the dagger away, instead adopting an aggressive posture and watching the newcomer I couldn't see. "Who are you?"

"Should I tell her, John, or do you have that covered? Toshiro, let the kid go."

Toshiro complied, and I smiled as his hold on me ceased. I pushed myself off the wall and turned to face my rescuer.

He was a shade under five-seven, built like a seasoned soldier with only the necessary muscles. Someone deemed it fit to grace him with the broad shoulders of a professional swimmer and the features of a gentle father. His salt and pepper hair matched his brows. Eyes the color of polished acorns managed to glint in the darkness.

He smiled, the perfect white contrasting his well-bronzed skin. The red leather of his designer jacket matched the bricks around us. His jeans were well worn, as were his boots.

"So, kid?" He arched an eyebrow and broadened his grin.

I bristled and developed sympathy for Cassie. It was not fun being treated like a child. I cleared my throat. "Cassie." I waved a hand past Toshiro to my eloquent friend. "This is my mentor and greatest friend—"

"And the man who bails him out of trouble...which is starting to seem like all the time nowadays." He gave me a reproachful look.

I shrugged.

"My name is Quentin Denholm." He extended a hand towards Cassie.

She pursed her lips and looked at me before stowing the dagger. She took his hand and Quentin pulled it to his mouth, pressing his lips against the back of fingers.

I groaned. "Aren't you far too old to be trying to flirt and woo women in their early twenties?"

He flashed me a smile. "Being an old man is precisely what makes this fine. I'm old and charming. I'm being polite."

"I'll say." A hint of color touched Cassie's cheeks, and I ground my teeth.

"So, John, old boy, what have you done this time?"

Toshiro opened his mouth, but Quentin waved him off. "I asked him, not you, *boy*." There was something in how he said it that made it demeaning.

Toshiro's eyes widened for a microsecond, and his face tightened. Toshiro was so much older than me that it was laughable to think about. But Quentin, he was old enough to baffle the world's leading archaeologists and historians. I almost believed that he had forgotten more things and events than experts would ever know. If he were the sort to forget things. He wasn't.

"So, kid, what was it this time?"

I told him. I left out the parts about who Cassie was, referring to her as "she" or "her." I went out of my way to exclude what she could do. I trusted Quentin more than anyone or anything in all of time, but I'd die before spilling an ounce of that information near Toshiro.

He was an honest man, a duty-bound man; that didn't make him a good man. Members of his order would the let the world burn if it meant keeping the balance. He would gladly see Cassie killed if it meant preserving neutrality.

Over my dead body.

"Oh, John..." Something cracked in his voice. He sighed. "You've really gone and done it this time, haven't you?"

"I'm not a man of half-measures. If you're going to do something, best to do it right, no? You taught me that." I gave him a weak smile.

He grunted. "I clearly taught you to be an insufferable wiseass as well, hm?"

I didn't argue the point.

Quentin stepped towards me, rubbing the heel of a palm against his right eye. "Right, then. The court's likely convened. They've decided on your outcome already. But you know how these things go."

I nodded.

"Pomp and ceremony. They'll give you a retrial. Then kill you."

"The hell they will!" Cassie's lips peeled away from her teeth in a feral snarl.

"I like this girl, John. She's got the right attitude."

"What's the point, Quentin? I'm dead. You know it."

"Bollocks. If they're retrying, it means I've got time to try something of my own."

Toshiro placed himself between Quentin and me. "You will not interfere in this. I will take Jonathan Hawthorne—"

"Stuff it, boy. I'll take him. You've hounded him and us long enough. Go on." Quentin made a gesture like he was shooing away an irritating animal, going so far as to cluck his tongue.

Toshiro looked like someone had just pissed on his ancestors. His hand flew to the hilt of his blade, pausing as his eyes shut tight and he composed himself.

Quentin waggled a single finger. "Uh-huh, you lot aren't allowed to judge and act like that. If you've got my boy trumped up for not following the rules, you best follow them yourself, Toshi."

Toshiro's chest swelled for a moment. I really believed he was going to draw and take Quentin on. In all honesty, I wished he would. I wanted to see the outcome. Quentin was not a pushover.

"I will remember this disrespect, Quentin."

"Good. Kids these days are scatterbrains from what I can tell." Quentin smirked.

Toshiro huffed and snapped his hand. A Way opened. It resembled the sort of vortex that forms when unplugging a filled bathtub. A swirling mass of smoke and fog roiled together, endless shades of gray fighting and blending, all being swallowed into a mouth. It was certainly an interesting shape for a Way, but I should've expected as much.

Toshiro motioned with his hand. The cloak I held faded through my fingers. A mass of smoke flitted towards him and took form. His cloak wrapped itself around his body.

"Woah," Cassie whispered.

Toshiro passed through the Way like he was made of nothing more than air and dust particulates. I breathed a sigh of relief as he left.

"Never liked that sprat." Quentin spat on the ground. "Right, then. Come on." He walked past us and the troll's slumped body, heading out onto the street.

"Where are we going?" I almost felt stupid for asking.

"Your place, kid. I'm old, knackered from the trip, and a guest. Invite me into your home, eh?"

Cassie grinned. "I *really* like this guy." She let out a laugh, recovered my gun, and followed him to the curb.

I scowled and hugged myself, slipping my hands under my shirt to rub my chest. Being one of the Timeless does not mean I am immune to the cold and its effects.

"Wait for me." I stomped after them, giving the troll's separated head one last look. I swallowed. Any further antagonizing on my part and Toshiro would have given me the same treatment.

I came to a stop behind Cassie and Quentin. My mentor fished in the pocket of his coat. He pulled out a flat, expensive looking smart-phone, tapped his thumb on the screen, and placed it to his ear.

"Cab's on its way. Now, we wait." Quentin turned to Cassie. "Are you cold, dear?"

She shook her head. "No, John gave me his coat. I'm good." She pulled the sides of it, wrapping herself deeper in its warmth.

"I'm fine. Thanks for asking." My teeth chattered. I couldn't see my lips, but I imagined them turning blue. I was losing sensitivity in my fingers.

"Well, kid, you should have brought a coat." Quentin kept his eyes straight ahead and his voice level, but I could almost picture his smirk. He buried both hands into the pockets of his coat. One came back out, holding a vial no larger than his pinky finger. "Catch." He lobbed it over his shoulder without looking.

I stumbled forward, fumbling as the vial struck my palms, sending a short jolt through my skin. Cold weather and hard objects do not mix. I glared at the back of Quentin's head, imagining it plastered with a snowball.

Petty actions like that are beneath members of the Timeless.

I threw a snowball anyway. It struck the back of his head, flattening into nothing at the moment of impact. It wasn't a hard throw, but he staggered nonetheless.

"Wow, childish much?" Cassie tilted her head and regarded me with an expression that tried too hard to remain neutral. The corners of her lips twitched. She fought to conceal a smile.

I threw a snowball at her as well. She had my coat. It was only fair.

"Ugh! Oh, hell-no-you-didn't." Cassie straightened up, brushing the dusting of snow off my coat's collar. "Game on." She knelt and scooped a handful, not bothering to form a ball, and threw the mound at me.

I took the unshaped lump of snow directly in the chest. I regretted starting this. My teeth jack-hammered together, aching a bit. I threw my hands up in a gesture of defeat and placation.

"Damn right," muttered Cassie.

I wobbled the vial in my hand. The translucent orange fluid sloshed from side to side. "What's this?"

"Liquid warmth, kid. Down the gullet and you're golden for the night. No more sniffles and chills."

I blinked, holding the diminutive vial up to my eyes for scrutiny. Using the tip of my thumbnail, I dug into the cork and flicked upwards. The top popped out and onto the snow. I downed its contents without thought. The solution hit my mouth, fizzing and rolling over my tongue with an orange, almost static charge. I winced as it made its way down my throat and into my stomach. "Brr, was that orange...soda?"

Quentin shrugged. "Some was probably used in the base. Don't ask me. I don't make the potions. I just buy them."

"And you happened to have warm-up potion on you?"

He said nothing.

Realization hit me in a manner as jarring as Cassie's hurled mini-mountain of snow. "You were the one following us, weren't you? The streak of light in the alleyway outside the diner—that was you. Toshiro's Ways don't open like that. And I'm fairly certain if Toshiro were stalking us, I wouldn't have seen him until he wanted me to."

"You didn't see him, did you? Technically, John, I was following him following you. Details—small things in life, but they matter."

"Why, Quentin?"

"You have to ask me that? You were in trouble, boy. When was the last time you had to go through trouble on your own? You do a fine job getting into it by yourself—but tell me—when was the last time you had to get out of it on your own?" His voice carried a tired weight.

"I'm sorry, Quentin. I know. I..." I trailed off as I felt Cassie's stare; she was watching the both of us. I cleared my throat and cracked my stiff neck. My fingers tingled with a newfound sensation of warmth. "Thanks for the drink."

He grunted.

I moved to stand by him at the curb, looking straight ahead.

"Aw, you boys are adorable, trying to share feelings and not knowing how to use emotions."

Quentin and I grunted in unison. Twin beams of dull yellow light rolled over the road, illuminating us as a taxi trundled forth. Quentin waved at the cab, stepping out on the road. The driver noticed and rolled to a stop.

Quentin beckoned us as he walked to the cab's rear,

opening the back door and motioning for Cassie to enter. He folded his hands over hers as he helped usher her in. "Ladies first."

Cassie's lips pressed together as she fought a smile.

Some inner part of me groaned at Quentin's elderly and charming act. It was something he had done for as long as I could recount. The act came off as a doting and indulgent grandfather, which is what I suspected he intended. Everybody loves the kind old man. It was a way for him to get what he wanted and remain in everyone's good graces.

He half clambered into the cab, hanging onto the door and looking at me. "Are you coming, kid, or do you need an invitation?"

I blew out a breath that came out as a hot plume of steam. The potion warmed me up the longer it flowed through me. "Yeah." I made my way to the car, snow slipping through the hem of my jeans. Some stuck to my socks.

I scowled as I met him at the door. He gave me a toothy grin I felt like stuffing with snow. He gave me a little nod and fell into the cab, hunkering down in the middle. I sat down, forcing us to feel a tad cramped in the back.

"You could have sat up front, kid."

"Stop calling me that." I glared at Quentin.

"Now you know how it feels."

I ignored Cassie's quip and leaned towards the driver. I gave him my address and fell back against the seat, cupping my hands behind my head to get comfortable. My eyes fluttered shut as the car lumbered forward. The cab swayed over the wintry road for a second, causing us to slide over the seat as much as we could in our crammed seating.

"So, John." Quentin exhaled through his nose, pausing for a long minute. "Tell me all of it, leave nothing out. I can't help you if you do."

I let out a dark laugh. "Help me? How? You know what I have coming, Quentin. Just watch out for her." I tilted my head towards Cassie.

"You're not even going to fight?" Quentin's voice was

tired, but there was a hint of steely resolution lingering within. He still thought I had a chance.

"How?"

"How 'bout we tell him everything. You know...like he said?"

Quentin let out a sharp bark. "She's smart, John. You could do worse for a partner if you're on the run. So do us all a favor, will you, boy? Tell me truth."

I told him.

He let out a lengthy whistle. "Damn, boy. You've made a real mess of things. We've got problems to deal with on two fronts now."

"Three. Don't forget the Marquis."

"Don't worry about him, kid."

Cassie bristled. "*I'm* worried. You weren't there. Asshole had fangs!"

Quentin chuckled; it still sounded odd to me. As long as I had known him, he had always had that British accent, but there was something about the way he spoke—the words he chose—that never completely sold me on the lie.

"I bet. Night Runners, I've found, are normally one of two extremes: beautiful to the point of being nauseating and effeminate, or hideous," said Quentin.

Cassie snickered.

"So, Quentin, do you have a plan?"

"I do. It involves taking your broken and battered behind back to your Hobbit hole, have you looked at, and then move from there."

"That's it?"

"One thing at a time, kid. How many times have I told you that? The best stories are written one word at a time. Every journey—single steps and all that. Take it as it comes."

I inhaled, exhaled, then repeated the process, stilling my mind. Quentin was old, wise, and crafty. If anyone could help me with my troubles, as well as Cassie, it was him. That did not make him any less irritating. I groaned.

I felt a hand on my shoulder. Quentin gave me a gentle

shake. "Rest, kid."

My lids felt heavy, so I followed his advice.

Chapter Ten

Laughter pulled me from my reverie. I blinked and let out a groan as I listened in to the conversation. Quentin was in the middle of a joke.

"And then I said, 'These are not the jewels you're looking for, love.'"

Cassie erupted into a fit of raucous laughter far louder than before. If the cab driver minded, he didn't show it.

I groaned again. "How long was I out?"

"Hm?" I could feel Quentin's eyes on me as he weighed what to say. "Long enough, kid."

"Felt like several hours."

"More like several minutes. How are you feeling?" Cassie's voice was a shade lighter, still colored by the laughter.

"Terrible. Quentin, your plan?"

He grunted. "Let's get you looked at first. Till then, leave it be."

I exhaled through my nose, letting some of the tension out. "Fine."

The cab slowed and stuttered, fighting to stop instead of slide. We rolled a few feet past the opening to a diminutive bakery. The cabbie twisted back and gave us the total. I leaned over and tugged on the edge of my coat, prompting Cassie to give me a strange look.

"Really? I've got nothing for the cold, though?" She clung to the coat.

I eyed her. "My wallet..."

She blinked and relented, slipping out of the coat and passing it to me.

I paid the driver in cash and donned my coat. Its weight was comforting. The door refused to open, and my heart rate sped up. A cab was a perfect place to be ambushed. Tight quarters, doors that can be locked on control, and too many other reasons to list.

The cabbie spat a curse and complained about the state of the cab commission and a list of things that flew over my head. "Give it a good *urpmh*!" He mimed ramming his shoulder into the door.

I did. The door swung open, straining the hinge before coming back as I hobbled out. It caught my battered arm. I didn't scream; instead swallowing the noise as an odd gulp.

Quentin put a hand on the top of the door, leaning into it to pull himself up. Not that he needed to. He may have looked old, but Quentin was far fitter than any man his age, and many younger.

I offered Cassie a hand, helping her out of the car. It would have been gentlemanly of me to offer her my coat again. I didn't. We were a few steps away from my home. She could tolerate the weather for several paces.

Another flare of pain ignited within my arm as Cassie bumped into me in her rush to pass. "Crap-crap-crap-crap!" She huffed a series of short breaths, hugging herself tight as she ran to the bakery. Her body jerked as she gave a quick tug on the handle of the unwilling door. "The hell?" She rapped her knuckles on it in rapid succession. Failing to get a response, she banged her fist against it.

I winced as it opened.

Tatiana stood in the doorway, her posture tight as she loomed over Cassie. Her fists were balled and resting on her hips. She quivered like a taut wire.

I sucked a breath through my teeth.

"Never, child, ever, for as long as you live, bang on this door. Do you understand?"

I drew close enough to see Cassie's eyes change in size, ballooning before shrinking as she cast them to the ground. "Yes," she mumbled.

"Good, now come in." Tatiana grabbed Cassie by a shoulder and ushered her inside.

Quentin sped up, overtaking me as he rushed to meet

Tatiana. She froze, her face contorting into a myriad of emotions as she no doubt wondered how to greet him. He flashed her a wide smile, one that I couldn't believe to be sincere. My belief was irrelevant as Tatiana smiled back.

Quentin capitalized. He took one of her hands in both of his, bringing it up to his lips as he brushed them across it. He gave a light tug, pulling her close as he shot up and kissed her cheek.

There was confident. There was brash. There was stupid. And then there was Quentin Denholm. My friend and mentor was a wondrous and baffling mixture of them all.

One did not take such liberties with Tatiana without repercussions. I waited for the slap that would leave his head ringing for days. First, he'd have to remove it from the wall it would be driven through. It never came.

Tatiana blinked. Her lips moved for several seconds, refusing to give voice to any words. Her cheeks reddened much like Cassie's had earlier, but she pulled Quentin inside.

I have lived for well over a century, to the point where I am a fair hand into my next. In all that time, one mystery still eludes me: women.

Tatiana turned to me and took a sharp breath that sounded more like a hiss. The door drifted shut as she ran into the snow towards me. I met her about five paces from the door.

"Jonathan, what happened? Your face—you look like you were beaten with a sack of potatoes."

"The potatoes probably came out feeling the better."

Tatiana gave me a look that said I wasn't funny. She took a step back, adopting the same posture as when she had opened the door. Her balled fists rested on her hips. She arched a pale brow and tilted her head a fraction to the side.

"It was trolls. I couldn't tell if it was one of the same ones as before. It's difficult to differentiate between ten thousand shades of ugly."

Her hand flew to my face, and I flinched. It slowed and came to rest above my brow, close to my temple. Her touch was soft, but it still sent a short-lived jolt through my head. She trailed a finger down the side of my face. A gentle tingle trailed its path. "You know better than to pick a fight with a troll, Jonathan."

"I do. I didn't pick it; the troll did. Picked me up as well and threw me into a brick wall."

Tatiana's lips quirked at the edges. "Poor wall." She didn't move her hand away from my cheek. Instead, she traced a small circle over the bruise that made me wish my face was numb. "Clearly you killed it. You're too smart to have shot it in public."

I tilted my head much like hers. "Shot it with what?"

She rolled her eyes and slipped her free hand into my coat. "With this." She patted the pistol. "I'm not stupid, Jonathan."

"No, you're not."

"Good." She patted my cheek and a dull throb tinged with fire blossomed over my face. I winced and let out a hiss. She responded with a little smile. "So long as you are aware. So how did you kill it—your knife?"

I didn't answer.

"I know about that too, and I know why you have a big, obvious sword dangling from your belt."

"Oh?"

Tatiana scoffed. "Because you are a man, and having a big sword hanging off your belt is a thing only a man would do." None of what she said made any sense to me. Maybe it wasn't meant to.

"That's not true," I said without knowing exactly what I was arguing against. It seemed like something to argue against on principle, however.

I don't know how Tatiana did it, but she managed to give me a look without shifting her posture. Her eyes remained still, but something changed in them. A hardness appeared that told me it was a mistake to open my mouth. I kept it shut and let her finish.

"The other reason is that you are clever, and you hide it well." She removed her hand from within my coat and gave the sword a tap with her fingers. "This is for the fools to keep their eyes on, right before you take them out with your dagger."

I shivered. That was a needlessly graphic image. "Have I ever told you that you can be an uncomfortable person to be around?"

Tatiana gave me a wolfish smile. "In another life, yes. One where, if I recall, I told you to keep a dagger close to your heart."

Pain washed over me, flooding my body and reaching my heart. "You've gotten your memories back?"

She turned her head to the left, looking past the street and to some place far away. Her fingers danced up and down as she waggled a hand in a so-so gesture. "Some. Not all. You know how it is with my kind. It's something we have to endure, yet a thing we never learn to deal with. Accepting it is hard."

I wrapped my fingers around the hand touching my cheek. "I thought you had forgotten. I didn't want to say anything."

"A woman never forgets. Remember that, Jonathan Hawthorne." Something in her tone and the look on her face made me unsure of whether to smile or swallow a gulp of air.

She touched another finger to my cheek, the two of them slid their way down my jaw and throat, settling near my collar. She gave it a good tug. "Let's get you inside and looked at. Then, you will tell me everything that is going on." It wasn't a question. It was a command.

I nodded and followed her inside the bakery. Warm, earthy decor greeted me and pulled some of the soreness away.

There's a certain aura that surrounds and fills places of love; passion; and hard, honest toil. It's the energy that fills homes and certain businesses, places where hardships have been endured, love has been nurtured and grown. Places like Tatiana's bakery.

I wanted to stay there and curl into a ball near the

crackling fire in the corner. I wanted to inhale the soft, sweet aroma of sugar-tinged spices. Things like cinnamon, caramel, and nutmeg. They helped combat the grogginess of my mind. But not by much.

The world skewed. My balance wavered and I fell. Or I would have had Tatiana not wrapped a lean, well-muscled arm around my waist.

She helped right me. "You probably have a concussion."

I grunted in acknowledgement. The thought of speaking sent an elastic *twang* vibrating through my skull.

She helped me hobble through her confectionary-filled sales floor to the back. If it weren't for my coat, the chilled air preserving her ingredients would have seeped into me like a cold towel pressed to my body. I didn't need that.

I needed liquor, or painkillers, or both. Not doctor recommended, but I was sure doctors didn't have a prescribed treatment for being hurled into a brick wall by a troll. They could only do so much.

Cassie and Quentin waited by the wire cage elevator, refusing to step inside without me. Or maybe it was fear. Some people seemed to harbor a certain discomfort around the rickety, shoddy-looking contraption. I had no idea why. It functioned perfectly fine.

"Quentin." Tatiana's bark snapped him to attention. "Get the doctor."

His face twisted into a mask of uncertainty before he composed himself. "Of course." He looked me over and made no comment about my sorry state. "That...*man* disturbs me though."

"He can creep you out as much he likes. He's a good doctor. Get him." Her tone left no room for Quentin to argue.

He moved out of my field of vision, spouting his discontent in a string of indiscernible grumbling.

Cassie rushed to undo the mechanism barring the way into the lift. Then she came by my side, adding her strength to Tatiana's. I didn't need it. I was capable of walking on my own...as soon as the world leveled. Tatiana surely didn't need the aid, but she accepted it without comment.

The pair eased me into the elevator, one of them setting the machine into motion. There was a raucous groan of metal before everything juddered into life. We descended.

The descent was almost magical. Almost. I could feel the lingering sensation of Tatiana's shop—her home—being pulled away as we lowered. My home didn't have the same love, passion, and time invested into it as hers did. It was a place for me to rest my weary body after my travels around the world. A place to lounge in between jobs and court appearances.

I read there, gained knowledge, and when I was tired, I scoured books for further information. For all my travels and the companions gained, I lived a rather solitary life. It showed, emanated from the aura of my residence. But still, it was home, and it was mine.

We stopped, and Cassie pulled open the safety gate. The sudden urge to let the strength leave my body overwhelmed me. I resisted, wanting to make a dignified collapse onto one of the many couches strewn throughout my home. Collapsing seemed a good idea.

The second I took an awkward, assisted step inside, it hit me. That familiarity of routine, of knowing everything had its place, knowing I was home. It may not have been as warm and inviting as Tatiana's, but it was all I needed.

A comforting warmth that had nothing to do with heat made its way into my muscles and bones. A gentle tugging sensation offered to pull me into a deep sleep. The crown of my skull felt like it was sewn with lead, weighing on my neck and dragging me towards the ground.

Tatiana had an issue with that. The back of my scalp erupted into a million pinpricks as my hair pulled taut within her fingers. The pain yanked me out of the groggy trance I was entering.

"Concussion—no sleeping. Stay awake...or else."

"I must have a thing for feisty, aggressive women."

Tatiana yanked my hair again.

Cassie laughed.

"And I never had a thing for men who talk too much, or think they are funnier than they are," Tatiana said.

"You did at one time." Getting the words out was hard. She ground her knuckles over my head, going so far as to twist them. I winced through the maneuver.

"Don't make her angry. You won't like her when she's angry." Cassie's body shook as she let out another fit of laughter.

"In another life I did, another time, Jonathan." Tatiana's voice came out dry and distant.

Hearing her say my name, even as far and removed as it sounded, was nice. It always had been. "Yeah, whatever happened to us, Tatiana?"

"I got old and started over. You know how it is with my kind."

"Yeah." I sighed. I could feel Cassie's eyes and ears on us as we ambled towards the nearest sofa.

"And *you* kept on going, getting into trouble and not aging a single day."

A smile touched my lips. "Jealous?" I hissed as her knuckles contacted the sensitive and lightly irritated skin atop my head. She stopped nearly as soon as she began. She smiled. I couldn't see it, but I knew it; I knew her.

They eased me onto a particularly good find, a loveseat of burnt sepia that I had found dumped outside an apartment complex ages ago. It was sunken in some areas and the leather upholstery was frayed, but it was comfortable beyond measure. It contoured to my body, letting me fall into it as it rose around me. A groan of equal parts pleasure and relief escaped me.

Tatiana's strong, slim fingers squeezed tight around my hand before letting go. "I'll fetch some food and clean towels." Tatiana turned on her heel and walked away.

I let my head roll past the armrest to get a better view of her as she left. I didn't regret the accompanying pain from stretching my neck in the slightest. The pain that bothered me was in my chest. It felt like my insides were hollow and being hammered. Watching her leave made my chest pang with every step she took.

Sometimes old flames still burn. And old or new, fire always hurts.

The seat caved in further. I felt Cassie rest herself a bit past the middle mark, closer to my legs. She leaned against me, taking care not to place her full weight on my battered body.

Cassie waited until Tatiana was out of earshot to speak. “So, you and her are a thing?”

My voice came out heavier than I expected. “We were.”

“Oh, sorry.”

I waved her off, letting her know it was fine as I let my arm fall over my eyes. The pain was getting to me.

Most people don’t know how pain works. They only have an idea. I have centuries of experience. Pain comes in waves, and it grows. It’s not an instant thing. Pain is not considerate in that sense.

The beating from the troll would linger, filling me with dull aches and throbs until I healed. The surprise and adrenaline from earlier were the only things suppressing it. Now they had faded. The floodgates opened, and with them came a dizzying array of soreness and discomfort.

“I heard the whole thing, you know.”

I didn’t reply, instead swallowing what moisture formed in my mouth.

“Her memories are gone?”

“Yes, Cassie.”

“How? Is she going to get them back? Is she okay?”

“Not so fast.” I pressed my hands to my ears. “Yes. Age. Time. Yes,” I answered in a staccato fashion.

“Age? She looks younger than you.”

“She is. Much younger. This time around anyways.”

Cassie gave me a sideways look, waiting for me to explain. I didn’t oblige her.

“Age is just a number, John.”

I could hear the subtle tone in her voice, the gentle reassurance that things could work out between Tatiana and me. I blinked, amazed that Cassidy cared about my relationship to that extent.

"It is, and it's more complicated than that. We grew apart. For the time being at least. She's a different person now. She may grow back into the one she was before, but there's no knowing for sure."

"She's not human, is she?"

I licked my lips, wondering what to say next. If the Ageless court didn't kill me, Tatiana might. "No, she isn't."

"What is she?"

"You'll have to ask her yourself. If she feels like answering you, she will. If not, then she won't."

She let out a sound caught somewhere between a growl and frustrated exhalation. "You know, this not explaining stuff is bullshit. You can't keep stringing people along, teasing them with bits and pieces."

I snorted. It sent an arctic jolt through the bridge of my nose, causing me to squint and contort my face. "Watch me."

"Maybe I'll just keep pulling, John, see what I can unravel."

"Sometimes that's not what happens when you pull on a string that's not ready to be undone. Sometimes, Cassie, strings are knotted, old, and frayed. Do you know what happens when you pull on those? They tear, break, come undone and are left in pieces. Don't pull on these strings, please."

"Okay, I'm sorry." She put more of her body on my legs, curling into a ball near the other half of the seat.

"It's fine," I mumbled.

A clatter of metal clanged and shuddered. I could hear the elevator grate slam to the side as it opened. The doctor hurried forward, carrying an orange duffel bag. Quentin lingered a few steps behind, moving in relaxed, confident strides.

George fell by my side, snapping his wrist and letting his bag fall. He moved with practiced motions, unzipping the duffel bag without looking, and sending a hand snaking within. He held up a rectangular container made of the same glass used for beer bottles. He shook his hand, and I saw something stir within. A thick gelatinous fluid rose against one side.

"What is it?" I wasn't fond of mysterious substances, not that George would poison me. If the day ever came where he wanted to kill me, he wouldn't be subtle about it.

"Don't ask." With a deft twist of his wrist, the top came off with a *pop*. It smelled like rich petroleum. "Just down it, Jonathan. If you can do it in a single go, it'll be better for you...and me."

"I'm just bruised. I need painkillers, maybe something to get me back on my feet."

Cassie shifted aside as the doctor placed a hand on my calf. His fingers tightened around the muscle, and my body convulsed like streams of molten lava were coursing through my veins. He let go and the sensation died. A moment that felt like decades passed before I remembered how to breathe.

I blinked away the spots marring my vision and worked to still the rapid rise and fall of my chest. "What...was that about?"

"This isn't the first whooping you've taken of late, John." He pulled my pant leg up. "There was whatever did this to you."

I shook my head the best I could, letting him know I was lost.

Quentin didn't let the good doctor explain. He was down on a knee and in my face, looking to my scarred leg and then to my eyes. "Where did you go in the Neravene?"

I answered him.

He spat, not a curse or a simple sound from the lips; he actually *spat* in my home.

My throat quivered as I let out a feeble burble. If I'd had the strength, it would have been intimidating.

"You're stupid. Do you know that? Both of you. You could have been killed, and then what? I can't help a pair of stiffs. That is not your domain, nor one for any mortal.

Dammit, John, *immortals* stay out of the Long Gardens."

I mumbled an apology. It technically wasn't my fault. I could have laid that at Cassie's feet, but the last thing the girl needed was more guilt or blame.

George cut in. "Look, whatever hit you in there left something inside of you. If I were a normal doctor and had a look at your blood, I'd say it is an infection, or something close to one. But since I'm not one of those blind crackpots, I'd say it's something worse. I can't be sure if it's magical in nature, but that's where the smart money would be. When I healed you before, I sopped up most of the blood and stitched you back together, even went as far as to suppress this stuff."

"You knew about it before?"

He gave me a steady look that said I should be grateful to be alive enough to complain.

"Thanks, George."

He grunted. "I thought it was a one-time thing; it's not. This stuff is spreading, John. Slowly." He gave a shake of the bottle. "I can make it slower."

"I'm sensing a 'but' here, George."

"But...slower doesn't mean stopped. This thing's going to overtake you, and when it does, it's going to burn you up from the inside out. It ain't going to be pretty. You'll be leaking worse than a cheap tire."

"He doesn't need to be pretty. Make him functional. We have a court to attend, yeah?" Quentin's voice turned dour. It was a fair reaction to hearing that his pupil, friend—and whatever else he considered me—was going to die.

Cassie remained silent and still throughout the exchange, almost still at least. I could feel the slightest quiver coming from her, like a bowstring settling after being pulled.

"Give me the stuff, George." I reached out for it, but he was kind enough to press the lip of the bottle to my mouth.

The second it passed my lips and hit my tongue, I fought the urge to retch. It was like an old fluid that had sat too long and congealed into something thicker than syrup. His medicine was pushing science's definition of a liquid... It was closer to being a solid. I forced it down my throat nonetheless. I shuddered from the jelly-like concoction. It was acrid and bitter, like it had been burnt in its making.

"Bwugh."

I writhed until Cassie centered her weight over my legs. A pair of strong hands pressed down on my chest. Quentin and Cassie held me still with iron strength. George took my calf in one hand, and my forearm in the other. He didn't do it to keep me from thrashing, but I wished he had.

A burst of static rolled over my skin before sinking deeper. It skittered under my flesh, dancing over my muscles from top to bottom. And that was it. A single instant of blinding pain, contortion, and electrical discharges—and then nothing. I was fine.

The aches, throbs, and burning faded. My muscles felt a tad rubbery, but that was the extent of my weakness. I certainly didn't feel like a troll had tried to put me through a wall. And that wasn't right.

"George." My voice was a dry, but speaking was easier. "What did you do?"

The elderly man let out a trio of coughs as he fell back sputtering.

"George?"

"Sorry, John. It was stupid, but I had to try."

"George, what did you do?" I brushed Quentin's hands aside, propping myself up on my elbows. "Get off me, Cassie."

She muttered something under her breath. "Should be so lucky," was all I managed to catch.

George cleared his throat. It was rougher than normal, sounding like it tore at the lining inside. "I tried *pulling* it from you. It wasn't a good idea."

"Are you..." I didn't finish the question.

"I'm fine. I will be at any rate. You, though—you only have an extension."

I raised an eyebrow.

"You feel fine, sure, but it's temporary. It's not masking the pain. I took most of that away. But I couldn't stymie the rot."

If I hadn't heard the last part of his statement, I would have grinned at his use of the word stymie. People seldom spoke like that anymore. "The rot?"

George pulled a handkerchief out of his pocket, going through the slow, careful motions of folding it bit by bit until it was no larger than his palm. He mopped his sweaty brow. "Whatever this stuff is, it's not poisoning you, John. It's eating you."

Cassie, Quentin, and I wore the same face of disgust and horror.

"Never seen anything like it. It's tearing you up from the inside, making you look like a jelly cup someone's thrown to the ground."

I could have done without the visual.

"I put it in its place. That's the best I can do. It'll flare up again, and it'll be worse. I won't be able to do something the next time." The words carried through my enormous home.

"So, what do I do?"

"Get help, better help than me. Maybe something from the other side."

"No." Quentin's voice ended the discussion before it started. "I'll have some of the other Timeless take a look at him." The way he said it caused George to glare at him; something must've caused him to take umbrage. "I don't know exactly what did this, but there are members older than me. They might be able to fix you, kid."

I pushed myself up, leaning back against the cushioned seat. A heavy sigh escaped me. "It's worth a shot, Quentin."

"Good. We're late as it is, and time may be on our side, but the court isn't fond of waiting. You've irked them enough, boy, disrespected them. Don't keep them any longer. Say your goodbyes."

An icy cord snaked through my body.

Quentin noticed it. "What's wrong, kid?"

I blinked and looked to the elevator. "Tatiana hasn't come back."

Chapter Eleven

Fear comes in many forms, and I was going through all of them.

Thin, copper strings went taut throughout my body and heart, thrumming and winding as they edged towards their breaking point. Tonal brass rang through my skull. Silver bells blared as I launched myself from the couch.

"Jonathan, don't be stupid. Lie down. Rest. We'll find her."

I ignored George's warning, pushing forward in spite of my spinning vision. Tatiana wasn't the sort of woman to linger or get distracted. That wasn't her way. She defined military precision to the point where I seemed lax in comparison, and I had served three times. If she hadn't come back, it was for a good reason—or a dangerous one. I wasn't fond of the latter.

Machinery clunked and groaned. Chains whirred as the lift descended.

The elevator wasn't empty.

Nor was it Tatiana who rode it down.

Two figures, both of which were too large for human proportions, came into view. A pair of parkas lay at their feet—one blue, one black.

My teeth grated against each other. I started my series of unfortunate events when I'd crossed paths with them days before.

Trolls.

They huddled in the relatively small confines of my elevator, not bothering to mask themselves beneath glamour. The lift came to a shaky halt and the naked trolls surged forward. They didn't bother opening the gate, instead using their bulk and speed to tear through it, mangling the metal around them. Each creature let out a sound that could've been used as a substitute for industrial machinery starting up.

Roars echoed back as George, Cassie, Quentin, and I rushed to meet them, screaming in defiance. My world swayed back and forth like the platter of a turntable in the hands of a disc jockey. It didn't stop me from using my long gait to take the lead and meet the closest troll head on.

In contests of strength, facing a troll is a one-sided proposition, mortals cannot win. The strongest human is nothing more than a rag doll for them to toss about—and then eat.

Trolls are every mother's nightmare. They love to play with their food, or bludgeon it; it's all the same to them.

None of that deterred me. I was past rational. I could feel my heartbeat in every inch of my body, a percussive throb as realization washed over me and rage took hold. The only way they could have come down here was through the bakery. Through Tatiana.

The monster may have been generously layered in grotesque muscle, but that didn't mean it was smart or skilled. Its squashed face twisted into a hideous mask of contempt as its hand flew towards me. I let my momentum carry me forward as I released the strength I was using to remain upright. I sank and tumbled below its swat. Pivoting my body as I rolled, I drew my saber and lashed out. The blade grazed the back of the creature's knee.

The troll lurched, its anguished howl carried enough force to jar my head further. There was no reprieve for the intruder. Cassie's kimono fluttered at the hem as she cracked her whip. The iron barb burrowed into the troll's shoulder. She gave a forceful tug and pulled it free. Flesh tore and the monster stumbled further forward, struggling to make a decision as to what wound to address. Both injuries billowed noxious dark smoke as the edges puckered. Discoloration spread like a dye in water, a miasma across its body as the metals wreaked havoc on its being.

I reversed the grip on my blade, arched my back, and

went for the killing blow. The troll released a sound like a diesel engine on startup, a raucous snort-growl as its body snapped to motion. I couldn't move in time. The broad of my back ignited in pain as the troll's back-handed blow caught me, sending me soaring over a table and onto the ground. My landing rattled every bone in my body to the point where I wondered if George's treatment would hold.

It did. I shook my head and rose.

The second troll turned its hand over, reaching down and under my loveseat. With a remarkable display of brutish strength, it hurled it aside as it advanced towards Quentin and George.

If I were a better man, I would have felt sorry for it. I wasn't.

George moved like a predatory insect with darting bursts of speed I wouldn't have fathomed possible for a man of his age. In a simple succession of three steps, he maneuvered into the troll's blind spot. The elderly man twisted his body at the waist. He turned and a bony fist cracked into the monster's elbow. There wasn't enough strength behind it to cause the troll anything other than a moment of irritation. It breathed out through its nose, turning to disregard George and focus on Quentin.

It was too much to take in, like trying to keep track of both a chess game and a tennis tournament at once.

Cassie's troll reached into that deep reservoir of fury that blots out all pain and fills you with adrenal fluids. I could only imagine how much of an adrenaline surge a troll could muster. Its eyes were red and wept mucus secretions from the corners. A possible reaction to its contact with mortal metals. What bits of spittle didn't fly from its mouth hung in strands between its lips as it screamed. The beast stormed towards Cassie.

She backpedaled, casting the whip into frantic, terror-driven lashes. The troll's hand shot out like a child trying to grasp a butterfly. Its fingers closed around the portion below the tip and pulled. Cassie came off her feet as the whip left her grip. Her knees and shins struck the floor as she collapsed. The troll was atop her a second later.

A feverish pulse ebbed in both my temples. My skull felt too tight for my anger, which seemed to be bottled and growing. It could have been a side effect of the potion Quentin gave me earlier. My extremities tingled and my skin flushed and prickled. I was hot, angry, and planned to do something about it.

Every fibrous strand in my body vibrated and knotted with my scream. The effort taxed me to a point George would surely complain about later, but I pushed it from my mind. I had the troll's attention as I barreled towards it. I left the air and tucked the saber along my chest. A wide, gray, yellow-nailed hand flew through the air, ready to swat me like a mosquito. The troll's hand fell.

It missed me. I sailed under its arm and stabbed. I collided against its ribs and drove the sword beneath the meat of its breast, pushing the blade through to the other side. That much steel buried in its mass alone would kill it. But I had pierced its heart.

There were no screams, no furious protest from the troll as it passed. Its fingers jerked in a spasmodic fashion. The creature tried to raise its arm, almost succeeding in its effort to press its hand against its chest. It failed. Its eyes clouded as its chest and distended belly lost their grayish hue. All color was replaced by a green so dark it could have passed for black. Its skin dried and crackled. Steam billowed from the fractures in its tissue. The troll's body erupted into a flash of green flame.

Nothing remained. Not even dust. But there was an echo. A horrendous roar, more felt than heard, filled the area around us. The second troll moved with startling speed, ignoring George and Quentin. Even from where I stood, I could see its eyes burning with a single objective.

Kill Jonathan Hawthorne.

Both my mother and Quentin had warned me that being the center of attention was a good way to die. I hated it when my elders were right. I was also told that one shouldn't go down without a good fight.

Quentin and George were unarmed from what I could tell. Cassie was composing herself, and the troll came closer. I approached him and released a yelp, stopping mid-step to dive out of the way.

A flash of silver stole my gaze as it hurtled towards us. It hit the troll like a battering ram of metal and wood. An honest-to-God spear lodged in the monster's throat, parting its flesh like a surgical blade against the rind of a rotten fruit. The troll crumpled as blood poured from the wound. It pawed at the spear only to contact the metal. A violent hiss sizzled like oil hitting a pan. The blood boiled and steamed. Globules ricocheted off the metal and arced to the floor, bursting into minute plumes of green flames. The troll disintegrated, following its companion into nothingness.

Tatiana stood off to the side, panting. Her cornflower blue t-shirt was tattered and stretched tight against her chest. At first glance, I could've mistaken the stains across her clothes as raspberry preserves. They weren't.

Thin streams of blood snaked from under her sleeve, trickling over her bicep and down to the floor. It looked like she had rubbed a balloon against her hair. Every strand of wheat-colored hair appeared frayed and wild. Her black sweatpants were in the same shape as her shirt. There was a wild look in her eyes. They were dilated, wide, looking at us and through us all at the same moment. That wasn't what held my attention however.

Her soft green eyes were replaced with something else. They were sapphire blue, deep, luminous, rich and dark. I became lost in them. Her head turned with the slow movements of a predator settling on its prey. We locked eyes. I heard a thousand different iron tones at once, a thousand swords crashing against one another. I heard the screams of victorious battle cries. I heard the screams of dying men and women.

Songs floated through my head. Songs that promised me a glorious afterlife with endless drink, merriment, and all forms of revelry. Songs that begged me to fight and take as many as I could with me. Songs that promised me greatness and death.

"Tatiana!" Quentin's voice jarred me back to the present.

My stomach roiled, and I fought it from emptying its contents. I failed. I doubled over, clutching my knee as my other hand pressed to my stomach. A thin film of fire lined my abdomen as I heaved.

A gentle weight fell on my shoulder; Quentin gave me a double pat on the back. "Let it out, kid. Their stare is worse than any hangover I've ever had. And I've drunk with her kind before. They know the meaning of bottoms up."

Poor choice of words. I retched again.

"Better, John?"

I coughed and gave him a shaky thumbs up. I blinked away the tears and risked looking at Tatiana. The hypnotic, deep blues faded back to a worn, muted green. Her eyes shook, confused, and her lids were lined with a hint of moisture.

"I'm bleeding." She blinked, staring at the wounds like she was seeing them for the first time. "John?" Her balance wavered as she struggled to stand upright. "It hurts."

Oh, Tat.

I ached more in hearing her say that than from the beating the trolls gave me. A slow, rhythmic pulse boomed just above my right eye. I winced, steeling myself against the discomfort.

Tatiana let out a small hiss and held her hand against her side. She pulled up the shirt, and I echoed the sound she made. A nasty bruise lined her ribs, the size of a troll fist. A blow from a troll could crush a mortal's bones. Tatiana had held up rather well, considering.

"George." My voice was coarse, like I had swallowed a load full of sand and gravel. "Tend to Tat, will you?"

She shook her head, regretting the action a second later when she put a hand to her head. "You two." She motioned with a finger to Cassidy and me. "Take care of them first, George."

"No," I said.

She blinked several times and tilted her head like a dog hearing an unfamiliar sound. "What?"

"No," I repeated through a series of small coughs. "You and George live here, in my building, in *my home*." I put as much weight and heat into the words as possible given my condition.

Her eyes went wide at the statement. I had a feeling that if I continued, Tatiana would lodge the spear in my throat next. I didn't care.

"We struck an accord, all personal feelings aside, you're going to abide by them." She adopted a look like I had slapped her. In truth, she was the more likely to slap someone—namely me.

"George, help her."

There was a second of silence, which could have been used in an old western. Tumbleweeds could have rolled by at any moment. It was broken by a long, low whistle from Cassidy.

"Someone's in the doghouse."

I blocked out her comment. "George!"

The old man shivered, snapping erect in response to my tone. He cast me a level look. George wasn't used to being shouted at. But he complied.

"Alright, alright," he grunted. George bustled over to Tatiana, extending a hand towards her bleeding arm. "You're not going to want to sit for this, Tati."

She nodded as he brushed his fingertips over the muscles of her arm, not the least bit concerned about the blood. His lids fluttered, and his breathing slowed.

When George worked, it was normally on me, battered and bruised from some trouble I had fallen into. It was rare for me to see his process as an observer.

Tatiana's breathing fell in step with his, dropping in frequency until it was no longer audible. Her eyes shut, the bleeding ceased, and a healthier color seeped into her skin. The pair of them sighed in perfect synchrony.

"Well, well, that was a rare sight, even for me." Quentin rubbed his jaw, a small smile on his face. "Didn't know you could pull that on someone like Tatiana."

I gave him a hard look, one he responded to with a mild shrug.

"I'm fine, by the way. Don't mind me. Nope, not like I went toe-to-toe with Fee Fi Fucking Fum the troll!" Cassie huffed and kicked the leg of a nearby table. "I'm still in a"—she tugged at the kimono with a hand—"whatever this crap is. What's a girl have to do for some new threads?"

"That's a giant you're referring to, Cassie."

"Whatever! We were jumped by trolls...in *your* place! I thought you said we were safe here. You promised me that."

Those last words cut me deep. I did make that promise, and I failed. But it was something I was going to correct.

"I'm sorry, John." Tatiana crossed the distance between us. "I tried, there were—"

I cut her off with a wave of my hand. "It's alright." I dropped my voice to a whisper. "It's alright. Do you mind taking Cassie in the back?" I hooked a thumb over to the door at the end. "Get her a change of clothes. You too—you could use a..." I stopped when she raised an eyebrow. "Please?"

Her lips twitched but she said nothing. She beckoned Cassie with a hand and brushed past us, looking over her shoulder and giving me a quick grin before turning back.

"Finally." Cassie breathed and set off after Tatiana, hitching up the ends of the kimono as she ran.

I suppressed a laugh. A sound like a dog lapping water caused me to turn around. George's tongue slid up against his fingers, smearing Tatiana's blood as the rest coated his mouth. He released a pleasurable sigh. His eyes flickered, reminding me of a drug addict getting a fix.

"George, can you please, not here?"

He gave me a dirty look. "I don't tell you how to be a one-hundred-year-old ass, do I? I'm tired, Jonathan. You know what it takes for me to heal someone, and you know my price. If you think you can start bossing me around, you can find yourself another healer." George slid his first two fingers into his mouth and sucked. He kept them buried in his mouth when he spoke next. "I think I'm going to go back there with Tati and the young woman. Besides, there's a door back there that will let me resupply my stock, yes?"

"Seventh door, right-hand side." I sighed and rubbed the heel of both palms against my eyes.

A door slammed shut. George moved fast, which was a good thing. I wanted to be alone for this.

"Well"—Quentin dusted off his coat—"that was unpleasant."

I whirled around and lunged, grabbing his collar in both fists as I drove him back.

"Bloody... John, what are you—"

"How did they find out where I live? How did they find me, Quentin? How did they find my goddamned home?"

"Why would I know?"

I pulled back, tightening the muscles in my body as I hauled him off his feet. Quentin didn't rise much more than an inch, but it made an impression. "Cassie and I were safe before. We came here earlier and nothing followed us out of the Neravene. We traipsed through the Grand Marquis' domain, insulted him, and still, no Night Runners sat waiting or watching my home. But you—you and Toshiro followed us, didn't you? The instant you're in my home—my home, Quentin—that's when the trolls find me?" Spittle left my mouth. My throat went raw and I ached inside. "They found my home? They found a way past Tatiana? Past her?" I shook him until my biceps could endure the fire no longer and I let him fall to his feet.

I should have held out longer. My jaw cried out as Quentin's fist crashed into it, sending me tumbling to the side, I lost my footing and crumpled to the ground. Quentin was atop me in a second, straddling me as another fist came down. My shoulder throbbed. Another blow. My ribs flared. My other shoulder ached as his fist connected. He repeated the cycle, avoiding my head. I would have realized it sooner if my body wasn't being tenderized.

"Stupid—arrogant—damnable—always-thinks-he's-right—infantile—pillock!" Each word was punctuated with another punch. "Dammit, kid." His fingers went under my jaw and he lifted my head. Quentin's eyes were bloodshot, strained with hairline streams of moisture. "You really think I would do that to you? Dammit, John, you know me better. You're tired, you're hungry, you've been beaten senseless and pushed into too many corners to think straight." He stopped supporting my jaw and wrapped his hands around my shoulders. Quentin gave me a firm shake. "Oh, kid." He took a deep breath, and shook his head, not looking at me anymore. "Think, boy—think! You've known me close for a damn sight longer than anybody else, even the Elders in the court. Would I ever put you in real danger? Me?"

I blinked away the tears. "Quentin, get off of me. Please...sir."

He blinked and let out a snort, but his posture softened and he let me go. "Sometimes I have to beat the sense into you, don't I?"

I exhaled through my nose and stayed silent.

"Now think, John. Something is playing you—playing us. Trolls? When was the last time trolls had this much initiative? When is the last time they thought anything out? When is the last time you saw trolls this organized? You know as well as I do, the free fae are too wrapped up in their own world and problems. When they're not terrorizing people, kidnapping and killing them, they're offing each other. Especially when it comes to tribes of trolls that haven't signed on with one of the courts. Someone or something is pushing them on you, John. Do you honestly believe they would be after Cassidy Winters of their own desire? Are they that smart?"

I felt terribly stupid. I couldn't even look him in the eyes. "No."

"No. Why would they care? So she can open whatever doors she wants in the Neravene and bugger the rules. What good is that to a troll too dumb to understand the importance of it? There's an angle we're missing here. Until we find out everything, refrain from jumping to stupid conclusions and laying a hand on me or so help me...Jonathan Hawthorne, I will shove my shoes so far up your bunghole you'll be stuck flossing your teeth with my laces!"

"Yes, sir."

"Good. Now, if you're done having your ass handed to you by trolls and old men, make yourself presentable. We have a court date."

Chapter Twelve

I had almost forgotten about my trouble with the Ageless court. Courtesy of trolls assaulting my home. I groaned.

"You can't hold them off, John. You're lucky I managed to stall them this long. We're due. Remember, keep your head. Deal with one problem at a time. First the court, and then I promise, boy, I'll help sort this out with you and the girl. I can't do that with the court breathing down my neck and yours."

"Right, right." He had a point. There was also an endless wealth of knowledge amongst the eldest members of the Timeless; some of them were bound to have answers. Any extra information would be a boon. "I'm bringing Cassie with us. We can't leave her here. Not after this."

"Agreed. With what she can do, maybe the court will have an idea of what to do with her."

I got to my feet and brushed myself off. Each movement reignited minor pangs from Quentin's beating. As if on cue, metal groaned and I turned to see Cassie coming out of my never-ending hall. Tatiana trailed a few steps behind. The pair of them wore clothes that defined the term "polar opposites," and each outfit was equally as startling.

Cassie wore a black sweatshirt, hooded like the one she wore before...almost. The hood fell to her brow. White triangles lined its edges, resembling a set of teeth. Two bulbous, lizard-like eyes sat above. They had a cartoonish look to them. A pair of notched ears protruded from its top. Her sleeves continued the effect of the dragon motif apparel.

I had to blink several times to ensure I wasn't imagining

it. A snug pair of faded jeans hugged her hips, ending in the same sneakers as before. That wasn't the shocking bit. Her whip was gone, replaced by a sheath for the antiquated sword. The half-moon pommel was well worn.

I didn't have to see the blade to know it would have been at home on the set of a Viking movie. The weapon would have been equally at home in the hands of a Scandinavian warrior a thousand years ago. She still wore the dagger on her hip. A strap of brown leather made its way diagonally around her chest, holding something to her back. I could see the outermost end of a polished bronze circle.

A shield. A specific shield. I couldn't see it all, but I didn't have to. I knew what it looked like. An intricate tribal band outlined the edge, its design made via empty spots in the bronze plating. At the center was a cap of protruding metal. Twin birds were etched into it. Twin ravens to be exact.

Tatiana, what have you done?

The Nordic beauty moved up beside Cassie, holding a short sword in her grip, another antique. She pivoted, snapping her torso and popping her hips as she thrust the blade into the air in front of them. Tatiana repeated the motion, slowing it down and pointing out the subtle transitions in the different movements and balance to Cassie. The young woman nodded studiously.

Tatiana grinned and sheathed her weapon. She was dressed in simple clothes that belonged in a historical documentary on Scandinavian people. Dark, earthy hues that somehow brought out more of her fair complexion. She whispered something in Cassie's ear, and the pair of them burst into laughter.

"What's going on? Where's George? Cassie, why are you dressed like..." I had no way to finish the sentence, resorting to gesturing to her outfit.

Tatiana answered for her. I wish she hadn't. "She's a shield maiden. You're going to need one." Her face remained neutral, but there was a glint in her eyes.

"She's dressed like a...shield maiden? What is that

sweatshirt? Cassie, where is the whip I gave you?"

"A whip, John? You can't keep treating her like a child," Tatiana chided.

"It kept creatures away from her. It gave her distance and safety!"

The Norse warrior didn't budge, shifting her weight and crossing her arms. "Safety? What safety?" She might as well have slapped me. "John, they came into my bakery, into your house, *our* home. She needs to be taught how to fight, how to survive in both worlds. No more babying. No more running for her. She's going to have a home. If not out there, then here." She gave me a stare that ended my argument before I could make it.

I changed subjects. It was safer. "So what about you, Tat? You're not dressed for battle."

Her lips pressed into a thin smile. "I think I have had enough for one day."

The simple statement could have knocked me back. Tatiana wasn't the kind to shy away from a battle. She loved it. It was part of her job at one point. I hoped it never came back to that though. I kept that opinion to myself.

Tatiana looked around the room. "Someone needs to keep an eye out here. If trolls came looking for you once, they will come back again. Trolls are not smart."

"No, they're not. Not if they're looking to pick another fight with you."

Her lips quirked at one corner, turning into a lopsided grin.

Quentin shook his head and exhaled in frustration. "This is wonderful—emotionally amazing and fantastic for the pair of you, really—but can we drop the romantic subplot revival and focus? John, time, court, trying to avoid my cherished friend and pupil's execution—save myself having to deal with all the paperwork that will come with your death." He tapped his wrist. "Tsk tsk."

"Right, we'll get going." I pulled my coat tight. It was more a comforting act than necessary. "Cassie, you're coming with us."

"Oh? Where? Troll killin' time?"

"To meet the Ageless court."

"The stuffy, uptight bastards who want to shove their collective feet up your ass? Yeah—no. I think I'm, um, fine here, thanks."

Quentin sniffed and moved towards the elevator.

"What's his problem?" Cassie quirked a brow and stared at Quentin.

I tried not to laugh. "He's one of the stuffy uptight bastards on the court."

Cassie's mouth parted. Her lips moved, trying to come up with some witty reply to save herself. She couldn't.

I turned to Tatiana, wanting to cross the two steps between us and do more than talk. But I couldn't—I didn't. "Do you want to... I mean, Quentin and I, and Cassie as well..."

"Woah-oh—no. Nah uh. I'm not sitting here for this." Cassie took a single step back, turned and slinked away.

I bit my tongue and refrained from making a comment about her leaving me. I remembered a dozen times where I could have left her, but I didn't. Thinking about it gave me a vindictive pleasure.

"Jonathan." Tatiana stood an inch from me now.

A warm flow of air wafted over my mouth and nose. Each of her breaths was a welcome feeling—a feeling I missed.

Life is complicated, a spider web of dizzying events and infinite complexities, and throughout it all, the simple things can sometimes outweigh them all. The little things carry power. Like feeling the breath of someone you love. It stirs something in you, memories of times long gone, hope for new times to come. Things like that help lessen the pain, physical or something deeper. They help soothe the fears of what's to come.

"You're scared."

"Terrified. Tat, I broke the rules. You don't do that to the court. The rules have been there forever. Nobody has broken them. They didn't come down on me the first two times because they didn't expect anyone to be dumb enough to break them a third time. I did. I—"

My lips squished together under the pressure of her index finger. "Jonathan, stop talking."

"But..."

She pressed harder, pushing my lips against the front of my teeth for a moment before stopping. "You've lived a long time, John, longer than many and yet, not as long as some. You're scared of losing that now. You're scared of not knowing when, for the longest time, knowing is what you did. You're scared of letting Cassie down. This is what you do. You get involved, John. You help people. They're punishing you for being you. Don't let them. Fight them. Fight the trolls and whoever else is coming after Cassie, you, and our home. Fight."

I nodded weakly and fell against her. Tatiana held me tight. There was strength in her arms. The woman was carved out of old-world wood, never mind the warrior's muscle. She had an inner fire built over the ages that gave her strength. That was the strong, reassuring heat I felt at that moment. It radiated from her, burning away my doubts.

"You've done so much good with your years, your money, and knowledge. You're afraid they will take that away from you. It's not the end. My life is a cycle: I lose it, and my memories, and start anew. I've seen the end, and it can be scary, but it's not dark. Not with friends and people you love by your side. And mark my words, Jonathan Hawthorne, this is not the end. Say it."

"It's not the end, Tat. I'll make sure of that." It was an effort to speak with her finger against my lips, but I managed.

"You will, or I will personally find you in Valhalla and spend eternity kicking your ass before heroes and warriors. They will laugh at you. I will call you a sissy, and it will go on forever." She tried not to smile, but it made its way to her eyes.

I snorted and shook my head. "I don't think I could live in a forever where you are doing all of that to me."

"Good. Neither can I. Your hard head would break my bones. Eventually."

I pulled her finger down and away from my mouth. I took her hand in mine and held it for a second. I wished I could have stretched it out longer. "Thank you, Tatiana." I bobbed my head in the direction of the steel door and the hall beyond. "Walk with me?"

"Of course, but there's something you should see first."

I arched a brow. "Oh?"

"Come on." She gestured as she moved towards the elevator where Cassie and Quentin waited. I lingered for a moment, casting a look behind me.

"How's George?"

Tatiana stopped. I could see her neck muscles tighten. I imagined the ones in her back were doing the same. "He's...fine. He will be, at any rate. He's doing his... You know how George is after healing. He gives up a lot of his chi helping you. Not to mention his regular clientele."

I grunted. George earned his keep in my home. If he needed some time to himself, he would have it. It was preferable that way. Tatiana and I were not fond of watching his recuperation process. "I'll leave him be then. Show me what you wanted. Is it important?" The question was innocent enough and asked without malice.

Tatiana didn't move save for turning her head enough so I could see one eye and interpret the entirety of the look she gave me. It told me that if this wasn't important, she wouldn't have bothered. I felt stupid and bowed my head accordingly. She sniffed, looked ahead, and walked away. I had to break into a little jaunt to catch up to her.

"About time." Quentin gave me a heated look. "Think this heap of rubbish will still work?" He jerked a thumb to my lift.

I moved past Cassie and Quentin, inspecting the poor state of the lift. The trolls had done quite the number on it. I was surprised it had taken their weight and carried them as far as it did. The front gate was destroyed, warped and sitting a few feet in front of the elevator. The metal that once held it in place was now bent at the edges, pushed out and weak. Apart from the superficial damage to what amounted to a safety measure, there was no structural damage to be overly concerned about. The gate served to prevent people stepping out of the lift while it was in motion. The linkage, gears, and mechanical assembly necessary for motion all seemed properly functional. But there was only one way to find out.

"She may not look like much, but she's got it where it counts."

Cassie burst into a fit of snickering, throwing her hands over her mouth to stifle the sound. "Good one, Solo."

We all looked at Cassie, dumbfounded. Her eyes widened and her mouth went slack. She blinked several times. "You mean you never... None of you? No! This is wrong on so many levels. If we survive this, marathon."

We exchanged quizzical glances. Quentin threw in a shrug for good measure. I shook my head and stepped into the elevator. Cassie literally hopped into it behind me. The metal shook from her impact. I eyed her. She pursed her lips and looked around the lift as if something else had caused the shudder. I sighed.

"Tatiana?" I made a flourish like a butler beckoning someone to enter. "You said you had something to show me." She entered, giving the elevator a wary look. "Quentin?"

"Sure." He shrugged and stepped in. "We won't have to deal with the court if we die in this deathtrap."

I inhaled slowly and repressed the urge to groan.

Everybody is a critic, especially the elderly.

The lift handle was cool in my hand as I applied pressure and cranked it back. An ungodly snarl sounded, like a bear waking early from hibernation. The elevator shivered and rattled, but it rose. I took a step forward, turned on my heel and gave my friends a smug grin. The three of them rolled their eyes in unison. It was mildly insulting.

The trip consisted of four different kinds of silence. Mine was a grim, dark silence. The sort a hanged man carries to the gallows. Tatiana's was the silence of shock and rage. A quiet fear of being violated, assaulted in her own home, and the whispers of retaliation. She wanted payback. Cassie carried the silence of uncertainty, lost in all of this without a clue as to what came next. Quentin Denholm was the embodiment of silent anticipation. Waiting for the elevator to stop. Waiting for the Ageless court. Waiting for answers.

Four kinds of silence did many things to your nerves—none of them good.

I breathed out in relief as the too-quiet ascent ended, and was the first to exit. My anger over the state of my home washed away when I saw the back end of Tatiana's bakery. Racks were twisted and mangled. Fruits and flour caked everything. There was an indentation the size of a truck tire in one of walls.

Gods and darker things, what did that?

An industrial fridge of polished metal was upturned, resting against the wall with flexible piping hanging over its edges. Driblets of water plopped to the ground from its hoses. All manner of liquids and culinary debris were strewn throughout the place. It was like a hurricane had torn through. That hurricane being Tatiana.

Three trolls lay among the wreckage. Ichor and blood coated their bodies and the floor around them. Two of the trolls sported puncture wounds consistent with a spear. Their bodies were covered in a necrotic rot—metal poisoning. There wouldn't be much left soon, or at all.

A series of lacerations decorated the third troll's legs. I counted eight different cuts. The largest concentration of blood and gore centered around the creature's groin. A chunk of its loincloth was shredded. I eyed Tatiana askance. She caught the look.

Tatiana nudged Cassie with an elbow and leaned over. "If it's soft, dangly, and can be squished or stabbed, go for it. Eyes and balls. See how long a troll fights then." She gave Cassie a wolfish smile.

Cassie looked at the trolls, registering the scene and carnage around us. She nodded in understanding. "You know, girl, you scare me. I like you. Good tip."

"Always listen to one of my kind on matters of combat. If you can do that, you'll be fine." She whispered something in Cassie's ear and waved a hand to the mess before us.

Cassie's skin blanched, looking pale against the black dragon hoodie. Her eyes ballooned, and under the bright lighting, interesting things happened to them. The fire-like gems caught the light and sparkled as she gawked at Tatiana in awe. Cassie stared on as Tatiana tapped my shoulder.

"Hm?"

"They wrecked my bakery, John." There was a hint of expectation in her voice. "All to get to you two." She gestured with a waggle of her index finger.

I swallowed. "I'll pay for it. Of course. Don't mention it."

Tatiana nodded and moved towards the front of the bakery. I motioned for Cassie and Quentin to follow me as I rushed after Tatiana.

The warrior paused and waved to the double doors. More accurately, she gestured to where they had been. The only evidence of their existence was a leg-sized piece of jagged wood and the splintered fragments behind us.

"That's real wood, Jonathan, old wood. *Old,*" said Tatiana.

"I'll replace it." The benefit of old age and a fortune is that it compounds nicely over time.

She ignored the comment and positioned herself in the middle of the bakery. There was surprisingly less damage. Some broken glass, fallen pastries and confectionary items, and a baseball sized hole in the wall. A single troll lay on the carpeted floor, its thick blood seeping into the carpet. It was lucky to be dead. Anything that dirtied Tatiana's carpets would be put through hell. It looked like the troll already had. Several fist-sized holes peppered its broad chest.

I whistled at the tight grouping of entry wounds. "Shotgun?"

"It was." Tatiana went over to a corner and knelt to pick up a mangled firearm. The shotgun was twisted into a sloppy U-bend. "One of them snatched it from me, but not before I put their leader down."

"Leader? How can you tell?"

"That's what I wanted to show you. Look at its hand, John."

I did, and a winter fist gripped my heart. Ice water pumped through my veins. In between the obscenely thick, grime-covered sausage fingers of the troll was a rectangular piece of plastic. The bag was no larger than a Post-It note. Plastic bags were hardly a threat, but they could be when carrying the right items. The troll's bag was.

"Is that..." I licked my lips, at a loss for words.

"Yours, John," Tatiana answered.

"Dammit, kid. They've got you by the short hairs now."

"What is it? What are you talking about?" Cassie pushed her way past Quentin and Tatiana, peering down at the troll. She squinted to get a better look. "Is that...hair and blood? Eyugkh." Cassie stuck her tongue out, eyes squeezing nearly shut in disgust.

"Oh, shit." I buried my face in my hands. This was bad.

"What's the big deal?"

"Thaumaturgy," I spat.

"Uh, and for the members of the audience who aren't up on their thamah thingies?"

My head felt like it was seated between a pair of oversized vice-grips. A terrible, acute pressure arced through my skull. An infinite number of questions with no answers had that effect on a man.

Quentin jumped in to explain. "It's a transitory type of magic, Miss Winters, short lived with no permanent effects. It revolves around a few principles. One of which is, 'Once whole, always whole.' Pieces that are separated from a larger whole still retain properties and a link to the original. A connection if you will. In this case, John's hair and blood. A practitioner, or someone with proper knowledge, can create a conduit to that person with said items. You can use it to track people—or worse."

"Like voodoo?" Cassie made an unconscious gesture to

touch her hair.

"Very much so. You've got a sharp mind. But there's a catch. It only works if the nature of the items, or things they are from, haven't changed. If John shaved his head, the hairs wouldn't work. Or if he dyed them."

"What about the blood?"

Quentin smiled. "Really sharp. Blood is harder to distort. It's why it works so well for tracking things. But it can dry out unless something is added to it. Don't ask me what. I'm not *that* adept at this. If John abused his body with copious amounts of alcohol or drugs, that could, in theory, work. Best not to put into practice, however."

"Got it. Keep dying hair. Continue being fabulous, and don't bleed." Cassie ran her fingers through her hair and gave it a modelesque flip.

Quentin snorted in amusement and Tatiana chuckled.

I would have joined in if I wasn't burdened with a singular question. "How did they get my hair?" My knuckles cracked and my fingernails dug into my palm. "How did they get my blood? How did they accomplish Thaumaturgy?"

"They didn't, John. They couldn't—can't." Tatiana's lips pressed tight.

I stared at her. "Someone did."

"She's right, kid. It's like I said: they may be a free tribe, but someone or something is pulling these fae's strings. We're low on time and answers, John. We're due before the court, but after we're done, I think I know who you should pay a visit to."

My heart froze.

"Who?" Cassie looked between the three of us.

"John, no." Tatiana shook her head.

"The Faerie Queens," said Quentin.

Chapter Thirteen

Cassie sputtered. "Fa-wah? You're shitting me."

I shook my head. "I wish he were. They're not nice, they're rarely honest, and they're powerful. Terrifyingly so."

"Faeries?"

I nodded.

"Like tiny wings, Tinkerbell, and short skirts?" Cassie's expression was priceless.

"If by that you mean large, wingless, powerful beyond measure, hauntingly beautiful, and worthy rivals of lesser Gods—then yes." I gave her a knowing look.

"And you want to meet them?" Cassie looked to Tatiana. "Are boys always this stupid?"

Tatiana blinked before bursting into a torrent of laughter that subsided into a fit of giggles.

"Yes," growled Quentin, "but we have another court to pay a visit to first. Now." There was nothing but urgency left in his tone. His color peaked; he was genuinely worried.

"Let's go." I turned to Tatiana. "They found this place once, Tat."

She stared at me but said nothing.

"Be on guard; be careful."

"I will. You take care of yourself."

I gave her a lopsided smile and a thumbs up. I hoped it reassured her more than it did me. "How do you plan on reaching them, Quentin? I don't have a Way that can get us to them, and I have no idea how to describe it for Cassie."

He pointed out the window to a cab, sitting at the curb with its dull yellow lights illuminating the falling snowflakes. "Called it while Cassie and I were waiting for you to finish your soap opera arc with Tatiana."

A low growl formed in Tatiana's throat, audible

throughout the bakery.

I refused to turn and look. Eyeing a predator is a bad decision when they're angry.

Quentin rolled his eyes. "I'm countless millennia older than any of you sprats. I can say what I want." He grunted with enough force for it to come partially out of his nose and throat. Quentin said nothing when he stepped out into the snow.

I followed, giving Tatiana one last look. Cassie squeezed by me as I stood in the doorway. The three of us clambered into the cab without a word. Quentin gave the driver an address I wasn't familiar with and we set off.

"How long?"

"Relax, kid. Short drive."

"Faeries..." said Cassie.

"Yes." Quentin watched me out of the corners of his eyes as I answered. "Think of the tales you heard as a child. Now disregard them all. They are tricky, deceitful, serve only their best interests, and make the Marquis look like a child at wordplay. As crafty as he is, they are craftier. It's in their blood, Cassie, in their magic. Not all fae are bad. But so far I haven't met one with my well-being in mind."

"And trolls are fae?"

"Quick," muttered Quentin from his near dozing state.

"They are. That's the one thing to take away from the tales. They got a great deal right about the kinds of creatures that comprise the fae. But their structure is complex. There are three courts, each as distinct as their queens. Each court filled with a variety of fae, a countless number, including tribes of trolls. And don't get me started on the endless kinds of trolls there are. But...one weakness pervades all fae."

"Iron—steel?"

"Yes. Cold iron is a poison. It's too mortal, too human for faeries."

"Eh?"

"Iron is a part of us." I touched a hand to my chest, right above my heart. "It's in our blood, every inch of our being, flowing—forever. It's our life-force, part of us and the Earth. Cold iron is part of *our* side—ourselves. Faeries can smell it, and they hate it. Iron is strong. It's in our blood, and if you're a poetic person, you can argue that it's the iron that gives us our strength. Our mortal iron will if you will."

"Say that ten times fast."

I glared at her. "Cemeteries used iron gates in the belief it would prevent the souls of the dead from wandering out. They were right; they just didn't know how right."

"Why steel?"

"Steel is iron alloys and carbon. It still holds the same properties. It's stronger and not so prone to rust, making it quite handy." I reached over and patted the sword on her hip. "When it comes to the fae, steel cuts just fine."

"So technically, if you shank a queen with enough iron or steel, you can kill one?"

"Of course, it would be no different from fighting a lion with a thumbtack. You're welcome to try, Cassie. I wouldn't advise it, however. Just because iron can hurt them doesn't mean they will give you the chance to use it on them. The level of magic they possess is frightening. It's on par with the rising of the sun and moon."

She whistled. "So they're comic book strong. Got it."

"And it's second nature, comes to them as naturally as breathing."

Cassie clicked her tongue against the roof of her mouth and nodded. "No messin' with mama faeries, gotchya."

"Tatiana was right. I can't keep shielding you from this. They're after you. We know that. We just don't know who exactly. But you have to prepare yourself. You have to learn how to fight, how to deal with the supernatural—as many kinds as you can. You're going to have to learn proper etiquette..." I paused and gave her a look. "We can take our time with that one."

She pursed her lips.

"Cassie, I'm going to have to teach you everything I can. It's going to be a lot, and you're going to have to work at it. Your life depends on it."

"Wow, way to lay it out all heavy on a girl. Ultimatums much?" She leaned over and rested her elbows on her knees. Sighing, she looked out the car window at the passing buildings and snowfall. "I know my life's on the line, John. Thanks for not dipping on me through this."

"Wouldn't dream of it."

"Thank you." Relief flooded her voice.

"That was well said." Quentin nudged me before turning his gaze towards the window. He paused, licking his lips before glancing out the rear. "Well, if that isn't odd..." Quentin jabbed an index finger at the window.

I shifted in my seat and followed his finger. A car—an inflated lawnmower seemed more appropriate a label—trailed behind us in the snow. It wasn't so odd a thing to have the little car following us. It was a shade of green that screamed of the seventies. A chrome grill filled the space between the headlights. The AMC Gremlin drew closer.

The cabbie, whose eyes seemed to sink before snapping themselves wide and alert, registered the car's approach. His lined and worn face warped into a mask of irritation as the Gremlin came too close for comfort. The driver pressed his lips together and spat more in gesture than actuality. He lowered the window and stuck an arm outside. "Oy-ye!" The Latino man waved a hand, motioning for the car to pass. On the slick roads, tail gaiting would lead to an accident. "Oy-ye!" He waved again.

The driver of the Gremlin honked. I couldn't see them clearly, squinting as I tried. "Gah." The cabbie let out a long, distasteful groan. He waved again, answered by another honk. His gesture morphed as a singular finger protruded from an otherwise closed fist. "Vete al Diablo!" He closed the window, shook his head in disdain, and wrapped both hands back on the wheel. The cab driver grumbled something indiscernible in Spanish as he led us through the snow.

There was a noticeable burble from the engine of the Gremlin. It was too short a warning. Everyone lurched forward, only to be reeled back by the seatbelts. Metal and polyurethane crunched when the Gremlin rear-ended us.

"Hijo de puta!" The driver's eyes were more alert now. Another growl emanated from the engine before Detroit steel pitted itself against the right corner of the car and pushed.

They were trying to spin us. Professionals. In this weather, it wasn't too difficult a feat to achieve. Doing it without losing control of their car was the trick. They succeeded.

Buildings spun. The falling snow looked like a whirling dervish. Everything swirled then shook with an impact only several thousand pounds of metal could make. We struck a lamppost, our heads pulled to the side in unison. My vision blurred for a moment. Overall, I felt fine despite the situation. A benefit of the fear-driven adrenaline rush.

The three of us released varying groans. I cradled my head. "Is everyone okay? Cassie? Quentin?"

Cassie groaned and shifted uncomfortably. "I feel like I was in a car accident. How 'bout you, old man?"

Quentin grunted. "Like I was in a car accident with two smartasses."

"Smartass," Cassie shot back.

"Takes one to know one, kid."

"Get out of the car!" I barked, pushing Cassie into the door and putting an end to their bickering.

Cassie froze before I growled and galvanized her into action. She opened the door with enough force to send it swinging and scrambled out of the car. I followed with Quentin in tow. The cabbie rubbernecked, looking to us as we scampered out of the vehicle and to the green Gremlin that had caused the accident.

I had a bad feeling.

The driver muttered something under his breath, steeled himself with a breath, and exited the car. Before he could do anything drastic, Quentin called over to him. "Son, do you have insurance?" The driver nodded. "You might want to call it in," he said as the Gremlin's lights shut off and the engine died.

The Gremlin's door opened, and a man so large it was near comical stepped out. I would have put him at seven feet tall, easily. Not to mention the sheer amount of bulk he carried in his body. It was like watching a professional strongman wrestle his way out of a clown car.

"I have a feeling you're going to need a new cab." Quentin shook his head.

The driver was having none of it. "Oy-ye cabron." He shook a fist at the mountain of muscle. "Look here—" He fumbled for words as the man fully exited the car and the vehicle shook.

The man weighed a good deal. How swell for him. He was healthy. It was bad news for us. The haphazard driver was wearing a gray tank top—in winter. His arms made my legs look small. He wore rugged jeans and boots. A potato would have felt like a pageant contestant if held next to the man's bald, sloping head. A sleek, black object sat between his gloved hands.

That's interesting. Nothing to cover his arms against the cold, but he wore gloves.

"Pistola!" The cab driver turned and darted towards us. I recognized the word.

"Down!" I screamed.

Quentin pulled Cassie to his chest and fell against the body of the car, lowering himself with her. I dove away from the vehicle over a mound of snow, crashing into an aluminum trash bin. The driver tumbled across his hood, landing hard and scuttling over to Quentin.

A five-count burst went off. It sounded muted, like someone was banging a phonebook across the hood of a car, rather than an ear-splitting staccato of thunder.

Automatic, silenced, professional. It was not a good sign.

For most people, automatic weapons conjure scenes of gunmen in black suits unleashing a torrent of cracking lead, riddling a large area with holes. Hollywood fiction. Submachine guns are notorious for their ability to spew bullets quickly, but not with accuracy. The recoil is horrendous. But in the hands of a professional, they can pin people down efficiently.

The gunman unleashed another well-placed salvo. He wasn't trying to hit us. None of the bullets impacted the car or zipped through the trashcans at me. They were above us and to our sides. He was keeping us fenced in. Not an effective technique unless he had unlimited ammunition; otherwise he'd run dry by the time he was done advancing.

The cold from the snow reached my marrow as I realized what was happening. Our gunman hadn't been riding alone. I pushed myself up to all fours when the unmistakable *click* of a shotgun's action filled my ears.

"Tch, I wouldn't if I were you. Then again, I haven't seen what one of these can do up close," one of the assailants purred.

I lifted my chin to get a better look. My teeth clacked together and an electric jolt rocketed from the bottom of my chin to the top of my skull. My vision flared white and red as I upended, falling backwards into the snow.

"Not smart, are you?" she said.

I certainly wasn't. My sight cleared and I made out my assailant. She was garbed in a tight leather jacket, the sort armored for motorcycle use, with pants and boots to match. Fair skinned, even amidst the snow, with sable hair shaved close on the sides of her scalp, save for the top where it fell like a horse's mane. She wore gloves like her hulking partner. Citrine shone within her eyes, a hungry look.

The woman's comrade ceased firing. A terrible quiet fell over us. It lasted half a second.

The cab driver shook his head and did the unthinkable. He ran, shouting, "Mi madre me dijo que ser un carnicero."

His mother was right; he should have been a butcher. It was safer given the current situation.

"The rest of you: move and the Timeless loses a knee." The woman trained her shotgun at the center of my left leg. She stood a safe distance from me, never letting the barrel of the weapon get too close. Caution—the sign of professionalism in thugs or whatever she happened to be. I didn't appreciate the trait at that moment.

She let out a sharp, piercing whistle and made an intricate motion with two of her fingers. Her brutish companion grunted in acknowledgement. "Keep your gun on the other two. If they move, kill them."

That caused me to blink. The entirety of our troubles of late was due to Cassie's ability. Not a single creature was willing to put her at risk, and now someone was willing to kill her to make a point?

I licked my lips and took a risk. "What do you want?"

She looked at me in genuine surprise, a half-smile coming over her mouth. "You can't be *that* stupid?"

I heard a smattering of grumbles in Quentin's clear, concise voice that amounted to, "You'd be surprised."

"Yeah, he's not exactly Stephen Hawking," said Cassie.

The gunman—gunwoman—ignored their comments. "We're here for *you.*"

It's been said that a change of pace could be a good thing. I felt the need to disagree with that. "I'm assuming you'd like my cooperation?"

She titled her head to the side. "It would be in your best interest."

"Piss off, you tart." Quentin moved to stand before the walking goliath let out another burst from his weapon. "Son of—" He reeled from the close proximity of the rounds.

I needed to find a way to stall. "Drop the glamour and let's talk."

"Well, well." Her mouth twitched in amusement. "How did you know?"

"Your eyes, your hands."

She arched an eyebrow. "Oh?"

"You're emotional right now, overexcited. Your glamour's not hiding your eyes. They're yellow. The gloves took me a bit. You two were afraid of touching anything steel, even brushing against the car door would've hurt."

She clicked her tongue. "Impressive. Maybe I was wrong about you being stupid."

"I have my moments, like this one. You should leave."

"Or I could have been wrong." An arrogant smirk

spread across her face. "Why should we leave? We have you, if you haven't noticed."

"Because you're not well versed in the mortal world. You caused a car accident and let the cab driver get away."

"So?"

"You shot off a submachine gun, silenced, but still loud enough to draw attention. Who do you think the driver is going to call? Not his insurance. The cops. Gloves won't protect from bullets."

"And waiting for them to arrive won't protect you from us," she countered.

She was smart.

You have to hate the smart villains.

"Last question—who sent you?"

She laughed. "You think you can attack a freestanding lord of the Neravene...and walk away?"

"Ah." I didn't know how else to respond.

"There's a bounty on your head, preferably still attached."

The Ageless court might present a problem to her aims. Poor her.

"Well, that's that come back to bite us." Quentin almost sounded bored.

The street lamp above us flickered. That happens from time to time on any given street. There were six lamps on the block, strobing without stop. My stomach knotted. "How big is the bounty?"

Her face scrunched. "Why?"

"Because I don't think you're the only ones out to collect it."

The street lamps went out.

Chapter Fourteen

There's something chilling about having the lights go out. Humans draw a certain comfort from artificial light, never mind the convenience factor. The truth is, we're afraid of the dark, still to this day. Most people won't admit it, but without some form of man-made light, we're easily terrified. The light fleshes out our surroundings, banishes the unknown and bathes us in the familiar. Take that away and what's left? Darkness and everything it can hide. It doesn't matter if it's empty or not. It's the possibility of what it can hide that scares us. And it should. The dark brings darker things with it.

It wasn't complete darkness; I didn't think such a thing existed within the boroughs of New York. But the sudden loss of light was noticeable and disconcerting. What came next, more so.

An odd sound, like playing cards striking the spokes of a bicycle wheel, echoed around us. A second echo cried out. Then a third. They multiplied exponentially in the space of a few seconds. And I couldn't pinpoint their source. The throaty clicks subsided to a chittering...which died off.

Quiet.

The "woman's" glamour vanished. Stark, high cheek bones replaced her average and unassuming face. Ashen-gray skin made her Night Runner eyes stand out all the more. Her hair went white, still keeping the punk-like style it was cut in. The elf's mouth was open, fangs bared as she swept the area for a sign of the newcomers.

It was a mistake. One I took advantage of. I didn't bother getting to my feet. Scrambling, I plowed into a low tackle as I collided with her below the hips. The shotgun didn't go off from the impact, another movie trope. It did, however, blur into motion as we fell. I released my hold and tried to shift my weight. The stock struck my chest.

"Ooof," I coughed from the blow.

Snow plumed into the air as muted thumps sounded around me. "Yah!" I rolled clear of the bullets and struggled to my feet.

The Night Runner was quicker, already bounding to a standing position. "Idiot!" she hissed to her companion. "You nearly hit me."

I turned to gawk at the dimwitted gargantuan. The term definitely applied now. His glamour had vanished as well. He wasn't a Night Runner or a troll. I wished he was.

The creature stood at thirteen feet tall, layered in a shaggy blanket of brown hair. Marble-sized eyes peered out from ridged brows, with a sloping skull that jutted and rose too high to ever be confused for human. Its lips were thick and fleshy, flecked with spittle. The muscle concerned me the most.

Actually, it was fairer to say it was one of the top three concerns the ogre presented.

It was covered in grotesque, bulbous muscles from head to toe, in proportions that made trolls look dainty. Its hands were the size of snow shovels, covered in thick crepe bandages to protect it from metal contact. The gun looked like a toy in its hand, or would have if the ogre held it in that manner. Nails, long enough to qualify as talons, held the submachine gun in a pinched grip. It must have been a delicate one to not crush the weapon. A single nail managed to squeeze into the trigger guard.

It would have been comical if I wasn't staring at an ogre pointing an automatic weapon at me. The gun was a hindrance; the ogre didn't need it once it dropped its guise.

The same train of thought must have crossed the beast's mind. Expensive composite material shattered between its nails. It flung the remains aside in contempt and lunged at the hood of the cab.

The ogre's nails pierced the hood like it was made of wet cardboard. Paint and bits of hood peeled around its fingers. There was a wrenching sound as the hood's locking mechanisms gave way. The ogre held the hood above its head.

I swallowed and moved as fast as my body would allow. I lost track of everything that happened. The ogre grunted, the hood flew towards me, and an incalculable number of shrieks filled the air. I dove. The hood cried out as it struck the ground, warping, cracking, and falling apart in too many ways to describe. Snow showered me as I landed. The shotgun boomed.

Quentin's voice cut through the auditory carnage. "Run!"

"What is it?" My throat burned but I got the words out.

"Don't talk. Listen. Run!"

I did. Quentin hauled Cassie to her feet and led her away from the cab. I followed on the sidewalk, trying to catch up to them.

"No!" snarled the she-elf.

Snow erupted as something zinged by me and hit the ground. There was no clump of pellets that I could see. I gulped. *Slugs.*

The ogre screamed, a cavernous sound so deep and resonant it would have made a better foghorn. I snuck a look back and nearly lost my footing as a result. I counted a dozen simian-looking creatures clambering over the ogre's body. They resembled small monkeys shaved clean, their skin covered in chitinous scales of a sickly green. Bat faced, with the wings to match. They clawed at the ogre's fur with scalpel-sharp, carapace-covered talons. They cut through its thick hide with ease. Saliva frothed at their mouths, coating their protruding fangs. Their reed-thin tails flailed as they danced over the mountain of fur and muscle, tearing its flesh apart.

I had thrown up enough for one day.

The Night Runner threw her head back and released a blood-curdling war cry. She tucked the weapon to her chest and fired at the ogre. The steel-coated lead rounds pulped one of the creatures unfortunate enough to get caught in its path. Brilliant chartreuse flames streaked across the ogre's arm. It staggered, twirling into a violent spin from the force of the slug. Steel wreaked havoc across the fae creature's body. Steam hissed spitefully into the air. The ogre batted at the flames, trying to subdue them. It might have succeeded had the diminutive beasts not capitalized on the situation. They swarmed the monster and gouged at its tissue.

Another crack of thunder from the shotgun. Another crushed fiend. Another problem for the ogre. No loyalty among thieves or bounty hunters. The mountain of fur and muscle bucked under the weight of the scaly, monkey-like beings. They made quick work of it. The pack separated flesh and sinew from bone in a matter of seconds. It was like watching a group of paranormal piranhas.

The shotgun boomed, scattering most of the pack; the Night Runner subdued another one. The monkey monsters shrieked in unison. It was an earsplitting keen, one that was answered. A second scream called back through the night. The sounds morphed into something more sinister. Playing cards in spokes again. A low series of guttural clicks and growls.

Shit, this is going to draw the attention of every officer in the state. That was, if we were lucky. At the rate things were going, the National Guard would be getting involved soon. The pack erupted into a frenzy. They charged the Night Runner. I came to my senses and ran harder. I didn't want to watch.

Boom—boom—boom! The Night Runner discharged her weapon until the inevitable—silence. She let out a defiant roar.

I kept my eyes ahead as the fiends answered her cry. There was a lone, long scream that drowned out all other sounds and thought. I caught up to Cassie and Quentin who had moved up to the sidewalk from the street. "What now? Where are we going?"

"And what's with the Oz posse? Someone gave them a major makeover." Cassie glanced at me, taking care not to look back over her shoulder.

"Gremlins. John, Cassie, quit talking. Run!" Quentin

sped up, his feet barely touched the ground as he pulled ahead.

"He's kidding, right, John? Gremlins?"

"Wrong guy to ask. I thought they were fictional."

"They don't seem like goofy pushovers."

"They're not. Did you see what they did to the ogre?"

"No, I was too busy running!"

"Run faster!" Quentin barked.

The gremlins let out a chorus of howls that caused my skin to crawl. It came from all sides. I looked to my left. I couldn't count the number of shadows bounding over the nearby rooftops, stalking us. And there was a group on the streets pursuing us. At least their wings seemed more decorative than functional. They were still fast, however.

"Ah!" I stumbled sideways, a throb making itself present in my ankle. It wasn't bad, but noticeable.

One of the scaled fiends perched on my shoulder. I swiped an open hand at it and missed. The bastard leapt into the air and came back at me, claws spread, fangs bared. I couldn't risk falling to the ground simply to evade one of the gremlins. If I fell, the rest would be on top of me in seconds. I didn't feel inclined to do the Ageless Court's work for them. Those stuffy coots would have to work for it, and the same went for the gremlins.

I twisted, sending my elbow back. A sharp twinge went through my waist. The bony joint connected with a *crunch*, sending the creature back. It let out a surprised yelp and set after me with renewed effort. I normally appreciated perseverance, not at that moment however.

"There!" Quentin gestured to a building coming up.

It looked officious in nature. Red brick, white columns, a similar design to many other unremarkable, government buildings.

"A courthouse?" I said.

"I can't do what she does." He gave a brusque nod towards Cassie. "Only way I know to get us to where we need to be." He broke off to catch a couple of breaths. "Cab would have taken us here anyway."

I understood his plan. I didn't like it. A federal building was rarely empty despite the late hour. We wouldn't be welcome with a pack of gremlins chasing us. Oh well.

Quentin tore his way up the stairs. Cassie followed, her face strained with effort. My foot hit the first step when the leather of my jacket parted. Hot agony streaked across my lower back in three parts. I came down hard on the next step, my knee shuddering from the impact.

I whipped around and swung out in a blind, openhanded blow. The inside of my palm stung as it connected with the hardened surface of the gremlin's body. It flew aside, hitting a low stone wall hard enough to crack it. The creature wasted no time in getting back to its feet. I lumbered up the stairs sideways, keeping an eye on the creature. Its friends weren't far behind. At least it had learned a lesson in caution. It didn't jump at me, instead choosing to bound up the stairs in a serpentine pattern. I kept my head on a swivel, watching as it darted around me with surprising agility.

"John, come on!" Quentin waved at me, holding the door to the building open.

How did he get that open? I didn't let the question keep me from following his advice. I ran.

My sudden increase in speed set the gremlin off. It trumpeted in fury and jumped after me. I didn't bother to look at it. I raced up the stairs, clearing two of them at a time. Cassie and Quentin entered the building, leaving the door cracked enough for me to jump through. I did.

My forearms and elbows absorbed the shock of the landing. The door slammed shut behind me. A noticeable *thunk* sounded against it. Cassie dropped to a crouch, her eyes shimmering like gemstones under the lighting of the building.

"You okay?"

"Little shit grazed my back." I pushed myself to my knees to find Cassie holding out a hand. I took it and she pulled, leaning back and using her weight to help haul me up. "Thank you." I brushed myself off and twisted to get a look at the state of my back. The motion caused the area to tighten and stretch. Needles erupted throughout it.

"It's not bad, John," she said.

"Feels like it."

"You'll live, kid. Now let's keep moving." Quentin locked the door and set off at a brisk walk. "That won't hold them long."

The light flickered. "Or at all." I said.

"How are they doing that?" Cassie cast a quick look to the door and then to the lights around us.

"Gremlins fear many forms of light. Fire, the sun, man's light. Anything that's not the stars and moon. They can conjure small tufts of Myrk, a type of magic that can shroud sight and light sources. It disrupts electrical things, too. So move!" Quentin crossed into another hall with us in tow. We turned a corner and jogged up a lengthy flight of polished stairs. So far the place appeared to be empty, a small relief.

The building darkened. My relief went with the lights. Our footsteps were noticeably loud as we plodded over the stairs. They echoed through the halls.

"Quentin, how good is a gremlin's hearing?"

High-pitched wails filled the building, and they sounded close.

"Good, damn good, John."

With the sudden loss of light, it was hard to adjust to the dark. There was no starlight or ambient glow from the windows of nearby homes. It was as dark as it could get. Something skittered across the polished floor below us. Claws against marble. They were at the foot of the staircase.

"Run faster!" Quentin yelled.

And then the things in the dark set after us again. Their chittering intensified as they gained on us.

"Any time now!" I growled.

My vision adjusted just enough to see Quentin clear the top stair and send his hand into his jacket. He pulled out something too small to see, clenched tightly in his fist. "Keep running, and don't look back."

The object left his hand. It tumbled through the air, sinking to the ground. Glass shattered, and I looked back.

My eyes welded shut against the explosion of carmine light. A hellish scream accompanied it, peppered with gremlin shrieks. The superheated blast buffeted us. I threw an arm up to shield my face. Dry air brushed my cheeks and neck. I could almost feel blisters forming. The light subsided. When I opened my eyes, part of me wished I had kept them shut.

The walls were scorched, most of the drywall gone. Bits of the marble stairs resembled a frozen waterfall. The polished stone dribbled like tar, deformed and blackened. The windows on the far side were more accommodating to fresh air now. Each could fit a truck through the gaps. I couldn't make out what happened to the glass or where it had gone. Ash and soot blanketed the area as well as hung in the air.

I rubbed my fingers against my eyes, brushing what I could away, and turned to Quentin. "What was that?" I spat as particulate drywall—and likely gremlin—invaded my mouth.

"Alchemist's fire, not a great amount or decent quality. Couldn't reach my usual supplier in Virginia, had to settle for a rank amateur grade at best."

That was amateur?

"What's wrong with you old guys?" Cassie's face was covered in a liberal coating of ash. It was hard not to laugh as she vented her frustrations. "Throwing fireballs and crap? I swear to God, if you burned my eyebrows off, I'll..." She trailed off, her eyes widening as she ran her fingers through her hair. "Did you...singe my hair?"

A dangerous quiet fell over the scene.

I broke it. Not the smartest decision I've made, but in a century plus of living, I've made worse. "You usually carry things like that, Quentin?"

He gave a grunt I took to be a yes.

"Do you have any more?"

"No."

"Rather shortsighted given the situation, isn't it, sir?"

He sighed. "It's never enough when it comes to children, is it?"

Cassie let out a low growl. "You're lucky. If you had any more of those things, I'd be shoving one up each of your asses."

Quentin threw his head back and laughed. A chorus of screams cut him off. He grimaced, "Should've known there would be a larger pack. Come on, we have seconds at best."

We scampered up the remaining stairs as Quentin took a deep breath. He raised his hand, fingers splayed. Lambent streaks of silvery-yellow trailed each of his fingers as he waved them through the air. Within seconds, he wove a net of pure light before us. The entire crosshatching of light flared into a single mass of white.

"Into the Way. Hands and feet inside at all times, and no kicking and screaming, kids. In! In!" Quentin made an exaggerated wave as he ushered us towards it.

Gremlins clawed their way up the ruined stairs, what remained of the walling, and banisters. Cassie jumped through the Way without a second thought. I ran after her, pausing next to Quentin. "Regret getting involved yet?"

He smirked. "No I—" A gremlin flew between us. Quentin's hand struck my chest, pushing me through the Way. The last thing I saw was my best friend buried under a dozen monsters.

The Way shut.

I landed on my feet. The world tipped to a sharp angle, and I stumbled back a few feet, waving my arms for balance. Two palms pressed against my back, helping me steady myself. The stone walls and marble were gone, replaced by something much older.

Arches of steel hung above, rows of them filled with small intersecting beams of metal. Old, thick branches wove their way over and around each arch, adding a bit of earthiness to the works of man. Brick walls, now green under years of moss, made up the high walls. Bits of yellowed cement lines were visible between the clumps of greenery. Running water trickled behind me.

I turned and saw an opening in the wall to our left, wide enough to fit a train. Water cascaded down the steps, streaming to form a small pool in front us. More showered in from the opening above.

There were stairs ahead, leading to a building of worn stone and a design that couldn't be found in the mortal world. Aged stone columns, panes of glass reflecting golden light, and doors made of a wood that seemed to carry a hint of burnt orange in their coloring.

It was surreal, even with everything I had seen in my life. It was like a subterranean greenhouse of metal and earth. It was beautiful. And I didn't care.

Cassie breathed out. "Woah."

I turned back to look at the empty space where we had fallen through. "Take us back."

"What?"

"Take us back, Cassie—now."

"You're kidding? John, I...don't—"

"Now!" My voice echoed through the cavernous structure, shaking loose foliage hanging nearby.

Cassie shuddered, taking a step back from me. "We were there for a minute or two tops. There was barely any light. I couldn't make anything out. I don't remember it well enough, John."

I stared at her, hard. "Take us back."

Her lower lip quivered before it settled. "I can't."

"Can't, or won't?"

"John..."

"He's my *friend,* Cassie. We're going back."

"I know, and I'm sorry, but I can't. And...don't hate me, but I don't want to."

Never mind the water falling around us, trickling and pooling. Never mind the gentle whistling of the wind. It was all silent to me. For a moment, at least. I spoke in a dangerous whisper. "What did you say?"

Cassie moved her mouth to speak.

I cut her off with a wave of my hand. "He risked his life

for me, Cassie. He risked it *for* you. We both did. This wasn't his problem, but he made it his. This wasn't my problem, but I made it mine, for *you*! And *you* can't go back for him?" I never raised my voice above the soft notes of the wind.

She looked away, lowering her gaze to the pool of water. Her body shook. She rubbed her arms, and I swore I heard a sniffle.

"Cassie...please. Just open a Way. I'll go by myself."

"What if I don't want you to?" She turned her head, her eyes were wet and slightly reddened.

"He's my friend."

"And you're mine. You can hate me for it, but I don't want to let you go back there."

"Let me?"

Her shoulders shook as she sniffed again. "I can't send you back, and if I could, I wouldn't."

"It's not your call, Cassie."

"It sort of is."

I felt like sand in a bottle, only the bottle was broken. I sank to all fours. The stress, the pain, the loss—all of it hit me at once. The grains of sand went everywhere, and I fell apart. I didn't bury my face in my hands. It was easier to stare at the grass as my eyes stung. Moisture streaked down my cheeks. Rogue drops kissed the blades of grass below.

Cassie came over to sit beside me. Her arm slipped around me, and she pulled me close. She didn't say a word as I sobbed; she just held me.

Quentin did more than offer me support and good advice; he saved my life, all those decades ago. He showed me a world of infinite possibilities and more. I owed my life as a Timeless to him. He took me in, taught me. The man walked me through endless worlds of magic and wonder. I owed him everything. He was more than a friend.

What do you call someone who stood by your side for over a century? Guided you through trouble and more? He gave me the tools and knowledge to prosper in a world of monsters and magic. Quentin was my friend, but he was also my mentor—and at times—a father. And I'd left him behind.

I didn't know how long had passed before I stopped crying.

"I'm sorry, John." She pulled me in for a tighter hug, one I was too tired to return.

"So am I."

"What do we do now? I have no idea where we are or where to go?"

"I don't know. Quentin had a plan to deal with the court. What it was, I have no idea. I'm not overly fond of confronting them as things are. I may not have a choice though."

"You do not," said a heavily accented voice.

I jumped to my feet, hand on sword, turning and drawing my blade. The world flashed through streaks of electric whites and yellow. I staggered back, clutching my forehead, which was in the act of stinging and throbbing. It was an impressive hit.

Toshiro stood garbed in his gray cloak and robes, his sword sheathed, but it hardly mattered. He held it an inch from where my head had been before I reeled from the blow. The scabbard felt like it left quite the mark. There would likely be a welt.

I scowled. "Why did you do that?" I rubbed the area, picturing it swell under my fingers. My fingers came away red. The gash could have been worse.

"You drew your weapon to attack me, I defended myself—without causing you harm."

I gestured to my forehead and raised an eyebrow. "Without causing me harm."

"Serious harm," he amended. "Enough to keep a child in line."

I took in a deep breath, working to keep my voice level. "I am not a child."

He waved his weapon to both Cassie and me. "You are—the both of you—children. Reckless, endangering people...stupid."

"And you're an ass...an old curmudgeony assbiscuit."

Cassie went as far as making an obscene gesture with one of her hands.

Toshiro blinked and tilted his head, trying to make sense of all she had said.

"She took the words right out of my mouth. Some liberties were taken, but she got the gist of it." I glanced at her and mouthed, "Assbiscuit?"

She winked back.

Toshiro shook his head. "Rude. Childish. Come." He took several steps towards me, and I tensed. He paused and blinked. Toshiro took a slow, long look around us. "Where is Quentin Denholm?"

I licked my lips, swallowed the lump that formed and looked to the trickling waterfall. For a while, the running water was the only sound.

Toshiro pieced it together. "Ah, how?"

"Left him behind. It wasn't my choice. He pushed me through."

Toshiro nodded in what looked like understanding. "Yes, he would do that for you."

"Gremlins jumped him." Cassie's fists tightened. A series of light cracks followed.

"He was a good man." Toshiro shut his eyes and inclined his head. It was a small, yet perfect bow.

I glossed over his apology and focused on a single word. "Was?"

Toshiro stared at me. "Alone, with untold numbers of gremlins." He shook his head. "I am sorry, but Quentin Denholm has passed."

Toshiro may have lived for a score of centuries, fought in countless wars, and had endless experience in fighting, but it didn't matter in that moment. His eyes widened and my fingers dug into my palm as my knuckles connected with his face. I could feel the impact ricochet into the meat of my shoulder. Toshiro's head snapped to the side.

I didn't train like he did or have any boxing experience, but I had something else. My height, reach, weight, and in the moment, the sort of anger that gnaws at you—to the bone. It was enough to send him crumbling to the ground.

Toshiro's legs flared into action, scissoring around my calf and knee. There was a sharp twist and my leg gave way. I toppled. Cassie shouted something incoherent. One second I was upright, the next, I was looking at a wedge of glinting steel. The chisel-tip of his sword hovered a breath above my left eye. If I blinked, I could be sure to lose an eyelash or two.

"Reckless, foolish, like Quentin at times."

I growled, tensing my body. The sword moved a micrometer. It was enough of a warning to tell me to not bother. Toshiro didn't turn to look at Cassie, who drew her dagger. "Do not, child." He nodded in my direction, and Cassie got the message.

She hissed but sheathed her blade.

"What did you hope to accomplish by hitting me?"

"It felt good."

"Hai, and it will not bring your friend back. He is gone. Hear it now, accept it, and let it go. That is the way of life, no matter the years we are given. Timeless, Gray, or not, we all fade."

"I'll believe it when I see a body."

Toshiro shook his head in a weary manner. "There is no time for that." He pulled his katana back in a flourish, stowing the weapon. "Rise. The court awaits. Judgment needs to be passed."

"Why the rush?" I pushed myself up, brushing myself off as Cassie came to my side to help.

"Because I have other concerns to attend to, and I am pressed for time."

"So, what's that got to do with hurrying John up? He just, we..." Cassie trailed off.

"I wish to carry out his sentence and return to my business." Toshiro said it so casually that chills ran under my skin and into my blood.

"Maybe they'll be in a forgiving mood?" Cassie gave me a weak smile and shrug.

"I can hope."

"Hai, but do not cling to it, for hope is a weak root to hold onto."

"Cassie was right. You *are* an ass."

Toshiro ignored the insult. "Come, judgment awaits."

My body felt like it was held together with frayed rope. I was falling apart by the second. Cassie was likely feeling the same. We had been pushed, prodded, and chased for a long time without a good rest. "Toshiro, wait."

He didn't stop. "You have delayed the Court long enough. Come." Toshiro reached into the folds of his clothes and pulled out a clean rag. He tossed it to me.

I caught in with a swipe of my hand and dabbed the area above my brow. With a flick of my wrist, I tossed it back to him. "Cassie and I are tired, my best friend is trapped in the mortal world with gremlins, and I would like to rest. We both know where this trial is going. They can wait to cut my head off for another few hours. I'm not going anywhere, but I would like a good sleep. We both would."

Cassie nodded.

Toshiro paused. "The girl will be given a place to rest. You will come with me, be sentenced. Then you can rest...forever."

I threw my hands up in futility and followed him.

Cassie fell into step by my side. "They really gonna..." She broke off and mimed holding a sword in both hands. She twisted her hips and slashed.

"Likely so."

"And you're cool with that?"

"Gods, no."

"So why are you going?"

"Because I have to. And...if something happens, before anything happens..." I paused and took a deep breath. "I'm going to make a case for you. They have to hear me out at the very least. If they do, if they realize your gifts and importance, they will keep you safe." I didn't add the silent, *I hope*.

"Yeah—no, not cool with me. I'm not letting them go

Mad Queen on you. If things go bad, we can bounce. I'll make sure of it."

"There will be no...*bouncing*." Toshiro turned to give us both a stern look.

"He's right. If we did that we'd be hunted down—more than we already are. It wouldn't be prudent."

Cassie snorted. "Yeah, but since when have we been doing things the smart way?"

She had a point.

Toshiro led us up the stairs and into the stone palace. The scenery changed. A lone, short hall comprised of pale gold stones led to a single door of polished ebony. It was simple, and yet beautiful.

The simple things often are.

He gestured to the door. "I will show the young woman to where she can rest. You will go inside and face your consequences." Toshiro's tone did not help settle the discomfort in my stomach and heart.

"I'm going with him." Cassie took a single step forward, enough to put herself in front of Toshiro and myself.

"You cannot." Toshiro said nothing further, but the act of putting his hand on the katana's hilt spoke volumes.

"Listen, Toshi." Cassie leaned against the stone wall, and I fought to quiet a laugh. The warrior gritted his teeth as Cassie touched a finger to the tip of her nose. "Little tip on life: you've lived a long one, and if you want it to last longer, don't go around telling women what they can and can't do." She moved her finger from her nose and tapped Toshiro on the tip of his.

He blinked, and took an uncertain step back. He looked to me for help.

I shrugged. "Don't bother arguing with her. I tried, believe me."

"Good." She threw her arms together in a self-satisfied manner.

The door was cool as I placed my palm against it. I breathed out, shutting my eyes for a moment. "Judgment. I've always hated that word." I pushed the door open.

Chapter Fifteen

There are countless shades of every color, including white. The room we entered pushed me to recall as many as I could. Except it wasn't a room, but an endless expanse of white in all its forms. The floor was a single piece of polished pearl that stretched beyond where the eye could see and probably further still. The sky was a prismatic mix of porcelain, powdered bone, and ivory.

I reeled from the intensity of it. There was no light source in sight, but the place was illuminated nonetheless. The train of forest colors stood out against the backdrop. The figures wore robes of neutral earthy tones, rich verdant that could have come from any number of fields and woods. There were browns of mud, deep soil, and bark. They sat on curved chairs that looked to be carved from chunks of the moon. Stone the color of salt, marred by spots of charcoal. I felt them staring at me from within their deep hoods. There were thirteen of them. An important number. They waited in silence.

Cassie nudged me. "Say something. This is creeping me out."

"Say what? And it's creeping me out as well."

"How about a knock-knock joke? Break the ice. I know one about a polar bear."

"No."

"Alright, I got this." She interlaced her fingers and stretched her arms. I heard light cracks.

"Cassie, no—"

She walked forward several steps. "So." She projected her voice well through the area. "A hundred-year-old coot and an awesomely witty, and attractive—if I do say so myself, and I do—chick walk through a black door. They come face-to-face, not literally, with a bunch of hooded figures about to pass—"

"Enough." The figure at the center spoke, his voice drowning out Cassie's like the crack of thunder over hail.

Cassie looked down, taking a step back. "Nobody expects the Spanish Inquisition," she muttered.

I pressed my lips into a tight smile, reminding myself that I mustn't laugh. In truth, part of me wanted to see her make it through the joke. It would've stalled them, if only for a few seconds more. In the moment, even a few seconds would have helped me feel better.

"Jonathan Hawthorne," boomed the center speaker. He rose and pulled his hood back.

I knew him. A sloping brow and mountainous crags defined much of his face. They were the sort of features you would expect from a man in his earliest days upon the world. Neolithic, hard, and brutish. His hair was thick and straggly, pulled into a tight tail and tied with a length of gold silk. A coarse wire brush beard of black lined his solid jaw. His eyes were deep brown and stared me down with weight. The robes were loose but enough to conceal how powerfully built the man was.

The eldest of the Timeless. The most conservative. The strictest and most judgmental. Wonderful.

"For your ease and so we may hear the most accurate and understandable recounting of your transgressions, the inquisition will take place in English. Is this acceptable?" the eldest said.

When you have all the time in the world to live and travel, you learn many things, like languages. I may have spent most of my time obsessing over the paranormal than studying the many forms of man's word. So the concession came as a pleasant surprise. They could have done the whole thing in Latin, which would not be to my advantage. Stuffy old language anyhow. Spoken by pretentious old pricks and governing bodies of wizardry, I've heard.

"Yes, that is fine. Thank you." I bowed my head.

Two figures came in on either end from a fold of white

light. They stopped at the ends of the semi-circle seating arrangement. They were garbed like Toshiro, robes in a gradient of grays. A European sword of considerable length was strapped to the back of one figure. The other held what looked like an authentic rapier in one hand, sheathed and not fasted to him in any manner. Both their hoods were up.

Always a good sign...

The eldest waved a hand to make sure he held my attention. "Jonathan Hawthorne, you are called before the Ageless Court to explain your offenses in breaking your oaths of impartiality. You will have a chance to explain your actions, defend yourself, and make a case for leniency or forgiveness. Do you understand?"

I nodded.

"You stand accused of involvement in mortal affairs and the supernatural. Involvement in the event recorded as the First World War. You were fully aware prior to intervening that you were forbidden from doing so. You are responsible for forty-three mortal deaths, and thirty-seven paranormal. The deaths of the supernatural are waived. The mortal ones...are not."

It was a fair point.

"Second. After your first indiscretion and despite being reprimanded, you took part in the underground French resistance in the Second World War. You killed significantly more mortals, totaling the sum of one hundred and twenty-nine. Was the first war practice? A warm-up for your bloodlust? The court is well of aware of how and when you became a Timeless. Once a warmonger, always one. The—"

"'That's enough!" barked a figure five seats down. It was a woman's voice, and strong. Her voice carried an accent I couldn't make out. Something from the Indo-Pakistan region. It managed to hush the eldest without drawing a harsh rebuke from him. That was something impressive. Not many could speak to him like that, even on the Court. "Dragging in the boy's life before becoming a Timeless is meaningless. Don't try to paint him like some delinquent, or even a threat. I could always regale the Court of your beginnings—clubbing things, grunting and chest pounding. Pot, meet kettle." A robed sleeve, too large for the woman inside, pointed from the eldest to me.

I bit my tongue and buried the raucous laugh as a series of deep coughs.

One of the figures near the end, third from last, made a series of subtle hand motions. They were deliberate and clearly intended to draw my attention. Some of the nearby members titled their heads and looked at the figure. The motions stopped as they leaned back and tucked their arms across their chest. A single hand slipped out, the fingers pressed to the palm as their thumb stuck up visibly.

I blinked. *A thumbs up?* I stared at the figure, squinting and leaning forward, anything to get a peek within their hood. No such luck, but I didn't need it. The figure raised their hand and waved it with childlike enthusiasm. My laughter echoed through the endless space and the Court went silent. I swallowed the remainder of the laugh and muttered an apology.

One figure shook in their seat with what looked like amusement.

Bastard. It couldn't have been. My mind felt smothered and unable to process everything as relief flooded me.

The eldest carried on. "Leaving out Jonathan Hawthorne's life prior to joining the ranks of the Timeless, he has still committed offenses that need to be addressed. You were warned of what a third transgression would entail, and were summoned here three days ago on probation. In that time, you committed not only your third, but fourth offense. Interfering with the mortal world by associating with..." He stopped short, pausing as if searching for the right word. He made a callous hand motion towards Cassie. "That strumpet."

Cassie leaned in towards me. "Strumpet?"

I inhaled and shut my eyes. This was not the time for this. "It means prostitute."

She took it better than I thought. Cassie pursed her lips and nodded. "Okay, okay. I'm cool."

I breathed a sigh of relief. It was premature.

"Aw-hell-no-he-didn't." She shook her head and marched towards them. I ran after her, catching her by the arm. "Call me a hooker? I'm going to shove my foot so far up your pruney butt you'll be coughing periwinkle, jackass!"

Mustn't laugh anymore.

The eldest of the Timeless shook his head. "Disgraceful. Since taking up company with *that*"—he looked at Cassie again—"you've endangered the Timeless. You assaulted a lord of the Neravene. You started a war."

He wasn't wrong. But I did it for the right reasons. Then again, the road to hell was paved with those. But I stood by it, and if I was heading there, I was going to make sure Cassie didn't follow.

One of the members threw back their hood and rose. Quentin flashed me a quick wink, and gave a gawking Cassie a lopsided grin. He left the row of seats and positioned himself at the front, facing the court. "That's rubbish and you know it. We all know what kind of man, excuse the term, the Marquis is. And we all knew what getting into bed with him meant. This was inevitable; he would have betrayed us eventually. I know Jonathan, and I've heard his account of it. The Marquis assaulted him."

"Personally?" The eldest arched an eyebrow. The single word carried through the space.

Quentin faltered for a second, visibly so. "Yes, he did." Many members leaned closer to one another and muttered amongst themselves.

"Only after your protégé threatened his person."

"Garbage, and you know it." Quentin cut through the air with a swipe of his hand. "Members of his court attacked them."

"Members that did not swear to uphold any word of safe conduct. That word was given by the Marquis and him alone."

He had another point. I didn't like the eldest of the Timeless before. I certainly didn't like him now. I imagined him coughing periwinkle. It brought a smile to my lips.

One hundred years of age doesn't mean you have to bury your inner child. You age better if you hold onto a little petulance and let it out now and again.

The eldest made a dismissive gesture with his hand. "Hawthorne played a game with the Marquis, and lost. He was outwitted and has to pay the price."

"So we give him up to some conniving low lord and bow and scrape and what? We're Timeless; we didn't get here by bowing, but by learning. We know what his ilk are. We know how good their word is. We know how to beat them, if we need to."

"Are you saying we need to? That we should let this happen?" The eldest's voice stirred many of the Court to sit up straighter, their posture going rigid. He knew how to manipulate his crowd and how to play on their fears. "We're not warriors. We're scholars, observers; we record." He waved a hand at the two gray robed figures at either end of the seats. "Their role is to take action. True, neutral, and unbiased action. That is their function, not ours, or did you forget?"

"Fine." Quentin ran a hand through his hair. "Then get them to act." He pointed to the Order of the Gray members like the eldest had. "You want to play by the rules. There, they can act. One of us was attacked, played, and you're not even asking the most important question."

The eldest leaned forward, resting his chin on steepled fingers. "Oh?"

"Why?" The single question reverberated through the room. Many members went silent. Others tilted their heads in curiosity and spoke to one another. Quentin tipped his head towards Cassie, and my heart lurched. "That girl can open Ways—all of them—any of them from what I can tell."

The silence grew. I didn't think that was possible, but it was. It was the sort of silence that left me almost able to hear my own blood pumping.

Another member leaned forward and removed their hood—the woman with the eastern accent. She looked like someone's grandmother—kind face, a sort of frailty that almost seemed endearing. Her dark features were contrasted by an unruly shock of white hair that she did not bother to manage. She looked at Cassie, examining her. "Is it true, child?"

Cassie turned to me for help.

"Might as well. We came here in part for their help."

She bit her lip and nodded. "Yes."

"Hm." The old lady pressed her lips together and nodded more to herself. The rest of the Court mirrored her actions, or so I thought; it was hard to see within hoods. "Dangerous," she said, the word carrying throughout the room.

I could feel the weight of the judgment being passed down—not on me, but Cassie. I decided to quash it then and there. "Yes, she is. She can be. That's the point. Don't you get it? The Marquis wasn't hostile until she piqued his curiosity. Think about what she can do. Think about what she can do in the hands of the Marquis. For that matter, in the hands of some of the more volatile, unbalanced lords and ladies of the Neravene."

Cassie's mouth barely moved, but I was able to make out what she said. "Dude, what are you doing?"

"I'm trying to impress your importance, the fact that you are technically a weapon." It was not an easy feat speaking with my lips pressed that close together.

"Oh yeah, sure, tell 'em I'm dangerous. That's the way to make them like me. Think they'll give me a spot next to you on the chopping block? It's always been on my bucket list—kick bucket with best friend." She shook her head.

I didn't respond. Instead, I addressed the court. "Think about it. She can be dangerous in the wrong hands. A woman who can open Ways at will, bypass defenses, even ours. You're worried about me starting a war. I did it to keep her safe. She could be used to start and end a dozen wars. Any lord or lady of the Neravene could use her to accumulate enough power to rival Gods, the Faerie Queens, or worse. Is that what you want? I started a war to keep her safe because she could be used for a terrible purpose. But more than that, I started a war to keep her safe because she is my friend."

The court listened and kept silent. I took it as an invitation to go on.

"We are supposed to observe, take note, and watch humanity. For what? To stand idly by when they're in danger. No. Not anymore. I'm done with it, and the Court, if that's what this means. She was—still is—in danger. We're not supposed to be removed from it; we are supposed to be part of it. Time and humanity are two different things. Somewhere along the line and ages, you have all forgotten that. What good are knowledge and experience if we don't use it to help people like this?" I jabbed a finger towards Cassie.

"She doesn't deserve to be in danger. To be chased by trolls and Night Runners. She should be making terrible, stupid mistakes that many people her age make."

I could feel Cassie staring at me. "What are you trying to say?"

"Hush, I'm trying to save both our hides here."

Quentin took over. "Jonathan is right. We have endless knowledge among us, but it doesn't take that to realize what it would mean for this young woman to be taken into the Neravene. If she was used by any freestanding lord or lady, it would create a series of wars like we have never seen. There are so many things kept in balance, not only in our world, but the worlds beside ours, and she could throw them all off."

That comment hit a nerve. Every hood fell back. A variety of faces of all ages stared back. Every face paled, looking to one another for an answer. Every face settling in the end, on Cassidy Winters. I recognized the signs: some weighed her a threat. Others saw her as an irritant, something to be ignored or pushed away from sight. A few saw her as a human being, a child on the run, scared and needing help.

I appealed to those. "Please. Help her." Three words,

with enough emotion and power to sway the minds of the Ageless Court. That was the hope at least.

The eldest member stepped forward, raising his hands to stifle the murmurs that broke out. “Enough. No more deliberating. It is time for judgment.”

Chapter Sixteen

"Arbitration." His voice was clear and carried into an echo that spawned more.

It took me to the count of twenty to remember how to think properly again. Arbitration. Not a decisive judgment. But...he was giving me a chance to decide my own fate. Our fates really.

Quentin's posture sank in relief. A good sign. He must have been hoping for this. If only he had let me in on the plan. Though I suppose if he did, I wouldn't have done what I had.

Nothing ever goes according to plan. Sometimes you have to keep people in the dark to get them to act in their best interests. It's not something that leaves you feeling good, but it's a harsh necessity at times.

I could see it in Quentin's face when he turned back to look at me, flashing me a weary smile. His face seemed to carry more lines than normal. He had less shine to his skin. I didn't know what he did before the Court, but whatever it was, it had taxed him.

"Psst, what's arbitration?"

"A sign we might have a shot."

"How?"

"They're going to take a vote to push this issue to the discretion of one man."

"Oh great, so do or die by one asshole instead of a group of them; that's always great."

"The person they're going to choose is truly neutral, a rarity. They are a member of both the Timeless and the Order of the Gray. They can carry out action, but live as one of us. They watch over humanity, learn, observe, and—I hope—sympathize."

"I push for a vote of arbitration." The eldest faced the members and waited. Some nodded in agreement. Some didn't. I kept count. Five in favor, five against so far. My collar grew hot. Quentin nodded in favor and eyed the dark-skinned woman. She followed his lead, as did the sickly pale man with thinning blonde hair. Eight in favor, including the eldest, which was a surprise. That settled it.

I breathed out and let my shoulders sink.

"Arbiter," he called.

Nothing happened for a moment after the eldest spoke. A film of light split the room vertically. It was fluid, bending to an unseen current of air. If it weren't from the smoke billowing from the crack, it would be near impossible to see amidst the white backdrop. Something stepped out of the Way.

The Way shut like a giant taking a deep breath. He was tall, near seven feet. The man was a walking pile of contradictions. Whip-cord thin, his robes hung loosely around his body. His skin clung to him like it was stretched tight, a black tarp pulled too tight. And yet, his posture was perfect, and straight. He carried himself with more strength than I imagined possible for someone with his build. His head was clean-shaven. Thick, dark brows hung above clouded eyes.

He was blind. Despite that and his malnourished appearance, he gave off the aura of a king. I would know, having met a few. I couldn't bring myself to take into account everything I was pulling off of him: regal, powerful, yet frail in appearance. Tired, yet still doing his duty. Every member of the Court lowered their head in deference to him. It seemed like the smart move. I put a hand on Cassie's shoulder, giving a slight tilt of my head to show her what was happening. She got the message. We lowered our heads as well.

"You called?" I couldn't define what I heard in his voice. When the Arbiter spoke, it was like listening to a hurricane speak.

You can't have a conversation with thunder, its voice

overwhelms yours; it's too broad and powerful. But if you could, that's what the Arbiter sounded like.

I wasn't the only one rocked by his voice. Cassie teetered before collecting herself.

"We did." The eldest kept his head bowed. "We would like you to provide a solution, or settlement, to a problem."

I looked up and the Arbiter faced me. We met eyes. A torrential flood hit me. I took a step back and averted my gaze. I didn't know how a blind man managed to carry that much intensity in his eyes, but he did.

"Surprised, Jonathan Hawthorne?" When the Arbiter said my name, it felt like I tripled in weight.

Never underestimate the power of names, and never underestimate what a person of power can do with your name.

"Yes," I said. There wasn't much else I could reply with.

The corners of his mouth turned into a smile. "Why?"

"Because you came through the frickin' Eye of Sauron," Cassie muttered.

The Arbiter's smile slipped for a second. He looked at Cassie and threw his head back, exploding into laughter. It was a rich, rolling laugh—infectious. Cassie laughed, so did I, a few members of the court joined in. It the midst of an inquisition and judgment, it was rather nice.

After the laughter subsided, I looked at the Arbiter without meeting his eyes, which was something of a tricky feat. "You heard your name being called from the other side of a Way?"

The Arbiter said nothing.

"You're blind, yet I get the feeling you see pretty well."

"Better than you know. And I see more than you think."

I raised an eyebrow. "Oh?"

"I see what happens if you fail in finding the power after Cassidy Winters. I see you standing before the Faerie Queens. I see you breaking, Jonathan Hawthorne, driven mad by the ghosts of lifetimes past. I see you lost among the bones of dead gods and nameless things. I see you holding your chest and stomach together, trying in vain to keep yourself from spilling the last of your blood."

"Oh..."

Cassie gave me a light tap. "Um, how good is Madam Cleo over there?"

"Very good." The Arbiter had a thin smile on his face. "And I see you, Cassidy Winters, beside yourself in anger and grief, tearing through space and time." When the Arbiter said Cassie's name, I saw her eyes flutter and her balance waver. "I see you in chains of iron and thorns—cold—your face marred with tears and blood. I see your eyes lose their fire, replaced by hollow lenses and an empty light."

Cassie's eyes widened and she swallowed, her skin blanching.

I didn't blame her. I felt the same.

"I also see what happens should you succeed."

I was afraid to ask. I know how that sounds, but after hearing what I had, even success seemed like it would have less than pleasant consequences. "And what is that?"

"The world goes on. You live." He paused to jerk his head in Cassie's direction. "She lives." The Arbiter jerked a thumb over his shoulder towards Quentin. "The smartass lives. I live. Good reasons for you to succeed."

"Well, when you put it that way," said Cassie.

"Indeed." The Arbiter turned to address the Ageless Court. "I have decided."

Once again—three words with a great deal of power and weight behind them. Not to mention the anticipation.

"And what is your decision, Arbiter?" The Eldest spoke in a neutral voice, no curiosity coloring his tone. He wanted an answer, and he would accept it, no matter if he agreed with it or not.

"Let them continue unhampered," said the Arbiter. "If they succeed, Hawthorne and Winters will avert disaster for both the mortal world and those within the Neravene. If they fail, Hawthorne's punishment will no longer be a concern for the Court, nor will his life."

Though I agreed with his decision, mostly because it got me out of trouble, I wasn't wholly appreciative of how he phrased it. He could have been a little less nonchalant about my death.

The Eldest pursed his lips and shut his eyes, thinking. He exhaled, and after a moment said, "Very well. Jonathan Hawthorne, you are free to go."

Cassie piped up. "I noticed he didn't say anything about me."

"You were never on trial, Cassie."

"Could've fooled me."

I snorted. "I had to explain how important you were, and the necessity of keeping you safe should I be killed."

"That's because you're lazy and don't want to take responsibility." She sighed. "Always looking for the cop out, aren't you? You can't dump me on a bunch of stuffy old coots."

"Who's stuffy?" Quentin stood a few feet off and to the side, hands on his hips as he wore a look of mock indignation.

I looked past him to see the council dispersing. Some members broke off to form cliques. They made deft motions towards our little trio. I couldn't hear what they were saying. I had the feeling that I didn't need to, nor want to.

You know when you're being spoken about.

"You're stuffy—you stuffy lookin' nerf herder!" Cassie grinned and threw her arms around Quentin.

He laughed, returning Cassie's hug. "Good to see you too." Quentin turned his attention to me. "Jonathan." He gave me a curt nod.

"How did you—"

"Survive?"

I nodded several times without saying a word.

"Funny thing that. Once you two passed through, they scattered."

"Why would they do that?" It wasn't like gremlins to give up a free meal. I stared at him, waiting for an answer.

He shrugged. "My best guess is that they were either after you, or the girl. Maybe both? You two are wanted by different parties, maybe the gremlins thought they'd nick the pair of you and cash in twice the pay? They didn't seem too interested in me after the Way shut."

"But...I saw you get buried under a group of them." I blinked, pressing a hand to my head. None of it made sense.

Quentin shook his head. "You're right, and they would have torn me up properly if I hadn't gotten away."

"And how did you do that?" Cassie eyed him sideways.

He smirked and held an index finger to his mouth. "Secret."

I groaned. "What about the courthouse?" I remembered what Quentin had done, the damage he had left behind. Someone was going to have to deal with that. "You could have burned the place down."

Quentin raised his hands, turning them over in a helpless gesture. "I needed to be in a courthouse to open a Way here."

"What, why?" Cassie's face scrunched into a tight mask of confusion.

"Because, most people, even Quentin, cannot open Ways like you." I made a gesture similar to the ones she used in making a Way. "Everything may be interconnected, but it's not easy to run along those tracks. Besides having the knowledge of opening a Way, you need to be in the right place, somewhere with the right energy. To bring us to the Ageless Court, we needed to be in a place similar to it. So, a courthouse was the best bet. A place of trial, judgment, sentencing—"

"And old people in robes eager to punish you; I got it," said Cassie.

"Still, Quentin, you threw fire in a courthouse. What if the fire didn't go out?"

"It wouldn't be the first building burned down in New York of late." He rolled his shoulders in a halfhearted shrug. "Remember that hotel a year ago, the Premiere?"

I nodded.

Cassie looked between the pair of us. "What?"

"Some idiot, so I heard." Quentin scratched his chin as he tried to recount the details. "He was fighting an Elemental. I don't know what the poor slob did to get on one's bad side. The hotel wasn't left in serviceable condition after that. It's only just getting back on its feet."

I couldn't argue with that. New York did seem to be going through an increased number of oddities recently. The paranormal sort at that. I sighed and shook my head. "Fair enough. What now? We've gotten the Court off my case, but we're still at a loss about the powers behind the trolls—worse, what else could be after her."

"And you, kid, don't forget that. The Marquis' put a nice price on your head. It's going to be more than trolls after the pair of you. Honestly, I'm surprised there haven't been more things setting chase after your hind ends."

"There will be. Your journey will be fraught with even more danger from now on." I hadn't seen the Arbiter approach, another thing I found disturbing about him. "But you are—all of you—focusing on the wrong thoughts."

Quentin tilted his head as he regarded the Arbiter. "Hm?"

"Why has only one kind of troll pursued you for so long? Why are they truly after Cassidy Winters? Power? But for whom? Themselves? Someone else? If the latter, then why are the trolls doing their bidding? Are they being coerced? Is it an order? If so, who wields enough power to compel them? Is it simpler than that? Are they being paid? The proper questions lead to the proper answers."

My head spun under the Arbiter's rapid fire questions, but he had a point. And he had even better questions. But I had one for him. "Why are you helping us? Are you even allowed to?"

He cracked a smile. "Allowed to? Helping? Hm..." The Arbiter rubbed his jaw, his smile widening as he did. "I am simply asking questions. No harm in that. You could say it is in my best interest, and yours." He inclined his head, exhaled, and deftly moved two of his fingers. With such little motion, and barely an exertion of power, he opened a Way.

Cassie's ability to do so was nothing short of amazing. But she had little control over it. She was getting better each time, but the Arbiter was *good.* Cassie picked up on that.

"Wow, nice moves. Think you could give me a lesson after we're done with trying to save our collective butts?"

"If you succeed, it would be my pleasure." The Arbiter made an extra low bow to Cassie. He stepped backwards into the Way and vanished.

"So we've got our next bearing. Follow the trolls," I said.

"Yeah, because that always goes well. Follow the spiders, remember that bit?"

Quentin and I gave Cassie strange looks.

"Ugh, you two are hopeless."

"So what's your plan, kid?"

I glowered at Quentin. "Find some trolls, and go from there."

Quentin blinked, sighing and pressing both his hands to his eyes. "I didn't just hear that."

I shrugged. "It's the best option I can think of."

"Think again." Quentin's voice was a tad muffled behind his hands.

"Yeah, seriously, John, no *bueno.*"

"Look, all we know is that trolls are after you. They're part of the Faerie domain. Someone or something in the Fair Lands wants you, Cassie. They are our only link at the moment. We need to find them, follow them, or interrogate them if we can."

Quentin rolled eyes his. "Wonderful idea, John. Maybe you can find us a cooperative one while you're at it, hm? One who will tell us everything we need to know, and be kind enough to drop us into the domain of one of the Faerie Queens. Honestly, kid, we would be better served looking into the troll's backer a different way. Always follow the money."

I blinked as an idea hit me. "You know what? I think I

might be able to pull all of those things off."

Both Cassie and Quentin's eyes widened. Quentin recovered first and eyed me askance. "Do tell, kid."

"Yeah, John, what's up?"

"I think I know someone who might be able to help. Someone who can take us from being hunted...to doing the hunting."

"Oh?" Quentin crossed his arms, waiting for an explanation. Cassie copied his look.

"Yeah, I'm going to need pennies. Lots of them."

Chapter Seventeen

They exchanged puzzled glances. "Uh, pennies? Um, John, hate to break it to you, but pennies aren't worth what they used to be." Cassie paused for a moment. "Were they ever worth anything?"

I shook my head. "No, not really. But sometimes it's not the worth we attribute to things. It's the worth others give it. One man's trash, another man's treasure."

"Right...it's still a penny." Cassie rolled her eyes.

Quentin looked at me like I was insane. "Where are you going with this, kid?"

"Times Square, if I can. I don't suppose you can take me back there?"

"Sorry, I can't. But..." Quentin trailed off and stared at Cassie.

She returned the stare and nodded. "I think *maybe* I can pull it off?"

"You don't sound too confident," I said.

She shrugged slightly. "It's been a while since I've been to Times Square. I'm still learning this whole bouncing around thing. It's not as easy as I make it look, you know?"

"She's right, John, it's not. Maybe you should bother to learn instead of hopping through the ones buried beneath your place."

I held my hands up in a gesture of defeat. "You win. I'll stop pressing it. All I know is that we need to get back there. How we do it isn't that large a concern."

Cassie rubbed her hands together in an excited manner. "Alrighty, I think I got this. Times Square." She blew out a breath and shut her eyes. The tip of her tongue slipped out between her teeth when she bit down on it. Her brows furrowed in concentration. "Snow, light, lots of people rushing around, and trolls. Trolls in the alleys. Right, Times Square."

I hated to chime in while she was focusing, but I felt like I had to. "Cassie, nothing's happening."

One of her eyes peeped open. She managed to glare at me before shutting it.

I took it as a hint to shut up.

Cassie moved her hand but something was off. It wasn't the usual fluid and decisive movement. Her hand trembled, and there was a moment where it clearly spasmed. She parted the air and a Way opened. It just wasn't the sort I expected.

I took a step back as Quentin had a more dramatic reaction, leaping a few feet to the side. The Way was a horizontal cut, pulsating yellow light, the sort aged headlights of a car would give off. Clouds of smoke surrounded the light, billowing and ebbing as if alive. Streaks of horrendous red lightning crackled through the clouds.

Cassie opened her eyes. "Holy shit!" She flailed her hands and stumbled backwards. I rushed to put a hand behind her back to keep her from falling. The Way snapped shut with a violent hiss. "What was that?"

"I don't know. You opened it."

"I didn't mean to. I just thought about Times Square."

"And what exactly did you think about it?" asked Quentin.

"Huh? I don't know." Cassie looked away. "Everything really. Times Square isn't a fun place for me. I've been chased through it. I remember pushing people aside, trying to get through and away from things. I remember sitting on the curb—cold—or against walls and hoping someone would give me cash. And then there's the trolls... They started this thing. So not a lot of fond memories." She rolled her shoulders but didn't turn her head towards us.

"I'm sorry. I know it can't be easy to go back. I know you're feeling apprehensive about it."

"That's a good word for it."

Quentin put a hand on Cassie's shoulder. "It's alright,

kiddo, don't push it. I can't pretend to know everything about how you do what you do, but the Ways are more than just places. They're feelings too. They are attached to emotions, ideas, even time. All of those things on a level that's beyond the understanding of many. If Times Square has bad memories for you, it's going to affect your Ways, and not in a good manner. Part of you wants to avoid it. If that's the case, then avoid it; otherwise, your subconscious will do it for you. It's possible that Way wouldn't have taken us to Times Square, and we've got enough trouble without adding being lost to the list." He patted her several times.

I sighed. This wasn't good. Without Cassie, we didn't have a way back. Something I felt the need to voice. "So how are we getting back?"

Quentin gave me an apologetic look. "Well, I know somebody who might be able to get us there."

"Why do I sense a but?"

"But...you're not exactly their biggest fan, nor they yours. I'll be back."

Cassie folded her lips together, the edges of her mouth pulling into a smile as she shook. "Mustn't say it." Whatever it was, she kept it to herself as Quentin moved towards the few remaining members of the Court.

There was a grunt from behind that pulled my attention. Cassie was the first to face the source. Her eyes narrowed. "You."

I took my time turning around, moving in a lazy half circle. Sometimes it paid not to turn around. I followed Cassie's lead, narrowing my eyes. "You," I mimicked.

Toshiro stared back neutral faced. "Yes." He tilted his head and looked past me to Cassie. "You are well, child?"

She bristled and ignored the question.

His gaze returned to me. "You are alive, tsk." His eyes fell to the floor, and he shook his head. The disappointment in his voice was the largest show of emotion he had displayed since we had run into to him.

"No, no, don't get broken up on my account, Toshiro. I know how hard my death would have hit you. I'm fine...really." I gave him a flat look.

"I would have been saddened by your death, Jonathan Hawthorne." He sounded like he meant it. "However, it would have been a just sentencing."

"Execution."

He ignored my correction. "You are a good man, but you made mistakes. I follow the path of neutrality, you know this. Regardless of your nature and the motives behind your actions, you committed offenses and must be punished for them. It is only right. I can mourn your death and believe it to be just. Life is not black and white."

"No, it's shades of gray to you folk, isn't it?"

Toshiro bowed his head in agreement. "Hai."

"And that's why I could never be one of your order. Life's more than that. It has its gray areas, and there are times when it's fairly cut and dry between black and white. There are moments, Toshiro, where it's not so easy to pull the trigger, or swing the sword in your case."

The Japanese warrior's eyes lost their focus for a brief moment. He looked at me like I was speaking gibberish.

I guess that's why he wore a gray cloak, and I didn't.

He didn't respond right away. It must have been hard for him to know I had bashed him over the head with a philosophy that made little sense to him. Toshiro may have believed in a harsh code, but to him, it was a fair one. Life wasn't about getting even, passion, or doing the right thing. To a member of the Order of the Gray, life was about taking *no* sides. It was about keeping balance, even if that meant doing terrible things, blurring lines and borders between right and wrong. It was a cold, hard code. One I could never live by.

"I think you may be right, Jonathan Hawthorne." It bothered me whenever he said my full name. "The world is not what it was. Sometimes I wonder if there will ever be true balance, true neutrality." I wanted to interrupt him and let him know that I honestly didn't care what he thought, but it sounded like he was trying to make a point—an important one. "Things are always in flux and slipping between the roles of good and evil, harmony and discord."

I didn't know what to say to that.

Fortunately, Cassie did. "Deep, bro, real deep. We've um...got stuff to do, so we'll let you sit here and percolate on the mysteries of life. I'm gonna go grab our old dude"—she made a quick hand motion to where Quentin was, in deep conversation—"and we're gonna skedaddle. Cool?"

Toshiro's head shook in the slightest of motions. It looked like he was fighting a stroke. He gave Cassie a quick look before turning to me. There was a silent plea for help on his face.

I shrugged. "I speak youngster about as well as you."

He frowned and turned his attention to Quentin. Toshiro arched a brow and gave me a level stare. "He survived." A simple statement, if only his tone suggested as much.

"Yes, surprised?"

Toshiro nodded. "You told me you saw him fall under a swarm of gremlins. Unlikely odds for any man, even him, or myself."

"What's your point?"

"You don't find it odd that Quentin Denholm survived—without a scratch?" Toshiro gestured with an upturn of his chin. Quentin did seem fine. Better than fine given what he had gone through. He was still in talks with a handful of Court members, laughing.

"So what? I'm glad he made it out fine. Most people would be. It's the expected emotion when your friend comes back from a trip to hell. You want them to be fine, and he is."

"Except, it is not normal. He should not have survived. He has. To do so without bearing any marks or injuries is strange." Toshiro had a point.

I tried not letting it show on my face, but doubt has other ways of getting to you.

It's a shadow that casts your sense of reason and logic into darkness. Thoughts become muddled, and eventually, doubt escalates to fear. I glanced at Quentin out of the corner of my eyes. A weak pulse filled my stomach, like it was nursing its own heartbeat.

I shook my head a bit harder than necessary. It helped free me from the train of thought I'd been nursing.

Paranoia comes free with doubt.

"You should go, Toshiro."

His face made it clear he had no intention of leaving.

I made myself clearer. "Now." I winced as my knee felt like someone had taken a club to it. I bent over, running a hand over the joint and giving it a squeeze. Cassie noticed the pained expression. Toshiro picked up on it too.

"Something wrong?"

I glared at him. "Basketball injury." Cassie let out a muffled laugh; I tried not to redirect my glare at her.

Toshiro knelt and brushed my hand away, replacing it with the both of his. His head was uncomfortably close to my gentleman's region. I coughed louder than necessary to get his attention. "What are you doing?"

He ignored my question. In one smooth movement he dropped his hands to my ankles, lifted my pants, drawing a startled yelp from me, and regarded my leg. He eyed me then returned his attention to my knee and the surrounding area. Toshiro pointed to my calf. "You're sick."

I jerked my leg back. "I was a really bad basketball player." The humor was lost on him.

"I have never seen anything like that."

"I told you to go, Toshiro. Take the free advice."

He inclined his head. "Very well, but do not push friends away, especially ones who can help. Take the free advice." His mouth did something funny, something an average person would call a smile. That didn't make sense. I was certain Toshiro was incapable of smiling...or having fun. He turned on his heel and made his way towards the exit.

"Alright, maybe he's not so bad for an uptight, 'I must kill everyone for the scales of balance' sort of guy." Cassie mimed a series of dramatic sword slashes with her empty hands.

"No, maybe not so bad." I watched Toshiro exit the

building, still surprised by the amount of concern and humor he had shown.

People are strange. That bit never changes.

Cassie made a dismissive wave towards something behind me. "Don't look now, but Quentin's bringing company."

I looked anyways. Sometimes adults should heed the advice of kids. Quentin approached with another member of the Court in tow. I would have been happier had he come back alone. "Quentin." I gave him a curt nod as I turned to face the Eldest Timeless. My lips twitched in anticipation of speaking, but I didn't know how to address the man before me. We had never really met one-on-one. How did you address the man who wanted you to be executed? Thankfully, he didn't leave it to me.

The Eldest held out a solid, calloused hand, with thick hairy knuckles. "Hawthorne." If there were any hard feelings between us, they weren't going to be found in his voice. He sounded like we had been having a polite conversation for a while now. "We've never been properly introduced." Up close, his voice sounded like he swallowed a tractor engine. It was a deep, rumbling thing. "Most call me Malcolm." There was a wisp of a smile on his face.

I knew a fake name when I heard it. It was too rehearsed. But it was common practice among the Timeless and paranormal.

His hand was still outstretched. I took it, and my jaw shut tight as he squeezed. All of the Timeless were mortal, as far I knew at any rate. Which is why the amount of strength he exerted was particularly impressive. I could feel my bones nearly slide against each other. There was no sign of effort on his face. He wasn't even trying. Malcolm let go an instant later. I tried to act like it was a simple handshake. "I'm sorry, Hawthorne. I forget modern day people aren't as strong as they used to be." His eyes shone when he said it.

"I'm fine," I grumbled. "Interesting choice of words."

He flashed me a smile that showed too many teeth. They looked like the sort you could find within early primates, larger than normal, sharper too.

I was right. "How old are you? It must be an impressive number for you to be the Eldest of the Timeless."

"Old enough." It was a good answer, and he made it clear he wasn't going to elaborate further. I took the hint and let the matter go. "Quentin told me you could use some help returning to Time Square."

"Yes; although to be honest, I don't see why he would go to you, or why you would help us." I could have worded it a bit more tactfully. "You didn't appear to be keen on aiding me during my trial—"

"I called for arbitration, did I not? It was a chance for you to save yourself. You're welcome."

"You'll forgive me if I believe that had more to do with Quentin than you."

Malcolm turned his hands palm up and brought them to his side in a gesture of resignation.

"So how do you plan on helping us?"

Malcolm directed his attention to Cassie. "By getting you to help yourselves."

Quentin had remained silent the whole time, something it looked like he was going to continue doing. I asked him a silent question with a tilt of my head and subtle arch of my brow. He didn't answer.

"Remember, Hawthorne and young Miss Winters: most people, Timeless included, struggle to open Ways."

"If you're trying to impress us with how difficult it is just before you miraculously manage to open one, spare us."

He exhaled in frustration. "I'm trying to explain that I can open three separate Ways at most." I admit, three wasn't much when compared to Cassie, but it was three more than I could manage. I was impressed. "But what I can do is help her get you back to Times Square."

I breathed out through my nose, squeezing my eyes shut for a moment. Something didn't sit right with me. "Why? What are you getting out of helping us?"

His eyes widened, and his face flashed through a series of quick expressions. "I trust the Arbiter's judgment; you don't live as long as I have without trusting the right people. This young woman," he broke off to make an offhanded motion towards Cassie, "is in possession of a remarkable gift. I trust the Arbiter, and you, about the danger her abilities pose in the wrong hands. Before you ask, yes, you had to be put on trial. You know our laws; you swore to abide by them. I recognize the severity of the situation, and I worked in tandem with Quentin to get you out. You are out. Gift horses, be grateful."

Something in his tone made me realize that I should express my gratitude. I swallowed and muttered a quick thanks.

Malcolm placed an oversized hand on Cassie's shoulder, causing her to flinch for a second. "It's okay, child. I'm offering you a comforting hand, and some advice, if you want to hear it, that is."

Cassie shot him a skeptical look before her features softened. "Alright, I'm listening."

"Quentin told me you're having trouble opening a Way back to Times Square."

"Something like that."

"Your problem isn't your magic. It's in here." He pressed a finger to one of Cassie's temples. "You're thinking of everything you hate and fear about Times Square. That is the wrong way to go about it."

"Well, I don't have oodles of good memories about the place."

"Then borrow someone else's."

Cassie blinked. "Huh?"

"Follow my lead, little one." Malcolm shut his eyes and inhaled. "Breathe and picture what I tell you. A carousel of electric colors, one for every person bustling through the busy streets of Times Square. A raucous symphony of laughter, shouting, car horns, and construction. The smell of numerous food carts, automotive fumes, and the cold, fresh chill of falling snow. Times Square is a metaphor for New York City, a five block brightly-lit hive of activity. Repeat it, over and over. Keep telling yourself those things. I want you to believe that *is* Times Square."

Cassie bit her lip and nodded.

"Now open your Way."

She did. I don't think there will ever come a time where I won't find Cassie's Ways beautiful. It had the appearance of a mirror in liquid form. A puddle of reflective glass, twice my height, and several times the width. Quentin and Malcolm let out appreciative whistles. All conversation within the chamber stopped. I could feel the eyes of every Timeless turn towards Cassie's Way.

Malcolm cupped a hand to his mouth, his voice still managed to come through. "Well—well, hearing about it is one thing—"

I clicked my tongue against the roof of my mouth. "But seeing is believing?"

"It most certainly is. It most certainly is. The Arbiter knew what he was doing."

Quentin put a hand on Malcolm's back and patted him twice. "It's why we pay him the big bucks, eh?"

Malcolm didn't respond.

"Oh before I forget, here, kid." Quentin reached into his robes. A series of jingling and clinks came from under the heavy cloth. He removed his hand, revealing a fistful of pennies in all conditions. Quentin didn't give me a chance to extend my hand before he dropped them.

I stumbled forward, bringing my palms together and fumbling to catch the coins. A few rogue pieces of copper bounced off the ground. I fell to my knees and snatched them up, contorting my face into a series of lip-curling snarls as I grumbled. One penny felt the need to be particularly difficult and rolled away. I smacked the coin palm first into the ground.

Maybe I was harboring a bit of tension and hostility. I rose to my feet and pocketed the pennies. Quentin and Cassie watched as I did, exchanging a quick glance.

Cassie tugged on a lock of hair and kept her eyes on my pocket. "You gonna tell us what those are for, or do we have to guess?"

"Better. I'll show you." I flashed her a grin.

Quentin shrugged out of his robes, revealing a similar attire to what he had on before, and turned to Cassie. "I hate it when he does that."

"You and me both."

I ignored them and stepped into what I hoped was a Way to Times Square.

Chapter Eighteen

For the record, Malcolm was right. Times Square was five blocks of frenzied activity. A rush of every color imaginable swarmed my eyes. I squinted in the face of sunlight. When we'd left New York, it was night.

Time flies in the Neravene.

My foot caught on something and nearly twisted. I stumbled and crashed into someone.

"What the hell, man?"

I shook my head and pawed blindly at the person in front of me, trying to right myself.

"You just...what the hell?"

I blinked until my vision cleared. The street was filled with people as you'd expect. It was broad daylight, and a glimmering Way hung in plain view. Not to mention the fact I had dropped out of it. A split second later, Quentin stepped out, looked around, and parted his mouth.

"Ah. Well, that was bound to happen when we all go gallivanting around like that. This is why I prefer to travel normally."

Then Cassie came through in a fashion only she could have pulled off. She threw her arms up in triumph. "Booyah bitches! Can't keep a good girl..." she trailed off when she noticed the crowd of people gawking at us. "Uh...down. Ta-da?" She bent at the waist, spread her arms out and rolled her hands in a flourish.

I shrugged and went with it, clapping my hands as hard as possible. "Isn't she amazing? Come on, folks." I motioned for the crowd to get involved. "Come on, come on!" I reached out for the first name I could think of that wouldn't jeopardize Cassie's identity. "Give it up for Alexis Summers, the new talent hitting the streets of New York with her scarcely believable teleportation act." I clapped harder.

There was a second where it was just me, then the air exploded in howls and cheers. I sighed in relief.

Quentin leaned in and whispered. "Alexis Summers?"

I shook my head. "Long story, don't ask."

Cassie nudged us both with elbows. "It still sounds like a stripper name. But, crap, when we settle all this, I really need to milk this Ways thing. I could kill it on stage."

"And if you attract that kind of attention, something could kill you." Quentin grabbed Cassie by the arm and led her through the crowd.

Thankfully, many of them were still enamored by the Way. I stuck close to the pair of them as we slipped out of the main grouping of people and turned a corner just as the Way shut.

We were halfway down the street when Cassie stopped. "Hey, I know this street. This is where I first bumped into you." She searched me with her eyes, looking for an answer.

I gave her one, sort of. "It is. We're looking for somebody. I just hope he's still here."

I pushed past her and kept my gaze fixed to the building walls on my left, watching for anyone slumped against them. I was rewarded with the sight of an elderly, disheveled man. He was buried beneath layers of tattered clothing and blankets. A face of dark leather covered in wiry steel hair. Even amidst the numerous New York street odors, I could smell the underlying sweetness of cotton candy.

The homeless man held out a hand, narrowing his eyes in the face of the sunlight. "Spare some change?"

"Sure." I held up a single copper coin. His eyes widened despite the glare of the sun. It was a good performance as far as acts go. "Penny for your thoughts?" I tossed him the coin.

He caught it in a smooth movement that should've been difficult for someone of his look to perform.

When it comes to the paranormal, looks are always deceiving.

"What are you looking to know?" The homeless man pulled his gaze from the coin, directing it at me before returning to the penny.

Quentin sniffed the air several times, blinking and shooting me strange looks until it registered. "Are you crazy, boy?" He pulled me away from the beggar and reached into his leather coat.

I put a hand on his arm, stopping him. "I'm not crazy. He gives good advice."

"Oh?" Quentin stared at me like I was insane. He had good reason to. And maybe I was a bit crazy.

"I do." The homeless man flipped the penny into the air, watching it tumble in amusement. He snatched it out of the air with the same skill and speed from earlier. "I told him to run a few days past. Could've kept him out of trouble. But it seems like your boy-o here has a problem running into it, rather than from it."

Quentin guffawed. "That he does."

I waved them both off. "Yes, yes, I'm trouble. I get it. My question." I cleared my throat. "What do you know about trolls moving around the city of late?"

He had a good poker face, I'll give him that much.

"What's that? Trolls?" He ignored me and looked to Quentin. "Your boy here do drugs?"

Quentin pursed his lips as if in deep thought. "Hm, it's possible. He's always been a problem child."

Cassie laughed. I followed suit with a mock one. "Ha...ha, very funny."

"But the kid's smart, always has been. Quick on the draw, and besides"—Quentin stopped to tap the tip of his nose with his index finger—"the nose knows. Those blankets and thick layers don't mask the smell as well as you think."

"Smell?" Cassie scrunched her face before taking a few whiffs. "I recognize that. Woah!" She took several steps back, looking at the homeless man in a panic. "He's a—" She glanced at Quentin and I. "What are we doing talking to one of them?"

"Alright, alright." The old man reached under his bundle and withdrew his bottle. He took a quick swig, let out a rather violent cough, and held his hands up, motioning for us to calm down. "Quit shouting." He braced against the wall and came to his feet. With a nod to the alley at our side, he said, "Follow me."

"The hell we will! Right, John?" Cassie's color paled when she looked at me. She didn't want anything more to do with alleyways or monsters. Understandably so.

"It'll be fine, Cassie, trust me." I gave her a thumbs up and a smile. She settled a bit.

"Famous last words," grumbled Quentin. I scowled at him as Cassie's posture tightened.

Sometimes old people cannot help being grumpy curmudgeons.

"We'll be fine." I put more weight and stone into my voice, glaring at Quentin as I did.

He rolled his eyes and hunched against the cold, slipping his hands into his pockets. We followed our guide into the alleyway. The sun did a good job of casting light into the otherwise bleak passage. It made things far less intimidating.

We fear the dark because it obscures, it hides things; it's the unknown. Man always fears the unknown. It's for that same reason we love the light. It reveals, casts the darkness and shadows away. It illuminates and brings into clarity what hides in the dark. It's the little things like that in life that help. When in doubt, or in fear, shine a little light. It makes things less scary, trust me, I've lived a long time.

The homeless man made it nearly to the end of the alley before he stopped. "Okay, you three mind spreading out, blocking people from looking in?"

I obliged and took a spot near the right wall. Quentin stood beside me.

"Oh great, yeah. Let's all line up for the big, ugly monster to eat us." Cassie sighed but did as we did and took up a spot near the other wall.

The old man eyed each one of us individually. "Now,

don't freak out and start caterwauling. Last thing we need is more attention."

Cassie huffed and shook her head like she couldn't believe she was doing this. "Right, wouldn't want any witnesses. Why do I listen to you two? You're a bad influence."

Quentin let out a laugh that was more a succession of light puffs of air leaving his nose. I resisted, working to be the mature one.

The homeless man tugged beneath the collar of his heavy coat, pulling out a woolen train of Autumn colors. It was a well-made scarf, and equally well-worn. Thick and warm. He took care in handling it as he undid it and set it atop a nearby bin. There was no further ceremony, nor any point in removing the rest of his clothes. The scarf was likely the only real piece of attire anyhow.

"Remember"—he sounded like his throat was churning cement—"stay calm."

It wasn't a subtle shift in appearance. The air rippled and the man's skin took on a mottled purple hue. His frail appearance looked to have tripled in mass. Thick, sculpted bare arms came into view. His ears tapered off to points at the end, but he was not elven kind. There was a high rising, thin blade of hair cutting into the air above his head. A puce Mohawk. Two pieces of sullied ivory, thick as my thumbs, jutted from his jaw, lifting his lips as they curved upwards. Silver glinted from his nose, ears, and above his brow.

Trolls come in many shapes, colors and sizes. They're a well varied species. I'm an open-minded and progressive man. Diversity isn't great when it comes to monsters. It simply means there are more kinds of them that can kill you.

He didn't dwarf me like the trolls from earlier, though that didn't mean much. The monster was a hair's breadth shy of seven feet. But he appeared better put together than the first batch of trolls. Different as well. He wore an open leather vest, the sort bikers did. The rest of his outfit continued the leather motif.

I watched Cassie without turning my head. Her chest

rose rapidly, as I'm sure her breathing did.

"No, it's cool. I'm calm. Yup. We're standing 'bout ten feet from a tusked troll who's a member of a biker gang. Why should I freak out?"

The troll laughed. It sounded more like an awkward fit of deep coughs, but it was a laugh nonetheless. Laughter is a universal language. Some laughter just needs to run through a spot of translation is all. But it served its purpose. Cassie's breathing slowed, and her posture lost some of its tightness.

"Alright, now we've gotten that out of the way, what can I do?" He ran a hand through his hair, and scratched under his chin. He was nervous. Hard to believe. He was the biggest and strongest thing within a mile at the very least.

I raised my left hand and held it out, fingers splayed in a calming gesture. "I'm reaching into my coat for something."

The troll nodded and took no threatening action. It was a relief, believe me.

My fingers brushed against discs of cool metal. I pinched one and removed it from my coat. I held it up for him to see, then flicked it towards him. The troll caught it, like before.

"Many thanks."

"So what's with the whole penny thing? I mean if we're trying to bribe info out of monsters"—Cassie broke off to shrug—"no offense, dude. Shouldn't we be, you know, paying better?"

"If you were bribing a man, yes. But since I'm not"—the troll held up the penny and smiled—"these do just nicely."

"It's tradition, Cassie. The supernatural revolve around it. For trolls, it's long since been a thing for them to demand payment for passage," I said.

"Paying tolls to get by." She nodded in understanding. "Gotchya."

"It used to be a copper. Times change, and one's best bet is to pay up with pennies." I stuffed a hand back in my coat and rummaged around, making a noticeable jingling noise. The troll's ears twitched, and his eyes lit up. He understood there was more where that came from.

"Poor for a man, rich for a troll." The creature spread its mouth into a wide smile as he tumbled the coin through his fingers. "So it's information you're after, is it?"

"It is," I said. "By the way, you speak rather good English for a troll."

"Thank you. Spend enough time with them, listening, taking their money—it's pretty easy to pick up the language. Flattery won't get you anything extra though." He waved the penny between two fingers. "This is what will get me to talk. I'm practical."

"Fair enough. Some days ago you told me to run from a pair in parkas. You and I both know they were trolls."

He nodded.

"Do you know why they're here? What they're after and the why?"

The troll shook his head, his Mohawk wobbling as he did. "Not all of it. They're chasing something, or someone from what I've heard. Don't know the specifics. Not my tribe, not my problem."

He had a good point. Trolls were notoriously competitive within their own circles, and doubly so with other tribes. They didn't care much for the finer details or problems other tribes faced. Not unless they could use it to conquer those tribes. Trolls were also bad liars. It took too much effort and skill. They preferred blunt—honest talk.

"Sorry, human. Anything else?"

I shook my head. "They were independent, no markings belonging to any of the courts."

"So?" The troll lifted an arm and flexed a bicep. It was an impressive one.

I didn't show any reaction.

Big arms weren't the most impressive thing. But I looked anyways. A marking of black ink stood out on the muscle. It was a filled in circle, lines springing out from its center like rays from the sun. A rather primitive-looking symbol.

I arched an eyebrow. "Really? Why them?"

He shrugged and tilted his head. "Personal choice, found them to be the better court for my needs and desires. Besides, my whole tribe is sworn to them."

"Oh, well, if everyone's doing it. I mean, when all the cool kids jump off a bridge or smoke crack, you gonna join 'em?" Cassie waved an admonishing finger, and the troll laughed again.

"Our lives are more complicated than that. But now isn't the time to talk about it. What else can I do for you? This coin's value is running out—quick." He gave the penny a little rub.

"That's fine." I sifted my hand through my pocket. "I have loads."

"Good to know. It doesn't do me much good in your pocket though, does it?"

"No, it doesn't, which is why I'm ready to part with it for a large service."

The troll turned his head partially away from me and eyed me obliquely. "What kind of service?" He kept the penny dancing between his fingers.

"I need you to get us into the Fair Lands. I want to meet the Faerie Queens—all of them."

The penny dropped.

Chapter Nineteen

There was no horrible clang, though I wished there had been. The troll's mouth moved soundlessly. He looked over his shoulder as if something was about to burst through the brick wall and kidnap him. Maybe he was praying for it. He licked his lips, stopping when his tongue brushed against one of his tusks.

"You want me to what?"

I smiled. "You heard me. I want you to take the three of us into Faerie."

"The *two* of you." Quentin took a step back. "If you go through with this plan, I'm not tagging along. I can't."

"You should listen to the old man." The troll cast another wary glance over his shoulder. "He's got the right idea. I can't take mortals into Faerie."

I snorted. "Really? Because it seems like that's one of the things faeries love doing. Luring hapless mortals into their domains, tricking them into their possession. Every Fae loves having playthings, servants, and mortals to twist around."

The troll looked at the ground but said nothing.

I had a point, and he knew it. I turned my attention towards Quentin. "And why won't you come along? Or why can't you?"

"Faeries have long memories and love revenge. Let's leave it at that, kid." Quentin gave me a look that told me to drop the subject.

"Your friend's not wrong. You shouldn't do this. And it isn't worth this." The troll dragged his massive boot across the ground, kicking up snow and sending the penny into the air.

I pulled my hand from my pocket. A fistful of copper

caught the troll's attention.

Whatever the value, money always talks. It's no different for the paranormal. You simply need to offer the right price, and be able to pay it. Thank God trolls are cheap.

He didn't take his eyes off the coins but he was still on guard. "What says I need it? I collect plenty of coins sitting on the street. Lots of it is worthless, but I pull enough copper. I'm rich enough."

And typically, trolls are stupid.

It must have been my bad luck to run into the one smart one. I moved my hand back towards my coat, taking my time and making a show of doing it. "You could be a bit richer. Every coin counts. Besides, there's good money on these streets. I know it; I've walked them. I bet you're pulling more bills and larger coins than what you really want. This...is a good hunk of change." I raised and lowered my hand, making sure he caught a good glimpse of the coins.

It was worth noting that most pennies today were made from zinc and only copper plated. That was enough.

Sometimes it's the idea of something more than what it truly is that matters to the supernatural.

The troll folded his lips as much as his tusks would let him and licked them. "All of them." He sounded hungry.

And trolls were greedy. Something for which I gave silent thanks.

"Of course, here." I held out my hand.

He crept forward, watching me carefully. Cassie bristled and went rigid as he approached. I didn't blame her. The troll lunged. I shut my eyes to keep me from overreacting. A giant troll rushing me was not a welcome image. I'd been charged by enough of them, but you couldn't blame all trolls by the actions of a few. Then again, all the trolls I'd ever met went out of their way to harm me. I could feel the coins leave my grasp as the troll's fingers brushed against my palm. My insides felt like cold snakes were writhing through them. I suppressed the shiver.

At the end of the day, trolls were predators. I couldn't show any fear. I opened my eyes and found him back in his spot at the end of the alley.

"So, you'll take us?"

He nodded.

"Right then, this is where I bow out, kid." Quentin stuffed a hand into his coat and removed a mass of hairy, decrepit-looking fingers. "Here." He tossed it towards me.

My first instinct was to let whatever it was fall to the ground. I caught it, the small hairs tickling my palms. It took me some seconds to realize the gnarled digits were a part of a vine. "What is this?"

He crossed the distance between us, put a hand on my shoulder and whispered. I took it all in and repeated it to myself several times to ensure I memorized it.

"Got it, kid?"

I nodded.

"Remember, crush it, and throw. Simple. Just...don't throw it at one of the queens, please."

I nodded again. "I get it. Dangerous. Be careful."

He clapped me harder on the shoulder. "Good lad." Quentin touched his first two fingers to his forehead in a quick salute. He bowed and strolled out of the alley.

I stowed Quentin's gift in the removable inner lining of my jacket, lifting it enough to place the vine within. The troll watched as I did but said nothing.

"Ready?" He looked at the pair of us.

"Yes. Cassie, you?"

She intertwined her fingers and stretched her arms above her head, cracks ringing out as she did. "Sure, this is the best lead we've got to figure things out, right?"

"I hope so." I didn't know what else to tell her. I believed it was.

Sometimes belief can get you through a lot of trouble and hard times. And sometimes it's just too hard a basket to put everything into. For me at any rate. Faith is hard. Then again, the greatest and best things in life often are.

So, for Cassie's sake, I changed my tune. "Yes," I amended. "I believe so."

She inhaled and nodded. "Then, yeah, I'm good. Let's

roll, troll."

I sighed.

The troll stared at Cassie and then me in confusion.

"She has that effect on everyone. It's been like this since I met her."

The troll pursed his lips and scratched his cheek with a finger. "I'm sorry." He turned and placed his hands against one of the brick walls. He brought his hands closer until the tips of his fingers touched. In one smooth movement, he separated them, sliding his hands across the rough surface.

I winced. That must have hurt.

Thin lines of sapphire arced over the bricks. Troll blood.

He looked over his shoulder. "A troll grants passage when tolls are paid. Remember that."

"I will," I said.

He grunted and spread his hands further. More flesh scraped and something flared to life within the blood. Light blossomed within the fluid, and a Way opened in the brick wall. Compared to the other Ways I had seen of late, it looked rather dull. A wide, unassuming mass of light the color of wet Earth. It was crude, but if it did the job, I wasn't going to complain.

"In you go." The troll jerked a thumb to the Way. I took a step towards it when he held out a hand. "Wait!" He pulled away from the wall and knelt to the ground, closing his fingers around something. He rose to his feet and held out a penny.

I didn't reach for it. "I figured you'd want to keep every coin?"

"You figured wrong. Think of it as good luck. Even a penny can go a long way, especially in the lands of the fae. I give good advice, remember?"

"You do." I took the penny and passed it to Cassie. I could see the silent question on her face. "Priorities. We're going there for you. Any luck we can save up, I'd like to keep it for you." Cassie said nothing, but she shook her head, leaving me to pocket it. "Alright, let's go." I took

Cassie's hand and stepped into the way.

***

I touched down on flat grass that had grown wild. The fae did not believe in lawn keeping, and given the look of the place, they shouldn't have. Beautiful failed to describe it.

Picture a prairie of rich greens and wildflowers, only with colors defined by a master painter. Everything was more vivid, brighter—detailed. There were shades of colors you couldn't hope to find in the mortal world. In the distance, small hills that looked like they had been pulled from the pages of Tolkien. It might have been the other way around, but it didn't matter. Sunlight rolled over the place without being blinding, a gentle glow. Looking up, I had the feeling that the sun never set in this place.

"Wow," Cassie breathed. "This is my kind of place."

"Welcome to the outermost lands of the Morning Court." The troll waved an arm to accentuate everything before us. "You're in the domain of the Dawn Lady. Tread carefully and with respect. If you can do those, you will be fine."

"It's a good thing we brought a guide," I said, not taking my eyes off the scenery.

"No...you didn't."

"What was that?" I hadn't finished turning when the troll spoke next.

"I promised to bring you here. I said nothing about bringing you back." There was a sound like a stubborn jar lid being removed. The troll was gone, and his Way went with him.

"Wow..." Cassie's voice dripped with sarcasm. "The troll ditched us. Didn't see that one coming." She looked at me and I could feel the judgment. "Did you?"

I shrugged. "He got us here. You'll have to get us out."

"Right, because it's that easy."

"We will figure it out, Cassie. We've been doing it so far. Until then, we walk." I put a hand to my brow in an effort to focus my view. Looking at the hills ahead, I decided to correct my statement. "We walk a lot."

Cassie gave me a resigned look and accepted it without further complaint. As we walked, I made a mental note that the next time I asked a troll to deposit me in the Fair Lands, it would be closer to where I wanted to be.

Silver linings came in many shapes, and in our case, temperatures. It wasn't hot despite the sunlight. It was like a spring morning that hadn't let go of winter. Cool, but not cold. It was refreshing. The long blades of grass brushed against the exposed bits of our skin, namely our hands, and pressed globules of dew to them. It felt nice.

It's a shame that all good things have to come to an end.

An arctic jolt of electricity coursed through my calf, ringing my knee. It settled in my thigh. I hobbled, arms flailing for support and balance. The grass didn't offer either of those. It didn't stop instinct from taking hold however. I grabbed at the lengthy blades. They didn't help, but they cushioned the fall. I lay there, fistfuls of grass in my hand and an equal share in my mouth, blinking through the convulsions racking my leg.

"John!" Stalks of grass bent as Cassie brushed them aside. She kneeled at my side, her hands an inch from my body, unsure of whether to touch me. "You alright? What happened?"

Grass has a taste of its own. Nothing else comes close, except other grasses. In my experience, they are all equally unappealing.

"Auckh." I coughed and spat out the twisted lump of vegetation lodged in my mouth. "I fell."

"Yeah, I saw that. Timber and everything. Are you good though?"

I shut my eyes and drew a long breath. I needed it. The spasms subsided, but my leg felt like a tourniquet was cinched around it. "I'll be fine. It's my leg." I gestured towards it with a nod.

"It's getting worse." It wasn't a question.

I tensed the muscles in the limb, letting go after several seconds. A coolness, almost like a swipe with an alcohol swab, filled the area. The pain left, but my leg felt a tad distant. "I'm not sure, to be honest. But that seems the safest bet."

"That's why we're here though, right? Answers for me and a fix for whatever is giving you Gumby leg."

"Yes." I got myself to my knees, but pushing up from there was difficult. "I'm going to need something to get us there, Cassie."

She remained silent, asking the question with her eyes.

"A hand." I reached out towards her, meeting empty space for a second. Soft, strong fingers met mine, and Cassie hauled.

It doesn't matter how long you've lived, what you've seen and endured. Sometimes we can all use a hand. It's a simple gesture with a lot of weight behind it.

I made it to my feet, and Cassie slipped an arm under my shoulder to keep me upright as I teetered. My infected leg quaked for a minute before settling.

"We're not going to get very far if your leg keeps getting worse."

"We'll get as far as we can as fast as we can." I gritted my teeth and clenched my jaw until it became a new source of pain.

"And how far will that be? Don't know if you noticed, but this is a pretty big place. Heck, I can't see an end to it."

"As far as we need it to be. We have to. Neither of us really has a choice."

"Well, when you put it that way, let's hurry up before we're mobbed by Hobbits or something."

I snorted and leaned on Cassie. She helped usher me forward. Most of the feeling returned to my leg. It wouldn't be much longer until I could walk properly again.

Cassie used her free hand to brush aside the grass. "Ugh, this stuff's going to slow us down. Hold on and don't topple over again, oldie." My support was gone and I bent at the waist, squeezing the muscles along my back to keep me from falling. I pulled myself up, put more pressure on my infected leg, and let out a sigh of relief. It was short-lived. Cassie drew her sword.

"No!"

My warning came too late. Her steel blade cut through the stalks, parting them just above waist height with ease.

I wished that was all it did.

There is a reason mortals should not tote steel in the Fair Lands. Steel is poison to more than just the fae. Imagine being able to spark a wildfire with a flick of metal.

And fire always spreads.

The stalks slashed by Cassie's sword were the first to change color. Losing their brilliant green, they blanched to a shade of gray that belonged in an old movie devoid of color. There was a *snap-hiss* as the severed blades of grass lost all flexibility. They hung suspended for a moment, reminding me of slivers of glass, before shattering violently.

I had only a split second to watch in equal parts awe and terror as the finger length slivers of glass hurtled everywhere. "Down!"

Cassie followed the instruction without hesitation, collapsing flat against the ground. I wasn't so lucky. It felt like someone dragged a hot surgical blade across my cheek. I hit the earth and heard the whistling of blades zipping over us. It didn't stop.

I gawked, unable to process it. Every bit of grass past the chunk Cassie had slashed changed. Blade after blade lost color and form. I didn't risk rising to my feet but imagined everything ahead as a field of pure glass. There was a horrible cry, and I shut my eyes, not wanting to see the glassy knives hurtle towards us. We must have been lucky.

Flecks of glass shot into the air, collapsing like they could no longer hold themselves together on a microscopic level. Shimmering particulates rained down around us, each glinting and reflecting the sun. It was almost beautiful, if it weren't for the barren plains of gray before us.

Cassie got to her feet and swallowed. "Um...did I do that?"

"Yes."

"I'm sorry, John, I didn't..." She turned away, unwilling to meet my eyes.

The truth was, I wasn't mad. It was a mistake. They happen. Some could cost you your lives, but at the end of the day, Cassie did it to help me. "It's okay."

"It is? Do you think anyone heard that?"

I laughed. "Yes, Cassie, on both accounts. But the good news is, I don't think we will have to go far to find any of the fae."

"Yeah?"

"They'll find us. And they won't be happy." I looked over my shoulder and found that the effect hadn't spread behind us. That was something to be grateful for at least. We could've destroyed an entire field. Some jobs were better left undone.

"Come on, we should move. We don't want the fae to catch us in the middle of this."

"Think we should drop our weapons? They can't be happy about people bringing steel into their digs."

"No to both. What's done is done, and besides, you've dealt with some fae already. Would you care to repeat those experiences without a weapon?"

Cassie gave me a heated glare.

"And for the record, the fae are rarely happy about people coming into their domains regardless. The only exemption being when they kidnap them."

"Noted." Cassie held out her arm for me to take.

I shook my head. "No, I'm fine. Go on, but stay close."

"Got it." She sheathed her sword and took the lead.

I didn't want to admit it out loud, but it was easier moving without the grass. Telling Cassie that could possibly encourage more reckless behavior. Between the two of us and our poor impulse control, I didn't think that would be a good thing.

We crossed the first hill when the operatic call of thunder shook the air and ground. Cassie and I turned our heads upwards in unison. The sun wasn't dimmed in the slightest, nor was there a cloud in sight. The thunder sounded again—and it didn't stop. It picked up, becoming the frenzied beat of drums. The ground shook in concert with the increasing booms. It took me a second to realize they were footsteps—lots of them.

Cassie gave me a wide-eyed look. "This is one of those, 'Run,' moments, isn't it?"

"Yes, I'd say so."

She eyed my leg. "You up to it?"

"I'll have to be." I took a deep breath and braced myself.

Cassie didn't wait, taking off at a sprint. "Fly, you fool!"

I groaned and took off after her. "Cassie, chases are marathons, not sprints."

"Speak for yourself!"

"I'm speaking for both of us."

If only I knew what was doing the chasing, I wouldn't have wasted the energy running. The sounds grew closer—louder—and distinctly clearer. It wasn't a singular boom being repeated. It was hundreds of them. Hooves. Mounted creatures, or worse, the creatures themselves. The Neravene was always full of surprises.

"Okay, that really doesn't sound good!"

"When did anything in here ever sound good?" My leg held up fine all things considered. There were moments where it shivered and felt like it was lagging behind the other. At least it didn't fail me completely.

The hoof beats were past just being heard. I felt each individual one as a tremor that shook its way into the small bones of my feet and up into my gut. My belly quaked and I forced myself to look behind.

Many creatures rode horses. They were wonderful mounts when well trained. There were few that didn't need a steed. The ones chasing us *were* the steeds. How fortunate...

They overtook us in the span between my last and next breath. It was an impressive display of speed. A countless number of men and women came into view. Their bodies were smooth and carried the flat, hard muscles of Olympic runners. Their skin was the color of dull talcum powder and just as smooth. The sunlight did interesting things to their bodies, making shimmering specks appear like on the surface of a pond under bright light. What little resemblance they had to humans ended at the waist.

Cassie stopped abruptly and tumbled into a ball, coming back to her feet awkwardly. "Holy My-Not-So-Little Pony!"

"Centaurs," I corrected as several dozen encircled us.

Their waist-length hair matched the colors of their equine bodies, bobbing and dancing wildly as the circle grew tighter. Each wielded a shaft of dark, polished wood that ended in a sharpened spade of some odd-looking metal. Like silver too bright and carrying a glow that seemed unnatural. I was lucky enough to get a closer look as one centaur leveled their spear at me.

It huffed out an angry snort and placed the tip of the spear at eye level with me. With a shake of its head, it threw back its dark hair, revealing a pair of small, tapered ears. "Name yourself! By what right are you here? You are trespassing on the domain of Morning Court!" The centaur shifted and I wished I had missed the action, but I recategorized *'it'* as a 'he'. He narrowed his bottle-green colored eyes.

It's difficult to give an answer when a weapon's an inch from your eye. Far worse when you're surrounded by dozens of jumpy equine fae.

I did my best. "You'll excuse me for not relinquishing my name to a group—a rather large group at that—of fae." I fought the impulse to move. I wasn't fond of the idea of being skewered or trampled.

The centaur snorted a loud burst of air like from a power tool. My nose twitched just from hearing it. He pulled the spear back and gave it a twist. The slender rod whipped around. Its butt struck. There was a sound I could barely make out, like something hard striking flesh. It felt like it too. A band of white obscured my vision. Lengths of nauseating ropes twined within my gut. I doubled over, clutching my stomach and breathing hard.

"Answers."

I looked up without lifting my head. The centaur's spear was trained on Cassie. She was smarter than I was.

"Alexis Summers. Here because the class trip to Washington D.C. was canceled. Blows cause my permission slip was signed and everything!" She was braver than me as well, crossing her arms and pouting in mock disappointment.

The centaurs bristled, giving each other quizzical looks. I was glad Cassie had that effect on more than just people.

I righted myself, slowly, so not to give myself vertigo, and gave the centaurs what they wanted. Almost. "My name is my own, to keep and to speak. End. But we're here on an urgent matter. We wish to address your queen."

That got their attention. The spear faltered in the centaur's grip, dangling between a few loose fingers. Their faces lost all expression, becoming blank masks. As far as requests go, I couldn't have asked for a larger one.

A female centaur shook her head. Her hair fell away from her chest. Centaurs didn't believe in undergarments. How freeing. A sinister smile tugged at the edge of her mouth. "What makes you think you will have the chance to meet our queen? What makes you think you'll leave this field alive?"

Only the corner of Cassie's mouth moved. "Yeah, what makes you think we'll leave here alive? I'd like to know that too." She flashed the creatures a quick, false grin.

I gave them a grin of my own and tapped a finger to the tip of my nose. "Curiosity."

The female centaur quirked a brow in amusement, turning her head to regard the rest of the herd. "Oh? Do tell."

I matched her expression. "How often do humans wander into your domain?"

She pursed her lips, looking to the sky before addressing me. "Not often. When they do, they make poor sport. Humans don't run very fast." Her mouth spread into a chilling smile.

I ignored the discomfort it gave me. "No, we don't. But we're a surprising bunch. You have to give us that much. And that's what we've brought. Surprises, and questions.

Would you like to hear them?"

There was a chorus of laughter followed by enthusiastic nods. The centaur—centauress? The female one—brushed her mane back and stared at me in amusement. "Oh yes, we would."

"Excellent. Take us before your queen, and you can hear them as I ask her."

Several centaurs guffawed at my bravado. The one who had hit me earlier bucked before settling down. He gave me a level stare. "Very well." He made a sharp turning gesture with his head. The group of centaurs tightened around us. "Take them."

I sank a bit, holding my hands up to calm them. "We can walk. We'd prefer it in fact."

"It's a long walk mortal, quite long."

I grimaced.

The centaur nodded towards his back. "Get on."

"What?"

His eyes went flat. "Get. On."

I stared him down. "Give me one good reason to trust you."

"Because, mortal, we can kill you and save the bother of taking you to our queen. Because, without us, you will be walking for a very long time—in *our* domain—alone. Walking through hills that harbor more than just my kind. And not all fae you encounter will be as nice as us." He may have been part horse, but the smile he flashed belonged to a large cat. "The first option holds a great deal of appeal to me. I could run you through with my spear; you'd run, but not fast enough. We could trample the pair of you. That has always been a personal favorite of ours." He looked around the nearby crowd and nudged some of them with his elbows. There was a low murmur of approval. "Or you could come with us to see our queen, as *you* wished, in the manner *we* say."

"Well then"—I shrugged—"if you insist."

The centaur motioned with its head again. I went towards its flank and paused. Centaurs didn't come with stirrups. "How do I get on?"

The horseman sunk to its knees. It was a simple action, yet I couldn't help but feel the contempt in his body language. Not that I was an expert in centaur body signals. I eased one leg over its body, hesitating to lower myself fully. I looked over my shoulder to see Cassie seated and pressing herself against the back of the lady centaur. There wasn't much choice. I followed suit and sat down.

"Woah!" I clung fast to the back of his arms as he rose in a single motion. "Calm down, Silver."

He ignored the rather brilliant reference. "Hold on tight to my arms."

"I bet you say that to all the men who ride you."

The centaur let out an irritated puff of air and shook his head much like a horse would do. I made no comment on how odd it was considering he had the torso of a man. But I followed his advice.

He turned his head a fraction to the side, just enough to glance at me out of the corner of his eyes. "Ready, mortal?"

I nodded. I'd admit the prospect of riding among a group of centaurs to meet the Dawn Lady was terrifying. So I watched Cassie, who seemed rather calm despite everything, and asked myself what she would do? I found myself grinning rather foolishly. "Hi-yo, Silver. Away," I whispered.

The world rushed backwards. The centaur's lengthy mane followed, blinding me as it flew into my face as well as around me. Cassie let out an undefined scream, something caught between sudden terror and surprised delight. I shut my eyes and held on. My thighs ached and burned within a minute. I squeezed tight to the creature's body with everything I had to keep myself from sailing off. The next minute had me wishing for a saddle. My gentleman's region wasn't built for bareback riding. The centaurs didn't take this into consideration. I filed it away as a complaint for the queen.

"This...is...awesome!" shouted Cassie.

"Quiet," snapped a voice I pegged as the female

centaur.

I remained silent.

"Do you know"—my mount stopped speaking and spent a handful of seconds breathing hard—"why we insisted you ride atop us?"

I shook my head, then realized how stupid the action was. "Why?"

"Have you seen what happens to a rider thrown from a galloping horse?"

I swallowed.

"Have you seen what happens when they are thrown into a stampede?"

The fist-sized gulp of air felt like it doubled in mass as it remained lodged in my throat. I forced it down, feeling it in my chest before it subsided and buried itself in my stomach. "Empty threats." I managed to fill my voice with enough gravel to sound unfazed by its questions. "You're fae. You want to see what happens next. You want us to reach your queen."

"Oh, aye. But one last thing for you to think on, mortal."

"And that is?"

"What makes you think the Dawn Lady will give you the answers you seek, or let you leave? Better yet, what makes you think she will let you live?"

He had good questions.

I wished I had the answers.

Chapter Twenty

We rode in silence for half an hour, or so I imagined. The scenery changed too often for me to keep an accurate count, or as accurate as a person could make in a place that had little regard for time. We passed over plains and fields, through lush forests teeming with life and magic, places that could have been plucked from stories and imagination. Babbling brooks and creeks went by. Refreshing droplets arced into the air and showered us as the centaurs plowed through. In the entire time, I hadn't come up with an answer for the questions my ride posed earlier.

So I asked my own.

"Why haven't you said anything?"

The centaur grunted.

"I don't suppose I can ask your name?"

He grunted again. It was a dark and dismissive thing.

"Of course not." I scowled and looked back to Cassie, who was holding onto her centaur's shoulders, leaning back and enjoying the ride. By now, my entire nether region was too sore for me to feel the slightest hint of enjoyment. I was sure my scowl was going to remain long after we dismounted.

"About what?"

I blinked at the centaurs sudden interest in actual words. "What?"

"Why haven't I said anything about what?"

Ah. "About where you found us."

"The hills, or what remained, you mean."

I exhaled. This could go wrong, and quickly. "Yes."

The centaur said nothing. He didn't need to. My mind raced. I imagined the gears turning within the creature's brain. It took me seconds to figure out what it was thinking.

In that time, we crossed another impressive amount of distance.

Horses run fast. Centaurs redefine the word. A little magic goes a long way.

"You said nothing because you were going to lay it before your queen."

"Yes."

"You think that if you tell her we brought and used steel in The Fair Lands, she'll cast judgment and punishment against us."

"Yes."

"And is that want you want?"

There was a beat where nothing happened but the world passing us by.

"Yes."

I didn't need to ask why. We destroyed a part of their home, inadvertently yes, but faeries care little for intent. At least as far as the intents of mortals are concerned.

"And don't think you will get the chance to use your weapons. Keep them sheathed, or you'll find out just what each one of your bones sounds like as they're trampled on. It doesn't sound good, and it feels worse."

I believed him.

"And what do you think she'll do?"

The centaur faltered, just a bit, but it was noticeable.

"What?"

"You want your queen to kill us, or at the very least, give you permission to do it. But what do you *really* think she will do? Don't you think she'll be just as curious as you as to why mortals would seek an audience? If there's one thing Faerie Queens love, it's mortals. Mortals to manipulate, mortals to take, mortals to bind." I could almost hear the doubt running through his mind. "She'll be most curious as to what one of the Timeless is doing in her realm too."

I should have kept my mouth shut.

Hindsight is twenty-twenty.

The centaur slowed too quickly for me to adjust. The

muscles in my legs cracked, and I bobbed up. I landed a split second later. My eyes were plastered shut as tight as possible. I focused solely on breathing. I also developed a dislike for equine creatures.

The centaur resumed its pace, once again taking the lead among the herd. The bouncing resumed as well. My dislike for horses grew.

"One of the Timeless."

"Yes." My voice was a pitch higher than normal. I refrained from speaking and adopted my earlier scowl.

"Well, this certainly is interesting. I don't suppose you could tell me what you're doing here?"

I breathed out through my nose three times and exhaled once through my mouth for good measure. "We're looking for your queen." He couldn't see my smile, but I'm sure he could feel it. I certainly felt him bristle. "How much longer?" I didn't risk taking a hand off him to shield my eyes as I squinted towards the Sun. It hadn't moved since we arrived...

"We're here."

"What?" I blinked the spots away from my eyes and looked ahead. The centaur stopped. I didn't make the same mistake as before. The bob caused me to wince, but fortunately, that was all it caused. I couldn't see the rest of the herd. Just our two centaurs.

The sun was gone, replaced by a skyline of trees all around us. I hadn't noticed the transition; it was that fast and smooth. Light fell in varying shades of bronze and gold, illuminating all within the thick grove.

Cassie breathed out in awe. "Wow, this...is something."

"Yes. Yes, it is."

Every tree had a brush of fine auburn hairs growing around its base that twitched and bowed under the gentle sway of wind. The trees were a mix of nameless browns and greens. Roots, vines, branches shivered and swayed like they were conscious of our presence. I took another look around and decided they were.

Orbs of light no larger than an infant's fist pulsed in

dizzying beats that made night clubs seem calming. They were disorientating, and, if you stared too long, hypnotic. I squeezed my eyes until they ached. A thin stream of fluid lined my lids. I brushed it away and turned to Cassie. Her gaze was locked on an area where a grouping of primary colors throbbed and flashed.

"Cassie." No response. "Cassie!" Her head turned too slowly for me to be comfortable with. I gave her shake. It did nothing. "Cassie!" I shoved her and kicked a clump of dirt onto her prized sneakers. She looked at me, or rather through me, before blinking. "Eyes on me, kid." That did it.

She blinked several times, working through a series of facial expressions before scowling. "Thought I told you to stop calling me that, Gramps."

I smiled. "And I thought I told you to be careful."

She pursed her lips then nodded. "Touché." She pointed her index finger without looking at the area she had been transfixed by. "So what are those things?"

"Wisps." There was something in the centaur's voice that sounded off.

"Fool's fire, or ghost lights," I said. "They're small creatures that lure people closer and then recede. They're infamous for getting travelers, fae and mortal alike, lost and killed."

The centaur was silent.

I faced him. "You knew." I wasn't asking.

He remained silent.

"What would have happened if we kept staring?" Cassie's head turned a fraction of an inch back towards the light. I saw them too. I understood their allure.

"If you stare long enough, one of two things can happen." Her attention turned back to me. Good. "First, you fall into a trance deep enough that it's like a waking coma. You'll stare forever—entranced. You won't eat, you won't sleep. Then you'll die. It just depends on what kills you first. It's never hunger. Dehydration or the lack of sleep causes you to hemorrhage."

Cassie shivered before composing herself. "Gee, how

pleasant. Do I want to know the other option? Let me guess, it ends in death too?"

"They lure you into whatever environment they call home—bogs, swamps, and forests. Then...something large and nasty kills you." Keeping busy was the safest course of action to keep our eyes from wandering back to the lights. I dismounted.

The action prompted Cassie to follow suit and keep her attention on everything but the Wisps.

"Do they like to eat the remains or something?"

"No."

"Then why do they do it?"

It was a good question. Sadly, my answer wasn't reassuring. "It's their nature. When it comes to the fae, some things are too ingrained." I eyed the centaur. "Like being an ass." The centaur's eyes went flat. "In many ways, the fae are closer than anything else to nature. They do things because of that, because that's what they are; that's their nature. The Wisps get nothing out of it." I shrugged. "You might as well ask why the wind blows. It just does."

"Believe it or not, that's creepier than if they killed for kicks and giggles. Killing just because... That's frightening."

"I believe it."

Both our mounts watched and listened to our exchange in curious silence. I guessed they didn't understand the little complexities of humans. Our natures were vastly different after all.

Humans have their own natures, yes. But not all of us embrace them. We suppress, rebel, fight to change or improve them. It's a concept the fae and many creatures aren't familiar with. The ability and will to act how you want—not how your urges dictate.

The fae are what they are. Those that have read their faerie tales know how terrifying that is.

"Where's the queen?" I watched the centaur for any sudden movements.

He snorted in discontent. "My liege is up ahead." He nodded to a small break in the trees. "I've done my duty."

The centaur and his companion turned to leave.

"Yes, you have, haven't you?" Both of them stopped, their heads swiveling to watch me. "You brought us exactly where you said you would. In a lovely copse that just happens to be inhabited by Wisps."

"It is the location of my queen's court." His response was too carefully delivered, too rehearsed.

"Of course it is. And warning us about the Wisps just happened to slip your mind? You were true to your word. Accidents happen, don't they? You fulfilled your duty. If two humans happened to be lured to their deaths by a group of Wisps, well, how is that the fault of a centaur?"

Both centaur's eyes narrowed to slits. They moved closer. My hand went to my hilt. Cassie did the same. "Wait!" I pulled my hand back, and Cassie gave me a puzzled look. "Don't." Her look intensified before she moved her hand away as well. I met the centaur's eyes. "Clever, but not clever enough. Leave."

They bristled, posture tensing. For a moment, I thought I really would have to reach for my weapon. Thankfully the pair plodded away, but not before leaving me something to think about.

The male centaur looked over his shoulder, and smiled. "Thank you for sharing part of the young woman's name with us. In these woods, sounds go far, names further. No telling how many ears heard it. No telling whose ears it will reach." His smile grew. "There are many things we can do with a mortal's name."

Cassie's eyes widened, and she gave me a nervous look. I didn't let it show that their threats scared me. It was more for Cassie's sake than mine.

"Yes, but you can only do that with a full name. Good luck getting the rest. Go on." I clucked my tongue like I was ushering a horse to move on. It didn't go over well with them.

"How long before we learn yours?" he said.

I didn't respond, leaving them to turn and finally leave. We were left on our own to confront the Dawn Lady. It could have been worse.

"Come on." I took off towards the path ahead. "We have an important date, and we can't be late."

"Great." She didn't sound enthused by the meeting. "I know the story. I'm not a fan of rabbit stew."

I smiled and entered the thin pathway. The trees grew thicker on either side, forming an almost impenetrable weaving of bark. I waved a hand for Cassie to follow and stick close.

There was no response or acknowledgement. I turned around. The trees looked like they were bending or my vision was. The path seemed impossibly long, like it was taffy stretched to a ridiculous length. The ground was the sort of red you find on rusted iron, deep and dark. Looking at it made my head spin. I turned my attention to the path behind. No sign of Cassie. I turned around and reconsidered which way was forward, and which was the way we had entered.

I blinked and had to think again. They looked the same. The trees bowed and waved. I put a hand to the side of my mouth. "Cassie!"

Silence.

I spat at a nearby tree and reached into my pocket. My fingers closed around a smooth disc. I pulled it out and set the penny on my thumb. "Heads, ahead. Tails, the other way." I flipped it. Heads. "Okay then."

I ran. The trees grew closer as I sprinted, the path shrunk in width. As much as it pained me to do so, I stopped shouting Cassie's name. The centaur was right. You never knew who or what was listening in the Fair Lands. I'd find her. I had to.

I slowed my pace and turned my body to fit into the narrow opening ahead. My lungs ached as I exhaled the much-needed air from them. My profile thinned, albeit temporarily, and I edged my way through the trees.

Light.

That word held many meanings to many people. In this instance, they'd be wrong. I was given a first-hand glimpse of what the word truly meant.

The warmest colors imaginable spread across my face and body, bringing the comfiest of sensations with them. Every inch of my body felt like it was sinking into balmy sands as soft as powder. I wanted to stand there and bathe in it. A tiny hammer gonged within my skull, reminding me where I was and how bad an idea resting would be.

The light did more than make me feel like relaxing. It showed me what Cassie and I had come looking for.

The Morning Court. And it was in full attendance. Wonderful.

"John!" I faced the direction the voice had come from. "John!" I winced as Cassie crashed through brambles and flew out of the trees. I had no idea how we had been split up. She came to a complete stop the second she broke through, reacting to the light much like I had.

But there was more than the light to pay attention to. Worn, cracked stone tiles were laid out before us in the shape of a cross. Two statues of an inhumanly beautiful woman stood on either side of the stony pathway. All roads led to a circle of the same stone tiles surrounding the Court.

And it was ever the sight.

Tables crafted from wood the color of sunburned oranges and apples. A beautiful mixture of those two hues. All along their shape, tiny carvings of faerie creatures, lore, and more. There were nearly a dozen tables—all of them occupied by Morning Court nobility. All of them surrounded a tree stump that dwarfed a single story home in height and width. A path led to its base, becoming stairs to a crown of moss-covered stone that lined the stump's lip. It wasn't the stump itself that made me hold my breath. It was what sat atop. Or rather *who.*

Two reed-thin trees stood on either side, no taller than me, their red leaves in full bloom. Between them, a throne of stone too large to belong to any one person. The light from earlier dimmed and showed the fine detail on the arched back of the throne. The carvings reminded me of early light-worshipping societies and their rudimentary drawings of the Sun. The figure seated on the throne reminded me of the Sun itself.

Bright and radiant like a large star, she was blindingly beautiful. The Dawn Lady sat with her legs crossed, leaning casually with her chin resting on a palm. The corners of her mouth were pulled up in an amused smile. There was something catlike about it. Her eyes were closed, but I had the feeling she saw everything around her despite the fact. I wanted to shout to Cassie and get her attention, but even the thought of it felt like disturbing a prayer or a gathering of monks in meditation. The Court seemed that tranquil a place.

I waved a hand, hoping the motion would be enough. It was. Cassie took note and didn't utter a word as she ran towards me. I sprinted to meet her somewhere in between. The entire Court watched us. If they cared, they didn't show it. They didn't show much of any reaction in truth.

"Hey." Cassie leaned forward and placed her palms on her knees. "So, what gives back there? You disappeared."

"Funny, I was going to say the same to you."

"Guess the joke's on us."

"It's like that when it comes to faeries."

Cassie nodded to the figure atop the stump. "That Queenie?"

"Yes," answered a voice that made me feel like strings of ice wired my body.

We looked to the Dawn Lady as she rose from her seat. The strings quivered and tightened with every step she took. Tighter and tighter, tensing to a breaking point that seemed like it would never come. It was a musical piece of silent terror that wouldn't quite reach a crescendo.

Some women are breathtakingly beautiful. Some sights and places are too grand and all-encompassing to be described. If you were somehow able to blend the two, then you might just have a being half as entrancing as the Dawn Lady.

She appeared young enough to make a man feel guilty for thinking the thoughts her looks could suggest. In reality, she was likely older than the earliest civilizations in the mortal world. Her hair was the color of lemon marmalade, cut short in a pageboy style. Sun-kissed skin peeked out wherever her body wasn't covered by an outfit of green bark. It was woven together to look like a dress that hugged her body tight. Solid, yet clearly flexible, it left her arms and legs bare. She had legs any man would notice. Her mouth was a small and attractive Cupid's bow. It fit her youthful face and sharp nose.

Then she opened her eyes. Ours closed in response, or tried to. I couldn't bring myself to look away. It was like glaring at a pair of suns, unshielded.

Some things are jarringly beautiful; they shake you to the core and demand your full attention.

This was one of those things. It felt like my eyes were compressed in a vice while balloons were inflating inside them. I didn't know what would happen first. Would they burst, or be crushed?

"Apologies." Her voice carried the same pressure behind it.

There was powerful, and then there was Faerie Queen powerful. I gained a new respect for the fae. The Dawn Lady shut her eyes and the pain vanished. It didn't leave quick enough for my tastes however. My fingers dug into soft earth. I hadn't realized I had fallen. Twin streams of moisture lined either side of my nose. I brought my thumb to the inside of my eyes and wiped the trail. It came away red. I blinked and my eyes stung like they were filled with glass dust.

"I forget how..." she stopped as if searching for the right word. "*Fragile* mortals can be at times."

A round of deep chuckles came from the base of the stump. Fae lords and ladies no doubt. I gritted my teeth and tried not to show any weakness—any more, technically. Easier said than done.

I didn't know how, but the tissue in my throat felt like a dry sponge, shriveled and cracked. My lips pulled together as I sucked, trying to work whatever moisture into my mouth I could. I was rewarded with a globule of spit likely no larger than the tip of my thumb. I swallowed it. It wasn't an appealing thing, but it brought me a bit of relief. In the moment, I was willing to take whatever I could.

"Are you okay?" I didn't turn to look at Cassie.

"Yeah, although if this is okay, okay sucks hardcore."

I snorted, the action caused a pang in the top of my throat.

"Whatever does the Morning Court owe the pleasure of these two mortals to?" The Dawn Lady's words were like a current of soft air infused with honey. They made me want to answer her in full. I swallowed the urge.

I took several breaths and pushed myself up. It was shaky finding my balance, but I did. I made every effort to look the Faerie Queen in her eyes. Thankfully, they were no longer burning orbs. They looked rather normal, no different than any stranger's on the street, except for the color of her irises. They were polished citrines, sparkling prisms of every gold and yellow imaginable. Another feature of her beauty.

She smiled and my heart missed a handful of beats. "Well, do I have to ask again? I'm not accustomed to that in my domain." She looked around to the attendees. They laughed as if she had said something hilarious. I didn't get the joke.

The lords and ladies of the Morning Court looked exactly how you would imagine a noble faerie to look. Take every desirable feature you had wished for and been denied, and give it to them. Then ask an artist to go over them and bring them to a point beyond haunting perfection. People did not look that good; they *could* not look that attractive with all the computerized aid in the world. That thought made me wary.

The most beautiful things are more often than not the most dangerous. Nature, by design, makes pretty things deadly.

I ignored them and snuck a glance towards Cassie, who was still standing. I kept my surprise to myself. A simple look from a Faerie Queen, and I had collapsed into a heap. Cassie received the same look but remained standing. She looked like she was nursing a rather large headache as a result. Cassie looked at me, and her eyes fixed on mine. She brought an index finger just below one of her eyes and scratched the area.

"You're bleeding."

"You're not." I rubbed a fist against both my eyes to clear away whatever was left of my blood.

Cassie's face scrunched in confusion. "Should I be?"

"Good question. I don't know."

"Fa." The queen sighed. "Thrice it is then." We turned our attention back to her. It wasn't good for one's health to ignore a Queen of Faerie. "What are two mortals doing in my realm?" She spread her arms out wide, gesturing to everything around us and further beyond. Her gaze leveled on us, and her mouth twitched in anticipation. The rest of Court turned to watch as well, in silence I might add. It was disconcerting.

Cassie managed to make it look like she was staring ahead while glancing at me out of the corner of her eyes. She made sure her mouth moved as little as possible. "Give her a good answer. I get the feeling that Fireball Eyes isn't the forgiving type."

"No," said the queen. "I am not. And...Fireball Eyes hears all within her realm."

Cassie visibly gulped. But I knew how to address the queen now.

"Yes, you do hear all in your realm. So you know why we are here, don't you?" It came out a tad more brazen than I expected.

The noble fae in attendance looked at me wide-eyed. If it bothered the queen, it didn't show. It likely wouldn't. Faerie Queens did not take kindly to slights, no matter how small. She would have killed us in an instant.

Since she hadn't, I decided to continue. "We seek an audience with your grace, Monarch of the Morning Court."

Her mouth didn't move but her eyes glowed in

amusement. "Oh?" She descended the steps, drawing closer to us.

I mimicked Cassie and gulped.

You're not supposed to show predators any sign of weakness or fear. But when a tigress walks towards you, confident and in her place of power, it's not an easy thing to remain calm.

"To what end?"

"Knowledge." The word filled the grove and made it to the ears of every fae in sight.

She smiled. "Now, there is something interesting. Knowledge, power—often priceless. It never comes without a price." Her smile grew, the glow in her eyes growing with it. "You know this. So tell me, what have you brought to pay for it? What do you know worth anything I might share, hm?" She was ten feet away and getting closer.

I could feel her from that distance. I was sure if she had wanted me to, I could have felt her the second we entered her realm.

It was like lying bare next to a warm hearth. A lulling heat that promised a wonderful sleep and better dreams. I fought against the desire to rest. She was within arm's reach. The Dawn Lady paused, sniffed the air, and her eyes fell to my infected leg.

"Mm..." She stepped between us, circling me. "Someone has been wandering through the wrong gardens." She pursed her lips and waved an admonishing finger at me.

I felt like a child being chastised for playing with fire. "I made a mistake. It is one of the things I would like to speak to you about."

The queen turned, ignoring me as she tilted her head and sniffed again. "Fa. What we speak about will be decided upon once *I* choose if the Morning Court will entertain your presence further, or not." She didn't look at me when she spoke, but there was something in the "or not," that made me shudder.

The Dawn Lady moved into a new circle around Cassie, regarding her carefully. She sniffed once more. "You"—she blinked—"are something entirely...appealing." There was a hungry undertone in her voice.

I didn't like it. Cassie didn't seem to either. Her body tightened.

"Dawn Lady, please, we're pressed for time." I tried bringing the conversation back to why we were here. I couldn't have done it in a worse way.

The Faerie Queen looked at me like I was an adorably ignorant animal. "Oh, child. Time passes for all. It passes with little regard for you in the larger scale of things. Especially so here. Time means little to us." She waved to her court.

"I'm infected." There had to be something I could do to get her to help.

"Yes." Her features sank. She seemed genuinely saddened by my pain. It hurt to see something so beautiful upset.

She bent at the waist, bringing her face to the ground. A strand of green sprouted and bloomed into a white flower. She plucked it and stood up, holding it between her thumb and forefinger for me to see. "But all things die." She spun the flower and the petals withered until they were no more. "All things fade."

I nodded in agreement. "They do, but if there's anything in your power that makes it so I don't fade because of this"—I gestured to my leg—"I would be very grateful."

"Gratitude only?" She bit her lip to keep herself from smiling. "A poor price for my services."

"Hey, a little bit of gratitude goes a long way...or something?" Cassie shrugged. She wasn't helping, but she tried. I couldn't begrudge her for that.

"Fa. But you have so much more to offer." The Dawn Lady gave me a look that made me feel like I was on a menu.

Her finger came to rest below my chin, and electric jolts shot through my body. They subsided, becoming something else. A pleasurable tingling overtook every inch of my being. I didn't want it to stop, but it did.

"A mortal man is always welcome here." Her smile became something ravenous, and I knew where she was going. She tilted her head towards Cassie. "Or you could pledge the girl into my care. She would be well provided for. A mortal handmaiden could prove...useful."

The fae loved mortals for too many reasons.

In the end, it always came back to free will. The fae are bound by countless rules, and many of those forbade them to involve themselves too openly, too deeply in the world of mortals. Every action comes with a consequence. That only applies to them. Humans, however, can do as they've always done—anything they want. We can suffer repercussions as well, but they are byproducts of mortal laws, which to the fae are nothing more than flimsy rules based on morality. Their rules are harsher and ironclad. But if a human were to be in the service of a Faerie Court, by proxy, they could be used to act out the will of their queens. A living loophole. A dangerous one.

It was a rare thing for someone to willingly bind themselves into the service of the fae. It wasn't so rare for a young, beautiful fae woman to seduce an equally young and stupid man into a night of debauchery. Come nine months, the fae would have a child of both worlds. A child raised to think like the fae. A terrifying prospect.

"No thank you, milady. I'm afraid we will have to decline those offers."

"Shame." She turned and waved a dismissive hand. "You are of mild intrigue, so you may leave." It sounded like she was doing us a great favor. She wasn't.

"I'm afraid that's not an option..." It wasn't the smartest thing to say to a Faerie Queen.

She paused. There was a subtle twitch in her body. "What...did you say?"

"We're not leaving. We can't. Not without answers."

A silence formed over the already quiet court. The sort that fell before a storm came ashore. It wasn't good for my nerves either.

The Dawn Lady turned. A flicker of burning light

returned to her eyes. I wasn't keen to repeat my prior experience. I averted my gaze, focusing on her Court instead. They must have had the same idea. Their eyes were trained somewhere between the ground and the general area of my torso. Nobody wanted to eye the Faerie Queen.

Great minds think alike.

"Answers have costs, and you have nothing to buy them with, do you?"

"That depends." I kept my eyes fixed on the ground. A flicker of electric green danced just on the edge of my vision. I looked up. The Dawn Lady's left hand was no longer bare. Verdant tendrils, living and hungry, streaked over her hand and arm. I could feel the heat from where I stood.

Fael fire. It was dangerous, difficult to control, even among the fae. I didn't think she would have that problem. The fire was akin to magical napalm, clinging to any surface it made contact with, and spreading until it ran out of fuel. It could burn a great many things with little regard to whether they were flammable or not. Magic didn't do a good job of playing by any rules besides its own. Suffice it to say, Fael fire wasn't much good for useful things like cooking, unless you were flambéing a person. I found myself highly allergic to the stuff.

I licked my lips and turned my gaze back to the ground.

"Depends on what?" There was a curious edge to her voice.

Good. Curiosity I could take advantage of. I just hoped I wasn't pushing my luck. "Do you like secrets, oh, Queen?"

The flames crackled and dimmed in vibrancy. *So far, so good.*

"Mm." Not much of an indication as to whether she was intrigued or not, but I had nothing else up my sleeve. Before I could speak, she decided to tear my approach to pieces. "What secrets would those be? That you're Jonathan Hawthorne, one of the Timeless? That you're ill because you were foolish enough to wander through The Long Gardens?"

Ill was an understatement, and in all honesty, Cassie dragged me there.

"That the Grand Marquis has put a bounty on your head—"

I had her. "Do you know why?" I looked up and met her gaze this time, holding it.

She blinked. "Because you attacked him—a freestanding lord of the Neravene. An insignificant one, yes, but all the same."

Insignificant. I reminded myself who I was dealing with and buried the smile trying to force its way across my face. "Do you know why that was necessary, Dawn Lady?"

"Hm..." My smile must have found its way to her lips. She grinned in amusement, eyes twinkling. "Secrets indeed. Why?"

Cassie gave me a quick look of warning. She had a point; this could put her in immediate trouble. A distant throb in my leg reminded me that I was already in danger.

"He broke his word of hospitality—in a manner of speaking. We defended ourselves."

Her curiosity didn't seem placated however. "But it begs the question, *why* did he break his word? That carries a heavy penalty in the Neravene."

This is why I do not like dealing with faeries. There is such a thing as too many questions and being too curious. Frankly, it's a pain in the ass for even the most patient of people. Admittedly, I don't have the best level of patience.

Some members of her court had even less than I did. One of the tables erupted into frenzied action. A particularly tall fae whipped around with a sword trailing in his grip. It lodged in the gullet of a bipedal tusked creature that looked like a cross between a pig and a bear. I couldn't remember what the being was called. I was distracted by the garnet fountain of blood spurting from its throat.

It was a bold move—stupid, but bold. The upstart didn't last long. One Court member's glamour faded. He stood taller and wider than the cab of an eighteen-wheeler. Easily the largest troll we'd encountered. It clobbered the fae swordsman with a fist the size of a sports car's tire. There wasn't much fight left in the blonde haired fae. It was a shame he wasn't alone.

Screams echoed from the other side of the grove. A mud brown ogre systemically dismembered an elven woman, starting with her head. Several fae of varying species swarmed him.

You can always feel when there is a gun placed near your head. Even if you can't see it. There's a certain pressure that fills the space near you. The veil dropped.

She was dressed in full leather. It suited her punk hairstyle. Tapered ears, bright eyes, and fangs that were visible when she smiled. She would have been attractive if it weren't for the scars. They must have been new. She didn't have them when last we met. That wasn't the most disconcerting thing. She held the shotgun pointed at my right ear.

"Miss me?" Her voice was a sensual purr. She was enjoying this. She shouldn't have been.

"I don't even remember your name." I smiled.

The Night Runner smiled back. "I didn't give it."

It was the wrong time for smiling. The Faerie Queen's face was a mask of unequivocal, silent rage. It was the sort of quiet that hovered over graveyards and other places of death. I clenched my jaw and hoped it wasn't going to be our graves.

"Enough." One word, that was all the Dawn Lady said, and that was all it took. She might have whispered it, but it came out like a whip crack.

Every single being within earshot impacted the floor. My body was driven by instinct to focus solely on breathing. I've heard people speak of being under the weight of the world. In that moment, the weight of the world would have been a relief. My insides felt like they were being compressed from every side imaginable. The air was forced from my lungs as fast as I could suck it back in. The grove spun like a forest-themed top. The Dawn Lady spun too, and I realized she was equally attractive from every angle.

Until her eyes ignited. Over the decades I've met a countless number of supernatural beings, all of whom I believed were powerful in their own way. I was mistaken. And the Dawn Lady was kind enough to provide that lesson.

I couldn't scream, though I wanted to. I couldn't pull my gaze away; I couldn't shut my eyes. I had no choice but to look. It was like looking into a fire for too long. All I saw were flames, spinning and dancing. The bright colors blended together, somehow finding a way to become even brighter, until all I could see was the purest of whites.

White turned to black.

Chapter Twenty-One

"The Arbiter..." Cassie broke into a fit of shivers. "Was right."

"I know." I coughed several times. "I have the sneaking suspicion he knew he was right, or was going to be."

"Know-it-alls." She made it sound like a curse. I had to agree given the situation.

I arched my back, trying to keep my skin away from the wet, chilled stone. Being pinned upright to a wall was not part of the plan. The chains and manacles kept me from stretching too far. Shame.

I squinted for half a minute before giving up. Adjusting to the dark was possible, but it required a modicum of light. Absent that, it was near impossible.

"I'm cold, John." Her voice told me that much, and that she was likely only an arm's length or two away.

If what they did to me was any indication—they had taken most of her clothes as well, leaving her as bare as possible. Torture didn't work hand-in-hand with hospitable treatment.

I pulled my arm. It jerked to a halt as a circlet of metal dug into my wrist. "Can't be metal," I mumbled.

"What was that?"

"Sorry, trying to think, be rational, work through this."

"Oh." She sounded distant. The cold was getting to her.

Temperatures can cause a lot of problems for a person. They can also exacerbate depression. Cold, isolation, uncomfortable positions—all of them can break people mentally. And when it came to torture, the fae might as well have written the guidebooks.

They're not known for being a cheery race.

"It helps, Cassie. Thinking about facts, logical things

that you know are true no matter what. It helps ground you. I know things are bad—"

She snorted. "Ya think? I know they're bad. They're *always* bad. That's what happens to me, John. I warned you to stay away when we first met. I warned you!"

I pressed my lips together. There was a slight sound when she finished speaking, like a swallowed hiccup. A sob. I couldn't see her, and I didn't know if I wanted to at the moment. I imagined she was crying. She wouldn't want me to see her like that.

"These aren't made of metal, they can't be. Fae can't touch them."

"They feel like it. They feel cold."

"I know, Cassie." I groaned as the muscles in my back and shoulders knotted, and I collapsed against the stone. A solid blanket of ice pressed against my body, and my brain numbed for a moment. "It...has...to be...s-something else. Faeries can fashion their own alloys."

"Yeah...I'm sure that's...what that is." Her teeth chattered. "How long do you think we'll be down here?"

I forgot how I was going to respond. A sound interrupted my thoughts—high pitched, peppered with gurgles and what sounded like thrashing against metal. Thuds, bangs, and screams.

"Hopefully before that happens to us."

"You"—I could hear Cassie take several breath—"are such a cynic."

I snorted. My nose stung and my eyes ached from the action. My body was growing accustomed to the cold. I could speak clearly in bursts. It wasn't a good thing. "A cynic is what an optimist calls a realist. I simply cannot abide an eternal optimist."

Cassie snuffled and then let out a peal of laughter that morphed into dry coughs. It was short-lived, but it was nice to hear her laugh. "So, you said to be logical? That's supposed to help?"

"It keeps your mind off things like the cold and the situation."

"Okay, fact: I'm chained up in a dark dungeon next to an old man. My mother would be ashamed of me right now."

I laughed. My lungs tightened, but I ignored the pain.

"I wonder what else she thinks about me?"

"What?"

"My mom—wonder if she misses me."

My chest ached and the cold wasn't causing it. "Of course she does, Cassie, of course she does."

She sniffed. "Fae."

"Where?"

"No. F-a-y-e. Cassidy Faye Winters. My mother called me Cassie most of the time. But you know what I remember the most?" Cassie's voice cracked. "My middle name. She always used to call me her little Faye when things were bad, if I was sad, or anything was wrong in my life. Wish she was here to say it now. Things are pretty bad."

"They are, but we'll get out of here, Faye."

A long, quiet moment passed between us.

"I cannot abide an eternal optimist... Thank you, John."

The muscles in my face felt taut. They didn't want to stretch on account of the cold. I grinned anyways. "Right now, in this dark, I'd say optimism is our best bet."

She didn't reply.

"Cassie?"

"Yeah, sorry, but optimism is a stretch. I'm not going to lie. I don't see it."

"See what?"

"The out. It's been one thing after another, all of them crazy. It doesn't feel like I'm getting out of this one. If we are...then how? Where's the light, John?"

"I don't know. I wish I did. It's dark, yes, but the thing about the dark, Cassie, is that isn't permanent. I've been alive a long time. Old man, remember? In all that time, I've seen a lot of dark. Do you know what else I've seen? Do you know what I've found to be true?"

Cassie was quiet.

"That the sun always comes up. Guaranteed. It only

takes a little bit of light to wash away the dark, Cassie."

"And what about the day it stops? There's going to be a day it doesn't come up. What if that's today?"

She was right. One day it would happen, but it wasn't today. "Sometimes it doesn't come up, you're right. I'm not going to lie about that. It can get dark—truly dark. I remember some nights during the wars—"

"Which ones?"

"All of them."

"Oh."

"I didn't think the night could get much darker. I was wrong. Some things find a way to blot out the light, and that's okay, Cassie."

"It is?"

"Yes, because the thing about light is...you don't have to wait for someone else to shine it. Sometimes you have to do it yourself. I know you're scared right now. So am I. Even with what we have both gone through, this is something new."

"You mean you don't always get stripped and locked in dungeons? You're not the man your dating profile said you were. I'm offended."

My laugh was a series of sharp exhales through my nose and mouth. A fist-sized cold spot formed over the back of my head where I rested it against the stone. "That's good. Laughter helps at a time like this."

"I don't suppose we can laugh our way out of this? Maybe if start yelling some jokes?"

"Even *you* aren't *that* funny, Cassie."

"I want you to imagine me kicking you in the shins, real hard. Both of them. Right now. Because if I could, I would."

I snorted. "My point was that sometimes things look bleak and there's no hope in sight. The thing I learned about dark times and hope is they're not mutually exclusive. Hope is something you give yourself, Cassie, no matter how dark it gets. Sometimes you have to be your own light."

Footsteps. The door creaked open. A pillar of amber light washed over my face. I squinted and tried to make out who was there.

"I didn't think it would be so literal, ackh!" Cassie jangled the chains as she turned her head.

"Who's there?"

No response, only footsteps. They were heavy ones. A good reason to be uneasy. I could feel them shake the mountings of our shackles. Whatever it was, it was big.

"Who's there?"

The footsteps grew louder. The light grew brighter.

I may not always be fond of the rules, or following them for that matter. There was one I was particularly grateful for, however. There were some rules even the fae had to follow, from the lowliest to the highest. It didn't matter your rank, kind, or power—many creatures were bound by the Rule of Three. Thrice said, once fulfilled

"Who's there?" My rang clearer, echoing through the room.

"Murg." A smell like week-old restaurant garbage clung to my nose like olfactory acid. It stung my eyes and made me regret asking my question in the first place.

"Whoa that's rank."

Murg grunted. Cassie and I were given another whiff of its breath.

"I don't suppose Murg can speak without opening his mouth?" I turned my face away and not because of the light.

Cassie snickered.

"Murg is a she." The voice that answered came from further behind.

I wagered it was the source of the blinding light and our current predicament. There was a strange current over it, like it was coming from underwater

"Do I have to ask three times for your name too?"

"Do you really have to?"

"What can we do for you, Dawn Lady?" I didn't need to see to know that she was smiling.

"Mm." It wasn't much of an answer.

The light dimmed to a faint, gentle glow like a candle. Her outfit hadn't changed, nor had her appearance. The light did wonderful things to her silhouette, making every subtle curve, and not so subtle ones, stand out. Her eyes softened to their golden yellow hue. I preferred them that way.

"Yo, do you bring all your guests down to your dungeon, Queenie? By the way, two stars. You get one plus for the faerie allure and what not. It's damp, cold, and you took my clothes."

The Faerie Queen arched an eyebrow and bit her lip. Something crossed her mind. I only wished I knew what.

I hissed through my teeth and my body tensed. "Please don't antagonize a Queen of Faerie."

"Three stars."

I choked in a fit of trying not to laugh, failed, and swallowed the laugh.

The Dawn Lady put a finger to the side of Cassie's temple. Cassie shuddered under the touch, especially when the Faerie Queen trailed her finger down and stroked her cheek. "You're brave. Not many would speak to me like that."

"Oh, I'm freaking terrified. You've got me down to my undies, and you're starting with the foreplay. Being a witty smartass is just my thing in these scenarios."

"Brave." The queen pulled away from Cassie, but her attention didn't waver.

I decided to become her new focus. "Bravery is something you give yourself, no matter the method. She is brave. I would appreciate it if you left her alone rather than pushing to see just how brave she can be."

The Faerie Queen's head turned in a slow manner that spelled trouble. "There is bravery, Jonathan Hawthorne..." Chains rattled, stone shook, and my body followed as she spoke my name. And she didn't raise her voice in the slightest. "There is also stupidity. Tell me, are you stupid?"

I shook my head. It seemed a better choice than answering aloud.

"Good."

I was trying to be. It wasn't smart to anger a Faerie

Queen.

The Dawn Lady touched a finger to her lip, looking me over as she did. "Now, what to do with the two of you?"

"I was wondering the same thing. I couldn't come up with the answers. Would you be kind enough to enlighten us?" Perhaps I should have stayed quiet.

Murg let out a dark chuckle that shook her entire body, which spoke volumes considering her troll bulk.

"Enlighten." The queen rolled the word around her mouth like it was the first time she had heard it. "Now there is an idea." She held a hand a few inches before my face. A faint light shone over the skin of her fingers before they ignited into flames.

It wasn't easy maintaining my bravado, much less my composure. I tried anyways. "Let's try a different question: Why are we here?"

Silence, if one didn't count the occasional crackle of flames and Murg's snuffling.

"I could have imprisoned you for any number of reasons, Jonathan Hawthorne. For bringing steel into my domain. For touching said steel to my land and harming it. For colluding with assassins—poor ones albeit. And lastly, because I am the Queen of the Morning Court. Need I any other reason?"

She had good points on all accounts, especially the last. "No, no, you don't. But you can't expect me to believe that any of those are the reasons why my friend and I are chained here."

"Oh?"

"We both know the assassins weren't there for you. There are many kinds of idiots out there, but I don't know of anyone stupid enough to attack a Faerie Queen. They weren't with us. They were here for us. You know that."

The flames vanished. "I also know a great many other things." She waited for me to ask the inevitable, so I did.

"Such as?"

"That Cassidy Winters is quite the remarkable young woman."

Both Cassie and I went rigid.

"I know all there is to know about what transpired in the Grand Marquis' domain. The Night Runner didn't keep silent for long—they seldom can. I wonder..." she trailed off as she knelt to a crouch beside my ailing leg. "How long could you last if..." Her fingertips rested against my calf. Something coursed through her fingers and into the muscle of my leg.

All I could see was the ceiling. It shook and vibrated as I thrashed. My screams sounded like they came from miles away until, eventually, I couldn't hear them myself.

"Stop it!" Chains jangled as Cassie struggled.

The queen didn't listen.

"Stop!" she screamed.

The pain continued.

"Stop it, you bitch!" Cassie's voice was garbled and sounded several notes too high.

She did. The pain ceased immediately, no lingering throbbing or aftereffects like before. Whatever the Faerie Queen had done, it was clear she had complete control over it. The queen rose. It was a slow and deliberate movement. I didn't have a good feeling about it. The impromptu torture session didn't help.

The Dawn Lady glared at a spot just above Cassie's head. The wall exploded, showering Cassie in debris and leaving a basketball-sized hole behind it. The Faerie Queen lowered her gaze a fraction of an inch. The same thing happened. Her eyes trailed down.

"Okay! Okay, I get it. Sorry." Cassie tilted her head to the side, away from the queen's glare. The Dawn Lady stopped. The corner of her mouth pulled into a satisfied smile. She had made her point.

"I have killed beings for less."

Cassie nodded.

I remained silent.

"The thought still entertains me. I know what you can do, child. I know the threat you pose to my domain should you be convinced, or coerced, into helping other lords and ladies. I *should* kill you—both of you."

"It seems to be the trend of late." I managed to shrug my shoulders.

The queen's lips twitched. I remembered her display with the wall. I should have adopted respectful silence, but if I said nothing, it could last a lifetime.

"It's murder." My voice was a low whisper.

"What?" She looked lost—surprised—as if she didn't expect the argument.

"Murder. You could kill us, of course, and no one would ever question you for it."

The queen stared at me like I was an idiot stating the obvious. In a sense, I was.

"But it would still be unwarranted murder. Pointless. For a Faerie Queen to kill like that...it's rather pathetic, don't you—" My head rocked to the side as a whip-like crack echoed through the stone room. Electricity coursed through my cheek, and my jaw felt unhinged.

It took a while for the room to settle and my eyes to stop spinning in their sockets. The inside of my mouth filled with the taste of metal and salt. I let my head hang and the bloodied spit fall from my lips. The Dawn Lady had a powerful slap.

I looked up and met her eyes. They weren't burning, but I had the feeling if I did something like that again, they would.

"The young woman is a threat—to everything. Her *gift*"—she said the word like it was a curse—"is unnatural. No being should be able to manipulate the Ways like that. What is to stop the other queens from using *her* to usurp another—usurp *me*? What is to stop another lord or lady, or being of smaller stature, from using her to conquer each other—from upsetting the balance?" A dangerous light crept into her eyes. "What is to stop me from using her to conquer the other queens?"

My heart stopped as I considered her final question. It was another handful of seconds before I could respond. "Balance."

The queen froze.

I pressed my position. "We both know what's at stake if one of the queens oversteps their roles and takes on another. Balance—it's hard enough to create, and harder to keep, no?" The queen stared heated daggers at me.

"Balance." The Dawn Lady said it like it was a word long forgotten. "All the more reason to kill her. Temptation, abuse, upsetting the balance."

"John, your negotiating skills blow centaur wang."

"Don't do this, please."

The queen was resolved. "What do two mortal lives matter? Mortal lives are fleeting; I am eternal. Tonight, two mortals may die, but tomorrow, the sun will rise as it always has, and I shall continue to be its herald."

"Maybe so"—it still hurt to speak—"but you'll die without knowing."

Of all the things I had said and could have said, *that* got her attention. "Knowing what?"

"Who else wants Cassidy Winters? Who else is making plans for her? Who else wants your throne?"

I was mistaken. She hadn't frozen before; she was merely still. Now, she could have given lessons to stone. I'd hit a nerve.

Her voice was a whisper with a knife's edge to it. "You presume a great deal."

"I do, and I'm right. The two you captured were after my head. But you looked further into the matter. You know Miss Winters is being chased by far more than an irate, small lord. Free fae are after her. Fae with no loyalties, but why? Who's pulling their strings, and for what purpose? You want to know because if you let this go, if you kill Cassie, you'll never know who. You could have traitors in your own Court sponsoring this. The best threats are the ones you can't see. You know this."

"I see all in my domain."

"And what about outside it? In the mortal realm? In the small pockets of the Neravene you don't control?"

The Dawn Lady turned to Murg and made a quick

thrust of her head. Murg nodded and plodded out of the room. The Faerie Queen waited until Murg had left before she turned back to face me. "You are right."

Words I never thought I would hear from a Faerie Queen.

"I *am* curious. Maybe you will live; maybe you won't. I leave the choice with you."

Cassie looked to the queen, then me. "What?"

I had the same question. I heard Murg's footsteps as she approached. She came into view through the door. Something was thrown over her shoulder. Murg tossed the figure to the floor and lumbered out of the room.

Their clothing had been stripped from their body, forcibly by the looks of it. A few rogue bits clung to their skin, which had paled like they were low on blood. Given the copious amounts coating their body, it seemed like a safe assumption. Her hair was splayed in a wild fashion over the stone floor. The Night Runner's naked body looked like it had been subjected to every form of torture I could imagine, and some I couldn't.

The Dawn Lady regarded the figure on the floor, then the both of us. "Like I said, I leave the choice with you."

The Faerie Queen left the room, taking most of her light with her. A dim glow remained, just enough for me to make out a silhouette.

The door shut, leaving us chained in a room with one of the creatures sent to kill me.

The figure stirred.

Yellow eyes shone in the dark.

Chapter Twenty-Two

"Do something, John..."

"Like what?"

"I don't know, something smart and tricky. Dude, you just got a Faerie Queen to step off."

There was a groan, and it didn't come from either of us. The Night Runner twitched. Her chest heaved, and she breathed in weak, ragged gasps.

"I don't think she's a threat, not anymore."

"She could be faking it. I know I would be." Cassie gave the Night Runner a dubious look.

"Do you think you'd be able to after a Faerie Queen had you tortured? The Dawn Lady is old, Cassie—older than humanity. She's watched every form of torture come into being, not to mention having a hand in creating some."

Cassie shivered.

"The Faerie Queens have never been known for being nice. And the Dawn Lady is the most temperate."

Cassie sputtered. "That... She's the most stable?"

I nodded.

"I don't think I want to meet the other queens."

"I'm feeling the same way, but it might be necessary."

"Stop..." wheezed the Night Runner, "talking."

We both fell silent. The only sounds were her breathing, slow and labored. The Night Runner didn't look like she would last the night. Despite the fact she was after my head, the thought of her dying like that didn't sit well with me. Quentin would have called me a bleeding heart. He would have been right.

Cassie leaned as far forward as her chains would allow. "Hey, are you okay?"

The Night Runner exhaled, and her chest slowed its

movements.

"Stay awake. If you slip into unconsciousness, you might not wake again." I hoped the warning would galvanize the elf to fight the fatigue and pain. Of course, it was never that easy.

"I managed for this long," she said on a slow, long exhale of breath. "That bitch is cruel." She let out a rueful laugh. "I kind of like her."

"What happened?" Concern flooded Cassie's voice.

Even in her current predicament, she still showed concern for someone else. She deserved better than being stuck with the cards she had been dealt. The sad thing about life was people seldom got what they deserved. I resolved to make sure Cassie would.

The Night Runner turned to her side, coughing and sputtering as blood and saliva dribbled from her mouth. "Have you ever been crucified before?"

"I can't say that I have, but I can imagine." I gestured with a nod to the chains.

"No, no, you can't." The Night Runner coughed like there wasn't a hint of moisture left in her throat.

"Fair enough." I didn't want to hear the rest.

"They put me on a cross. The things holding me in place—thorns, and not the kind from your side of the fence."

I took in a sharp breath that sounded more like a hiss.

She chuckled. It was drowned out and turned into a gurgle. The Night Runner wracked her throat, and more fluids pooled onto the floor. It was thicker this time, noticeably so. She was spitting up more than just blood and spittle. She didn't bother wiping her mouth. Between that and her fangs, it made her look all the more frightening in the dim light.

I shuddered.

The Night Runner coughed until she was able to speak. "It hurts...when the first thorn breaks through your skin. It's a mix of fire and ice. It digs deeper. Little barbs hook into the meat of your body. It burns your tissue, and something else makes your mind go numb to everything but the pain. No other thoughts. It's like your brain is submerged in a frozen lake. The only thing you can focus on is the pain. That makes it worse. You start thrashing, hoping you can break the vines. It doesn't work like that…" She was interrupted as her body went through a fit of convulsions. She retched. The Night Runner wasn't going to be collecting her bounty.

She lay there, still, breathing for a series of quiet moments. "The more I moved, the more thorns dug into me. The vines grew tighter. After a while, I couldn't even scream."

I knew what that felt like.

Cassie turned a shade lighter.

I needed to change the subject. "What happened to your friend?"

The Night Runner didn't answer.

"What happened to the troll you came with?"

"The queen gave him to Murg. I think there's still some of him left—some."

I tried to keep my stomach from roiling. Trolls have a horribly efficient way of dealing with each other. I didn't know what to say, but Cassie did.

"I'm sorry."

The elf laughed harder. Pained moans peppered it. "Sorry? You mortals are…precious." Her features went tight as her face slipped into an anguished mask. "I tried to kill you, and you are apologizing to me?" She let out a sound like something caught between laughter and crying.

"Normally I would ask if you were still trying to kill us, but you're not a threat anymore, are you?"

"No." Another fit of coughs. She managed a weak nod towards Cassie. "*She's* the threat."

I kept the edge from creeping into my voice. "What do you mean?"

"I'm not stupid." Her words were drier and more strained than before. "You hear things in my line of work."

Cassie watched our exchange without moving.

"What sort of things?"

"At first, it was just why the Marquis wanted you. Then it was why he wanted *both* of you. It wasn't long before word spread about the mortal girl and what she could do." A gruesome smile crossed the Night Runner's face. "Bigger bounties went out once everyone knew."

"Define everyone." I buried the burble of fear crawling up my throat.

"Every free fae." Her smile widened. The bloody ichor coating her fangs didn't help the image. "Any small lord or lady with their ears to the ground knows. Anybody looking for an edge, a weapon."

Cassie turned her head and let her gaze fall to the floor. Her posture softened. It was clear the Night Runner's words were getting to her.

My muscles coiled and knotted. Pushing against the chains was useless, but I tugged on them regardless. "Stop. Talking."

"Or what? You'll kill me? I'm already dead." She was right about that. And she was wrong about Cassie.

"She's not a weapon. She's a person." I stopped fighting my restraints and let an edge slip into my voice.

The Night Runner chortled like a dying toad. It wasn't a pleasant sound.

"She's a kid." I could feel Cassie turn her head to stare at me. "An itty, bitty child with her whole life ahead of her and—"

"The only thing stopping me from kicking your ass right now, old man, is these." Cassie gave the chains a shake that sent them rattling.

The elf made a wet snort. By the looks of things, she didn't have long. I didn't know what was helping her hold on.

"I like her. Shame about things." The elf's features sank.

"About the bounty on her, or you not being able to collect it?"

Her smile stretched as wide as she could manage. "Yes."

I wanted to make a comment about her being a

smartass, but I refrained. "There's lots of things to be ashamed of. For instance, your current state."

"Same...as...you."

"True." I nodded. "But this is temporary. We have a way out."

Cassie didn't say anything, but her eyes bored holes into my skull, asking the question.

The Night Runner scoffed and gagged before spitting up another clump of congealing fluids. "I had one of those too, did me as much good as yours will."

"Oh?" If she had a plan, I wanted to hear it—failed or not.

She laughed. It was a sad, broken thing. "I'm afraid—" She broke off to inhale. It didn't sound good, stretched, dry, and ending in coughs. "It was too simple."

Cassie pressed her further, but kept her tone gentle. "What was it?"

"Bribery."

I did my best not to laugh at her, not that I could have. My mouth hung open at her audacity. "You tried to bribe a queen?" I no longer felt stupid for my boldness before the Dawn Lady.

"Of course not." She spat and finally mustered the strength to wipe her mouth with a hand. "Just a fae. The *queen* left as soon as I passed out for the final time. When I woke, one of the Daoine was standing watch."

"Daoine?" Cassie perked up.

I took it as a good sign that she was still curious. The dungeon hadn't broken her yet. If I acted fast, maybe I would keep it that way.

"They're the tall, graceful, human looking ones—if humans looked perfect. Like the queen, only with less power," I said.

Cassie mouthed a silent, "Ah." Then she regarded the dying Night Runner. "Why didn't it work? Didn't offer enough?"

"Too smart, too loyal."

That was all the reason needed for why her plan didn't

work, and all I needed to come up with one of my own. My mind turned to easier prey. Then it was pulled from those thoughts as the Night Runner's breathing slowed.

"Hey, hold on you stubborn, irascible, elf bitch!" Hot iron flooded my voice.

Anger is a great tool to jar someone into coherency, or some form of it at least.

Cassie watched as I berated the Night Runner.

It was odd. Before, when she had the shotgun placed to my head, I wished she were dead. I was getting my wish. Sometimes that could be something you came to regret. She wasn't a threat anymore. She wasn't much of anything—just broken.

Her chest followed her breathing, slowing, before stopping altogether. There was no final sigh, no last words or breath; just a pair of yellow eyes that lost their glow. They were unsettling before, and they still were. Dim orbs of pale yellow gave us a hollow stare. I couldn't meet that stare, so I faced Cassie.

She cleared her throat and blinked several times. "Wow, there must be something wrong with me."

I said nothing.

She cleared her throat harder, trying to keep her voice level. "I mean she tried to kill us, and still, she didn't deserve to go that way."

"No, she didn't."

"John..." Her lips trembled, and her voice followed, "I don't want that happening to me—to us."

"It won't."

She didn't hear me, or didn't want to. "She's right though..."

I shut my eyes as Cassie spoke. Our surroundings, the Night Runner, they got to her. In fairness, they were getting to me.

"No. Cassie, weren't you listening?"

"Then tell me why this is happening? All this and still no answers. Why can I open these doors? Why am I so far away from home? Why am I here?" Her head fell back against the stone as she rested. Her voice dropped lower. "This is your world, John, not mine. I'm tired of being on the run. I'm tired of monsters." She sounded like it. "I don't fit in. I don't belong."

Every word helped the cold seep deeper into my body. My chest and lungs ached. I felt like I was made of lead.

"Cassie..." My voice was pulled straight from the damp stone behind me. "Shut up."

She did. My aches and throbs deepened for saying it, but I had to. "Cassie, this place is getting to you, all of this is tearing at you, and that's okay."

Cassie pressed her lips together and cleared her throat. "It is?"

"Yes. You're human." I let a bit of laughter into my voice. "A wonderful, sometimes crazy"—her eyes hardened into brief glare—"wiseass of a human."

"You say the sweetest things." Her face was stained in tears and grim, but the smile she flashed reached her eyes.

"That's what I'm talking about. You're human. That means having ups and downs, being afraid. You're allowed to be. We're in Faerie and surrounded by paranormal beings of immense power, endless trickery and deceit. It's okay to be scared and feel out of your depth. We both are. But don't for one second think that you don't fit in. You do. Maybe not here, but you do fit into the world and larger scheme. I don't know how, but you do."

"Yeah?"

"Yes. The thing about the world is that it has no extra pieces. It's a great, big ball. Take away even a single piece—no more ball. Every piece, every person, and every thing plays a part. The world needs all of those ingredients. It's better off with them in it, the good, and sadly, the bad. It's better off with *us* in it. With *you* in it. It needs you. I need you. You're my friend."

She swallowed and licked her lips, turning her attention to her feet for a bit. "Thank you, John, for everything." She nodded to herself. "Gimme a bit, but I'll be good. Thanks."

"Good, because I've got a plan to get us out of here."

"You do?"

I thought of the deceased Night Runner and the flaw in her plan.

"I do." I raised my voice and flooded it with all the energy I could. "Murg!"

Chapter Twenty-Three

"What are you doing? Are you *trying* to get us killed?"

"Murg!" My voice reverberated through the room, but I needed it to carry down the halls.

"Okay, it's official—you've lost it. Please turn in your leadership of the crazy adventure card. You *want* to bring the giant ugly—" Cassie cut herself off as the door creaked.

It opened, and the blubberous troll filled the doorway.

"Hey...Murg, we were just talking about you, girl. How you doing?"

I folded my lips and bit down. It was the best way to keep myself from laughing. "You changed your tune quick." I winked at Cassie.

She glared back.

Murg lumbered forward, shaking the room. Dust and particulate matter fell from above. She stopped an arm's length away. For the sake of my nose, I wished it were several arm's lengths away—long arms. There was tantalizingly sweet, and then there was nauseatingly sweet. It wasn't hard to imagine where the troll fell.

"What want? Murg hungry." She smacked her thick, frog-like lips.

"Oh, good, hear that, John? She's hungry..." Cassie's stare grew heated.

"I did, and I'm pretty sure Murg is already well catered for that, aren't you?"

Murg's lips spread. It wasn't a pretty smile or sight. Her teeth were half rotten, chipped, and damaged in every way imaginable. They were also coated in a dark fluid. Bits of ragged flesh sat in odd corners of her mouth.

I closed my eyes and held my breath. My stomach settled seconds later.

"What want?"

Cassie must have been infecting me somehow. I nearly told Murg that I wanted her to eat a dictionary. I'm certain Murg would have indulged the 'eat' part of my request. I cleared my throat and prayed that my plan worked.

"I want to give you something—a gift."

Murg's eyes lit up. "Give what?"

"Yeah, John, what?"

"Something valuable. Something not easy to get a hold of in Faerie." I gave her my best and most sincere smile.

Murg leaned forward, shoving her face too close for comfort.

"Where?" She reached out and picked at my briefs with her fingers.

"Not there!" I flailed in panic, twisting my body away.

Murg pulled her fingers back. "Then where?" Her voice hardened, and her expression followed.

"Do you know where our clothes are—everything we brought with us and was taken?"

Murg's face scrunched in contemplation. She nodded.

"I need a favor from you. If you bring us our clothes, I'll give you the gift. It's cold here. You understand."

The troll's eyes narrowed. "No."

"I'm sorry?"

"Murg not dumb. You bring swords—*steel.*" There was a dangerous emphasis on the word "steel." To her credit, she was right on both accounts.

"You're right, but you don't have to touch them. You could wrap them up in the clothes, bring them here and drop them on the other side of the room. They can't harm you like that, but I want our things back."

Murg took a step back and shied her body away from me.

"Wait!" I was surprised when she stopped and looked back. "What if I promise not to take up our swords and harm you with them?"

Murg blinked. I wasn't sure if I had her or if she viewed me as a threat—one she'd crush.

"I'll swear it, thrice."

The troll turned back and stared at me. A minute later, she nodded. "Swear."

"I swear on my life that I will not take up my sword against you, Murg, should you return our clothing to us. I swear on my life that I will not take up swords against you. I swear it thrice, on my life, that I will not lay a sword on your skin."

Her nose twitched. Not much of a sign if she agreed or not. "Reward?"

"You'll have it, once you bring us our things, I promise."

Murg shut her mouth, and squinted, more to herself than me. "Okay." The troll moved towards the exit, shaking the place again. The door slammed shut with more force than was necessary. I had a feeling the doors were replaced frequently because of Murg.

"What was that about?" Cassie's hiss could nearly be felt on my skin.

"What?"

"Everything. What's up with the whole promising to reward the troll? And what's up with the whole three thing?"

"You caught that, hm?"

"I'm not stupid. Yeah, I caught that bit. You want to explain?"

"It's nice to know you're still eager to learn."

"Yeah, well, I'm all tied up at the moment." She shook her chains. "There's not much else to do. School me."

"Three's a magic number."

Cassie gave me a flat stare.

"I'm serious, there is as much power in numbers as names."

She arched an eyebrow.

"Three is a number of strength—of power. It comprises the triangle. The number can't be divided evenly—indivisible. It represents true balance."

"True balance?"

"What happens when two sides disagree? Nothing. True

balance has a deciding factor because balance wavers. It's something that teeters, back and forth. Three, not two. Think about the scales of balance, two sides that tilt back and forth but the third piece is hidden—decision. And decisions change. Three pieces, one resolution."

Cassie nodded.

"Three times of day. Morning, twilight, and night—"

"Three queens..." Cassie's eyes widened in understanding.

"Right."

"And they..."

I nodded.

"Oh, wow."

"The Rule of Three is part of nature, part of both worlds. Time is bound by it. The divisions of past, present and the future. The world itself. Earth, sky, and sea. In the Neravene, it's a binding rule. It can save your life. Remember it."

"I will. So that promise you made to Murg, you really can't hurt her? Bad promise. You think she'd hesitate to hurt us?"

I grinned. "Do you remember what I promised? What were my exact words?"

"You said you wouldn't raise a sword against her. What, you plan on pummeling a troll into submission with your fists? Good luck with that, buddy."

"Ye of little faith."

"Seein' is believin'."

I shook my head. "Not in this world. You should know that by now."

She scowled.

The door shuddered.

"Well, we're about to find out if Murg took your deal or not."

"Let's hope she did. I'd hate to think what the Dawn Lady would do to us if she found out."

"You—what she'll do to *you*; it's *your* plan."

I stared at Cassie.

She snorted. "I got your back, relax."

Kids, their humor is never as good as they think it is.

The door shook, looking ready to jump off its hinges. One last jolt, and the door settled. Murg's breathing sounded like an idling construction vehicle in the winter. The door opened and the troll's girth filled the way, blotting out the hall's light for a moment. Murg shut the door behind her and plodded in. Her hands were full.

I smiled and gave Cassie a knowing look. She muttered something about being smug under her breath. My coat was bunched and balled into a mess with the rest of my clothes and Cassie's. True to her word, there were no weapons in sight. I shut my eyes and hoped the troll hadn't bothered to dig into my jacket.

She held it up. A smile that would have made any dentist cringe played across her face. "Murg bring." The troll waved her clenched fist, sending the ends of my coat flapping through the air.

"Yes, yes you did. Thank you."

A little gratitude never goes amiss with the supernatural—especially the fae. Even the crudest of them appreciate thanks. And some appreciate the simpler things even more.

"I'm afraid we're a little tied up at the moment, Murg. I don't suppose you could let me down so I could slip into my clothes? We just want to get warm."

Murg's eyes flattened into slits.

I licked my lips and swallowed a trace of saliva.

"No." It was rather emphatic.

"Please?"

"No, first reward."

Cassie and I exchanged a quick glance. Her look said, "I told you so."

I stared at Murg and kept myself from scowling. "That hardly seems fair. What guarantee do I have you'll come through?"

The troll returned my stare, although rather blankly. I should have spoken in single syllable words.

"Do I look stupid?"

Murg gestured with her free hand, pointing a grimy finger to the chains. "Yes. You're stuck"—she jabbed her belly with her thumb—"not me."

She had a point. Having a troll outwit me wasn't one of my finest moments.

"We have to meet somewhere, Murg."

The troll stiffened when I spoke her name. "One hand." She lumbered towards me, reaching out with granite looking nails.

I winced as they drew closer. "I think there's a key involved, no?"

The troll ignored me, clamping down on the chain link closest to the shackle. She pinched her nails together, and the fae metal broke. It was an impressive display. I wish the troll stopped with the first one. Murg made a point of crushing the next dozen links. One. By. One. She gave me a level stare after finishing.

"Reward."

"Open my coat, please." I smiled as best I could. It felt tight, like my skin stretched too far.

The troll let the entirety of our clothes, save my trench coat, fall to the floor. Cassie let out a muffled groan. Murg held the jacket by both shoulders, eyeing me in anticipation.

"A little closer please."

She snorted like a car backfiring. I could feel it. Murg took a single step towards me. I angled my body, sending my hand into the folds of my coat. My fingers brushed against something smooth and familiar. I folded my lips and kept my expression neutral.

"Reward."

I nodded and pulled my hand back without removing it from my coat. "Let me just slip into my coat. Your reward's in my pocket. I can't exactly go anywhere, can I? You saw to that." A little flattery never hurt.

Murg gave a self-satisfied grin. I slipped my arm halfway through the sleeve, keeping the flat edge of what I held pressed to my forearm.

"Okay, check my right pocket."

The troll slipped a thick finger into the coat. Her eyes ballooned. The Murg's body twitched once, and she hooked her finger inside the pocket. It came out with the crook of her digit cradling a penny.

He *did* give good advice.

Murg grinned. "Copper."

I nodded. "All for you. One big, shiny penny. You can't find coins like this in Faerie. It's rare."

Murg's eyes grew larger upon hearing the word rare.

"Are you satisfied, Murg?"

The troll shivered and rolled her neck like a crick had formed. "Murg happy." She clutched the penny in her fist and turned her back to us.

"Don't spend it all in one place!" Cassie's smirk faded as the troll ignored her, head ducked and focused on her hands.

There was a heavy thud as the door slammed behind her. Wood cracked and splintered. The door hung as if its weight was too much for its support all of a sudden.

Luck. A terrible thing to rely on, but every bit helped. I would take any extra stroke as it came.

"So...that went well. We got our clothes back, you got a free hand to scratch whatever itches you want, and we're still stuck. Good plan. A for effort. F for execution."

I shut my mouth, but my laughter made its way through my nose as a series of light puffs. It wasn't long before I let it out completely.

"Oh snap, you've lost it. Great. Now I'm stuck in here with a senile old man."

I pushed my hand through the rest of my sleeve and brandished the dagger.

Cassie's eyes lit up. "You ninja! You going to pick the lock or something?"

"Or something." I grinned and pointed to my remaining shackle. "Of faerie make. What do you think will happen if I introduce it to steel?"

Cassie's eyes brightened and she smiled. "I think we

should find out."

I grinned. "Then let's."

Her smile grew into something feral, and her fiery eyes sparkled in the dim light.

I grimaced as I twisted my body so I could reach the shackle. The knife point hovered an inch from the faerie metal. I licked my lips in anticipation. I wasn't sure what would happen if I touched the blade to the shackle.

It was like throwing dry leaves onto a dying fire. Pale yellow and violent blue lights sparked into existence, arcing across the metal. There was a low groan as the shackle deformed. The fae material sank in on itself, darkening in color like it had been charred. It no longer felt as tight around my wrist. I jerked my arm as hard as I could. The metal crumbled.

Cassie whistled.

I bent at the waist and gave the same treatment to the shackles around my feet. The muscles along my back twinged like string about to snap. The dungeon hadn't been kind to my body.

They rarely are.

"Come on, come on, come on." Cassie fidgeted.

I was by her side in an instant. "Keep an eye out behind me."

She nodded as I pressed the dagger to the first of her shackles. After a series of lights belonging to a child's fireworks display, I freed Cassie.

"Thanks. Come on, let's get our clothes and bounce."

I stared at Cassie.

"Leave."

"Ah. Yes, let's do that." I let my jacket fall to the floor and scooped up my clothes. I turned away from Cassie as I slipped into them. A wolf whistle filled the dungeon, and I snapped straight. There was a fit of giggles behind me. I turned and scowled.

"What?" Cassie threw her hands up defensively.

I sighed and shrugged my way through my shirt. I tried not to watch as Cassie wriggled her way into her pants. It wasn't right, but it would be a lie to say a part of me didn't find it appealing.

I'm old, not dead.

I cleared my throat and turned my head.

"You're adorable."

I grunted and looked back. Cassie shoved her hands through her dragon styled sweatshirt and flexed her fingers.

"God this thing feels good, and warm."

"Let's go."

"You have an idea of how to get out?"

I shook my head. "No, but I have this." I waved the dagger. "And there's bound to be a fae nearby who does." I gave her a smile that was all teeth.

"Dude—no offense, but you can be scary."

"Good." I tightened my grip on the knife. "Because I'm going to have to be. It's time to show the fae that humans can be just as dangerous."

Chapter Twenty-Four

I centered myself in front of the door and took a step to the right, placing myself in line with its hinges. The planks making up the wood weren't in great condition after Murg's coming and going. I took a breath to steady myself, stepped back several feet, and exhaled. I ran forward and kicked, throwing all of my weight into the blow. My heel crashed into the wood. There was a crunch as the wood around the hinges gave way. The door fell to the ground with a weighty *thud,* much like Murg's footsteps.

Cassie hissed and swiveled her head. "Think anybody heard that?"

"If they did, it's all the more reason not to stand around gawking."

She narrowed her eyes and stuck her tongue out at me.

"Let's go, stay close." I stepped onto the door, which creaked and moaned as I walked over it.

"Yeah, no doubt. One itty bitty dagger and the two of us against a butt load of faeries. Great odds."

"At the end of the day, Cassie, odds are just numbers. Remember that."

She snorted. "Yeah, well, some numbers can get you killed."

She had a point. I made sure not to let her know it however.

Both sides of the hall were empty, for now. I silenced the paranoia within and chose a path. With a nod of my head, I motioned for Cassie to follow and moved. The hall was made of the same stone as the room had been. I placed a hand on the wall, dragging it along as we neared the first corner. The way ahead forked into two paths.

"Which way?"

I shrugged.

"Eenie meenie miney mo?" Cassie returned my shrug.

"We're escaping the Dawn Lady's imprisonment. I don't think that's an acceptable method of choosing where to go."

"Do you have a better idea?"

I blinked then sighed. I waved my finger between the two choices. "Eenie meenie miney mo." My finger settled on the path to the left.

"Works for me." Cassie nudged me with her elbow. "What do you think is at the end?"

"Well, look at it this way, we're going to find out when we get there."

"Yeah, not a fan of that."

"Neither am I." I jogged forward a few feet and settled into a more comfortable pace. The path was longer than the one before. It twisted and wound like a maze.

"Hey, John?

"Yes?"

"What happens when we get out of here? Like back wherever the forests and grass...and the flippin' sky are? Won't we still be in her domain?"

"Yes."

"And, uh, how are we going to deal with a Faerie Queen who can knock us out with a stare?"

I kept my voice low. "Let's hope we won't have to."

"So, a 'cross that bridge when we get to it' sort of thing?"

"Not in Faerie. Not in any of the domains of any of the queens."

"Eh?"

"Do you know what lives under the bridges in the Fair Lands?"

Cassie's gulp was audible. "Trolls?" Her voice was whisper soft.

"Can you think of an easier way to get a few pieces of copper here and there? Block the passage of anyone going anywhere and demand payment. That's what trolls do. They hamper one's passage and travels. Even the human trolls do it."

Cassie buried a light laugh in her hands.

"Keep it down. We don't want to be heard."

The air smelled of concentrated sugar. There was a burble like a piece of large diesel equipment thrumming to life. "Too late."

"Down!" I grabbed Cassie and pulled her to the floor.

A car crash sounded above us as the troll's hand reduced a portion of the wall into sediment and debris. Murg's lips were twisted into a sneer, and the whites of her eyes were threaded with red roots that seemed to throb. This was an unhappy troll.

"You tricked Murg!" She hefted a fist overhead and slammed it down.

Cassie pushed herself from my grip and scrambled to her feet. I rolled as fast as I could. The floor rumbled with a shockwave that vibrated through my ribs and into my teeth. My eyes spun as the force made its way to my skull. Murg pulled her fist from the crater and fixed her reddened gaze upon me.

Contrary to popular belief, being in the spotlight isn't always desirable.

Murg took two steps forward and reached out for me. I wasn't fond of that plan. I squirmed and backpedaled across the floor, making it just outside her grasp as her fingers tightened. Murg's other hand was balled tight, kept to the side. It almost seemed locked in place.

I settled the dagger into my palm and gritted my teeth. Murg charged, and I pushed myself to my feet. I sprang towards the troll and sank my weight. The troll passed as I tumbled into a neat ball and came up behind her. I pivoted and used my hips to help send the blade into a neat arc towards the creature's back.

There were three kinds of screams. The kind a pressure cooker makes when relieving itself. The defiant roar a man makes fighting a monster. And the sort only the fae can make when struck by steel and iron.

Murg's scream was a shrill and rolling cry. The skin and

muscle of her upper back split like wet paper. The edges turned an angry red and flaked into a crispy black within seconds. Murg whirled around, her eyes redder than before.

"You promised." It sounded like an accusation. Murg remained still, her body heaving in exertion. Her shoulders spasmed in what I presumed was pain.

"I did." I didn't drop my guard, keeping the dagger raised high before me. "I promised not to attack you with a sword." I gave the dagger a twist, making sure Murg took note. "Does this look like a sword to you?"

Murg's lips trembled. Her eyes narrowed, and her chest shook. "You tricked me!" Something deep resonated in her throat. It exploded into a roar as she rushed me.

Cassie moved before it registered.

My coat tightened around my body. I stumbled to the side as she pulled me away. The wall burst as the troll barreled through it.

"John." Cassie helped steady me from falling. "Maybe we should run now?"

"Good idea." I shook my head in an effort to clear it. All it did was make the inside of my skull throb. "Go." I gave her a gentle shove.

Cassie nodded and took off. I blew a puff of air through my nose and took three steps. The fourth step didn't come on account of the mantle of my coat hugging my chest. The hug tightened and my feet left the ground. Murg's breath tickled the back of my neck. The smell of cotton candy surrounded me.

"Murg going to throw you—hard. Going to smush you. Crush you. Make you flat. Then, going to drink you."

My mouth dried. As far as threats went, they were rather intimidating. Murg was certainly scary for a troll. "That's a graphic list of things to do to me, Murg. A bit redundant as well, if I may point out."

Murg snarled.

"I don't suppose it would be too much to ask you to skip over the repetitive bits of smushing, crushing and flattening me?"

Murg's deep rumble intensified. It was a pointed no. "Bye."

I shut my eyes and hoped Cassie had made it far enough that Murg couldn't follow.

An incoherent, warbling cry echoed through the halls. It grew louder, and closer. I opened my eyes. Cassie came into view, charging towards us, screaming like a lunatic. Murg froze. Her grip on me faltered, but not enough for me to free myself. It was quite the sight to see Cassie rocketing towards us like that. I couldn't imagine what was going through the troll's mind.

Cassie let out a bloodcurdling cry and leapt into the air. Her feet connected with Murg's belly in a ballistic missile of a dropkick. She fell to the floor the next second. Murg wasn't the least bit perturbed by her assault. The troll flicked her wrist and I tumbled through the air as I was callously tossed aside. I hit the wall and felt like I had been in a car accident. My vision seesawed, and I had the desire to retch. I buried the feeling as I saw Murg reach for Cassie.

Her mistake.

I matched Cassie's battle cry and lunged at the troll. The dagger bit into the meat of her shoulder. It was Murg's turn to scream. I tore the dagger free, making a mess of the troll's arm as I did. Ichor coated the blade and the surrounding tissue of the wound. Murg shifted her body, sending the back of her hand careening towards me. I sank to my knees and jabbed. The blade bit into the troll's knee. Murg howled and took a step forward before collapsing onto her good knee. Cassie seized the opportunity to jump onto the troll's back. Her fists pummeled the back of Murg's skull.

I sank the dagger into the troll's arm in rapid succession. Not once did Murg use her good arm to retaliate.

"Wait!" Tears and mucus coated the troll's face.

I held my arm steady, the dagger hovering a hand's breadth from Murg's eye. I waited.

"No more."

That was a first. I hadn't seen a troll submit before. Submission was part of the way their tribes worked, but it wasn't something they did to outsiders. In fact, I wasn't sure if it was even allowed against someone outside their tribe, much less a human.

"Why?" My voice was sawdust over gravel.

"Murg help."

I fought the urge to snort and spit in her face. "I distinctly remember that not too long ago, you proposed—what was the word—*smushing* me."

Murg blinked through her tears. "No more."

"Give me one good reason not to kill you now."

The troll gulped and looked to her many wounds. "Murg already dead."

I froze. She was right. If any other weapon had caused those wounds she might have been able to survive. Trolls are a hardy bunch. The steel was already poisoning her body. Murg wouldn't last much longer. Her breathing was already ragged and tight. I raised my hands and lifted all but my thumb and index finger from the dagger.

"Cassie, get off of Murg, please."

She gave me a look that told me what she thought of the idea. She wasn't a fan, but she hopped off the troll's back. Cassie skipped several feet away, giving Murg a wide berth. The troll met my gaze, her eyes shaking in their sockets.

"Murg, I'm going to ask you something now. You can say no. I'll understand if you do."

Murg nodded.

"Can you take us to our where our weapons are? Can you lead us out of here?" It was worth asking.

People, and even the supernatural, can surprise you.

A thought crossed my mind. Murg knew she was dying, and the dead have nothing to lose. Maybe my decision not to finish her was a bit rash. My fingers curled around the hilt of the blade, and I braced myself for the troll's answer.

"Yes."

"Good answer, Murg." I relaxed my grip on the weapon. "I don't suppose it would be too much to make you swear on it, would it?"

Murg's eyes lost their focus for a moment before regaining clarity. She looked her wounds over, then me. Her expression spoke volumes I wagered the troll could never give voice to.

"Fair enough. Do you..." I reached out with my hand, knowing I couldn't do much to lift the troll. It was the gesture that mattered. Sometimes gestures could carry as much weight as actions. Although, truth be told, I hoped Murg declined to take my arm. A troll pulling on the limb would likely tear it from my body.

Murg shook her solid, bulbous head and grunted. She pushed herself to her feet, wobbling a bit and placed an arm on the wall for support. The troll leaned forward, taking in deep, dry breaths. One last inhale and Murg straightened her body. "This way." She didn't turn back to look at us.

"Come on, Cassie." I waved a hand for her to follow as I fell into step behind the troll.

Cassie made her way beside me before I motioned for to stay several steps back. If anything happened, I wanted to place myself between Cassie and the troll. She would be safer that way.

A light poke drew my attention. I looked to Cassie and shrugged. She rubbed her arm and nodded to Murg's back, keeping her voice low. "Dude, look at her."

I did. The troll's wounds were festering. Sickly masses formed around the decaying edges of skin and muscle. It looked like a form of necrosis.

I felt a pulsating throb in my leg and shuddered. *Is that happening inside my body right now?* I shook my head and banished the thought.

The troll lumbered at the best pace she could manage. Her breathing grew drier and more strained from the effort.

"Murg," I said.

The muscles along the troll's back shivered and convulsed. She stopped and didn't look back. "Yes."

"Thank you."

Murg remained still, her head tilting up to regard the ceiling. The silence stretched longer. Whatever she was thinking, I could feel the weight of it. Murg's head lowered and she fixed her gaze ahead. "Welcome."

Of the things I could have expected her to say, that was the least among them.

The troll walked on, and we followed. Silence came along for the stroll too. I wished it hadn't.

There's something disconcerting about the quiet at times. It can be peaceful. It can stretch into awkwardness. And then it can unsettle you when you realize you're walking with a troll, deep underground in the domain of an angry Faerie Queen. I wished for noise other than thunderous footsteps.

A scream tore through the halls, causing my skin to ripple. I retracted my wish.

"What was that?" Cassie rubbernecked, her eyes wide and her posture quickly tightening.

Murg snuffled and turned back for a brisk glance before looking ahead. "Bad fae. Punishment."

Cassie looked to Murg then back down the hall. "Remind me never to be a bad fae."

Murg sniffed the air twice. "Too late." The troll took off, her pace quicker, causing me to lengthen my strides.

We walked for five minutes. After that, I lost count. Murg's pace slowed until she came to a complete stop. To say she didn't look good would have been an understatement. She turned her head and met my eyes. I sucked in a breath. Murg's face was matted with tears mixed with blood and something else. I couldn't make it out, something like sweat and a layer of almost liquid tissue. Her eyes were an unhealthy yellow, and ropes of throbbing red lined them.

She pointed to a door. "Here." Her voice sounded like breaking strings.

I pursed my lips and regarded the troll. In the short time I had come to know Murg, she had gone from impressively large and ferocious to frail and haggard. Her mass had shrunk. It was like looking at a starving greyhound. She had been a bear of a creature. Her body no longer gave off a cotton candy-like smell. Now she smelled like an astringent—cold, sharp, and harsh. The entirety of her skin was the color of eggplants. One of her fists was still clenched firm. I could see the muscles in her forearm quivering from the effort.

"Murg—" I cut myself off, shutting my eyes and taking a deep breath. "I'm sorry." It was an odd thing: one second she was trying to kill us, and the next, she was helping us. Death did curious things to people and the supernatural alike.

Cassie came to my side. "I'm sorry, too."

Murg blinked as best she could. The action caused strings of ichor and other fluids to thread between her lids. "Me not." Murg stopped and breathed in and out three times. "Way of things. You learn." The troll pressed her back against a nearby wall and leaned there. Murg's eyes fluttered and she sunk slowly against the stone until she was on the ground.

Murg the Troll passed seconds later. Her fist never opened.

"Wow." Cassie cleared her throat, breaking the silence that formed in Murg's death. "I didn't think that would happen." She cleared her throat again.

"What?" I kept my voice to a hushed whisper for more than one reason.

She rubbed her nose with her sleeve. "That I'd feel sad watching a troll die." Cassie turned her head away from me and pulled her hood up.

"I know what you mean. It's because you're a good person, Cassie. And maybe because there was a bit of good in Murg as well. People are complicated, so are the paranormal." I nodded to Murg's closed fist.

Cassie followed the gesture and then arched an eyebrow.

I knelt and reached towards the troll's fingers, prying them open with care. A copper coin sat comfortably in the center of her palm.

"She...held onto the coin? That one little penny?"

"What did I tell you about a penny's value to trolls?"

"I know, but still...it was just one. I mean, it can't have been Murg's only penny, could it?" Cassie blinked twice and folded her lips.

"Think back to when she attacked us, Cassie. Murg's fist was shut tight and she fought one handed. I'd wager that Murg held on to the penny since I gave it to her. She had no intention of letting it go. It meant a great deal to her. Copper coins mean a lot, but I told her it was rare. It was a mortal copper coin. She believed me. She valued it because *I* told her it was valuable."

"She believed it just because you said so? That doesn't make sense. I mean, why?"

I looked at Murg's prone form and sighed. "Belief is a power all its own, Cassie, never forget that. Belief changes people, and things—it empowers them. Or it can destroy them. This isn't the time and place for this talk though." I took Murg's giant fingers within mine and closed them. "Let her keep her penny, she earned it."

I got up and grasped the door handle. It wasn't locked.

The room was bare, damp and dark. It seemed to be a theme around the place. A room, just a room and nothing more. But one with a number of items heaped unceremoniously on the floor.

Among such things were a cavalry saber, a pistol, and a sword-shield combination that Tatiana would have disemboweled me for losing. Technically speaking, they were entrusted to Cassie, and she had lost them. I found them, and a great deal more.

A storage room. There were piles of things taken from all manner of beings. Belts, clothing, weapons—old and new. The temptation came over me to bring along sharper implements. I exhaled through my nose and shut those thoughts away. More swords wouldn't do me any good if I didn't have the arms to wield them. I stuffed my pistol into the folds of my coat, fastened my sword and turned to watch the hall.

Cassie finished seconds later. "Come on, we have to

find a way out."

"We do. I'm not sure how though, not when our guide is..." I glanced towards Murg's body.

"I can try opening a Way out of here?" Cassie shrugged.

"Do you think you can?"

Her hips shifted, and she adopted a challenging posture. I raised a hand by way of an apology. Cassie's eyes shut and she stuck her tongue out between her teeth, biting down on it as she concentrated. I waited for time and space to be brushed aside.

It never came. Cassie blinked and her eyes shook. She placed a hand to her head as her balance wavered. "Are you okay?"

"Yeah, I think. I feel like upchucking. Just trying made me feel sick."

"You're too tired. We haven't eaten well in a while either. Don't push yourself; we'll find another way out." My words didn't have an immediate effect on her. She still looked a bit crestfallen. "It's okay." I broke off contact to peer down the many paths. They were as confusing as they had been before. I imagined they were that way by design.

Dungeons are no good if they are easy for prisoners to navigate and escape from.

Cassie squirmed inside her sweatshirt, sniffing the air as she did. "At least it doesn't smell as dank and earthy in here anymore."

"What?"

"The smell—you didn't notice?"

I hadn't and followed her lead, taking a whiff. She was right. It smelled fresher, almost like the ground after a showering of rain. I looked at the path Murg led us through. It was canted ever so slightly, inching its way up. We had been traveling higher and higher the whole time, and it had escaped me. The shift in elevation was subtle.

Clever. I fell to the floor, flattening my body as best I could.

"Um, John?"

"I think I'm onto something, Cassie."

Her voice became a muffled grumble. "What is it with boys and dirt and shit?"

I ignored her, pressing my cheek to the earth and watching. One of the paths crept up higher than the rest. Our way out. I got to my feet and brushed the dirt from my clothing. "Come on, I found the way out."

"By kissing the dirt?" She looked skeptical.

I couldn't blame her. I growled instead; she got the point.

Cassie followed as I led the way. "How much further do you think this place goes on?"

"Hopefully not much. Keep your nose at work though."

She sniggered. "When in doubt, follow your nose, huh?"

"If it's good enough for a wizard, it is good enough for us." I glanced back and winked. "Watch the ground carefully. It rises along the right path."

Cassie nodded. "Gotchya."

My spine felt like it swiveled through my back as another scream carried through the halls.

"What do you think is going on down here?"

I raised an eyebrow and stared at Cassie. "You met the Faerie Queen. You saw her temper. Do you really want to know?"

Cassie swallowed and shook her head. "Guess not."

"Me neither. Watch my back."

"Always," she whispered.

The air grew thicker and fresher as we advanced. Soon it was close to resembling the quality we experienced in the Dawn Lady's court. I wasn't sure if that was a good thing. The air became something that could be felt as I inhaled, and light fell in beams through the holes and cracks around us. We were getting closer.

"Look." Cassie pointed to a path going off into a corner. It rose considerably higher than the neighboring ones. "If that isn't a clear sign of where to go, then I don't know what is."

I paused and took everything in. "It's obvious—too

obvious."

"Oh, come on. Not everything is a conspiracy in the world of magic and monsters, you know?"

"We just escaped a dungeon belonging to a Faerie Queen."

Cassie's lips twitched and her eyes flared. "You know what I meant, smart ass. But, hey, we can always stick around here—with the screams, the probable torture, and all the faeries around us. Then there's the whole bit about you being infected by some magical whatsit and the mystery of who's hunting little old me?" She crossed her arms beneath her breasts and stared at me.

"Yes, you're right, of course—"

"Of course." She smirked.

I sighed and stepped onto the path, my hand falling to the hilt of my sword. "Be ready for anything."

"The motto of my life recently."

"It's a good one."

Cassie exhaled. "What's a girl have to do for it to be Netflix and cake?"

There were some answers even over a hundred years of life couldn't give to you. I pushed ahead and ducked as my hair brushed against the structure above us. My back ached as I leaned forward to avoid scraping my head. The roof shrunk the further we went along. Planks of wood came into sight, narrow but sturdy in appearance.

"Stairs." I drew my saber and waved it towards them.

Cassie groaned. "My mortal enemy, we meet again."

I tried not to laugh. If I continued to encourage her, there would be no end to the jokes.

"In Faerie, everything can be a mortal enemy." My tone could have been lighter. Cassie sobered, and I realized that perhaps I should have just laughed at her comment. The first board took my weight with a solid thud. "Draw your sword, and keep your guard up."

She pulled Tatiana's blade from its scabbard and held it firm in both hands. I gave a nod to the top of the stairs and picked up my pace. Cassie kept herself a single step behind until we made it to the door. I placed a hand on the knob, twisted and flung it open.

My free hand came up to shield my eyes from the bombardment of light. I could only imagine Cassie did the same. The light refused to relent, flooding everything around us.

"Cassie, back up! Get downstairs!"

"What, why?"

I reached out blindly, hoping to shove her back.

"Fa. And so, choices made—my curiosity still lingers. Come, Timeless, let us speak."

Cassie's gulp was audible. "Out of the fire—"

"And into the frying pan." I tried peeking out from under my arm, but the light stung. "I feel like I should say, 'I told you so,' about how obvious the door was."

"No one likes a know-it-all."

Chapter Twenty-Five

The light dimmed enough so I could lower my arm and make out the Dawn Lady. She stood five feet away with a group of beautiful and heavily-armed Daoine. I took a step back, keeping my saber raised and pointed towards them.

"I think not." Her words snapped through the room, and my spine. "Stay where you are."

I did. I felt rooted to the spot, and by the looks of it, so did Cassie.

"You escaped, impressive. Not many can elude Murg in the tunnels below."

I kept silent.

The Dawn Lady turned her head from me to Cassie, and then back again. Her eyes closed and she nodded in understanding. "Fa. Murg has fallen."

The queen's voice stirred something in me. Waves of melancholy, heartbreak, and disappointment washed over me. I choked and sputtered.

"And how did poor Murg come to pass?"

Of all the questions she could have asked, the Faerie Queen had to pick that one. It wasn't an easy answer. Or one I wanted to give. It hardly mattered; the Dawn Lady was perceptive.

Her eyes drifted to the blade in my hand, narrowing on the blood marring its surface. The queen's gaze lingered on the knife for a minute of silence. She lifted her eyes and locked them with mine. They narrowed further. "Steel."

Every one of the fae around her stiffened. Their faces hardened with their posture. "That is the second time you have touched steel to something in my domain." Technically it was the third time if we counted the shackles. "Do you know what it feels like for a fae to touch steel?"

I kept still and silent.

Her voice sharpened, making my dagger seem dull in comparison. "Would you like to?"

I didn't have the chance to respond. She moved faster than I could register, appearing by my side instantly. Her body blurred. My muscles twisted as I was forced over, and the Faerie Queen's fingers dug into my shoulder.

"It's a pain that cannot be explained—only felt." She was right.

Heat blossomed in my infected leg and spread through the limb. It wasn't uncomfortable by itself; it was what came with it. Millions of invisible fangs sank into every nerve in my leg. If it weren't for the queen holding me, I would have collapsed to the floor.

My muscles spasmed and knotted. It felt like the insides of my body were boiling. Out of the corner of my eyes, I saw Cassie fidget before rushing towards me. The queen didn't break eye contact with me as she waved a blind hand. Cassie crumpled to the floor.

"Stop." I couldn't feel much of anything in my body, only the heat. My voice was coarse and almost nonexistent. "Stop, please."

She didn't. "Did you stop? Did Murg ask you to?" Her voice warbled, sounding like it was coming through walls. "Did she say please? Answer me!"

There are many terrible things in this world: hurricanes, wildfires, blizzards, and earthquakes.

They paled in comparison to a Faerie Queen's anger.

I choked on my own voice, pain, and what little fluid remained in my throat. "I'm...trying to." She released her hold but the knives pricking my body didn't leave. "I'm sorry."

The world exploded into bright, sharp colors as the queen's hand connected with my face. My chest bounced off the floor, and I lay there focusing on breathing. It was a small miracle that my lips hadn't split and that I still had teeth in my mouth.

"My Queen," said a voice that I couldn't pinpoint. One

of the Daoine I assumed.

My vision cleared, and I saw the Dawn Lady approach. She looked down at me, her expression a mixture of pain and anger. She held the stare for several seconds before turning away. "Pick him up."

Two Daoine rushed to obey her command, hauling me to my feet. The queen flicked her hand in a dismissive motion towards Cassie.

She blew out a large breath and sat up. "Ugh." Cassie eyed the queen and swallowed whatever she was going to say.

"Why didn't you kill me?" It wasn't the smartest question to ask. A sane man would have been quietly grateful and not pressed the issue.

"Because"—the queen stopped to take a breath—"the Dawn Lady is a role of many things—understanding, the warmth of compassion, and hot anger. My decisions are influenced by my emotions. I *care*. I care for those under my protection and in my domain. My power comes from those things, among others. Do you understand?"

I didn't, but felt I should nod anyways.

"It means I must also take care to balance those emotions. I am angry about Murg's death." A fire built in her eyes that died seconds later. "But killing you will not bring her back. What I wanted in a weaker moment, I resisted." She lifted her chin, almost in defiance; of what, I don't know. "Besides, you are already dead."

"Come again?" My body may have been burning, but chips of ice settled into my stomach.

The queen pointed to my leg. "You will be able to move, but not for long. I suggest you seek help."

Cassie interposed herself between the Dawn Lady and me. She snarled. "You *are* the help—or were supposed to be."

The Faerie Queen waved an airy hand. "Fa. Why should I? He took the life of one of mine. It is a small blessing I refrain from taking further action."

Further action. I understood what was happening. "The

infection, whatever it is—you've accelerated it."

The queen's gaze was unflinching. "Yes."

Cassie took a step towards the Dawn Lady, prompting her guards to bristle. The queen raised a hand, and they stopped their motions. Cassie quivered. Her face was a hard-set mask of anger. "Fix him...now." Her voice was a whisper that could have cut through steel cabling.

If only it were that easy to intimidate a Queen of Faerie.

"I cannot. I would not in any case."

"What?" Cassie looked over her shoulder to me for clarification. I had none.

"It is not my nature." The queen motioned with her hand, grass and all things green burst through the floor. "I am growth—life. It is not my nature to hamper the growth of something, even that." She nodded to my leg. "It is not my place."

Cassie puffed up and locked eyes with the queen. There was a noticeable difference in their height, all in favor of the queen. Then there was the power. But Cassie held her ground and stare with the Dawn Lady. It was something I planned to remember forever.

"Then make it your place," she growled.

I winced and took a step towards Cassie.

The queen looked past her, and focused her attention on me. "You should advise the child to take care of how she speaks, and to whom."

Cassie's fist clenched. "The child is right here."

The queen's attention turned back to Cassie. "For now."

The Daoine guard took a step back. I took one forward. The simple set of actions showed who was prudent, and who wasn't.

Prudence is overrated at times.

I covered the remaining distance and placed my hands on Cassie's shoulders. She glanced at me, and I eased her away from the Dawn Lady, taking her place in between.

"She can't do this to you, John."

"I can"—the Faerie Queen glanced at Cassie before

turning back to me—"and I will."

"So then, Monarch of the Morning Court, where does that leave me?" I had a feeling I knew what her answer would be.

"In need of help."

I was right. "So what do you suggest, oh Queen?"

Her lips spread into a wide, shark-like smile. The light in her eyes intensified and shadows played against the walls. "Leave. Run. Flee—as far as you can, Jonathan Hawthorne." An arctic lance shot through my legs and spine. "Leave my realm, if you can." She cast a quick glance to my leg and her grin widened further.

I nodded. It was good advice. Cassie didn't seem content, however. Kids.

"How 'bout something better than that? Like, go here, do not pass go, do not collect two hundred dollars, or run through these woods?"

The Dawn Lady arched an eyebrow and the corners of her mouth twitched in what looked like amusement. "Advice? Very well, *never* run through the woods in Faerie, child. Walk. Be silent. For those that inhabit them have wonderful hearing. They love nothing more than to take young, mortal women."

Cassie's expression slipped. "Um, I think we're good for now. I'll stick to fortune cookies from now on."

"Fa. Beware fortunes, they are fickle and ever changing."

Change. It hit me like a brick.

"Ah, now he sees. You understand where to go, who to see?" The queen watched me and waited for my answer.

I shook my head. "Yes. But why let me go at all? Why give me a chance to make it?"

"Oh child, who says you will make it?"

I blinked.

"The way from here to there is long, and not without danger. The paths are changing, like time, and her temperament. Do you understand?"

I didn't, not all of it at least, but I kept that to myself. "I do."

"Good." The shadows grew on the wall. Light ebbed and flickered back into clarity. "Now, run."

Chapter Twenty-Six

My leg felt like fire and smoke charred it from the inside out. Our legs pounded as Cassie and I clawed our way through tall stalks of grass.

"You think they're still after us?" Her breathing came in short, hard puffs.

An arrow scythed through the air and sliced through a stalk between us. I gave Cassie a look. "Yes, I believe they are."

"So, run harder, dude."

I did. The pain refused to subside. The heat remained, but I gritted through it. I only had one option: to make it to the border of the Dawn Lady's realm. If my leg failed me, I would die. If the infection spread too quickly, I would die. Another arrow landed near us. And if I was unlucky enough to be hit by an arrow, I would likely die.

It's been said death comes in threes.

Snickt. A trio of stalks fell from the arrows. Cassie glared at me as if this was somehow my fault. In a manner, I suppose it was. Something bothered me about the arrows flying around us. Something apart from the arrows themselves.

"Cassie."

"What?"

"Something's wrong."

"You don't say..."

"They're missing."

"Thank God!"

"They're fae."

A second of silence that felt longer.

She blinked rapidly. "Why am I not a Cassie shish kabob?"

"I'm wondering the same thing."

"Wonder and keep running!"

Another arrow lanced by, taking a bit of my coat along with it. In a fit of anger, I reached into my coat and withdrew my pistol. There was a violent *snap* as a round went off blindly behind us. There wasn't a scream to accompany the report.

Another volley of arrows impaled the ground around us. "It's a show."

"Yeah? Well, it's a good one—too good—very realistic. I hate it!"

"The Dawn Lady is driving us away, but she could kill us if she wanted."

"So why doesn't she?" Cassie stumbled.

I grimaced through a flare of agony in my leg as I reached for her. I caught her hoodie by the shoulder and kept her from toppling.

"I don't know." I cut off and focused on keeping my footing over a rough patch of ground. "I have trouble understanding you and Tatiana at times. What makes you think I could understand a Faerie Queen?"

Cassie managed to arch an eyebrow and shoot me a challenging look.

I changed the subject. "Look!" A dense grouping of trees came into view not more than several hundred feet away. "That's our way out."

"You sure? Won't they follow us?" Cassie picked up her pace, using her youth and coltish legs to put several lengths of distance between us.

I squeezed my eyes shut for a second and willed my legs to work harder, despite my condition. "If I'm right, they won't be able to." I sincerely hoped I was right.

"And if you're not?"

"You'll get that shish kabob you wanted."

"Not funny."

"Then run harder."

She did. I followed. Another report cracked out and for an instant, the arrows stopped. I squeezed off another round. A shrill yelp pierced our ears. Several outraged cries echoed in its wake. I let out a triumphant shout and pulled the trigger. *Click*. I faltered and had to correct my step or else fall to the ground. *Click. Click*. No matter how many times I squeezed, nothing happened.

I swore and pumped my legs harder. Whatever orders the queen gave her subjects, they appeared to have been thrown out the window. There was a chorus of spiteful hissing as the air filled with an uncountable barrage of arrows.

"Run!"

"I am!"

"Faster!"

We did. The trees closed. One hundred feet. Seventy-five. Fifty. I stopped counting and begged my body to give what more it could. We broke through the tree line and into the forest. Arrows sunk into the thick trunks like darts diving into a corkboard.

"Please...tell me we can stop?"

"Keep going until we reach a denser area."

"Why?" Cassie peered over her shoulder. "They're not following us."

Which was a relief. "And there's a good reason they're not."

She slowed her pace and gave me an accusing look. "You've led me somewhere worse, haven't you?"

"Worse is subjective." It was true.

"Yeah, so is bite me." Cassie came to a stop behind a tree three times my width. She collected herself, leaning against the tree and breathing deeply. "So, where are we?"

I placed my back to the tree and sank to my knees. It took me a bit longer than I would have liked to catch my breath. "A pathway. *The* pathway."

"Pathway to where, John?"

"The Twilight Lands. The realm of the Twilight Court and their queen."

There was no sound for several seconds save for our breathing. "Another Faerie Queen? Are you nuts? I mean, our first visit went so well, right?"

"She's different." Which was most certainly true. I didn't know if that was a good thing however.

Cassie said nothing.

"Her domain—her nature—is different from the Dawn Lady's, vastly so. One represents emotion, growth, the morning sun, all things life and in their youth."

Cassie remained silent, but she tilted her head closer, listening with intent.

"Twilight is more than just a shift in the time of day or light. It's a change in power. Remember that. It's a break between the dominion the other two courts hold over a day, and The Fair Lands."

"One court has better control over their time of day?"

I nodded.

Cassie let out a whistle as she understood the implications.

"The hours between dawn and sunrise, and sunset and dusk, is where the Twilight Court reigns."

"Balance." Cassie brought a thumb to her lips. She chewed on it before realizing what she was doing. She stopped, waving a hand for me to continue.

"Their queen represents many things, among them, change. A shift in time, power, change—in nature and all things."

"That sounds...important."

"It is." I gestured to my leg.

"Think she can fix it?"

"No, I get it now. That's not within her power. She can't reverse the damage, but she might be able to stop it from worsening."

"Good enough reason to go, I guess." Cassie followed my example and lowered herself, resting against the tree.

"There's more."

She let out a breath that was something between an exhale and groan. "Of course there is. Nothing is ever that simple."

"Not with the fae—no. There's been a shift in things in

the Neravene. Free fae, the trolls, have never acted like this before. They are only allowed limited involvement in the mortal world. Snatching children and people in the dead of night is one thing. Brazenly chasing you through the streets of New York—that's another."

"But what's stopping them, they're free?"

"Yes, but that means not owing fealty to a court. That doesn't mean they can run rampant. There are still rules, and if you break them, you risk the wrath of all three queens."

Cassie shuddered and looked away. It wasn't a pretty thing to think about. One Faerie Queen's anger had been enough for me.

"Okay, so whatever's pushing them after me has to be pretty scary if they're willing to risk a Faerie Queen smack down, right?"

"Yes, or offering obscene bribes in any and all currencies—money, power, information, and anything else useful."

"Wow, all that for me. Think it could be one of the queens?"

I prayed it wasn't. "The thought has crossed my mind."

"And?"

"I hope not, because then I would have no idea what to do."

"Oh...okay then. Fingers crossed that one of the Faerie Queens isn't tripping about her place in the grand cosmic scale of all things faerie and bitchy."

I snorted. The action made the insides of my nose itch and ache.

"I'm tired, John."

"I'm sorry, Cassie. We will figure this out, and then there will be no more running, I promise."

"I meant I'm tired now. The running and dungeon escaping worked a number on me. I want to sleep."

I looked around the dense forest. It reminded me of something from the other side of things, from home. It was purely simple. Nothing magical about it; nothing that stood out. Just a forest of green and brown, dirt and leaves. I glanced back at Cassie and flashed her a smile. "Sure, we can do that."

"You sure they—" She broke off and cast a look at the way we came. "You sure they won't come in?"

"We're between two domains, on neutral ground. If the Dawn Lady's subjects come in here armed and hostile...things would not go well. There is nothing physically stopping her army from entering. It's the implications behind the action."

Cassie raised a brow.

"It would look like she's attacking. They would risk starting a war."

"So we can sleep?"

"We can sleep," I confirmed.

Cassie gave me a quiet look that conveyed her thanks and slumped further, curling against the tree. I kept the smile on my face until I was sure she wasn't watching.

There were other reasons fae didn't step idly into the pathways between domains. I hoped none of those reasons took note of Cassie and me.

My eyelids fluttered. It felt like cement was flooding my bones and veins. Rest would have to wait.

I rose and shrugged my way out of my coat, carrying it with both hands as I made my way over to Cassie. I crouched, placing my jacket over her body. She didn't need the warmth, but I felt she might have needed the comfort.

A simple thing like a blanket, or a coat to cling to when sleeping, could offer a world of comfort. It was something she shouldn't have been deprived of in the moment.

I dusted my hands off and drew my saber. The immediate danger may have passed, but sometimes it was the things that weren't as obvious that could kill you. I wasn't about to let complacency be the cause of our death.

My fingers held tight to my blade as I walked several dozen paces away from her. I made sure to keep her sleeping form in my line of sight, should anything happen. Leaves and branches rustled above. I snapped to face the source of the noise. A handful of leaves and a few pieces of bark sailed to the ground. Other than that—nothing. I scanned the treetops anyways. Just as much nothing as before.

I lunged towards the nearest tree, the flat of my blade *thwaped* against the bark with a metallic cry. Nothing. Something hot and thick welled inside my chest, and I wanted to release it. I buried the angry scream and kept my eyes on the branches above. Invisible tendrils stroked the back of my neck; my hairs stood on end. I cast a quick look to Cassie. She was still there, fast asleep and content.

I took a chance and slipped behind a trio of tight-knit trees, moving deeper into the forest. My eyes were trying to keep track of everything above and around me. Soon, they ached and felt like wet paper left to dry too long in the sun. I pressed the heels of my palms to them. The pressure helped soothe most of the fatigue. I opened them and everything changed.

Light shone under lenses of ghostly blues and ultraviolet purples. They swam together in the sky above, painting a mesmerizing and ethereal picture. It was more like looking at a professional photograph of twilight than the actual thing. And what a photograph.

Gaseous indigo streaked through the clouds. Splotches of tangerine blossomed here and there. Twilight as only faerie could offer. And with the change of time and scenery, came a change of power.

When power changes, so do other things, like what creatures retreat, and which ones come out.

As if on a silent cue, softball-sized orbs of white light throbbed and pulsed in the distance around me. They darted and flitted through the forest at dizzying speeds. I had the feeling that if I kept watching, my eyes would be left spinning in their sockets for days.

One of the orbs ceased its hectic buzzing mid-flight. It hung in midair, bobbing in space before shivering in what looked like excitement. The pulsing light grew and flashed like a camera before hurtling towards me like a miniature comet.

I took a step forward and steeled myself. A silent countdown went off in my head. *Seven-six-five.* I shifted my weight, and dug my boots into the ground. *Two-one.* The saber arced through the air. It passed through the orb of light, but came out clean. I blinked and examined the blade's edge.

Chirping filled the air around me with the speed of a machinegun. I struggled to make it out.

"Ai-ai-ai-ai-ai!"

I whirled about, snapping the blade towards the sound.

"Eeeee! Watch it, beanpole!"

I froze. It spoke? I took two steps back and repositioned myself, keeping my guard up as I faced the shivering orb. "What are you?"

The light dimmed. My mouth parted and I was sure my eyes widened slightly. It was nearly half a foot in length, and seated upon something that was a bizarre cross between a diminutive pony and a dragonfly.

"Keep gawking, beanpole, it will make it easier for me to take your eyes," the little figure shrilled.

He—it sounded like a he—had angular, elfin features that on any full-sized person would have been androgynously beautiful. Curls of black hair fell to his ears and went well with his amber eyes. His skin was well-bronzed and much of it was concealed under what looked to be a dress made of moss green scales.

"You're…a dewdrop?"

"Oh-ho, what a most keen intellect and perception you are in possession of. Clearly, I am dealing with a genius of the highest order. Who knew they made humans that smart?"

I narrowed my eyes and waved the saber. "You're wearing a dress."

"Tunic!" The dewdrop quivered atop its strange mount.

"It goes down to your feet."

"Battle gown!" he amended.

I kept from sniggering and eyed his mount. It was a horse of pure white, its mane long and untamed, falling over the rider's thighs. The creature's front two legs appeared no different than a normal horse's, apart from their size. A series of braided dark cords crisscrossed their way from the hooves to its knees. Where the creature's rear legs should have been, its body narrowed, appearing pinched. It ended in a thick, fox-like tail. At least that's what I thought it was. The appendage whirred like the blades of a helicopter, as if it were keeping the thing aloft. That task was clearly being performed by the four dragonfly wings beating at an unperceivable rate.

I leaned forwards and squinted to get a better look at the creature's head. "Is that a horn?"

"Wuh-ho." The dewdrop leaned towards one of its mount's ears. "It has eyes that can see the obvious. What a wonderful thing."

I found myself regretting not cleaving the dewdrop more and more by the second.

"All Uniflys have horns." He said it like it was a well-known fact. Though if ever there was a name to describe the creature, Unifly was it, no matter how strange the name.

"And what a fine Unifly it is."

The dewdrop faerie bristled and looked around in an almost owlish fashion. "What are you doing here, biggun?"

I could have answered, or I could have gotten answers. "I'll tell you, if you tell me." I grinned.

The dewdrop puffed his chest. "Oh-ho, riddles, is it? Tell me, or I'll skewer you good!" He reached to his waist and drew a sharpened sliver of something.

I narrowed my eyes and focused on the object. It was a piece of whittled wood. It might as well have been a toothpick.

I eyed the tiny faerie and arched a brow. "It's not even a real sword."

His eyes flared and he quivered fiercely atop his mount. The faerie's face and ears flushed red. I almost thought plumes of steam would shoot out the side of his head.

"It most certainly is!" He zipped forward, thrusting with the tip of his weapon.

I flicked my middle finger. My nail struck just below the point. Wood snapped.

The Unifly hung in space, fluttering as its rider sat there, blinking. His eyes never left the splintered remains of his weapon. The dewdrop's lower lids welled with a lining of moisture. He flung the weapon to the side and spurred his Unifly. The creature bolted and perched itself on my nose. It was an effort not to go cross-eyed.

He hopped off his beast, and I felt a gentle weight like a leaf landing on my nose. The dewdrop marched up the bridge and stopped halfway. He crossed his arms over his chest and glared at me.

Eyes puffy and red, he jabbed an accusing finger at me. "You…monster! You foul, evil, wretched, giant, uncouth, dunderheaded, wooly-brained…human! How could you?"

My eyes watered from the strain of watching the little fae throwing its tantrum so close to the center of my vision. "You tried to stab me."

The dewdrop had the grace to look abashed, even if for a second. "Well, yes. You are trespassing in the realm of the Free Folk. We are the guard, the watchers; we are death!" A chorus of shrill cheers, enhanced by bobbing lights, erupted around me.

I bit my tongue and commanded myself not to break out in laughter. My body shook and betrayed me.

"You…find it funny?" The little faerie seemed beside himself.

"No, I promise." I raised a hand to reinforce my claim.

The dewdrop wiped his eyes with the back of his sleeve and stared hard. "You owe me a new sword, mortal."

I focused on him and blew a sharp breath. He was lifted from his perch atop my nose, and tumbled through the air. His Unifly sped towards him. The faerie righted himself in an impressive display of aerial maneuvering and landed on his mount.

"Rude! What else should I expect from a human?"

"You attacked me…"

"Syntax!"

"Semantics." I shook my head.

"That too!"

This was going to be a long, trying trip. I sheathed my sword and kept one hand up as a gesture of peace.

"Wise choice. A fight would not go well for you, mortal. You are surrounded." He put two fingers to his lips. A surprisingly loud whistle pierced the air.

The motes of light zoomed forward. They stopped five feet out, forming a circular perimeter around me. The lights died, and nearly one hundred dewdrops revealed themselves.

I raised my other hand as well. "You have me surrounded."

The faerie's eyes ballooned like he was surprised by the fact. "Erhm, yes, I do!" He flashed me a defiant and smug grin. "Now, you will answer our questions." He blinked and looked to the dewdrops around us. "Um, our questions?"

A fae on a bubblegum-pink Unifly buzzed over to him. She looked like a Brazilian model clad in a gown woven from starlight. She whispered in his ears, retreating after finishing. His eyes lingered on her as she flitted away.

I snapped my fingers.

"Ahem, yes, questions! What are you, and who are you doing here?"

I eyed the faerie askance.

He shook his head and tried again. "Who are you, and what are you doing here?"

"I'm traveling." It was best to be honest while being vague.

"Oh? From where? To where?"

I pointed behind me then pointed ahead.

"You think you're clever?"

I felt it best not to resort to sarcasm. "I'm heading to the Twilight Court."

Every dewdrop yelped. Their Uniflies sank away from me another foot.

"Not clever, not clever at all." His voice rose in pitch, and he kept his head on a swivel, looking over his shoulder as if he would suddenly come under attack. He dropped his voice to a whisper. "Why would you want to do such a thing?"

"You're free folk. Why not choose to be under the protection of one of the queens? Would it not be safer?" Tit for tat.

His face tightened and he clutched his stomach. "Thoeey!" He spat over his shoulder. "Hmph with the queens!" He thrust a fist into the air.

"Hmph with the queens!" echoed little voices.

The dewdrop looked around as if he was about to be caught doing something terrible, and his posture sank. Every other little faerie mirrored him. He looked at me out of the corner of one eye. "Do you think any of the queens heard us?"

I kept my expression neutral and stern. "No."

He breathed a sigh of relief. "Oh good. Messy thing, having to explain that to a queen. They do not take kindly to offenses."

I had an idea of what he meant.

"Um, where were we?" He scratched his head and looked to his entourage for help.

"Your name?" I figured it worth a shot.

"My name? Oh…" He blinked and caught himself before continuing. "Oh-ho, ha-ha. Excellent effort, mortal. Did you really think I was so stupid?"

He really didn't want me to answer that question honestly.

"Why would I give you my name? Don't you think I know what you could do with it?"

"I only asked because I wanted to know the name of the intelligent, rather cunning, and brilliant strategist of a fae who managed to lure me into this forest and surround me so effectively."

Dewdrops may be tiny, but their egos are the size of some states. Glowing praise goes far with them.

His cheeks flushed, and he blinked several times before turning to look at his fellow dewdrops. The faerie's lips pressed together and his body shook with excitement. "I did—I did." He practically vibrated atop his Unifly. "My name is Izzaroohoo Kallanhaen of the Big Tree!" The faerie with a mouthful of a name hooted and pointed at a particularly large tree nearby.

I bowed my head. "An honor to meet you, Izzaroohoo."

He beamed and bounced on his saddle. It took the little fellow a second, but he realized what happened. "Oi, you tricked me?"

I nodded.

"Most fiendish, well done! I don't suppose I can ask for your name now? After all, it is only fair."

It was. But not all's fair in Faerie.

"John." I didn't hesitate or give the appearance that there was more to my name.

"John." Izzaroohoo rolled my name around his mouth as if were trying to get used to the taste of a new drink. His eyebrows furrowed as his face turned pensive. "Are you sick, John?"

"In a matter of speaking."

"In the head?" He rapped his knuckles against his tiny skull.

"No."

"Are you sure?"

"Pretty sure."

"You must be. Why else would you want to visit one of the queens?"

"It's complicated. I need help."

"Well, of course, but not *that* help, not *their* help." His face made it clear that interacting with any of the queens was a horrible idea. He wasn't wrong.

"I don't have much of a choice."

"Well, can it wait? You should wait. Waiting is good." I couldn't tell what was moving faster, his mouth or his shaking head.

"Why?"

"It's not a good time." He gestured to the darkening skies and prismatic lights above. "If you're going to see the

Twilight Maiden, best wait until she's in a different mood."

I didn't say anything. I wasn't sure what he meant exactly, but I figured it had something to do with the shift of power and nature that just occurred in Faerie. "I don't think it can wait. Time is an issue."

He waved a dismissive hand. "Bah, you mortals are always in a hurry—never enough time. Make time."

I glared at Izzaroohoo. He sank further into his saddle and averted his gaze. "So what do you think I should do, oh wise and clever tactician?"

His chest swelled, and he bounced back to his previous position. "I think you should wait."

I shut my eyes and breathed slowly. As much as I hated it, the little dewdrop was useful...ish. At the very least, he had knowledge that might benefit me. "Do you know the paths through here?"

He nodded and bounced.

"Well that's something. Will you help me?"

"What will you give me?" An angry clamor filled the air. "I mean us—I meant us." He looked around to his fellow dewdrops with an apologetic expression on his face.

I didn't have much to offer the little faeries. "What would you like?"

"Honey?" His eyes looked like a flashlight had burst to life behind each one. dewdrops—like many little fae—had notorious appetites for sweets.

"I don't have that." I shrugged an apology.

The dewdrop pursed his lips and knitted his brows together. "Hmm." He cradled his chin between his thumb and forefinger. His eyes drifted down to my waist where they paused. He convulsed in a mixture of pure and uncontrollable glee. "Your sword!"

I exhaled and refrained from giving him a closer look at it.

"Yes-yes-yes-yes-yes!" His body shivered again. "You broke mine; I could use a new one." High pitched and frenzied shrills went off. "We, we. I meant we."

"It's several times your size…and weight." I patted the

hilt.

Izzaroohoo looked to the side, a bit abashed. "Well, that hardly matters, does it now?"

I breathed out slow and through my nose. Something was exceptionally wrong with this little fae. "What good is a sword you can't use?"

The faerie stopped, pursing his lips and furrowing his brows. A second later his eyes shot wide open. "Well, it's still a sword, isn't it?"

I gave up. "Yes." I nodded. "Yes, it is."

"Well, there you have it." He beamed, puffing his chest. "We'll take your sword thank you very much."

"It's steel." My words had a sobering effect. Thank God.

The dewdrop's expression faded. "Ah. Problems." He turned to address the surrounding crowd. "It's steel!" They shrieked and hissed in unison. He turned back to me. "What else?"

I sighed. I opened my mouth when another dewdrop flitted over to Izzaroohoo. Light-complected in every regard, short hair, and every bit as excitable as their scatterbrained leader. She chittered in his ear at a ballistic rate. Izzaroohoo nodded in concert with her words. It was dizzying to watch, like a conversation with caffeinated squirrels. They stopped just as fast as they started.

Izzaroohoo turned to me, his face hard. "Why didn't you tell me?"

"Tell you what?"

"About *her*!" He waved his arms and accentuated the word as if it explained what he meant.

"Her?"

He jabbed in the direction I had left Cassie. "Her-her-her-her!" Each word was punctuated with another jab.

I remained quiet.

"A girl! You brought a mortal girl!" He was beside himself with excitement. The dewdrop booted the flanks of his Unifly and zipped off.

"Wait!" I turned a shade too slow.

A micro hurricane of wing beats fluttered past me as every dewdrop followed Izzaroohoo. I ran after them. They were waiting for me as I skidded to a halt a few feet from the tree Cassie was sleeping under. The dewdrops hung around her like ornaments.

My voice was the sharp hiss of steam. "What are you doing?"

Izzaroohoo looked over his shoulder. "A girl!"

"I know. What…are…you…doing?"

"Watching."

My fingers flexed, and the small muscles in my hand knotted. I couldn't catch the fae if I tried. That didn't mean I couldn't entertain the thought of grabbing and throwing him. "Leave her alone. Let her sleep."

"Can we have her? We will take her!" Many of the dewdrops bobbed in agreement.

"No!"

Izzaroohoo looked crestfallen. "Why not?"

"Because, you cannot trade people like commodities."

"Why not?" He seemed genuinely puzzled.

Of course, human freedom was a peculiar, and unheard of concept to many fae. As far as they saw them, humans were prey, food, and tools. Things to be captured, tricked and lured—then bartered or used.

"Because that's simply not done."

"Why not?"

I pointed the saber at him. Izzaroohoo lost all interest in the moral reasoning behind my points.

"Ah, yes, well, doesn't matter much, does it? Heh." He shrugged. "Can you give us something else?"

Cassie groaned and shifted. "Urgh, what's going on?" She shifted again, bringing up a hand to rub an eye. "John, how long was I"—she smacked her lips—"out?"

"Not long. Don't overreact."

"What?" She blinked several times and sniffed. Cassie arched her back, shrugging out of my coat as she stretched her arms.

Izzaroohoo paid a bit too much attention. Before I

could do anything, both the fair and darker skinned dewdrops approached and cuffed him over his ears.

"Ow." He cupped his hands to his head. The dewdrop's yelp got Cassie's attention.

She looked up and blinked twice. My coat flew into the air as she flailed in panic. "Why's Tinkerbell riding a—"

"Unifly," I said.

"Right, yeah, sure, whatever." She cast a wide look around at the dewdrops. "Why are there tiny faeries everywhere? What did you do?"

I opened my mouth to answer, but Izzaroohoo had other plans. He darted to Cassie's face. "You trespassed upon our land. Now you will pay the price." He lowered his voice to sound menacing. It didn't work. "We will be taking you now, girl."

Cassie regained her composure immediately. She looked past the dewdrop to me, and then back to him, arching an eyebrow. To be fair, Izzaroohoo wasn't the definition of intimidating. She huffed out a breath that caused the faerie to cling to his mount.

He pulled himself together and shook his head vigorously. "Why are you mortals so…." He turned to his group. "What's the word I am looking for?" Another dewdrop flew over to him. "Ah yes, why are you so incongruent?" There was another whisper. "Oh, incorrigible."

I breathed several times, hoping it would calm my nerves. "Can we please stay on topic?"

Izzaroohoo shook his head and turned to me. "Ah yes, passage, guidance, offerings. Well"—he looked to the ground before eyeing me—"you don't have anything we want. Things do not look good for you, mortals." He drummed his fingers through the air in a manner that suggested it was supposed to be scary. Apparently, the faerie had forgotten his size. Frightening was a bit out of reach for him—literally. "You will be lost in these woods, forever, without us, of course." The dewdrop stuck his chest out and jabbed a thumb to it.

"Of course." My voice was dry. "There has to be something we can give you—within reason."

"Uh, John, what's going on?" Cassie rubbed the heel of her palm against an eye. "Part of me still thinks I'm out and this is a weird"—she broke off to regard the faeries—"really weird dream."

"They're offering to serve as guides through these woods, but there's a cost, of course."

Cassie's mouth twitched. "Of course. Isn't it dangerous to deal with faeries?"

I waved a hand to the little creatures. "Yes, but they're rather harmless, and we could use the help."

Cassie nodded, brushed herself off, and rose. She cleared her throat, drawing everyone's attention. "So, what can we get you—do for you?"

Izzaroohoo faced Cassie. He stood on the back of his mount and bowed at the waist. The dewdrop snapped to attention. "Izzaroohoo Kallanhaen of the Big Tree!" He hooted and pointed to the same tree as before. "It's the biggest tree around!" The dewdrop had the nerve to flash her a suggestive smile. He regretted it.

Two of his female companions zoomed in front of him, crossing their arms underneath their chests. He fell to his bottom and reined his Unifly back a bit. Izzaroohoo looked to me for help. I wasn't in a helping mood.

Cassie's lips folded. Her eyes shut as she fought the urge to laugh. "That's impressive; it really is a big tree." At least she was diplomatic. "Almost as big as your name." At least she tried to be diplomatic. "It's a mouthful."

Izzaroohoo blinked several times, too fast for me to count. "It is my name."

"Yeah, but you're in America now, so you're going to need something shorter, and easier."

"We're as far away from America as possible." I gave her a quizzical look. She returned it with one that indicated my point was irrelevant. I didn't see how.

She pounded the base of her fist into the open palm of her other hand. "Got it. You're, Izzy."

Izzaroohoo blinked again. "Izzy?"

"It's cool—different and easy to pronounce. Trust me, Izzy."

"Izzy…" His eyes narrowed and he tilted his head. "Izzy is a mortal name?"

Cassie nodded. "Yup. How about that for an offering, Izzaboobaboo…thingy? I give you a human name." She adopted a regal posture and look, raising an index finger like a sword. She brought it down gently to his head. "I dub you Sir Izzy, our guide."

I was sure the little fae's head would rocket off at any second. His face flushed and his head vibrated like it was a battery-powered toy.

He pumped his fist into the air three times. "Hoo." Another fist pump. "Hoo." A fifth pump. His compatriots broke into cheers and applause. "Names! Names!"

I couldn't believe it. Cassie was getting good at this. In a single effort, she offered the dewdrops something that cost us nothing, and made them our guides. She worded it in so subtlety—with the same skill any fae would have done. That's what made it frightening.

"Okay, I think we can work that out." She gave the dewdrops a great, big smile.

Flashes of light burst into life as the tiny faeries flew into a frantic buzz. Motes of all colors imaginable whirred around me as they fought to get into line. One by one, a dewdrop approached Cassie, practically quivering with excitement. Cassie was composed the entire time. Only the edges of her mouth gave away the smile she buried. Her finger touched head after head, naming them all. The entire ceremony took a handful of minutes.

The dewdrops formed a circle, strobing lights peppered us, making my temples ache. "Names!" Their cheers echoed around us.

Izzy held his hands up high, gesturing for quiet. They obeyed. "Thank you, beanpole and..." He looked to Cassie, bowing his head. "Now we celebrate—libations!"

"Libations!" the dewdrops echoed.

I raised my hand to silence them all. "We don't have any, but perhaps if we get a move on, we could attend to that?"

Every dewdrop's head lowered. Izzy looked up at an angle. "None? Not even one sip?"

"We have nothing."

Cassie came to the rescue. "If you lead us to where we need to go, maybe when we get out of here, you can follow me to get some soda."

Silence.

The circle closed into a tight-knit orb, rapid-fire chittering sounded off. Izzy popped out of the ball of dewdrops. "Soda? Is it sweet? Is it good?"

Cassie looked as if someone had drained her of all color. "Oh, you poor thing. Help us out and I'll show you the magic of soda." She shook her head, genuinely sad that they had never once tasted the sugary drink. "It's the best."

Every dewdrop's pupils dilated. She had them hooked in anticipation, and all for the taste of a beverage. I hoped we lived long enough to fulfill that promise.

"So, we have a deal? You'll lead us to wherever he says"—she thrust her chin in my direction—"for the names I gave you and the promise of soda?"

"Yes-yes-yes-yes-yes." Izzy bounced each time he spoke. "We will guide you through the perils of our land."

I kept from mentioning the land wasn't exactly *theirs*. I gave voice to another concern. "What perils?"

I shouldn't have asked. The Fair Lands were kind enough to answer.

The prismatic light passed into a darkness absent any stars.

"Oh dear," said Izzy.

A series of clicks, like cards in spokes, echoed around us. There was a low, guttural growl.

A dozen more answered it.

Chapter Twenty-Seven

"Ah, it seems waiting is no longer an option. We should flee."

"Sound plan. Lead the way." I struggled to focus my eyes and find Izzy.

"Oh, um, I see. You're mistaken." My gut roiled as Izzy spoke. "I meant that *we* should flee. I have decided that it is not in our best interest to help you. Thank you for the names. You can have them back. We'll be going now."

Click-clack-clack-clack-click-click-clack.

"Yes-yes, time to go."

"No you don't." I swept with a blind hand. I missed. "You agreed to her terms. Even the lowliest of faeries are bound to fulfill their word."

The clicks and clacks grew louder, and closer.

"Um, I'm starting to get really good at figuring out the sounds monsters make." Cassie was hard to make out despite being so close. "I wish I wasn't."

"What is it going to be, Izzy? Are you going to help us, or should I spread the tale of the group of tiny fae who broke their word? That isn't going to be good for the faerie community. If little dewdrops can break their word, what's to keep a Faerie Queen from breaking hers?" The diminutive fae hissed and flashed for an instance.

"No-no-no-no, bad idea. No, we don't want to get the queens involved—any of them. I think it's a good idea to help you, yes?"

I couldn't see Izzy, but I pictured him turning to his friends for agreement. They flickered once in differing colors.

"Yes-yes, we will lead you to safety. Come!"

A tiny gust of wind hurtled past my cheek. Izzy flying

by, if I had to guess. He looked like a comet, strobing and trailing a pastel limelight. A meteor shower came to life before us. Every dewdrop rocketed after Izzy, streaking through the air in a dizzying array of brilliant colors. A flashing orb of sunflower yellow settled near my face.

"Follow!" it chirped and took off.

I looked to where I thought Cassie was. "You heard the faerie, let's go. Don't forget my coat!" Something fluttered in the night. I reached out. My fingers brushed against my jacket. I turned and whirled it around, struggling to slip into it as I ran.

"Crap, I can't get this, argh!"

"Stop fiddling with your sword. Just run." Glittering orbs came in and out of sight between the trees. I tried to keep my saber up and ready.

"Got it." A nearby dewdrop's light glinted off Tatiana's sword as Cassie pulled it free. "Ah!" A dull, hollow thud filled my ears.

"Cassie?"

"Something hit me—the shield, I mean. Damn those things are like little cannonballs."

"Gremlins move fast. We should move faster."

"Good idea."

Clackclackclackclackclackclack.

I twisted on instinct, my arm sailing wide. The saber met some resistance before cutting through a large hunk of meat. There was no cry from the fallen gremlin.

The dead don't scream; they leave that for their companions.

The clacking intensified. I didn't want to stick around to see what a mob of angry gremlins could be like.

"Don't stop, keep your shield up, and if you're thinking about swinging your sword at something—don't think—do it!"

"Got it." Cassie puffed, keeping pace with me.

Two dewdrops slowed their speed, allowing us to catch up with them. Ultraviolet pink and electric blue pulses illuminated our immediate surroundings. Hunched simian creatures darted between the trees.

She paused behind a tree, hiding while catching a breather. "Don't suppose I can ask why it got all dark and spooky all of the sudden?"

I stopped beside her. "Neutral ground." Something clacked by me. I staggered and stumbled to the side, avoiding a blur of green mass. "It shifts according to the domain of the three queens. Morning." I swatted at something with the flat of my blade. There was a shriek. A fist-sized plume of fire erupted as the gremlin writhed and hobbled away. "Twilight hours." I took off, signaling to break into another run.

"And midnight, shit!" Cassie's blade hummed through the air. There was a *snickt* as she cut through a bit of gremlin.

"Yes, and now the neutral territories fall under her domain, even if it's for a short period. It's to deter invaders. They change so quickly that you can never tell when you'd lose your advantage in crossing. We just happen to be passing through at the worst of times."

"We *always* seem to do that!"

She had a point.

Another *thud.* Cassie yelped.

"Cassie?"

There was a scuffle of leaves, clothing, and loose ground.

"Stop!" I skidded to a halt. The dewdrops around us froze. My eyes moved faster than my head as they scanned our surroundings. A sound like knives scraping sent invisible ice picks into my spine. "Cassie?"

She groaned.

I honed in on the spot where I heard the sound. Cassie shook her head. The dragon hood flopped down. She was on her hands and knees. The sword had fallen from her grip and was a foot away. That wasn't the only thing on the ground. An ugly, lizard-monkey hybrid was recovering from its impact with her sturdy shield. It got to its feet, flexing its talon-lined digits. It opened its maw and leapt.

"No!" I moved, but not fast enough.

The dewdrops got there first. There was an explosion of flickering lights that belonged in an underground nightclub. My eyes reeled in their sockets. The back of my brain cried for a reprieve. Knots formed and bundled within my stomach. I was going to be sick.

The gremlin had it worse. It crashed to the ground, twitching and convulsing like it had lost control of its body.

"Attack!" screamed Izzy.

Where did he come from?

An electric rainbow of dozens of dewdrops swarmed the stunned gremlin. I heard what sounded like darts being thrown, and then I heard a gremlin scream. I had to say, it sounded pretty good.

"Protect the Namer! The Princess of Soda." Izzy's commands were met with raucous, squeaky shouts.

I clutched my stomach. I didn't know if I was going to vomit or laugh till my gut exploded. Princess of Soda? A second later, I had my answer. My body shuddered as the watery contents of my stomach left me. I fell to my knees, body quivering as my laughter carried through the night. Why settle for one or the other?

The spinning carousel of lights ceased their techno throbbing. A gentler glow covered the area around us, one I hoped would deter the other gremlins. Faerie light didn't seem to harm them like man's light, but it was certainly effective at incapacitating them.

"Are you okay?" I kept alert, peering through the dewdrops' light.

Over two dozen eyes reflected the multicolored lights from around the trees. That many gremlins. I licked my lips. The odds could have been worse.

"Yeah." She spat at the ground and recovered her sword, using it to prop herself up. "How bad is it?" She brushed her hood back, glaring into the trees.

"Bad."

Cassie spat again. "Always is."

"Izzy," I said.

He was by my side in a millisecond. "Yes?"

"What's the best way to deal with a small army of angry gremlins?"

He bit his lower lip. "Gremlins are always angry."

One good breath was I all needed to remain calm. "Izzy."

"Running is always a good idea. Flying is better, but you mortals stink at that."

Two good breaths were what I needed.

"Izzy…"

"Huzzah, I have it!"

"You do?"

"Of course he does, John. Izzy's a little genius. Give him some credit, right?" Cassie's compliments caused the tiny fae's face to flush red. She was good at buttering him up.

"We run—fast."

I was going to kill him.

"We lead them deeper into the woods. We go deeper into the Free Folk territory." Every dewdrop erupted into panicked chittering.

"Why does that sound like a bad idea?" There must have been a good reason every one of them protested it.

"It is dangerous, very dangerous. We will cross through parts that do not belong to the little folk."

Ah. Neutral ground wasn't so neutral after all. "And what else calls this place home?"

"Bigger things. Fiendishly fiendish fiends! Bigger than gremlins—scarier and hungrier!" The dewdrop was not good at putting one's mind at ease.

"Doesn't sound like we have much of a choice." Cassie pointed towards the group of glowing eyes inching forward.

The gremlins grew braver with each passing moment. I didn't know how long the dewdrops' light would deter them.

I nodded. "Lead the way, Izzy."

He flashed once and zoomed off. Several faeries followed him, serving as an advance guard. The remaining dewdrops formed a spinning ring around Cassie and me.

There was an impatient squeak. "Get closer together. Move!"

We obeyed, closing the distance between us. Cassie and I ran. Our sudden movement galvanized the cautious gremlins into action.

Hunched, scaly monsters jumped into the air, swiping their talons. All but one of them missed. A blinking mote of sky-blue disappeared. There was a screech like tires tearing across a road. Dewdrops flickered like ill-maintained light bulbs. They whirled around us in a furious tempo before speeding towards the spot where one of them had fallen. They circled the dewdrop and Unifly. They screamed.

Cassie and I received a firsthand accounting of just how many little faeries called this place home. Every color imaginable and, some with no names, came to life around us. Trees bloomed into view under lenses belonging to abstract paintings. Hundreds upon hundreds—if not thousands—of little folk dispelled the darkness. Cassie pulled her hood over her eyes, hiding part of her face in the crook of her arm. I stuffed my head into my jacket and placed a hand over my stomach for added measure. I didn't want a repeat performance of earlier, especially inside my coat.

Thunderous buzzing filled the air like a hurricane of hornets. Ear-splitting cries and a bombardment of lights found their way through the lining of my jacket. The noise grew and grew, threatening to continue until our ears likely bled.

The sound died as quickly as it had began. There was no winding down; it simply stopped. The frenzied staccato of pulsing lights were a muted, soft glow. I let my jacket fall back around my shoulders, and Cassie brushed her hood back. The lights revealed a grizzly scene.

The ground was caked in gremlin bits and blood. The lights gave the fluid a fluorescent sheen, none as powerful as the coating of blood on every dewdrop and their mounts.

"*They* did that?" Cassie's eyes were wide and her mouth

hung open.

I'm sure I had the same look. "Big things—small packages."

A green comet spun in a lazy circle around the fallen dewdrop. Izzy's light vanished as he sunk to the ground. He dismounted and knelt by the dead faerie. It was the fair-skinned woman who had thumped him over the head earlier.

Her Unifly was grazed across its torso. For something that small, it was fatal. I'm surprised both her and the mount weren't bisected clean. Pinkish-white blood blanketed her thigh down. Just a graze from a talon and her artery had been nicked. She'd bled out. The dewdrop looked paler than possible. Izzy hugged her. Glistening streams flowed from his eyes, catching the light coming from the other faeries.

The little folk sang.

If the greatest wind musicians gathered to play, they would've taken notes. The dewdrops' voices rose and sank, somehow carrying through the forest. I didn't know how beings that tiny managed it. As far as I was concerned, it was magic.

Through it all, Izzy's voice rang the loudest. The singing lasted a full minute. A part of me wished it never stopped.

Cassie rubbed her face with the heel of a palm. "That was beautiful. Izzy…are you okay?"

Izzy didn't respond, nor did the other dewdrops. They hung like silent candles. My teeth ground together as the muscles in my leg shook and ached. I had no idea what would happen if I left the infection untreated. I had no interest in finding out. I pushed the pain down to its place and took a step forward.

"Izzy, I'm sorry." I didn't know what to say. I didn't even know her name. "Izzy?"

The dewdrop ignored me.

"Izzy, we should go. We can't linger."

"Night has passed, so has its dangers, and it has taken its toll." The dewdrop lifted his fallen comrade as if she weighed nothing.

Pale sunlight crept through the trees. *When did that happen?* I was used to the Neravene's strange passage of time, but every part was different. The realm of Faerie grew stranger by the second.

"'Kay, I think their clock is broken. Twilight, night, and now morning? Dude, it hasn't been an hour."

"No, it hasn't." The change was so subtle that, with everything going on, I hadn't really noticed. Witnessing a death could do that to a person. "I guess it changes frequently as a form of disruption. Entering here means that one second your court has an advantage, and the next—disadvantage. That can lead to disaster."

"Doesn't seem like a good idea to travel these paths then." Cassie's eyes searched me. She was looking for the reason why I dragged her into these woods.

"No, but the lesser of two evils." I pointed back the way we had come. I turned to Izzy. "What are you going to do?"

Izzy carried the woman to his Unifly and lay her across its back. He mounted, pointed a finger to the sky, and made a circular motion with his hand. All of the dewdrops save for Izzy streaked into the air, trailing lights of yellow, red, and orange. They vanished from sight.

Light flashed from behind a tree. A trio of dewdrops returned a minute later. They formed a triangle around the dead Unifly and blurred into action. I didn't know how they did it, but a hammock woven out of grass appeared beneath the dead creature. The dewdrops fastened an end to each of their mounts and booted them into flight. They carried the deceased Unifly into the air and looked to Izzy for direction.

"There will be an accounting." He looked ahead, focusing on something that none of us could see.

"Izzy"—I kept my voice calm—"those gremlins weren't part of any Court. You can't expect anyone to answer for what happened."

He whipped his head to face me, his tiny eyes flashed with green heat. "It happened under night. Its queen will answer."

It was odd to hear such a small thing's voice carry so

much weight. I pressed my lips together. He was angry and rightfully so. That didn't mean I wanted to see the dewdrop challenge a Faerie Queen. It wouldn't go well.

I looked around the brightened woods and the corpses of the gremlins. I reconsidered my thoughts about dewdrops.

"We'll see to her properly, Izzy. I promise."

The dewdrop turned away from me, looking down at his friend. He brushed a hand over her eyes and muttered something only he could hear. I had an idea of what it was.

Apologies are easy to understand, even when they're silent.

Thorns raked the insides of my leg and I grimaced. Cassie caught my expression before I could hide it.

"Leg?"

"Yes."

"Let's move then." She brushed off her pants, tightened her grip on her sword, and set off.

I admired her resolve. She was adapting better to the Neravene the longer we stayed. She trundled forward, taking the lead. I settled my saber in my palm, cast a look to Izzy, and hobbled after her.

The dewdrops didn't move.

I stopped and looked over my shoulder. "Izzy?"

He shut his eyes and inhaled. The faerie slipped a hand through the reins and nudged his beast after us. In a second he was floating by my ear. "We will take you to meet a queen." A queasiness formed in my stomach. "But not the Twilight Maiden. We will meet the queen of all things dark. The Shrouded Mistress and the Bringer of Stars. We will take you to meet the Mother of Night. I will settle with her."

In that moment, I didn't know who to be more frightened of: Izzy, or the darkest of the Faerie Queens.

"Izzy, my condition, it's getting worse."

He gave me a look that told me he hardly cared. One of his kind had died helping us. He'd be damned if anyone stopped him from making things right.

"You can settle with her as well. I don't know the cost,

and I do not care. For us, the cost has been large enough." The dewdrop faced straight ahead once again.

Faeries came back into sight and followed his lead, looking forward. Their pace was a slow drift beside us. It was oddly beautiful seeing thousands of floating dewdrops around us.

"I'm not sure I want to, Izzy."

"No sane being would. Now isn't the time for sanity."

Part of me wanted to tell him that maybe it was. Rushing off angry and grieving to start something with a Faerie Queen wasn't a good idea.

"My condition is bad. I need the Twilight Maiden. Her domain is change. She could stop its progress. I'm infected."

Izzy sniffed the air and paid no mind. He clearly did not care.

"Izzy, please."

"She died helping you."

He was right. "I know, and I'm sorry, but if I don't get help, I might die. I promised her"—I nodded to Cassie—"that I would help her. I don't mean to break my promise."

"The Mother of Night can help you."

I had a feeling she could, but I wasn't sure if I wanted her help.

"Her domain is more than darkness. It is the end of things—all things. Her domain is where trees go bare, when things and beings creak and crack. It is where time goes to be forgotten and lost. She is the harbinger of the long night—of death." He gave me a steady look.

"All reasons why I'm hesitant to meet her."

"She can kill what's wrong inside you," said Izzy.

"Or me, and I'm opposed to that. I'm rather fond of myself—and life."

"She will not harm you." Izzy's voice was cold iron.

I opened my mouth to speak, then reconsidered. A thousand living plumes of light flickered behind us. Small in size, but large in numbers. It was one hell of an army to have at our backs. I smiled. "Thank you, Izzy."

He bowed his head. I matched the gesture. We walked

in silence, catching up to Cassie. I sidled up beside her and nudged her with my elbow. She took a step to the side, raising an eyebrow at me.

I arched one back. "Are you okay?"

"Are you?" She let her gaze fall from my face to my leg before meeting my eyes again.

"I will be." I hoped.

"Well, that's the point of paying this Twilight chick a visit, right?"

"It was." My words hung in the air for a moment.

Cassie blinked. "Was? Where are we going now?"

I told her.

"Oh, um, weren't we saving her for last?"

I nodded.

"So she's the Faerie Queen of darkness, death, gloom and doom?"

I nodded again.

"Right... So on a scale of one to ten, how important would you say your left leg is?"

I glared at her.

Cassie raised a hand to calm me. "Now, hear me out. Ten being very important, I can't live without it. One being...not so much, because you can always chop it off and not have to bother the scary Faerie Queen."

I sighed.

Her tone sobered. "There's going to be a cost, isn't there?"

"Probably."

"And if you don't pay it, she won't help you."

"Likely."

Cassie adopted silence, looking to everything in the forest but me. More trees, more flashing dewdrops passed—Cassie didn't say a word. I had a feeling she wanted to though. I gave her the time she needed to think.

She blew a light puff of air through her nose. "John?"

"Yes?"

"This is going to sound selfish, but..."

I waited.

"Pay it."

"I'm sorry?" She couldn't have been serious.

"Her cost—pay it." Cassie's eyes softened, she pleaded with them.

I said nothing. Honestly, I was reeling over how she could suggest something like that.

"John?"

I felt Izzy's eyes and ears on me the whole time. The next breath was long and slow, feeling heavier as I pulled it in.

My gaze fixed on Izzy as he flashed through shades of emerald, pine, and pastel lime. He looked me in the eyes, his expression grim. "A Faerie Queen's power is great; their costs are higher—always."

It didn't make me feel better. I eyed Cassie, letting Izzy's words speak for me.

She hugged herself and turned away. "I don't care about the cost."

"What?"

"I can't lose another friend."

Her words hit me like a nail being driven into a board.

I bit my tongue and let her go on.

"I didn't bail and run at first. I asked for help. I went to my *friends*." The word left her mouth with a sour note. "They told me I was crazy. One of them called the cops on me, so I ran. I haven't really looked back. I don't know when or if this will ever end." She gave herself a tight squeeze.

I placed a hand on her shoulder and gave her another squeeze. "It will. You'll be able to go home soon."

She looked at me, her eyes unsteady. "What if I don't want to?"

"I'm sure we can figure something out."

"Not if you're dead."

Ah.

"So, please, John, take the deal, if she gives you one. I need you around."

It *was* selfish, and it wasn't. I understood. There wasn't a doubt in my mind that if I were in her position, I would be asking the exact same thing. But some costs weren't worth paying—no matter the reward.

"She could ask me to do terrible things, Cassie. The queen *could* ask me to kill you."

She shuddered. "You won't."

"How can you be so sure?" I didn't look at her when I posed the question. It helped make my point.

"I guess I'm going to take it on faith. I'm not big on it, but, on this, I think I'm going to be." She seemed pretty sure.

"Fair enough, but we still don't know what the cost will be. It could be anything, any number of things."

Izzy flashed. "Yes."

"Whatever is it, we'll deal with it. Isn't that what you keep telling me?" A hint of a smile crossed her face. She wasn't deterred by any of this. I didn't know if that was a good thing or not.

"I guess that's as good a plan as any. How's this for an answer? I'll think about it on the way over there." I grinned.

"We're here." Izzy pointed ahead.

My smile faltered. Of course we were. I frowned and eyed Izzy askance.

There were no discernible markings to indicate a change in territory, the beginning of something new—anything. Nothing. The trees were a bit closer together. Some of them hunched towards one another, their branches crooked and touching like old friends trying to grab each other's hands.

I blinked and noticed there were rows of trees doing the exact same thing. A tunnel of arching trees and branches stretched back until the path was no longer clear.

It was something lifted out of a fairytale—the real ones. It wasn't foreboding in the slightest…

Cassie shifted under her hoodie. "It feels weird here."

"How so?" I peered down the path, narrowing my eyes. There was nothing I could see that would cause Cassie to shiver. I turned my gaze to her. "What's wrong?"

"You don't feel it?" She looked at me like I was missing

something obvious.

I shook my head.

She held a hand out, reaching towards the air between the trees forming the path. "It's like the air here goes cold. I can feel it pushing back, like there's an invisible wall of Jell-O." She shivered again. "Something ain't right. I'm getting a dark vibe. All's not well on the other side of this." She stopped and waved her hands in a dramatic gesture.

"Yes." Izzy's voice rose in pitch.

Is he frightened?

"This is the end of Free Folk domain. Beyond here lies Everlasting Night, a domain of darkness and darker things. That is what you are feeling. Cold, fear, hunger, and the creatures they belong to." Izzy touched the same spot of air Cassie did. "This…is where Faerie bends again; time shifts—so do light and power."

Cassie nodded. "Wibbly-wobbly, timey-wimey stuff beyond here, got it."

I followed their lead and raised my hand to the invisible barrier. Nothing. "I understand what's here, but I can't feel it."

Slender, warm fingers folded over mine. Cassie pushed my hand along with hers through the empty space. "How 'bout now?"

My hand pricked with the sort of warmth you feel when entering a hot room after being outside on a snowy day. The prickling ceased. Cold viscous sap took its place. It clung to my hand, chilling it to where the small bones inside ached and felt stiff. The frozen gel flowed into my wrist before Cassie pulled our hands away.

Warmth returned. Something else followed. Gentle, invisible currents of electricity rolled over and through my hand as she let go. I blinked twice.

A residual effect? It didn't emanate from the air ahead. The effect had come from Cassie. She was the source of that power. If we got out of this alive, I planned to take a long week of studying the Neravene and the Ways in my library. I opened my mouth and let out a slow breath. I was stalling, and for good reason.

"Okay." I sniffed and turned my hand over, eyeing Cassie. "Let's walk into darkness."

Cassie's hand fell into mine; I pressed my fingers over hers as she nudged me. "Could you not make it sound so terrifying?"

"It would be a lie otherwise." Izzy floated between us, doing little to boost morale.

I exchanged a knowing look with the both of them. We stepped towards the darkest domain in Faerie.

Chapter Twenty-Eight

Passing through was like walking into a powerful gust of cold, buffeting wind. It slipped through the openings of my jacket, pushing me back as if begging me to turn away.

I was sorely tempted to do just that.

We were surrounded by the sort of blackness found in the deepest reaches of the oceans. Places where the creatures lurking there had developed large, glowing eyes and fangs.

Large glowing eyes blinked at us in the distance. Presumably, whatever had those had fangs as well…

Pools of hideous orange watched us, sending only one message—prey.

I turned to Izzy's glowing form. It was a small reassurance, one that was snuffed out when I saw the faerie. "Izzy, where are the rest of your kind?"

He blinked, staring at me like I was asking a stupid question. "They remained behind."

"Why?" I fought to keep from turning around. Insects crawled over my skin. I could feel countless eyes on me.

"We've lost enough." He ran a hand across the dewdrop woman's body. "They stayed behind. The duty to settle with the Dark Queen is mine. The risk is mine." Izzy raised his head higher.

"That's commendable, Izzy; it truly is. However, I would like to point out *that.*" I gestured to the pair of fiery eyes.

"Ah…" The little faerie could have done better in responding.

"Hey, Izzy, John, um…don't suppose this would be a good time to be asking for another lesson in faerie monsters?"

"You took the words right out of my mouth, Cassie." I stared at Izzy. "Any idea what it could be?"

"They could be anything. The darkest of Faerie is home to many foul beasts."

"They?" I blinked and turned around.

They stared at us from all sides. I counted sixteen pairs of eyes. I was corrected a second later. Another orb of hot vermilion opened above each creature's pair of eyes. Three eyes. The list of possible creatures grew shorter. A fact I wasn't glad about.

"Oh." Izzy's light waned. "Well, that is most certainly not good."

"Izzy…" I kept from moving, going as far as to limit my mouth's motions.

"Barghest."

I swallowed the frozen lump in my throat.

"Yeah, that's either a really goofy monster…or something bad…isn't it?"

"They have three eyes, Cassie."

"Yeah, so really bad. I said that. Um, what are they?"

Izzy squeaked.

"They're a type of faerie hound," I said.

"So, faerie dogs. Doesn't sound too bad."

"Three eyes."

"Right, yeah, never a good sign."

"They're also known as goblin dogs."

"That ugly? Poor things."

"They have rows of fangs as long as your fingers, with four front ones that are even longer. They're built like leopards—long, shaved leopards that can jump, climb, and track scents for over tens of miles."

"Okay, not so poor things. Um, I take it I don't want to see these things up close?"

"I've never seen one, and I plan to keep it that way. I only know the stories about them. I don't know what they really look like."

"You do not want to, beanpole."

"Stop calling me that."

"But this is good." Izzy flashed viridian.

"Why is that?"

"Because you two are bigger than me." He puffed his chest. "The Barghests will chase you two first, and eat you. I can continue on my way to deal with the queen and seek amends."

"Only if the Barghests don't stop to get a faerie snack." Cassie's tone dimmed the dewdrop's glow further.

Izzy flashed again, and then his light went out. "I think our passage requires some measure of stealth."

"Good idea." Neither of them could see me rolling my eyes. I had the feeling the Barghests saw everything. "Why they aren't doing anything?"

"Don't give them any ideas, John."

"They are waiting, of course. Do you two not know how predators think? First they watch, then they watch some more. Watching is imperative to murderous beasts." Izzy's explanation wasn't helping settle our nerves. "Then, they attack!" He could have been a bit less enthused about the last part. "Barghests can outrun all of us with ease, and they are clever pack hunters." Izzy bobbed his head. "I don't think we can escape."

"Thanks, Tiny, how about a useful suggestion?" Cassie took a step closer towards me. She moved her sword. Every set of eyes followed its point and narrowed the next second.

"Don't. Move. Your. Sword." I reined in the urge to reach out and grab her arm. Further movement might have prompted another reaction from the faerie hounds. "Izzy…."

"Retreat? Retreating is always a sound strategy in the face of overwhelming and toothy odds. Especially when said teeth are accompanied by fearsome eyes and horrid, horrid-looking faces."

The Barghests let out a sound like motors starting in winter. Guttural growls echoed through the trees.

"Izzy, I have the feeling that you should apologize." I took a single step back. I shouldn't have. Every set of red eyes advanced a step.

"Ah, yes, I am very sorry if I have caused you creatures—mighty fine and intimidating creatures—any sort of offense and um…as recompense, I offer these two mortals to feast upon?"

"Izzy!" By Cassie's tone and posture, she looked ready to take a swing at the dewdrop.

"What? Can you place any blame on me?"

"Yeah, Izzy, we can blame you—a lot. Little buttmunch." It was nice to know that Cassie's creative vernacular wasn't suffering despite our predicament.

Izzy flared an electric green. "I most certainly do not munch on little butts."

I groaned. "Izzy, Cassie, quiet."

They listened—for once.

The Barghests advanced another step.

"We should go back." I eased Cassie back a foot. The Barghests growled, louder, and deeper than before. I inhaled and reached behind me, feeling for the barrier we passed through. Nothing. "Izzy?"

"Oh, well this is most unfortunate." He didn't seem proportionately disturbed considering our predicament.

"What is it?"

"It seems this particular path is…"

"Is what?"

"A one-way entrance only." Izzy let out a weak laugh.

I wasn't sure if the faerie could hear my teeth grating against each other. "So, we're in trouble, again."

"And it's your fault, John, again." I didn't appreciate her pointing that out. "So, what are the odds of us taking these things?"

"Picture fighting a group of sharks while you're weighed down by lead chains and are blindfolded."

Cassie mouthed the word, "Ah."

Izzy strobed in worry. My eyes stung, and I turned away from the only source of light. That was the moment I realized I was an idiot.

"Izzy, how bright can you flash?"

His face twisted. "I'm sorry?"

"The light." I pointed at him twice.

"Oh." He blinked as if he was suddenly aware of the fact that he glowed. His lips pursed and his body thrummed like a guitar wire being picked. Emerald light erupted, covering Cassie and me. "Is that sufficient?"

"How fast can you make it flicker?"

He blinked again, looking at me like I was crazy. I had gotten that look enough in the past few days. I was used to it now. "It's tied to our emotions and physical state. I am not a mortal commodity to be flashed and played with!"

I motioned to the Barghests. "Tell that to them."

A miniscule lump formed in Izzy's throat, one he swallowed. "Ah, excellent point." His face furrowed in effort. Green light strobed.

"Faster, brighter." The Barghests didn't approach. Good.

Izzy muttered something unintelligible about my request, but did as I asked.

"Okay, so now that Izzy's a one-fae rave, what good is that?" Cassie peered at the dewdrop through her hands.

I pointed to my eyes and then to the faerie hounds. "Night vision is a great thing to have in the dark. It's not so wonderful when—" I pointed to the pulsating faerie. "Deer in headlights."

Cassie grinned. "Nice, so what's the plan, run for it?"

I exhaled and gave myself a minute to think. I knew little about Barghests, but one thing was certain, they were pack hunters. I took in the ruby-like eyes and how they stared, unblinking. Predators loved a good chase. I wasn't inclined to give them one.

Bathed in Izzy's light, I motioned for he and Cassie to follow me. I took a step. The Barghests remained rooted. That didn't mean they stayed silent. Another rumble left their lungs in unison. It sounded like the onset of a storm rolling through the trees. I tested them further. I willed away the cold chains binding my left leg and took another step. The faerie hounds' eyes narrowed into angry red slits.

My legs felt like grains of sand flowed through them,

soft and ready to crumble.

Walking through a darkened forest full of goblin dogs has that effect on a man.

"Okay, so, they're just sitting there with a group stink face on." Cassie's head swiveled to all sides on alert for any further movement.

"For now." Izzy's light flickered and lost its brightness for a split second. The Barghests advanced several steps.

I hissed and glared at Izzy. "Keep the light up."

He did, pulsing brighter and creating a field several feet past where Cassie and I stood. Good, we had some wiggle room if we needed it. I hoped we wouldn't.

"Let's press things and see how we fare." I took three steps and broke into a measured walk, keeping my pace quick without pushing it. Cassie followed, Izzy floated above. The goblin hounds mirrored my advance, covering three meters instead of steps.

It seemed Faerie was fond of the metric system.

We pushed on, covering a dozen feet. That's when things changed. One of the Barghests broke from the pack and charged. It moved with liquid grace through the trees. A trio of red orbs closed the distance and its growls grew louder. The creature burst out of the woodworks and into Izzy's light. There were some views that stayed with a person forever; this was one of them.

The Barghest staggered and blinked in a stupor under Izzy's staccato of green light. It was a hideous cross between a hyena and leopard, with the mouth of a carnivorous fish. Shaved black fur with a large stripe of spiked hair running from the top of its skull to the base of its spine. It snapped at the air blindly, gnashing with teeth that could have easily skewered a limb. It was a wonder the creature could close its mouth at all.

"Bwa-ha!" Izzy pumped a single fist into the air. "Take that, devil hound!" His light intensified into a garish yellow-green that made my eyes want to water.

The Barghest seemed to hate it more than I did. It fell to the ground, trapped in a cycle of opening and shutting its eyes in disorienting pain.

"Not so fearsome now, are you? Great ugly brute."

"Izzy, stop antagonizing the demon dog." My hiss cut through the faerie's overzealous shouts.

"Why?"

I pointed my sword into the darkness. Reds eyes from all sides drew closer. "That's why."

"Ah, yes, the rest of them." Izzy's pleased mask slipped from his face. "I believe we should continue with our journey posthaste."

I shut my eyes and inhaled. This was not the time to hurt the little faerie. "Yes, Izzy."

He nodded and winked at Cassie. "Stay close, I shall protect you."

I exhaled through my nose.

"Rock on, Izzy." Cassie smiled back at him and pointed ahead.

"Don't encourage him, please." My words fell on deaf ears.

Izzy released a shrill hoot of triumph and surged forwards. We sped behind him, avoiding the thrashing Barghest as we paced. Killing it would serve no other purpose than to anger its pack. The last thing we needed was for them to be more aggressive. I didn't know how many of the creatures Izzy's light could repulse at once. I preferred to keep it that way.

The Barghest recovered and set after us, each of its paws tearing clods of dirt from the ground.

Some dogs never learn.

My legs quivered as we ran harder, keeping within the dewdrop's light. The rest of the faerie hounds decided they had waited long enough. They closed in.

"Ayeeeee!" Izzy's head bobbled as he looked to all sides. Demon dogs rushed us from every direction. "This is bad. Very bad. Very-very-horribly-bad. I blame both of you!" His light pulsed a weak, pale mint.

"You brought us this way!" Cassie pulled a few steps ahead of me, positioning herself in the brightest part of

Izzy's light. I couldn't blame her.

"Yes, well, that would imply that this is my fault, and that certainly can't be right." The dewdrop's face twisted in confusion. For something so small, he had an ego that dwarfed planets.

Two Barghests came at us from ahead, trails of gelatinous drool hanging from their lips. Izzy shut his eyes but flew on. I nursed the temptation to follow his lead, but kept my eyes open and a hand on my sword. If things came to it, I'd rather incur the pack's wrath than risk being bitten. A Barghest's bite never ended well according to the legends. Even being grazed was a one-way trip.

They split, increasing the distance between us.

"They're flanking us!" I slowed my pace to avoid risking a misstep.

Cassie caught on and shifted her attention to the Barghest coming to her side.

Izzy was ahead of us. "Back, fiends!"

His tongue protruded from between his teeth as he bit down. Izzy's eyes shut and his features tightened in concentration. The little dewdrop emitted a brilliant display of kaleidoscopic greens. Both creatures stumbled and lost a step. Cassie and I seized the moment.

I twisted, sending the saber arcing towards the nearest beast. It flailed as the blade nicked the tip of its blunted snout. Steam billowed as the tissue crackled and corroded. Skin peeled away, leaving a grim sight behind. Most of the muscle and skin evaporated from the creature's nose. I could see sinew and bone. It did nothing to diminish the Barghest's intimidating appearance.

The monster recovered quicker than I imagined it would. It bounded to its feet and snapped at my shin. I leapt back and swung blind. The Barghest yowled. One of its ears became notched, the steel imparting the same necrotic effect.

It wasn't enough. These things had a surprising level of tolerance to man's metal.

A yelp drew my attention. I cast a quick glance over my

shoulder. Cassie had hamstrung her foe, causing the beast to shamble back in retreat. Its red eyes never left us as it crept into the safety of its pack and the woods. I turned back to address the one before me. It was gone.

I hadn't given them enough credit. Their aggression was tempered enough not to be reckless. I hoped the rest of the pack wasn't comprised of smart monsters. A dumb one every now and again would be a blessing.

"How much farther, Izzy?" I had no desire to draw out this confrontation longer than necessary.

"Why would I know?"

"Because you brought us here!"

"How in Faerie does that imply I know where I am going? I know this is the path to Darkest Faerie. That does not—in any regard—mean I have been here before!" He shook his head as if I was the one being absurd.

"Izzy, find us a way out of here!" Cassie flashed him a glare before turning her attention to the path ahead. The dewdrop nodded and increased his speed. We followed.

Whoever was holding the Barghest's leashes was done doing so. They let go. The entire pack barked and set on us.

Izzy sounded like a miniature fire alarm. Cassie released a torrent of profanity and references I would never be able to understand. And I decided it was the perfect moment to regret many of my life's decisions.

The first Barghest leapt into the air, putting too much power into its jump. It soared by my head—missed—and found itself in the center of Izzy's light. Cassie and I gave it a steel death. Its dying howls spurred its pack mates.

One Barghest slinked behind my legs like a shadow, too quick and fluid to be struck by a sword. I bumped into Cassie in my efforts to avoid its teeth. The beast moved out of the light to try again.

Two Barghests took to the air, both going for Izzy. They missed, but Cassie didn't. The tip of Tatiana's blade burrowed into the belly of a Barghest. Its own momentum carried it forward, dragging the blade through its body as it gutted itself. Noxious fumes and intestinal bile filled the air.

The creature and its insides crackled and burned into nothingness.

Something snarled to my left. I whirled, sword flashing to meet it. I was too slow.

"John!" Cassie hit the ground, her fingers digging into the dirt as she was dragged out of Izzy's field of light.

"Cassie!" I lurched forward, dropping to my knees and reaching out with my free hand. I caught the ends of her fingers. They slipped through. "Cassie!" I scrambled after her, struggling to get to my feet with the flurry of movement around me.

Dull pain blossomed in my shoulder as something crashed into me. Spittle landed on my jacket, and a guttural breath huffed above me. My head spun. Three red eyes squinted through the now lime light. The Barghest snarled and blurred out of sight. I breathed a quick sigh of relief. It was short lived. Rows of spears broke the skin of my leg, piercing the meat of my calf.

My throat was scraped raw by my scream. Like sharks smelling blood, the Barghests erupted into a frenzied glee. Dark fur rushed towards me as the first lashed out with a *snink* of its jaws. I flailed and launched my right leg into a blind kick. Something crunched and the Barghest let out a yowl. A warm fluid slipped through the gap between my jean's cuff and my ankle. The pressure increased in my already infected leg and I struggled to see through the tears. Izzy's light grew dimmer.

The ground slipped away. I buried my fingers into the dirt much like Cassie had. My fingers ached as they clung to small rocks and solids bits of dirt. I raked at anything that would keep me in place. The Barghest shook its jaws, and the last of the air left my lungs in a scream. I let go, and the creature dragged me into the darkness.

The pathway receded from view as the Barghest pulled me into the thicket. Brambles and thorns clawed my coat, hoping to tear through and pick at my soft flesh. Red eyes closed in around me; over them—a basil light waned.

Izzy.

The dewdrop let out a noise somewhere between a whistling tea kettle and a screaming power drill. The high-pitched noise sent a hair-raising shiver through the hounds. They bowed their heads, eyes shut as they whimpered from the sharp keen.

The little faerie flitted closer towards me. “You shall not take him!” He threw back his head and let out another throaty roar. Izzy burst into radiant light comprised of greens for which there were no names. It was like looking into a star.

I shut my eyes and buried my face into the ground. My calf twitched, and dirt filled my mouth as I moaned in pain. The pressure was gone. I coughed and sputtered through bits of soil.

Izzy still burned brightly. It was rather beautiful. Every inch of me wanted to lay there and watch.

My leg grew cold. No red eyes in sight, good. I buried my hands into the ground and hauled myself to the shining dewdrop. “Izzy?” I racked my throat for whatever moisture I could. “Izzy?”

The faerie’s light dimmed to a gentle glow. His eyes were dilated, crazed. The irises carried an irradiated light. They calmed seconds later when he looked at me like it was the first time he’d seen me. “Are…are….” He shook his head, raising a hand to his forehead. “I think I should rest.” He tumbled off his Unifly.

“Izzy!” I crawled forward and fell flat as I sent my hand out to catch him. The dewdrop landed in my cupped palm.

He could barely open his eyes. His light was barely visible. “Are…you okay?”

“I am, Izzy. Thank you.” I kept silent about my leg. Threads of fire licked through the wound. Making it to the Faerie Queen was the least of my concerns.

“They took her. I am sorry.” Izzy let out a deep breath. His eyes fluttered.

“I know, Izzy.” I watched the dewdrop’s eyes close and his chest sink. “I know.” I closed my fingers around him as his light disappeared.

The forest grew darker.

Chapter Twenty-Nine

I lifted Izzy to my throat, brushed aside my coat, and slipped him into a pocket above my breast. His Unifly watched me in silence. I got the feeling it was acutely aware of everything transpiring before it.

My leg grew distant. Waves of icy foam swirled through it. I coughed and used my good leg to brush against the bad, pulling my jeans up as best I could. The small part of my leg I could see was the color of a plum. In all my years, I had never bothered to get a medical degree, but I was certain that wasn't a good sign.

I frowned at the bite mark. Blood should've stained my jeans and the ground far more than it had. Instead, it had turned to a stringy jelly the color of grape jam. The thick, dark syrup oozed from the wound. I could only imagine what was happening inside.

I stared at the Unifly. "I don't suppose you could help?"

The creature bobbed in the air.

"I didn't think so."

I sighed and sent my hand forward, burying my fingers in the dirt again. I inched forward. Every foot I dragged myself added more misery to my body. My leg burned as dirt and other material ground their way into the wounds. I could see my breath as I pulled myself along. The forest was growing colder. My throat dried and my lungs ached. I didn't know how much further I would be able to crawl like this.

Izzy's Unifly kept pace above me, hovering and carrying the fallen fae woman. The dewdrop had promised to lay his friend's body at a Faerie Queen's feet. I gritted my teeth and made sure he would be able to keep his promise. I clawed forward.

Cassie was taken, God knows where. I clawed forward. I was going to find her and make sure she was safe. I clawed forward. My best bet was finding the domain's Faerie Queen. My fingers tore up more of the ground as I dragged myself further.

There comes a point when the body can't be pushed anymore. A point when you break down. I told myself that this wasn't it.

I stopped, cold air tickling the insides of my mouth and throat. My chest heaved, and I looked up. Izzy's Unifly looked back. It watched me with what looked like simple curiosity.

"This is the best I can do."

The Unifly didn't respond. Of course, how could it?

I spat and threw my hand into the ground. The muscles in my back and arm strained. Nothing. I exhaled. *I'm not done, not yet.*

Then there are the lies we tell ourselves to inspire us, to drive us forwards. Sometimes they work. Sometimes they don't.

I screamed. It carried through the forest, echoing, but I was certain it went unheard. The Unifly fluttered ahead, and its propeller like tails slowed their flurry of movement. It lowered itself to just above my brow. The Unifly stared at me with his button-like eyes.

"What?"

It blinked.

Some creatures are incorrigible.

I licked my lips and formed a tight circle. Air filled my lungs and I puffed a breath through the focused ring of my mouth. The Unifly flapped through the torrent of air, its features tightening in disapproval.

"Do something useful or piss off." I grimaced. The pain in my leg doubled. Infected during the events in the Long Gardens as well as the Barghest's bite, I didn't know what would happen.

The Unifly rose and disappeared behind me.

I lay there, immobile. My breath shortened; my heart

felt like it was made of aged rubber. Every beat came too strong to be normal. The forest lost focus, and my head felt light. I wriggled my fingers. They didn't respond.

I had never met Death. I always imagined her like the stories, anthropomorphized into a hauntingly beautiful woman. Beautiful or not, I had no desire to meet her now. "Not yet, please." I hoped she was listening.

The collar of my jacket lifted. My shoulders were tugged as my coat went tight around them and my chest.

"What?" I coughed as my body rose.

My limp arms dangled by my sides as I was hauled to my feet. Technically speaking, I wasn't properly on my feet. My ankles bent as an invisible crane dragged my feet across the ground. A faint whir emanated from behind my neck.

"Impossible." I tried to shift and look back.

Something snorted, brayed, and whinnied in rapid succession.

It was an effort, but I managed to smile. I retracted my ill thoughts and comments about Uniflies. It carried me half a dozen feet before I let out a breath and tried looking back again.

How in the world is it carrying me?

Some questions are better left unanswered. Do not look a gift horse, or Unifly, in the mouth.

My ankles twanged as I moved along another dozen or so feet. The muscles in my injured leg ceased shivering. The rest of my body continued.

"I'd hate to be a terrible passenger, but I don't suppose you could pick up the pace? I'm dying."

Snort. Our pace increased. The little animal was growing on me.

Trees passed by, and I stayed wary of any red eyes hidden amidst them. It seemed a bit of luck had come my way. Our journey remained uneventful. My lids fluttered. I fought to keep them open. It was a long battle, filled with skirmishes against fatigue and my decaying body. I coughed, and a trickle of fluid rolled down my chin. It was red and congealed.

The Unifly carried me without complaint as convulsions and cold fits wracked my body. We passed through a section of forest where the path widened. The trees grew further apart and the darkness didn't seem as thick.

We slowed.

"What's…going on?" I scanned the trees. Nothing in sight to warrant stopping.

The Unifly brayed.

"I don't speak horse."

Snort.

A chord of cerulean fire streaked with onyx split the air before us. The Unifly released its hold and whinnied. My chin felt like it had been struck by a hammer. My head felt the same. I shook it clear and eyed the flames. It was another Way.

A hand burst from the flames, grabbed me by the arm, and hauled me into the fire. I shut my eyes, but I could feel the world tumble.

"Agh." My bones rattled and stone beat against my body.

A Unifly brayed.

I cleared my vision and looked up. Izzy's Unifly buzzed in a frantic panic. I wish it was the only thing I saw.

I lay on the floor of a hall that looked to be made of polished ebony. Columns of obsidian towered above me, running to a domed ceiling made of clear glass.

Somebody laughed. It was rueful. If the blood in my body wasn't already solidifying, the laugh would have done the job. I flopped over and looked up.

She sat on a throne made of onyx. Something burned inside the dark stone, a fire made solely of shadow.

I swallowed.

Her full lips spread when she saw it. They were the color of smeared blackberries. A sharp contrast to her skin, which was paler than moonlight. Her eyes were the soft color of mulberry. I hoped they stayed that soft. She blinked her soot lashes once, resting her cheek on a fist.

I coughed, and spittle landed on her floor. Air rushed

through my teeth in a sharp whistle. One does not drool on a Faerie Queen's floor.

She watched me. Her lips pressed together like she was trying to keep from laughing. At least, I prayed that was what she was doing.

She wore a gown of darkened slate so lustrous it made polished silver look dull. It left her shoulders and strong arms bare. The Queen of Darkest Faerie touched two fingers to her lips and rubbed them to one side. Her nails were painted the same color as her lips.

I took her suggestion and brushed a trembling hand across my mouth.

She smiled. For someone who spoke so little, she managed to say a lot. It was a rare skill.

One of the pockets in my coat vibrated, and there was a dry wheeze from inside.

The Faerie Queen arched a delicate, sable brow.

I managed a weak smile. I imagined it wasn't a pretty sight, not with the vast majority of my bodily fluids coating my teeth. The thrashing intensified within my coat.

"Darkness! Lightlessness! Oh wretched nothingness. I have succumbed to the long night. Aaaaaeeeeeoooo!" The dewdrop beat against my pocket.

The Faerie Queen's brow rose higher. She brushed aside one of the two locks of impossibly ink black hair that hung before her eyes. Her hair was done in an elaborate updo and held together in a tight bun with two slender sticks made of pure amethyst.

The queen had expensive tastes.

My pocket jumped again. I resisted the urge to smack it.

"Wait a tick, I know that smell. Beanpole, is that you?"

I lost my battle against the urge. My fingers struck the pocket in a fast, yet gentle, smack.

"Oi!" My coat fluttered as the dewdrop fussed and climbed out of the pocket. He slipped through my coat and flew out to face me. His eyes narrowed and he shook his head, his hair flipping about as he did. "Listen here, you tosspot!" He thrust an accusatory finger towards me. "How dare you—" He blinked and looked around.

I breathed out through my nose.

"This is most certainly not the forest. Where are we?"

The Unifly snorted and brayed.

Izzy's eyes ballooned to near cartoonish proportions. He turned his neck like the muscles had gone to rust. When he saw the figure lounging cross-legged on the throne, he made a whistling sound reserved for steam-powered machinery. The dewdrop zipped behind his Unifly, hiding behind its flanks. He peered out from behind it and glared at me. "Why did you not tell me this is where we were?"

I didn't have a good answer.

Snort.

"Yes, yes, I know, Barnabus, but still…"

I tried not laugh. This wasn't the place. Poor Unifly. Then again, there were worse names than Barnabus.

The queen spoke and my blood grew thicker and colder. "You have something you wish to say, mortal?"

I nodded, and avoided meeting her eyes. I could almost picture her lips quirking into a bemused smirk.

She regarded Izzy. "And you, little one—something occupies your mind as well."

"Indeed!" Izzy's voice regained its bluster. It's easy to be brave when hiding behind your magical, winged horse.

"And what would that be?" The queen's eyes shone.

I could hear Izzy's gulp. He breathed like a mechanical pump. His chest moved rapidly. His breaths slowed, and he steeled himself. The dewdrop edged around his Unifly, coming to stop at the legs of deceased dewdrop. Izzy's eyes shook. He bit his lip and lowered his head to the female's feet, brushing his forehead and hair across them. "I'm sorry," he said.

So was I.

He reached over and lifted her from his mount. The faerie carried her to the queen's throne. He paused a foot from her face and lifted the body higher.

The queen blinked. "What is this?"

"One of mine. She fell against gremlins." Izzy's voice

shook, but I could hear his efforts to steady it. Brave fae.

The queen said nothing. She merely stared.

Izzy licked his lips and took another breath. "She fell under your domain—under night."

A ghost of a smile touched the queen's mouth. "And where did she fall?"

The dewdrop didn't hesitate in his honesty. "Neutral ground. It doesn't matter. She fell under night and its creatures. I seek amends."

"And if I say no? What then, little one?" Her eyes hardened, and there was an undercurrent of threat in her tone. You don't press a Faerie Queen.

Some men are fire and steel on the outside, but when the moment comes, the flames are extinguished and the metal crumbles. Some men are only brave when it suits them. Then there are those who go through life quietly, shying from confrontation. There are moments when those men rise and prove they have ice water in their veins and a will of iron. This was one of those moments.

Izzy floated towards the queen, stopping a finger length from her nose. "Then I will settle with you." His voice was frozen steel.

The queen's eyes widened a fraction. She laughed. Izzy didn't. He remained statuesque, waiting for his answer. The queen beckoned with a single finger and Izzy closed the distance. She leaned forward and whispered something only he could hear.

Izzy inclined his head with reverence. "Thank you."

She leaned back in her throne. "We are concluded. Leave."

"I don't think I should just yet. See the long, scruffy one there, the one with the… Did you get bitten by a Barghest? Why would you do something silly like that? See what I have to deal with—"

The Faerie Queen's eyes flashed ultraviolet. "Now."

Izzy's snapped to attention. "Yes. Leaving. Now. Most excellent idea. Thank you, Queen. Yes, leaving. Many byes and farewells. Yes, bye." He zipped back to his Unifly, mounted it, and gave me a hapless look. "Bye." He waved and flitted off.

I was left alone with the darkest and possibly most dangerous Faerie Queen.

My face contorted as I pressed my lips together and kept from letting more blood dribble to the queen's floor. She watched me all the while. In retrospect, it was probably rude to ignore her.

"A little more light." She tapped two fingers to her left shoulder and then waved them in a wide arc before her. Moonlight filtered in from above, filling the entirety of the hall. She noticed me appraising our surroundings. "Do not worry. This place is well warded, and I have many halls. This is but one—a small one."

A small one? It was larger than rooms reserved for royalty in the stories. The only difference was the absence of ostentatious decorations. It was all rather sparse. Cold stone, monolithic and raw gemstones made up the place.

"Is it to your liking?"

I wasn't sure if that was a trick question or not. I bit my tongue.

"Silence may be golden, mortal, but it is also trying." She arched a brow and tilted her head. "So what brings Jonathan Hawthorne, youngest of the Timeless, to my hall?"

I cleared my throat and kept my voice as level as possible. "Necessity."

"Oh?" She leaned forward a tad. "Of what sort? The Barghest bite?" The queen gestured to my leg. "Or perhaps what else you are afflicted with."

My eyes widened.

"I can smell it from here, the rot inside you, and another queen's touch as well."

There was no point in lying. "Yes, but that's not all."

"Of course not." She flicked her hand through the empty air on her right. The air split in silvery currents of light.

"Hey!" A figure in a black hoodie tumbled through the Way, crashing to the floor. A sword clattered after her.

Cassie bounced to her feet. "You little turd muffin!" She blinked, realizing where she was and faced the queen. "Heh." A weak smile slipped over her face as she locked eyes with the queen. She broke contact to eye Tatiana's blade.

The queen smiled and waved a hand towards the weapon. "Oh, by all means—" Her eyes gleamed as she watched Cassie.

To her credit, Cassie didn't even entertain the thought. She raised her hands to her chest, fingers splayed, and stepped away from the blade. "Nah, I'm good."

"Wise, child."

Cassie bristled.

I coughed and waved at her.

"John, oh crap. You look like…crap." She rushed to my side, kneeling and easing my arm over her.

I shook my head. It wasn't worth it, not in my condition.

"You have one of the things you came here for. What now?" The queen's mouth twitched at the edges.

I made my move. "That depends on you, oh host."

She threw her head back and let out a rolling laugh. "Host? My, when did that happen? I do not recall welcoming you as guests. In fact, you are trespassers on my domain—trespassers coming from the Morning Court. How do I know you bear no ill will?"

That was one of the reasons you never try to trick a Faerie Queen. They're infinitely better at games. I thought it was worth a try at least.

"You don't." It was the only answer that seemed fitting.

"Indeed, but it seems you aren't in a position to be of any danger, are you?" Her eyes fixed on my wound.

"No, I'm not."

"Which brings us back to where we began—questions. Why *are* you here?"

I took a deep breath. "I need your help." I looked at Cassie, then the queen. "And *we* need answers." I winced as a lance tipped with thorns shot through my leg and into my lower abdomen. The pain was spreading.

"And what makes you think I can—that I will?"

My gums ached from the pressure of my teeth. I ground them anyway, gritting through the hot needles in my body as I hauled myself up with Cassie's aid. I looked the Faerie Queen in the eyes. "Because I know who you are."

One corner of her mouth quirked and she waited.

"I name you, Nox. Nocturne. Mother of Night. Mistress of Shadows. Queen of Veils and the Sightless, the Unseen." I bit my tongue and swallowed before naming another of her mantles. "Thread cutter."

A paper-thin smile touched her lips when I said it. I regretted it, but it proved my point. She *could* help.

"A—" I cut myself off. If what Izzy said was true, then she possessed another mantle. One I felt safer not to name.

The Faerie Queen's hands fell to the armrests as she rose. "I am. You've named me for my many faces, but you've failed to mention the most dangerous of them."

I mimicked her thin smile from earlier. It took a great deal of effort.

"Smart." She took a few steps towards me, appraising me with her head tilted only a fraction. "But you are right. I can help."

I waited for her to name her price.

She didn't.

The queen drew closer. She was taller than I thought, standing high enough barefoot to look me in the eyes.

Cassie backpedaled a few feet. She had the right idea. I wobbled without the support and tried to follow her. Except, I couldn't. My legs were rooted to the spot. The queen stopped. She was close enough that if I wanted, I could see if her lips tasted the way they looked.

Her arm blurred and the queen's hand pressed tight to the side of my skull. She pulled me close and I got my answer. She tasted like berries left out on a snowy day—crisp, cold, sweet. It was a kiss that made its way through my body, or so I thought. Frozen snakes coursed down my limbs, forcing their way to my mangled leg.

The muscles inside squirmed and throbbed. It felt like ice crystals were forming within. She didn't let up, holding my lips pressed to hers. My knees wanted to buckle, but her grip kept me from falling.

We parted after seconds that felt like hours, and my knees got what they wanted. I collapsed to the floor. I could see the air as I exhaled and panted. Another puff of misty air left my nostrils. If winter had a kiss, that was it.

The queen stood and watched me with measured curiosity.

Cassie's nose twitched but otherwise she remained neutral. "So, how was it?" Her voice was as flat as the expression on her face.

"I've always believed it poor form to kiss and tell." I struggled to catch my breath.

The queen lifted a hand to her mouth and laughed. "And it's poor form to keep a woman waiting for an answer. How are you feeling?"

I turned to Cassie first. "The kiss was…something." I focused my attention on the darkest Faerie Queen. "I'm not sure."

One of her eyes twitched. "Most stand when they speak to me."

Right, it was incredibly disrespectful to be talking to a queen when lying on one's ass. I coughed and held a hand out. "Cassie."

"Uh, John." Her eyes were wide. "Look at your leg."

I did. It took me a moment to process what I saw. My leg was coated in dried, thick blood of an unhealthy nature. Cold strings trailed and tickled through the limb, just beneath my skin. But as far as I could tell, I was no longer bleeding. I couldn't feel anything. My fingers dug into the meat of my thigh and I squeezed. Five acute points of pressure formed and throbbed, but that was it.

"You healed me? Why?"

"No, Jonathan Hawthorne." Something slithered down my spine when she said my name. "I did not heal you. I killed a part of you; there is a difference." She hadn't answered my question.

"Why?"

"Because the dead do not talk, at least, not for long."

"And that's what you want—a talk?"

"That, and something more."

I arched a brow.

"A chance to kill a little more of you." Her eyes lit with almost frenzied glee.

I didn't know what she meant exactly, but the feeling in my chest and gut told me it wasn't a good thing.

"So…let us talk—alone." Her eyes flashed.

Darkness swept over the room.

Chapter Thirty

Instinct and experience galvanized me. "Cassie!" She had been near me a second ago. I hoped that was still the case as I reached out blindly. True darkness wasn't something your eyes could adapt to. It was like a blanket of pure black had been thrown over me. "Cassie!"

My eyes welded shut as a torrent of light flooded over me. A pocket of warm air pressed against my cheek. I had felt it before. I twisted and swung an elbow towards it. The Darkest Queen batted my strike with a slap of her hand. She laughed. The light died.

I blinked and looked around. "Where's Cassie?"

"Safe."

Her smile did nothing to reassure me. We weren't under any oaths of protection or fair dealings. I couldn't take her word for it. Cold logic told me that if she wanted to, she could easily hurt both us. I exhaled and clenched my fist to vent my frustration. Lashing out in anger would lead to more trouble for Cassie and me. She'd been through enough. I had no desire to exacerbate the situation.

I licked my lips and softened my tone. "Very well. She's safe, and out of sight. I'm supposed to take your word that no harm will come to her, yes?"

She smiled in approval. "See, you *can* play the game. And, yes."

It would have to be good enough. I rubbed the spot on my cheek where she had breathed. A simple gesture, but it carried weighty meaning. The queen noticed and her smile faltered.

I cleared my throat. "You wanted to talk, let's talk then."

The queen backpedaled with effortless grace. It looked

more like she was sliding backwards than walking. She beckoned me with a finger.

I followed her. "What did you want to speak about?"

"Of the nature of names and things. The things you've failed to notice, and some you still need to see. Of all things you will do for me."

I lost my interest in talking. We came to an unassuming door. In Faerie, all that meant was the door looked ordinary. It was likely there was nothing normal about it.

The queen opened the door. I was wrong. The door was normal. The room wasn't.

"In."

I eyed her. "You're…"

Her eyes sparked into a bright color I had no name for. My head spun and her hand pressed against my shoulder. I tumbled into the room. It was a small miracle I kept my balance. The floor consisted of raised tiles, no two matching another in height. It made standing nearly impossible. I could've sprained an ankle stumbling into the room. It was only by some level of grace that I hadn't. Shame it wasn't my own grace.

The Faerie Queen stepped in after me. I took a step back and fell. My back and hips twinged as a tile jabbed them. She stood perfectly balanced on a tile the size of a credit card. It didn't look comfortable, but she showed no signs of discomfort.

I shifted my body. It resulted in a handful of tiles pressing against me. There was no comfortable way to sit, or sleep I wagered, in this room. I realized why she had brought me here. It was a cruelly simple design. The best ways to break someone had nothing to do with pain. She was old enough to know that. Given her history and nature, she might have pioneered the technique.

"So we're here—alone." I grimaced and shifted again. This was going to get old rather quick.

"Mmmm." It wasn't the reply I was hoping for. She shut the door, and the room grew impenetrably dark. I couldn't make out her silhouette. All there was to see were two rings of ultraviolet. "Let us start with the first of things—names."

I raised a brow, not that it mattered in the dark. "Any ones of note?"

Her eyes lowered to my level and drew closer. "The ones you know. Jonathan Hawthorne. Young, Timeless, brash, defiant, and meddlesome."

I was not meddlesome.

"You are but one of the pieces." Her eyes narrowed. A cold wire lanced through my skull. "Cassidy Winters."

I tried to remain still when she spoke her name. In truth, I didn't do a good job. I shifted and crawled back a pace.

"A mortal woman with the power to bend and travel the Ways as she sees fit."

She knew.

"That, young Hawthorne, is only the beginning of what she can do. The Neravene is not solely a thing of distance."

I swallowed as I started to understand what she meant.

"The child can upset the balance of a great many things." She gave me a look that made me feel infantile, of no consequence—a speck in the grand scheme of things.

My tongue moved and pushed saliva down my gullet, giving me some level of moisture to work with. "You want to keep her for yourself?"

Velvet laughter echoed in the small room. "You're not listening. To some, yes, she could be a tool to conquer. I am a Queen of Faerie. I need nothing."

"Not even another queen's domain?" I regretted the question the second I asked it. I winced in anticipation of her wrath. It never came.

"For a Timeless, you know so little." She sounded sympathetic. "What happens to a fire when left unchecked?"

I didn't know if she was being rhetorical. I kept quiet. Seconds passed before I realized she was waiting for an answer. "It burns everything."

"It consumes all—eventually itself—if left unchecked. *Balance.* All things require it, even the fae, even the

Neravene. That is why I have no desire to keep the child for myself. I know my role."

"And that is?" I could almost see her smiling in the utter darkness.

"All stories have a beginning, middle, and end, child." That was as much an answer as I could expect from her.

My heel braced against a particularly high tile. I pushed against it, placing my hands against the wall behind me for support. I got to my feet and looked into her iridescent purple eyes. "And my story? Is it just beginning? Or is it coming to an end?"

The queen met my gaze. "Your story is beginning, but a chapter will come to a close—*if* you can see what's before you."

A wet slap filled my ears as the bottom of my fist struck stone. "I can't see a thing in here! No more riddles and questions! Why are we here?"

The violet orbs vanished and left me with darkness. A rush of movement spurred me to turn. It was the wrong surface for fast movement. My legs wobbled, and I waved my arms to regain balance; it didn't work.

"Argh!" A fist-sized block impacted my ribs. They weren't broken, but the bruise would be nasty. I rolled to my side and righted myself, my chest heaving in exertion.

Fingers slid over my eyes and pulled my head back. My neck strained. Moving wasn't an option, so I ceased my struggles.

"As I said, to help you see. Darkness doesn't always obscure things, child. Light is blinding; it shows you a world of color, but you forget the shadows—and what moves in them. The dark forces you to rely on your other senses. You have a capable mind. Use it."

I growled and moved my hips. The pressure in the base of my neck increased. My spine felt like hot metal discs grinding against one another. I relented. The pressure lightened in response.

"Think," she urged. "Of names and motives. Why is the girl valuable?"

"We went over this."

"Then go over it again. Take your time—I have all of it."

I stilled my breathing. Anger wasn't going to do me any favors. Cassie was a doorway—a key through the Neravene. That brought her trouble, but in the hands of the right person or creature, that trouble would magnify. Power could and would be redistributed, concentrated and consolidated in the hands of a few, or—worse—one. The Neravene was a constant struggle, but it was balanced.

My lashes brushed against her fingers as I tried to blink. I understood part of it now. "It's about upsetting the balance—all of it!" I fidgeted, but her grip held strong.

"Go on."

I bit my lip and took a breath. Nothing. "It doesn't add up. Whoever—whatever is behind this can't get away with it. Someone would intervene."

"Who?" I could hear a pleased edge to her voice.

"The—" I broke off.

"And now he sees." She relinquished her hold, and I felt her move to my side.

I rolled my neck and shoulders, eyeing her as I crept a foot away. "So why haven't they?"

"Because you cannot fight what you cannot see."

"Of course, they don't know." My palms ground against my eyes and I snarled. "That means one of them…" I stopped and trailed a finger to the side of my neck. I swallowed and rubbed a hand through my hair, stopping where the troll had ripped out a few strands during the ambush in an alleyway. "No." I lashed out with a hand. My knuckles struck a solid surface. I winced and buried the pain. "They can't do that. They're not allowed!"

"You know to whom rules apply, and to whom they do not. Of all the creatures in all the worlds, what creatures have the ability, and desire, to go against their nature?"

Only one group served to carry out decisions. And one of their members was keen on seeing my throat slit. *The bastard showed up every time.*

I screamed. It served no useful purpose. It didn't abate the storm brewing in my chest and lungs. It didn't empty me of the hurricane of reds swimming before my eyes. It didn't quell the pressure building in my jaw and heart. So I screamed again and hoped it would do the trick.

"And now you know another name, Jonathan Hawthorne. You see the shadows moving in the daylight. What will you do?"

"Let me out, and I'll show you."

She chortled.

"You think this is funny?"

"You have a name, Hawthorne. Do not mistake that for answers."

She did a better job of calming me than I did. That alone was unsettling. I stared at her, waiting for an explanation. She was certainly more forthcoming with information than the Dawn Lady. I felt no reason to try and change that. It was a nice change of pace having some help with the answers.

"You're wondering why." The queen didn't pose it as a question.

I nodded in the dark, watching as her eyes tracked the motion.

"You know your tales of Faerie, but what do you know of the stories before those?"

"I've read over every creation myth at one point or another."

"And what of the things that precede creation?"

I didn't have an answer. A thought would have been nice, but I didn't have one of those either.

"Few mortals know of these stories. Less have heard them. These are the stories told to my kind. Tell me, Jonathan Hawthorne, what do you know of the Former?"

The name gave implications that caused my mind to run wild with thoughts. All of which I hoped were wrong. "Nothing. I've never heard the name until now."

"Hmmm." I could feel the weight of her eyes, judging me. "Of all the names you know and have come to learn, this is the most important."

It wasn't that important from where I was standing. I had learned another name, the one behind Cassie's difficult life of late. I considered that my priority. "And why is that?"

"Because, Hawthorne, there is a reason behind everything. Every action and goal is spurred by reason and desire."

"And the Former, whatever they are, are part of the reason Cassie is being hunted?"

"Yes."

"Why? I still don't know what the name means."

"In many ways, it means what it suggests." Her eyes quivered for a split second. A Faerie Queen's eyes...quivered. I was beginning to reconsider my priorities.

"Understand this, Jonathan Hawthorne: there is no such thing as nothingness. Every beginning comes from the end of another. Every end has an end in a new beginning. Do you understand?"

"I think so?"

"Think less then and understand."

It was easy for her to say.

"Before the fae, before the Gods of men, came the Former. Nameless beings born of the very things they represent."

"I don't follow."

She hissed and blurred from sight. I scrambled to find her. I did not want to endure another of her "enlightening" sessions. The darkness in the room wobbled and bent like it was fabric, not stone.

"The Former are not beings like you and I—coherent, rational, balanced."

None of those words described the Faerie Queen to me. I refrained from mentioning that aloud.

"They are driven by singular principles: order, chaos, destruction, growth, hunger, disease, and nihilism to name a few." Her voice came from every inch of the room.

I turned in place, taking care in my footwork to avoid a nasty fall.

"They are *old*, Hawthorne, very old."

I was beginning to put the pieces together and came to the decision that puzzles were no longer fun. "And I'm assuming they're powerful?"

The queen laughed, but it was not her usual fare. It warbled and cracked. It sounded bitter. "Yes, they are powerful. So much so that it was their downfall."

"How so?"

"They twist everything around them. They are not like us, the fae. We are tied to the nature of many things. They are *the* things."

My chest felt brittle. The tissue around my sternum stretched tight.

"Do you know where they are? Why they are forgotten? Why man and fae walk the world?"

I shook my head. "No, I don't. I assume you're going to tell me." My eyes snapped shut as the Faerie Queen came into full view. After being subjected to the darkness of the room, its absence was jarring.

"You are free because *they* are not. This"—she waved a hand to the room around us—"is where they are. And it isn't."

I swallowed and felt the need to make something very clear. "Forgive me, oh Queen, but I haven't the slightest idea of what you're talking about."

She looked down at me, and her lips pressed tight. It was a sad, sympathetic look. "There are some forces the mortal world, and the Neravene, cannot contain. So here and there, they are."

It's an odd thing, feeling your eyes grow to owlish proportions. An exaggeration, yes, but one that felt appropriate as I understood a little better.

"They're…trapped in their own domains?"

She gave a thin smile and lowered her head a fraction. "Yes. Unable to get out. Remember, a domain is shaped to the creatures that inhabit it. Their domains exist solely to contain their own power. Left unchecked..." The queen stared at me, and I fixed my priorities.

"I understand, but if they're contained, what's the problem?"

She arched an eyebrow.

Something fluttered inside my stomach. "It's not just about Cassie's ability to open Ways to other domains in the Neravene, is it? It's about her ability to open Ways that should remain shut. She can let them out, can't she?"

The queen's face was a grim mask, her mouth a thin crack. "And now he sees."

"So what happens if one of the Former gets out?"

Her color paled. "How much do you love your world, Jonathan Hawthorne?"

"A great deal."

"I feel the same about mine," she said.

"And that's why you won't hurt Cassie. That's why you won't hurt me."

Something flashed through her face and eyes. It was cold and hungry. "I won't hurt you, no. But who says I will let you leave?"

Checkmate.

I swallowed. "I'm sorry?"

She took a step back, placing a hand on the door. "You will remain here. I will attend to Cassidy Winters, and the Former."

"You're going to use her. A child." The bones in my hands felt too large as I squeezed.

She let out a single puff of air in a light laugh. "Child? That is the problem with you mortals. She is not a child. She is a key."

"Like hell she is! She is a young woman with her whole life ahead of her. You don't get to take that away from her." I took an unbalanced step towards the Faerie Queen.

"You already have."

I don't know what hit me harder, her words, or the smug look on her face.

I blinked several times. "What?"

"Look at what her life has become since taking up with you. Chased by trolls, small lords of the Neravene. Hunted, beaten, terrified." She gave a disappointed shake of her head. "Look at what you've put her through, Jonathan Hawthorne."

That wasn't true. It wasn't. Was it?

I shook my head. "No. She was already on the run. I—"

But she was right. I did bring Cassie to her.

"You've done nothing but endanger her life. You brought her before the Queens of Fae—to us, to me." A hungry light appeared in her eyes when she said that.

Something hot and ugly twisted inside me. "Maybe so, but what makes you think I would let you put her life in more danger?"

Her body shook and she put a hand to her mouth to contain herself. A second later, she burst into musical laughter. "*Let* me? Oh, dear child, what makes you think you could stop me?"

I didn't have an answer. An animalistic growl formed in my throat.

"I will take Cassidy Winters"—her voice hardened—"and ensure the Former never leave their domains." She made stone look soft. She would do exactly that and make good on her word. I'd expect nothing less from a Faerie Queen.

The air stretched thin. My lungs ached and struggled. The room spun. I shut my eyes and tried to calm myself.

"She will be my tool, my weapon, my proxy."

The last word made me feel like a pane of glass hit with a hammer. She wanted to use her for more than protection. Cassie was a pawn to her, one to help her gain more power. As if she needed any more of that.

"No." I shook my head and met her eyes, glaring hard. A thin smile broke over my face. "I can't stop you. You're right. You can keep me locked up here forever, but what makes you so sure you can do that to Cassie?"

All of the confidence slipped from her face. Served her right.

"What?"

"The very reason you need Cassie, why you are afraid of

her, is why you will never be able to hold her. It's as you said: she can let out the Former. Do you honestly think you can keep her here? She's been on the run for so long. What makes you think you could find her if she left?"

The queen frowned. Something dark flickered through her eyes and I had a feeling I was going to regret my outburst.

"And what would she do to ensure *your* safety, Hawthorne? You came here to be saved. I aided you. I saw the look on her face when you were healed. She cares for you." Her smile returned. "I'm sure there is nothing young Miss Winters would not do to preserve your life."

I grinned. "That works both ways, oh Queen. You can't persuade her to do anything without the proper leverage."

Her eyes lost their focus and she titled her head.

I took two measured steps to the side. I inhaled and snapped my head forward. Stone struck back, sending acute pain through the right side of my head. Tears welled in one of my eyes and my vision swam. I pulled my head back.

"You would kill yourself just to keep her away from me?"

I paused and glared at her. "To keep her out of your hands? Yes, I'd kill myself in a heartbeat."

"You know what is at stake. If Cassidy Winters isn't kept out of the wrong hands, billions upon billions could perish."

"Let them."

Her eyes widened, and she took a step back. "You'd condemn all those lives for one person?"

"I'd let all of it burn. Mortal side, Neravene—all of it."

"That's insanity."

"Humanity is irrationality. For all your years, wisdom, knowledge and power, you are vastly ignorant about humans." I could have chosen my words better. Her eyes narrowed into dangerous slits. I pressed on regardless. "*Every life matters*. If you're not willing to save one of them, how could you be willing to do what's needed to save them all?"

"That is completely irrational."

"What did I just say about humanity?"

"I could do horrible things to you. Make you suffer in ways forgotten by your histories."

"You could, and none of that would help you with Cassie."

The Faerie Queen stood an inch from me. I hadn't seen her move. I didn't see her arm move either. My cheek felt like it had been grated against a hive of wasps. I struck the wall and collapsed to the uneven floor. Something thick and coppery welled inside my mouth. I blinked at the floor for a while. My tongue pressed against the insides of my mouth, letting the saliva build around it. I opened my mouth and let the mixture drool to the floor. Seconds later, I spat the rest out.

The queen stood several feet away from me. She ran her hands down her gown to smooth it.

I coughed and wobbled to my feet. "What now?"

No answer.

A wise man would have remained silent and let things play out.

I am not a wise man.

"You want to stop the Former from getting out." It wasn't a question.

She remained still and silent.

"Cassie and I can keep it from happening. Let us leave, let us confront—"

"You think you can do anything? Even here, you are at *my* mercy."

I nodded. "Ma'am, I've been at the mercy of people, beings, and things greater than me all my life. It's never stopped me. Not once." The room finally ceased its infernal spinning, and the queasiness in my stomach abated. That was one hell of a slap.

She touched her forefinger and thumb to her lips in consideration. "Mhmm. You have suffered through a great deal. But this is something else entirely."

"Maybe so, but I deserve the chance to face it. So does

Cassie. Her more so than anyone."

"True. Very well, I will let you leave."

I choked on my next breath. "You will?"

She nodded. "But there are other matters to settle."

I swallowed.

"A name still remains."

I arched a brow. "Oh?"

"Mine."

My face scrunched as I tilted my head at an angle.

"You named me many times over but failed to choose one."

I did. There was a reason for that. I thought I was being clever by avoiding calling her by a name. I refrained from it, even in thought.

She took a step closer and I took one back. The process repeated until my back hit the wall.

Names don't simply have power. They are power. Names are identity. There is strength in that. When you define something with a name, you give it shape, form and power. The Faerie Queen had many names and mantles. Referring to her by one wouldn't diminish the others. It would serve to empower that one so long as I used it.

I looked to either side of the wall for an escape. It was a rather small room unfortunately. Her hand pressed against my chest and pinned me there.

"So..." Her eyes seemed to darken a shade and glisten. "Choose. It's rude to not use a lady's name."

I wanted to point out that was true for mortal women. Fae women didn't care much for that. But they did when it came to power. I held my tongue.

She leaned closer, putting her mouth to my ear. "No? Let me make it easy for you. Call me by the mantle I wear tonight. Call me Nox, Mother of Darkness."

It could have been worse. She could have chosen another name. I inclined my head. "Nox."

She pulled back a step and smiled. "Was that so hard?"

I grimaced.

Nox rolled her hand with a flourish. "Now that the

games are done, onto other matters?"

"Games?" I blinked and realized what had happened. "You were testing me? Pushing me?"

"Of course." She said it like should have been obvious.

In fairness, it should have been. Nothing was ever simple and straightforward with the fae.

"You never intended to take Cassie. You wanted us to do this. You're not getting involved with the Former if you can help it."

"Oh, no. I would have taken the child if you had proved less than capable."

Being wrong could be humbling. This wasn't one of those moments. I cleared my throat and moved to brush past her. My chest hit a stone wall in the form of her hand.

"We are not done."

"We are. We don't have time for any more of your games." I raised a hand to move hers away. I reconsidered when I saw the look she gave me.

"All I have is time. So long as the girl is here, the Former cannot escape."

She had a point. That didn't mean I had to like or agree with it.

"Please move."

"We still have one last matter to discuss."

I arched a brow.

"There is still the matter of *why* I should let you go. I did so desire to kill a bit more of you."

My blood ran a few degrees cooler.

"I do not need either of you to stop the Former. There is a simpler solution."

Murder. She was talking about murdering Cassie. My temples throbbed so hard I could feel it in the back of my eyes. "You won't harm a single hair on her head."

She pursed her lips in amusement. "I'm not interested in her hair or her head. I'm interested in *yours*."

Oh.

Nox watched me in silence. There was a look of expectation on her face.

I had it backwards. Cassie wasn't the pawn she wanted. I tried to take a step but her hand held firm. "What do you want?"

"You know."

I nodded. "I do, but I want to hear it."

"I will let you leave on one condition..." She let the words sit in silence.

It was a great technique. Nox knew exactly what it would do to me. My mind ran rampant with the thoughts and possibilities of what she wanted.

I wet my lips and took a breath. "And that condition is?"

The Faerie Queen of Darkness leaned close. The ultraviolet of her eyes flared with a maddening electric light. "I want you to perform a task for me. Not now, but perhaps on the morrow. A week from now. A year. I want you, Jonathan Hawthorne, to know that you are leaving by my mercy. That you will return to me at a moment of my choosing. I want you to know in every waking moment that you belong to me. You will stop the power pursuing the Former and still find no rest, no peace, no sleep. I want you to know that I will come for you in the dark, and set you to task for my purpose. You will not know when. You will not know what, until the moment comes. I want you to know that if you leave...you are mine."

I wish the room had stayed shrouded in darkness. My ankles felt like a sharp rod ran through them. The uneven tiling wreaked havoc on the small joints, and I suspected that I hadn't quite recovered from the queen's full-armed slap.

I looked away from Nox's gaze. She wasn't having any of that. In a single graceful step, she moved back in view, locking eyes with me.

"What is your answer? I could walk out of this room and leave you here for eternity, Timeless." A thin smile spread across her face.

She was smart. So long as she kept me alive, my torture would last forever. The room would see to that.

I shut my eyes and thought of Cassie—her earlier words. I opened my eyes and made my decision. I hoped I would live long enough to regret it.

"Yes."

Chapter Thirty-One

Her eyes burned in hunger and a feral smile appeared on her face. Nox's hands blurred through the air, weaving a tapestry of shadows and darkness around us. "Mine." Her voice rang in solemn iron tones. The room shook.

I already regretted my decision. But it meant being able to help Cassie, to keep her safe.

My wrists protested as the small bones compressed under pressure. The queen's fingers were slender rods of cool steel, squeezing with excruciating force. She held tight as the darkness coalesced into a tight cloud above her. The light intensified in her eyes. It hurt to look at them. I tried to turn away. I couldn't. The scene would be burned in my corneas for a long time.

A long time is longer still when you're a Timeless.

"And in the darkness, I will bind you."

The black cloud erupted into needles of blackness. Tendrils shot out, arcing towards my arms. They passed through the sleeves of my coat and struck my forearms. The coolness associated with antiseptics washed over my skin. I could feel every vein pulsate and grow cold. My fingers grew distant and paled. I sank to my knees but Nox held tight.

It lasted ten seconds. Ten long seconds.

She let go and I collapsed to the floor. Every breath burned with the taste of the harshest of hard liquors. My arms quaked, and even the simple effort of being on my hands and knees seemed too much. Her fingers closed around my biceps and I tensed. She hauled me to my feet like I weighed nothing.

"Was that so bad?" Her mouth quirked at the edges.

I coughed and sputtered. "I've had worse." I coughed again.

"Good, because you have worse still to endure." She took a step back and gestured out of the room with a wave of her hand.

I eyed the hazardous floor and stepped carefully to the door.

"After you." She inclined her head.

I coughed, scowled, bit my tongue from saying something that would earn me another slap, and exited the room. Nox lagged a step behind. I tried to keep concrete from settling in and stiffening my back. I didn't want the Faerie Queen to see any sign of the visible discomfort I had about her being behind me. There was a loud crash as the door shut, and I twitched.

Nox let out a succession of three quick laughs. "Apologies."

She wasn't sorry in the slightest. She was amused by putting me on edge.

The fae have a twisted sense of humor.

I exhaled forcefully through my nostrils. "Now what?"

She was by my side in an instant. I shuddered as three of her fingers trailed over one of my cheeks. The insides of my mouth felt like they had been swabbed with an ice cube. "Does it feel better?" She eyed me askance.

"It does. You have quite the slap."

Her lips twitched for a microsecond. "My bite is worse."

I believed her.

Nox passed by me, her midnight gown trailing behind as I stood and watched. There was a part of me that was relieved to see her leave. Another part enjoyed watching her go. I shut my eyes and took a steadying breath. There was trouble, and there was *trouble*. I didn't need my impulses stirring the latter sort. The Faerie Queen had me in a bind. I didn't want to add to that.

She lowered herself to her throne and rested her head on a fist. Nox watched me with clinical curiosity as I approached. I got the feeling she was sizing up her new investment. She tapped two fingers to her lips as she pursed them.

I wonder what she's thinking. Nothing good.

It was a fair answer.

"You understand what you're going to have to do, yes?" There was a dark undercurrent in her voice.

I didn't meet her eyes when I answered. "Yes."

"The girl will be in danger."

"She already is."

She inclined her head to concede the point. "More so. If by chance you fail…she will be taken. You know what that means."

"I have a vague idea."

"Let us hope neither of us have to see it clearer." Nox looked at the empty space behind where Cassie's blade lay on the floor. Her finger moved a fraction of an inch.

The air above the blade looked like an inkwell had shattered. A whirlpool of black spun through the air, spreading to the size of a compact car. It flickered through dark shades and throbbed.

Someone stepped through it.

"Eyuckh." Cassie squinted over her shoulder at the Way. "I feel like I need a bath—in frickin' ammonia or something."

I tried not to chuckle. "You're fine. There's nothing on you."

Cassie rubbed a hand through her hair, pausing to ruffle it. "John!" She broke into a sprint and leapt at the last second.

I was glad Nox had healed me. Cassie crashed into me. "Bwoof." I staggered back a step as we hugged. "How are you?"

She broke the hug and gave me a bit of room. "Fine. I was freaking out at first. I didn't know what she was doing to you."

What didn't she do?

I gave Cassie a weak smile. "We had a talk—a long, informative one."

"Oh, talking's cool." She leaned and dropped her voice

to a whisper. "Sure she didn't go all 'join the dark side' on you?"

I eyed Cassie and waited for an explanation.

Her posture slumped as she sighed. "Ugh. Did she convince you to join her evil army and offer you cookies?"

"No cookies."

Nox laughed. "No, but that can be arranged."

Cassie nudged me. "Can I trust the food here?"

"No."

"Oh, okay…because I have to keep telling myself I'm not hungry." She placed a hand to her stomach and frowned.

I turned to give her a sympathetic smile when I noticed something. The swirling black Way was still open. I peered into it for a moment. Nothing happened. I turned back to eye Nox.

Something chirped from inside the Way. "Yes, yes, I'm very well. Stop, you buffoon."

Cassie bounced in place, excitement riddling her face.

I groaned and rubbed my hand across my face.

Green light strobed against the black. A diminutive figure sailed out of the opening, riding atop a Unifly. Izzy's brows knitted. He looked over his shoulder into the Way, and shook a tiny fist at something we couldn't see. "Blundering, bumbling, buzzle-brained—" Izzy ceased his tirade as his Unifly chittered something. He blinked. "What's that?" Izzy twisted and looked to us. "Ah-hah! Success!"

The Way shut with the *snap-hiss* associated with opening a can of soda. The little faerie imitated the sound as he snapped around and glared at the Way like it had caused him some great offense.

"Damnable things." His face scrunched like he had eaten something overly sour.

I coughed twice into my balled fist. It got the green faerie's attention. "Izzy, what are you doing here?"

He looked at me like I was particularly slow on the uptake. "Rescuing the pair of you, obviously."

Obviously.

I rubbed the heel of my palm against my forehead. "Thank you, Izzy." It seemed the best way to placate the dewdrop and move on. He nodded and puffed his chest. I ignored him and turned to Nox. "I take it we are free to go now?" I shot a glance to Cassie then back to the Faerie Queen.

She inclined her head without a word.

"Excellent!" Izzy zipped to our sides. His face lit up like a Christmas ornament. He was too early, and too excited. "Where are we going?"

"*We*"—I pointed a finger to Cassie and myself—"are going somewhere. *You* aren't supposed to be trying to cross over with us."

Izzy sulked, his eyes dropped and his lip curled. He cast a disheartened look to Cassie. I followed it and met Cassie's eyes. She stared at the pair of us, deciding.

Nox settled it. Faerie Queens left you little choice. "He will accompany you. Consider it part of our agreement. Both of ours." She eyed Izzy, then me. "Do not discount what the little one can do, see, and hear. They have their uses and can be helpful."

Izzy swelled under the compliment. I could see why he was such a confident little bugger. He must have gotten lauded at every turn in his life.

Too much of a good thing can most certainly be bad.

I swallowed the growl and rubbed my face harder. A dewdrop flitting through the streets of New York certainly wasn't going to attract the wrong sort of attention. "Fine. We can't stand here arguing about it."

Izzy flashed an excited neon green and hovered closer to Cassie. At least he remained quiet.

"No. No you cannot. I presume you have an idea where to start your search?" Nox arched a brow as she tilted her head. She was scanning me, making sure she had made the right choice in letting me go.

I made sure not to disappoint.

I gave the queen a thin smile. "A certain establishment in New York that's neither here nor there. A certain man whose details are a little…foggy."

Her eyes widened and shimmered. Nox's mouth broke into a wide smile before she released a singular bark of laughter. "Oh, very clever. I like it."

"Thank you. I don't suppose you could open us a Way back?"

The queen ignored me, her gaze passing over to settle on Cassie. "I could, but I have to say, I am rather curious to see how *she* does it."

Cassie grinned. "Well, you know what they say about curiosity and…" she trailed off when she saw Nox's eyes. Cassie swallowed. "Yeah, no. Totally cool, um, right." She looked everywhere but to where the Faerie Queen sat. Her eyes stopped on her fallen sword. She licked her lips and chanced a slight look up.

Nox smiled and waved a permissive hand.

Cassie edged towards her borrowed sword. She took her time retrieving it, casting wary glances at Nox as she advanced. I couldn't blame her. She retrieved it and leapt back like her feet were scalded. After taking up a spot near me, Cassie fixed Nox with a half-smile. "Thanks."

Nox lowered her head a fraction. "Of course. Now, child, show me what you can do."

Cassie huffed a breath and pressed her lips tight. "Alright, where are we poppin' to?"

I told her.

"Okay? Random much?"

"Just do it, please? It's safer than arriving directly where we need to be."

Cassie eyed me askance. "Why's that?"

Nox leaned forward. "Because it's the most likely place to go for answers, and answers often lead to danger—danger that is likely to be watching for you."

Cassie's eyes widened. She shivered for a split second. "Thanks, Gotharella."

Nox arched a brow.

"Hehe." Cassie raised both her hands. "Sorry, I mean black totally works on you. Black is *so* in right now. It's chic, easy to work with, and slimming. Not that you need slimming. I, yeah…" She bit her lip and looked to me for help.

I sighed. I suppose it was too much to hope for leaving on a high note.

"Cassie, get us out of here before you get us into trouble."

She stuck her tongue at me before biting down on it lightly. Her face furrowed in concentration. Light breaths escaped her nostrils as her eyes shut.

A sliver of halogen blue light appeared in the air behind us. The Way was no wider than a string. It flickered and undulated through the air, waiting for us to step through.

I whistled.

Nox let out a sound like a large cat. "Mhmm. Clean. Efficient. Beautiful."

"Damn right I am," muttered Cassie.

I leaned over to her. "She means the Way."

Cassie moved her lips in imitation of a horse. "Pfft."

The Queen of Darkest Faerie left her throne and crossed the distance to us. She didn't stop her movements as she headed towards bumping into us.

We parted, giving her space to pass without breaking her stride. She never even looked at us. Her gaze was fixed on the Way. Nox paused a hair's length from the shimmering rift between worlds. She raised a finger to the top of the Way, letting it hover in front of it. She traced it down its entirety, and then...she touched it.

It was like watching a microwave with silverware inside. There was a heinous crackle accompanied by an electric blue flare. Smoke wafted from the tip of Nox's finger. The skin was just as fair and smooth as before. Her mouth twitched once. "Interesting."

The rest of us held our breaths.

Nox turned slowly. She fixed Cassie with a look that made it seem like she was looking through her. "If you ever return to my domain, we should talk, child—at length."

Cassie nodded mutely.

The Faerie Queen did not move her head, but her eyes snapped to my direction. "And you—we will speak again." Her mouth cracked into a smile that made me think of fairy tale character that had nothing to do with faeries.

The Big Bad Wolf.

I turned and suppressed a shiver. "Let's go." I placed a hand on the small of Cassie's back and urged her forward.

Her face remained neutral, but her opalescent eyes shimmered. "Age before beauty."

I bit back my reply and faced the Way. I resolved not to turn back and face Nox. Her smile still haunted me, and I had no desire for it to be the last thing I saw before entering a Way. I stepped through.

Arcing lights assaulted my vision. I hit solid ground, and winter brushed my skin. Snow peppered a grayscale of concrete monoliths around me.

There was a soft *crunch* of snow being compacted. Cassie wobbled before gripping herself tight. "Damn, it's gotten colder. So that's a thing…"

A warbled cry emanated from behind her. "Eeeeahooo!" A flashing mote of emerald light shot out of the Way. Izzy stopped by me, his Unifly visibly shivering as it hovered by my ear. The little faerie cast a wide look at the buildings around us. "So, this is the mortal world." He pursed his lips as flurries pelted him. "I don't like it."

Cassie snorted. "Everybody's a critic."

Izzy's body bucked as a violent sneeze overtook him. "It's cold. Wet. Gray. Bleak, and smells of…humans."

"You'll get used to the smell." I looked at the rows of townhouses around us and the larger buildings in the distance. Fortunately, the snowstorm had forced most people indoors. The streets were empty and soundless, save for the wind. Good. "Come on," I waved a hand and moved down the sidewalk. "Izzy, stop glowing."

He harrumphed. "First, you want me to glow, then you want me to stop. Humans." He said the last word like a curse.

Cassie sidled up beside me and bumped me with her

hip. "Where're we headed?"

"Trouble."

Cassie harrumphed like Izzy. "Not much of an answer."

I tugged my tattered and abused coat tighter around my body. "Let's just say that it's a good thing you're old enough to drink."

She gave me an oblique stare.

I ignored her and moved to make way for a pair of businessmen in long coats. They passed us and bowed their heads in simple thanks. Cologne overpowered my sinuses. I blinked and blew my nose, trying to get rid of the smell.

"Guckh. Less is more, boys." Cassie shook her head and massaged the sides of her nose.

I looked over my shoulder. There was no sight of our diminutive faerie escort. The pair of men stopped walking and engaged in polite talk, occasionally glancing at us. One of them leered at Cassie. She scowled in disgust.

Green light blinked twice in the corner of my vision. I looked without turning. Izzy and his mount perched atop a windowsill on the other side of the street. His body blared bright angry greens.

A warning?

I took a breath to calm myself—and then I smelled it. Underneath the cologne was a current of something else. Fresh cut grass and the smell of orange thyme. I sniffed again and my eyes widened.

One of the men spun and sank to his knees. The suitcase snapped open, left his grip, and sailed towards me. My shoulder caught most of the impact and I stumbled awkwardly off the sidewalk and into the empty road. "Don't run!"

Cassie did a double take. "Say what? Why?"

The glamour faded and two women stood there. Although the term 'women' wasn't quite correct. They stood a couple of inches under five feet and were mirror images of one another. One of their sharp and severe faces broke into a sneer. She held onto something sleek and black in her deerskin gloves: a submachine gun with a slender fitting over the front of it.

How modern.

"Take cover!" I pointed to a low brick wall that held a sign for the nearby apartment complex.

Cassie gave no sign of acknowledgement. She sprinted, bounded, and landed in a crouch on the other side.

The machine barked and rattled as it sputtered a burst of rounds. Brick snapped and spat chunks spitefully into the air. I slipped behind a parked sedan and peeked through the windows.

Their flaxen hair was bound into tight long braids that whipped when they turned to face me. Both their faces were carved from pale stone with sharp and severe features. Their lips curled in disturbing synchrony and the other blonde let her suitcase fall open. She removed something a bit more traditional and along the lines of what I'd expected at first. A state-of-the-art compound bow unfolded. She snatched up a small. black quiver. Neon tipped feathers protruded from it. Their sneers turned to razor-thin, cruel smiles.

I gulped and hit the floor.

There was a *thunk* where the arrow struck the other side of the car. Something hissed and crackled like frying oil. I rolled to my side and looked up. The arrow burst through the door panel, flying half an inch over my nose.

I hated arrows. I hated magical arrows more.

I scrambled backwards on all fours like a crab, scuttling to the next car. The submachine coughed again. Bits of glass showered the snow-covered street beside me. The car alarm tripped. Two arrows sank into the car at different points and silenced it.

They stripped out of their long coats, and their posture loosened in the comfort of their normal attire. They wore what looked like a flexible tunic made of strands of bark, woven together. It was the color of milk-infused tea. Their arms and most of their thighs were bare. Knee-high boots of the same material flattened the snow as they circled the car to get a better shot at me.

I disagreed with that idea. Fistfuls of snow flew into the

air as I clawed forward and got to my feet. Another burst whistled by, impacting the building on the opposite side of the street.

There was an irritated strobe of green and Izzy whizzed into the sky.

"Forget the Timeless." One of the twins turned to spit in contempt. "Get the girl."

Her counterpart grinned and leveled the gun towards the wall Cassie hid behind. She released a controlled burst of three rounds.

"Alive!" The archer hissed, and the gun-wielding woman's hand blurred into action.

I wasn't going to let that happen. I pressed my back against a large SUV and dug into my coat, hoping to find Quentin's gift. My fingers brushed over something like gnarled, dry vines. They crushed in my grip with a soft *crunch*. I brought the vines to my mouth and blew a gentle breath over them.

Quentin's words rang through my head. I repeated them. The vines undulated like snakes. My forearm convulsed as the muscles inside knotted. I could feel a static charge build.

I raced out from behind the vehicle and channeled my inner Cassie. "Go back to Middle Earth!"

Both elves turned to face me, their eyes wide. I snarled, shifted my hips and snapped my arm. The static charge arced down my shoulder into my palm. It collapsed around the vines as they left my hand. A sonic boom sounded as a lance of lightning shot forward. The air exploded with an electric blue discharge as the bolt of energy hurtled towards the gun-toting elf.

The windows of every nearby vehicle shattered. The air screamed spitefully, and snow vaporized into steam. Car alarms wailed a discordant tune.

I saw her eyes widen as she registered what was happening. The scream died as the light buried itself in her abdomen. Tendrils of smoke escaped from the center of her mass. Her body shivered as her hands inched towards the smoking crater. Her fingers stopped moving and she fell to her knees. The rum color left her eyes as her head sank. Her body followed, and she crashed into the snow.

A strange quiet hung over the noise. Nearby curtains and shutters were pulled open. Curious eyes peeped out to survey the scene. Cassie was one of them, peering an inch over the brick wall. Even with the all the snow-caked roads, the police would find a way to show up for something like this.

An inhuman scream drowned out the other sounds. The remaining elf's body trembled. Her eyes hardened and she nocked three arrows.

Highly impractical.

I dove to the side and covered my head. The arrows buried themselves in the snow. Steam billowed and the ground tremored. I got to my feet and ran towards Cassie. The ground erupted. Snow and chunks of asphalt rained down, peppering the parked cars.

Maybe it wasn't so impractical after all. I didn't want to stick around to find out.

"Cassie!" I motioned for her to get down as I jumped over the low wall. I landed hard, rolling and pressing myself flat to the ground.

Cassie fell beside me. "Holy shit! Did you see that lightning?"

"Of course. I threw it!"

Pebble-sized bits of brick crumbled as a sliver of metal protruded from the wall. That was a strong arrowhead. I grabbed Cassie, hauled her over me and rolled. "Move!" My fingers throbbed as I clawed through the snow, scrambling to get to my feet. Cassie broke into a full sprint, putting twenty feet between herself and the wall.

I was considerably closer when it detonated. Brick and mortar showered me as I ran. Larger chunks pelted my back like heavy-handed blows. I clenched my jaw and peered over my shoulder. The elf nocked another arrow. I had no idea what it could do, and I didn't want to find out.

Her lips spread into a cruel smile when our eyes met.

She wasn't planning on missing. It's a good thing Izzy of the Big Tree carried little regard for the plans of others. He streaked through the air between us, closing the distance before I could blink. The elf recoiled from the strobing orb of light. It seemed she wasn't used to being charged by a tiny dewdrop.

It's not a regular occurrence, even for the supernatural.

She leapt back and steadied her bow, vying for a clean shot. Izzy wasn't having that. He let out a shrill shriek of defiance and arced by her face.

Her bow sank into the snow as she stumbled to the side. She pressed a hand to her face. Wisps of steam bled into the winter air, spreading into wide plumes before dissipating altogether. Her body quivered and she swung a hand through the air to swat the little fae.

"Wretch!" Spittle flew from her mouth as her lips trembled. A slender gash marred the fair skin of her left cheek.

Izzy floated nearby, hefting a sliver of something metal. I have no idea how he held onto it without being burned himself.

"You have made a most grievous error, sylvan. Flee, or face Izzaroohoo of the Big Tree." He flourished the piece of metal in his hands. "Run while you still can." Izzy threw his head back and let loose with a belly shaking, "Muwhahahaha!"

"John, what are you doing?" Cassie stood at the end of the next block, jumping and waving her arms. I shook my head and ran.

Just keep her busy, Izzy. Try not to do anything stupid.

Izzy's maniacal laughter followed as I caught up with Cassie and we rounded the corner.

"Is Izzy trying to fight her?"

"I hope not." I grimaced and thought how an actual fight between the two would end. "I pray he's stalling her by doing what he's best at—being an irritant."

"Yeah, well, I hope Izzy kicks the snot out of Katniss." Cassie sank a fist into the palm of her other hand.

"The odds aren't in his favor. Sylvan are excellent marksman."

Cassie gave me a blank stare.

"Wood elves."

"Whatever. I'm still rooting for Izzy to take down Blonde Arrow back there."

Young people need to come with a dictionary.

I shook my head when I found what I was looking for. "There!"

I pointed to an antiquated gate layered in snow with hints of aged black showing beneath. It ran two-thirds along the length of the block and dwarfed me in height. The building behind it was far more impressive. A cathedral of old stone and style, hard to find today. It was smaller than the behemoths advertised in some brochures, but held its own awe and charm. It possessed something more important.

Its composition.

Cassie followed my lead without question. I rushed towards the gate. My fingers closed around the cold metal as the sleeve of my coat tore. A razor sliced through the top of my forearm, and I lurched back, sending the gate flying open. Cassie didn't need an invitation. She rushed through as I tumbled back.

The elf was engaged in a frenzied dance with Izzy at the end of the block. Her open hand blurred, and something made of dark glass hurtled past my shoulder. A cooling line ran over the area, and I realized my coat and skin had been parted with surgical efficiency. A throw like that should have been impossible with the snowfall as bad as it was. Not to mention the fact she was engaged in battle with the dewdrop.

Izzy seized his opportunity and surged forward. Another gash, another tendril of steam hissed into the air. The sylvan snapped her hands towards the dewdrop. Glass blades shaped like arrowheads seemed to materialize like magic. She slashed at him, missing every strike. Sometimes it paid to be small. She snarled and twisted. I realized her intent too late.

I stumbled through the gate as one of the knives bit into the meat of my shoulder. It filled the area with the sort of burn that came from pouring iced liquor into a wound. Cassie rushed to my side and helped me shut the gate.

The wood elf batted Izzy aside and darted to the gate. Her hands clasped to the bars, and she wrenched. The sylvan's skin screamed and hissed as she clung to the bars. She leaned forward, nearly pressing her face against the metal.

We locked eyes. Hers shook and danced with maddened light. She let loose an animalistic scream and finally released her grip. She fell back several steps, hands trembling, fingers twitching out of control. She turned her hands over, and I sucked in a breath that hurt my teeth.

Charred skin crumbled like burnt paper. She reached into a fold in her outfit and snapped her hand. A glass blade tumbled through the air. It struck the old iron and shattered into purple flame.

The gate remained untarnished.

She screamed again and whipped her arms in a flurry. Glass burst into flecks and beads of fire that died in the cold. The iron held strong. The elf stepped forward and eyed me. "Look at me." Moisture welled through the bottom of her lids. "Look. At. Me!"

I did.

We held each other's stares without fail. She gripped the bars again. Her face tightened and twitched in agony. "She was my sister... You killed her!" Saliva hung between her teeth as her face quivered in rage. "She was my sister!" Her fingers blackened and cracked like bad pottery.

I didn't know what possessed me to go over to her. I placed my hands on hers, gripped tight, and held her against the iron. "I did. I'm sorry."

Our eyes remained locked. She didn't care for my apology. I gritted my teeth, resisting the urge to turn away. My jaw hardened, and I steadied myself to watch, regretting that it had come to this. "I did what I had to do. I don't regret it, but I can still be sorry for you."

A burble formed in her throat and left as a snarl. The black portions of her skin could no longer endure the touch of iron. What didn't crumble to dust ignited. She thumped against the gate as she burned. Her final scream let out her anger, and let in the flames. She burned from inside out until nothing was left but stains in the snow and a puddle that froze over.

"I…" Cassie blinked and rubbed the heels of her palms against her face. She cleared her throat and looked away. "That was intense."

I grimaced and grabbed my shoulder. "Let's go." My voice was like ground stone as I nodded to the cathedral doors.

Cassie came to my side in a second. "John, why'd she do that?"

I coughed and looked back to the spot. "Honestly?"

Cassie bit her lip and nodded.

"I don't know. Loss pushes people to all sorts of ends—ragged edges they are all too willing to jump off of. They were sisters. It's not a stretch to believe they were very close. Maybe all they had was each other. Being an assassin is not an easy life. I've met some." I shook my head. "But I really don't know why she did it."

A silence fell between us. It was broken the next second.

"Oi! Dunderclunk!"

I groaned, and it wasn't due to pain.

Izzy flashed and waved outside the gate. "Grant me permission. I don't much care for this cold. You can't expect me to wait here, not after heroically saving your long, lanky bodies."

I scowled and trundled back to the gate. I'm not a spiteful man, but I kicked my foot through the snow. A heap of it showered Izzy and Barnabus. The pair of them looked disgruntled.

"Primitive…bark-brained…" Izzy's teeth chattered faster than he knew how to handle. I used the moment to open the gate and gesture with my hand. Izzy scowled. "Per…mi…sh…shun."

"I'm not the owner of this place, nor do I call it home. I can't do that."

Izzy's face tightened. "I'm supposed to help you."

"You're a dewdrop. How much of your power will you leave behind?"

"Bah." Izzy waved a dismissive hand. "That is beside the point."

I stared at him.

"Fine." He slumped and brushed a pea-sized drop of snow off Barnabus' head. "Tchk-tchk." He booted the Unifly into motion and flew forward. There was an instance of hesitance; it looked like he met an invisible wall. He grimaced as he passed through it. "That was wholly uncomfortable." Izzy shot me a look that said he deserved some form of recompense for it.

He wasn't going to get it.

I waved a hand to him. "Come on." I turned and the doors to the building opened. We all stared as a gentle, warm amber light filtered through. A man stood at the head of it. I would have liked to have said he had an unassuming appearance not worth remembering. I would've been wrong.

He eyed the three of us from behind black-framed glasses that contrasted the fairness of his skin. His eyes were a shade of icy blue that made the snow look warm in comparison. They settled on the green bobbing orb beside us. He smiled and I thought of toothpaste commercials. "You are welcome here, little one."

Cassie and I moved our mouths, but no sounds came out.

Izzy harrumphed and swelled his chest as he glared at me. He turned to the stranger and bowed to his waist. Izzy hadn't shown that level of respect to Nox. "Thank you."

The stranger nodded in acknowledgement. He took a finger and brushed away a few locks of flaxen gold hair. "You two are tired and hurt. Come in." His voice was soft and soothing.

I almost obeyed him as soon as he said it. The state of his clothes stopped me. A black dress shirt and clean, creaseless khakis. Pen tips protruded from his pocket protector.

It was winter, and that was all he wore. It was snowing…and not a drop touched him. Every snowflake miraculously found its way to the ground around him.

Cassie whistled then clamped a hand over her mouth, realizing what she'd done. "He's hot."

I glowered at her. Her cheeks flushed, and I attributed it to the cold. The man's face was too symmetrical—if there was such a thing. A model in a computer technician's clothing.

The man looked to the sky and his smile slipped. "Grey night." He frowned before turning back to us. "Come in, please. It's going to get worse."

Izzy needed no further invitation. He zoomed past us and into the cathedral. Cassie followed after him, pausing as she passed the man to give him an appraising look.

I formed an immediate dislike of the blonde-haired nerd. He arched a pale and expectant brow at me. I mumbled under my breath and trudged forward, nursing my injury. An oven's warmth radiated over the area, and I stopped as a hand fell on my shoulder. The stranger eyed me.

"You're hurt."

I thought that was obvious, but I refrained from being rude. "Yes."

I tried to brush past him and take another step. His grip held firm. My head filled with fog. I couldn't remember the last time I slept. Wetness spread through the knees of my jeans. The snow cushioned my fall.

"Rest. You have earned it."

I took his advice and blacked out in the snow.

Chapter Thirty-Two

Sharp notes of spice and toasted bread tickled my nose. A cushion pressed against my body and I stared up at countless chandeliers. They bathed the cathedral in an orange glow that complemented the candles around the wall. I groaned and pushed myself up. The floor was a black marble polished to a mirror finish. I turned to the sound of the chewing.

Cassie grinned between bites of a sandwich that caused my stomach to ache. She leapt from the pew and knelt by my side on the floor. "Here." She pushed a triangular piece towards my mouth.

I bit into it and shut my eyes to help savor the taste. I exhaled through my nose as melted pepper jack cheese and ham graced my mouth. The bread had a pleasant crunch, softened by the avocado.

Cassie offered me a glass of a dark fizzing drink. I took it and guzzled down the root beer. It was a personal favorite of mine.

"Is he awake? Is-he-is-he-is-he-is-he-is-he?" A softball-sized comet of green light rocketed overhead and circled me with dizzying speed. "How-are-you-how-are-you-how-are-you?" Izzy's chittering was like listening to squealing tires. My head spun.

I gave Cassie a look. "What's wrong with him?"

She frowned. "Sugar rush."

"Why?"

"He had soda."

"Soda!" Izzy hooted and cheered as he spun faster.

"How much?"

Cassie held up three fingers.

I shook my head and watched the faerie create a hectic

light show above. "Three sips did that to him?"

"Three sips? The glow stick drank *three cups!*"

I eyed my drink askance, then Cassie. "Root beer isn't caffeinated."

"No…but Pepsi is." She turned to shake her head at Izzy. "Little heathen."

I snorted, and a carbonated sting burned the upper portions of my throat and nostrils.

An ethereally soft voice pulled us away from the energetic fae. "You're awake. You're feeling better, I trust?" I shifted on the mattress lain on the floor. The blonde-haired stranger stood half a dozen paces from me. He approached with both hands at his sides. One held a book splayed open and pressed flat against his thigh.

I arched a brow. "Bradbury?"

"He gives good advice on writing." The stranger lifted the book and gave it a gentle wave. "Very Zen. How is your arm?" He lowered his head, letting his glasses slip to the tip of his nose.

I rolled my shoulder and grimaced. "A tad sore." Neat strands bound the tissue together. "Nice stitching."

The man smiled. "Thank you, but I'm out of practice."

His 'out of practice' was better than anything I could do. I flexed my fingers and my forearm throbbed. "Thank you for patching me up, and for the food."

He smiled. "Of course."

I rose from the mattress and extended my hand. "Do you have a name?"

His smile widened, and there was a faint glimmer behind his arctic eyes. "Names are a dangerous thing to share—aren't they?"

I blinked as he took hold of my hand. A static buzzing coursed over my fingers and faded in an instant.

What was that?

"But…" He held the shake and turned to look around the cathedral for a second. "Call me Church." He released his grip.

Cassie took a loud sip from her cup before giving

Church a half-smile. "No one likes a smart ass."

Church turned and matched her smile. "Then call me, Pot, Kettle."

Cassie blinked and decided to stuff her mouth with a palm-sized bite of her sandwich. She narrowed her eyes as she chewed, glaring at him.

I needed lessons from him on how to deal with Cassie.

"You don't seem the least bit disturbed by two strangers showing up in this storm."

He smiled but remained quiet.

"Nor...that." I waved a hand to Izzy. The dewdrop slowed his spinning.

"I'm not." Church sank to his knees and eased himself into a cross-legged position on the floor.

Cassie swallowed the last bite and wiped her mouth with the back of her sleeve. "So, who are you then?"

Church blinked, removed his glasses, polished them, and sighed. It was done with mechanical precision. "A concerned party."

"Wow, vague much, Blondielocks?"

Church tilted his head and looked at Cassie like it was the first time seeing her.

Cassie leaned back and eyed him like he was strange. "What?"

His lips twitched. "Nothing. For a moment, I was terribly afraid you might be related to someone I work with."

"S'what?" Cassie stared at him, waiting for an answer.

Church sighed. "Nothing." He turned back to me. "Now is there anything else I can do for you? Would you care to rest a bit more? There are spare beds upstairs for those in need. Or if you're in a hurry, a cup of coffee before you go?"

"Why are you being so kind?"

He blinked and his face lost all focus. "I'm sorry?"

"This." I gestured to everything around us. "You didn't have to help us. You didn't need to do anything."

The confused look on his face only grew. It was a good

thing Izzy was there to clarify. The dewdrop stopped by my ear. "It's his nature, John. You can't change nature. Though you humans certainly have the most absurd notions about trying to." Izzy shook his head.

"Right…thank you, Izzy."

The fae bowed as if he had done a great service.

I lowered my head in respect to Church and motioned towards the door. "Thank you again, but I think we will be fine. Cassie?" I reached over to the top of a pew where my tattered shirt and coat hung.

"Nonsense." Church's voice remained level but there was a clear note of steel in it. "I'll fetch something warm to drink and then you can leave. Life isn't a rush. The world isn't going to end if you wait a few minutes."

I hope you're right.

Church looked over his shoulder as he walked away. "I often am." I couldn't see his mouth but I had a feeling he was smiling.

I frowned and grabbed my shirt, donning it. It looked like it hadn't been through a blizzard and crumpled into a ball. It felt like it had just come out of the dryer and was pressed creaseless. Small tears still marred it. I eased into my jacket, wincing as my shoulder argued against the movement. At least it wasn't horribly inflamed, or worse, infected.

Cassie came to my side and plopped onto the pew. She tugged on my coat and gave me a look that said I should do the same. I did.

"What's on your mind?"

"You'll laugh."

I gave her a reassuring smile. "I promise I won't."

"Part of me is thinking that we should just stay here."

"For how long?"

Cassie looked away, first to the candles on the wall, then to the murals at the head of the cathedral. "As long as we can? I don't know. I just... How long are we going to have to do this?" She looked down to her knees.

I grimaced and rubbed the sleeve of my coat, sending

ants through the skin of my forearm. "If I'm right about the hunch I have, then not too much longer."

Cassie looked at me sideways.

I didn't elaborate. Nox asked tough questions, but the answers were worth it. It was what I did with them next that would determine things. I only needed to make the right choice.

And that is the hardest thing in the world to do. How do you know when your choices are right? And what happens if they're not?

I kept my dark musings to myself. Izzy came to an abrupt stop in front of my face. He stood atop his Unifly. I stared at him—waiting.

"So?" Izzy shook with impatience, going so far as to tap his foot on his mount's neck. Barnabus snorted and shook his head in disapproval.

"So, what?"

"What happened? Tell-spill-share!"

"What things?"

"With..." Izzy paused and leaned forward, cupping a hand to his mouth. "With the Darkest Queen of Faerie."

"Oh." My mouth twitched and I took a breath to still myself. I didn't need to blurt out anything unnecessary. Cassie perked up beside me. Her eyes were elsewhere, but her attention was focused on me. I cleared my throat. "We talked."

"About?" Izzy squirmed and fidgeted. I made a mental note to keep the little fae far away soda in the future.

"The nature of things. We spoke about names."

"What kind of names?" Izzy was resting atop the Unifly's head.

Cassie turned her head a fraction and shut her eyes. She was paying careful attention.

"The kind that can get you in trouble, Izzy. The kind that can get you killed. The kind that makes a young, innocent girl be chased by monsters." I glanced at Cassie. She looked back at me now.

"You know everything now?"

I shook my head. "Not everything, but enough."

"But you know who's after me?"

"I have a good idea."

Cassie bit her lip, then nodded. "Good enough for me. First dibs on..." She stopped and sank a fist into her open palm.

"If I'm right, you can have all the dibs."

She snorted and shook her head. "That doesn't make sense, but thanks."

"But-but-but-but still!" Izzy vibrated like a small car in winter. "You met *her*! You survived an encounter with the Darkest of Faerie Queens. And you left intact—sane! That is tantamount to besting her. She always takes a toll on those that meet her. Wait until I tell the Free Folk that *you* bested a Faerie Queen!"

"Please don't." It wasn't entirely true. Nox had taken her toll. Maybe not today, but one day—and one day was always closer than many seemed to think.

"Why not?" Izzy puffed up. "She isn't as mighty as she thinks." The little fae gave a defiant shake of his head. "Many should know that she couldn't take advantage of a beanpole of a mortal!" He laughed and pointed at me.

"And what happens, Izzy, if you spread that rumor?"

He blinked and stroked the underside of his lip with a finger. "Well, I suppose you will die a most horrible death." He shrugged as if it were no consequence.

"And what about the dewdrop that spread the rumor?" I arched a brow. "What happens to him?"

Izzy sank into his saddle as his eyes ballooned. "Oh…ah. Yes. Well. It's a rather stupid story anyway." He waved a dismissive hand.

"In my experience, there is no such thing as a stupid story." Church carried two mugs from which steam billowed. I could smell the cocoa from where I sat and reconsidered my rush to leave. "Careful, it's hot." He pressed a cup into my hands, and did so for Cassie as well. Church took a seat beside us and waited in silence.

I hissed at the first sip. It scalded the tip of my tongue

making it hard to taste anything. Cassie learned from my mistake and cradled her cup as she blew on it.

"Allow me, Soda Princess." Izzy nudged Barnabus towards her cup and flew into a tiny dervish above it. The steam died down. "There."

Cassie gave her a cup a sideways look, then to Izzy. She shrugged and took a sip. Her mouth spread into a smile. "Okay, that's good. It's rich."

Izzy sank to the lip of the cup and leaned over to almost bury his face in it. "May I try?"

Cassie didn't miss a beat. "I will cut you. Rule number one when dealing with women: don't mess with our chocolate."

He snapped to attention and saluted. "Rule number one. Understood."

Cassie grinned and sipped again.

I frowned, waiting for my chocolate to cool. I didn't think I was going to get the same helping hand from Izzy.

"You have a great deal on your mind." Church phrased it as a statement.

"I do."

"Don't."

I paused and looked up from my hot chocolate. "I'm sorry?"

"Don't. Clear it. Empty it. Sometimes there is such a thing as overthinking. It clouds your thoughts and makes you slow. The three of you will come out of this fine."

Cassie's posture softened. "Whew, that's a relief."

"It won't be easy, but the hard things in life never are."

"And…my calm's gone." Cassie smiled and took another swig of her chocolate.

I followed her lead and took a sip. It didn't taste like it came from a packet. It rolled over my tongue and clung to my taste buds. "It's good."

Church bowed his head. "Thank you. Melting chocolate is harder than I imagined, especially without burning it." He stopped and frowned for a second. "My colleague has a terrible propensity for burning things."

I felt sorry for his colleague. We sat there in silence, sipping our chocolate for a moment I wished would stretch on without stop.

"What are you going to do next?" Church watched me with an eerily neutral expression.

"Finish my chocolate."

"And then?"

I turned to Cassie and grinned. "Do you like clubs?"

Chapter Thirty-Three

Gray clouds rolled through the sky as we parted ways with Church. He waved from the entrance, though no smile touched his lips. It was a grim parting in my mind. Cassie didn't seem to notice. I planned to keep it that way.

We plowed through the snow-covered streets as best we could. Cassie sneezed and tugged on my coat.

"What's on your mind?"

"Are we really going to a club—now?"

I nodded. "Why, is something wrong with that?"

"This the best time for it?"

I laughed through my nose in little puffs of air. "You'd be surprised. This isn't the sort of club you're thinking about."

Cassie rolled her eyes. "Oh, great. Back to your cryptic crap."

Izzy hovered behind Cassie, his arms crossed tight and his face tighter. "I hate this." He snapped his head to look at every snowflake he could and glowered. "I hate this very much. Why do you tolerate this?"

"Yeah, I'll get on the phone with the weather channel and tell them to stop this, Izzy." Cassie shook her head.

"Do so, posthaste."

She sighed.

I looked over my shoulder. "Settle down in the back, kids, or I'll turn the car around."

Wetness spread over my hair, plastering it to my skull. I frowned and turned around. Cassie's lips were pressed tight, struggling not to turn into a smile.

I narrowed my eyes. "Which one of you did that?"

Izzy looked around as if there was someone else responsible. Cassie mimicked him.

Cute. One should never start a fight they can't finish.

I knelt and scooped up a handful of snow. In a swift motion, I sent the snowball into the air. Cassie stumbled back with an *oomph* as it struck her nose. I do not pull my punches in snowball fights.

She shook her head and brushed a hand over her face. "You…you…." Her eyes glowed with heat.

Izzy burst into raucous laughter and pressed his hands to his stomach. It was a poor decision. Cassie glared at me, then him. She mirrored my movements and snapped her arm towards the dewdrop. He was buried under a fistful of snow.

Barnabus and he sank a foot in the air, shivering as they shook off the snow. "How dare you?" Izzy's chest rose rapidly. "Crass. Terrible. Strange-haired—"

Cassie gave Izzy a look that could have melted the surrounding snow. She arched a singular brow and spoke in a low, controlled whisper. "Did you just talk shit about my hair?"

Izzy swelled further. If he puffed up anymore, he would burst. "Of course I did! Your hair is—*bwoof!*" Izzy swirled as a handful of powdered snow rained onto him. It was the only thing I could do to save him from his own stupidity and stubbornness. Izzy recovered and blinked. He looked to the pair of us. "You humans are maddening creatures."

Cassie snickered. "Likewise, faerie."

Izzy threw his arms across his chest and grunted. Cassie mirrored him.

"If you two are done fighting, can we move on?"

They both frowned at me.

I ignored them and walked. I made sure they didn't see my smile as I put some distance between us. It was a stupid thing, but sometimes when life is hard, the stupid things help. A snowball fight wasn't going to harm anybody. If anything, it let them get some of their anger out. And anger always needs an outlet—always. How you choose to let it out affects you. Snowballs don't lead to much trouble.

A palm-sized bit of snow impacted my jaw and brushed

against my eye. I blinked in time to see the second ball flatten against my chest. I looked down and then up at the pair of them. My eyes narrowed.

Izzy and Cassie burst into a fit of giggles.

"Stop it. It's undignified." I clenched my jaw and walked.

"Yessur, Captain Tight Pants."

I ignored Cassie's jab.

Snow crunched as Cassie trundled towards me. She gave me a gentle shove and folded a corner of her lip back. "So, where we're going—we going to have to ask for an invitation too?"

I arched a brow. "You caught that?"

She sniffed, wriggling her nose at the cold. "Yeah. Why'd Blondie have to invite Izzy in?"

"Principle of Foundation."

She wriggled her nose and scrunched her face. "Oh, right—that. So for those who might need a refresher?"

I raised my hands as if framing a distant object. "Imagine a place—a home, or something that has a sense of…" I trailed off, trying to find the right words. "A place like that church." I hooked a thumb over my shoulder. "Or a home that's been lived in a long time, love has fostered and more. There's a feeling in places like those—it protects them."

"Like a barrier?"

I nodded. "It's real. A threshold that creatures have to pass over. They can do it without an invitation, but at the cost of leaving a lot of their powers behind."

"Is that what happened back at your place?"

"Yes, it's why we had an easier time with the trolls."

Cassie scoffed. "Speak for yourself."

"If they didn't barge in and leave most of their strength outside, there's a chance we wouldn't be arguing in the snow now."

She mouthed a silent, "Ah."

"The Principle of Foundation is about strength, pillars of support. That's what homes and places like some churches are. So much goes on within their walls. A home is full of growth, love, and sometimes heartache. All of that forms something that doesn't really have words. It's an intangible thing, but it's real—it's there."

"And that can keep fae out?"

I waggled my hand. "It's a deterrent. It's part of mortal life, and a strong part at that."

Cassie nodded in understanding. "So is this club going to have one of these thresholds?"

I shook my head. "No, it's not the kind of place that could form one."

A handful of snow leapt into the air as Cassie's shoe kicked into a mound. "What keeps the nasties out?"

I eyed her and smiled. "The bouncers."

"Oh."

"They also keep the nasties in." I watched as she grabbed her arms and gave them a quick rub.

"So, who is it we're going to meet?"

I frowned and thought of the best way to put it. We passed an aged and defunct streetlamp when I found the words. "An important member of the other team."

"Huh?"

"There are two sides to every coin. Let's just say that he's the face of one of them."

Cassie remained quiet but pursed her lips and nodded.

A green light flashed once. Izzy came by my ear, and I found myself wishing he hadn't. "You know, for a mortal, you're awfully cryptic."

I took it as a compliment coming from a fae. "Thank you."

"It's irritating." He huffed and booted Barnabus towards Cassie's shoulder. She shot me a smug look after hearing Izzy's comments.

I smiled at his little jibe. It faded a second later. Snow crunched with a sound like a heavy truck over gravel. I turned to see a homeless man shamble around the corner. Woolen autumn colors snaked around his neck. There was a glint of copper tumbling through one of his fingers. I looked at the ground and saw a footprint that was close to a manhole cover in size. My gaze drifted back to the disheveled man.

He flashed me a toothy grin and held a penny pinched between his thumb and forefinger. "Thanks for this, by the way." He tapped the coin to his nose.

"This?" I eyed him askance. "Not these?"

His grin widened, and he sent a hand into a pocket. Coins clinked.

I raised an arm like a bar and eased Cassie to my side. "What can I do for you?"

The muscles in my back knotted as he took another step forward. He wasn't beholden to me any longer. Whatever services I had paid for were now complete. He seemed amicable as far as his kind were concerned. Still, I didn't want to do anything that might change that.

"Me?" He rolled the penny to the tip of his thumb and pointed to himself with it. "Nothing. It's what I can do for you." His smile grew to shark-like proportions as he jabbed the penny toward me.

"And what is that?" I inched a step back and made sure Cassie followed.

He reached up and sank three fingers behind the scarf. His head rolled from side to side as he tugged on the scarf. "Well, boy-o, since you left, I've been keeping my ears to the ground."

I watched him for any sudden movements. They never came.

He waited for a response, but I didn't indulge him. When he realized I wasn't going to say anything, he breathed an exasperated puff of air. "Ah, well, things are starting to get interesting."

I gave him a weak smile. "Are they?"

"Lots of players in the Neravene are gettin' interested in you. Lots of players that aren't batting for a team, if you know what I mean." He arched a brow and leaned forward.

"Yeah, no kiddin'." Cassie rolled her eyes. "We were jumped recently."

"No surprise, there's a big price out for you." He scratched his beard and turned his head slowly to face Cassie. He appraised her from top to bottom like a prized animal.

The look rankled me. I loosened my posture and took a step forward. "Are you planning to collect that big price?" My knees bent just enough in case I needed to spring into action.

He pursed his lips and made a popping sound with his mouth. "No. I'm interested in something more"—he snapped his hand through the air as if he could pluck the words from the sky—"lasting."

I arched a brow and Cassie eyed him askance. It was hard standing so close to him. Danger notwithstanding, it was the sweet smell oozing from him. I gritted through it.

Snow balled between his fingers as he rubbed them with his thumb. "Money is great, but do you know what fae like more than that?" He mimicked my raised brow and leaned forward.

I had a good idea of what he was going to say.

"Power."

I was right. "And what kind of power would that be?"

He nodded to Cassie. "The important kind."

She gulped behind me.

Our friend blinked and looked in the space above us. His eyes focused on the hovering green figure, noticing him for the first time. "You're far from home, little one."

Izzy shifted on his mount and pointed a shaking finger. "And you—you…smell."

I could almost feel Cassie rolling her eyes. "Good one," she said.

Izzy huffed a satisfied breath.

I snapped my fingers and locked eyes with the homeless man. "You won't put a hand on her." I stepped forward and reached for my sword.

His hands went into the air. "Not trying to."

I froze. "What?"

"I'm here to help."

That was new. He had to have a price. He did—power. But what power could he gain by helping us? It clicked a second a later. "Something is going on between the groups and domains in faerie."

He nodded. "As far as my kind go"—he jabbed a thumb to his chest—"chaos. Many are risking going tribeless."

Izzy and I whistled in unison.

Cassie gave me a nudge. "Clue me in?"

"Imagine being part of a large and powerful gang." Our new friend grimaced at the last word. I ignored his disapproval. "You have support—protection. But there are rules and if you break them…"

Cassie nodded. "Got it, you're out. No more crew to back you up."

"Yes," I said.

"It's not easy for one of us to make it alone." He tugged his scarf as if it were constricting him.

"Which brings us back to why you're here." My hand still hovered over my saber. I hoped he wouldn't give me a reason to draw it.

"I told you—power."

I finally figured it out. "Sides are being formed, aren't they?" He nodded. "And you want to be on the winning one."

He threw his head back and chortled. "You're missing the point." I glared at him as his laughter subsided. "This is turning into a contact sport." The homeless man rolled his shoulders and cracked his knuckles. "And you three are about to get hit hard."

It clicked. "You want to get involved in the fight. After all, what better way to get rid of the competition than in the heat of battle? You're using us like a magnet for any fae that wants her. If you can bump them off in a fight…"

The homeless man tapped an index finger to his nose.

Power. The lasting kind. He wasn't kidding. Removing any competition from other troll tribes, and possibly his own.

I extended a hand and offered him a smile. "I'm not one to turn down help." He grabbed my hand, and I tightened mine. "So long as there are no strings attached."

He raised several fingers into the air. "Scout's honor." The bones in my hand felt like cracked glass as he increased the pressure. I gasped and let go. "Don't get into a macho contest with a troll." He waggled a finger.

I shook my hand and scowled.

Cassie stepped between me and the troll. She jabbed him once with a finger. "Last time you helped us, you left us stranded. You took your dough and bailed." She accentuated each word with thrust of her finger, driving him back against a wall. "I should—"

Halogen light washed over us, forcing us to turn and shield our eyes. A series of crunches rang out as a vehicle came to a stop nearby. I turned and squinted. The high-powered light bombarded us from a fixture atop the SUV's roof. The Range Rover was noticeably modified, which explained its ease in navigating the snow. Every door opened in choreographed unison.

Slender figures exited the vehicle. They stood out against the snow like wraiths. The new arrivals were clothed in tight fabrics woven out of midnight. I squinted, trying to make out a feature to identify them. Burnished gold eyes stared back at me through the opening in their veils.

"Night Runners." I grimaced and shifted my weight.

Cassie spat and reached for her weapon. "Jeez, you had to go and piss them off."

I glared at her for a moment. "The blame isn't entirely mine."

She shrugged.

The black-clad assassins unsheathed a variety of blades that would have impressed a fantasy novelist. I swallowed and took a single step back. Cassie followed.

Izzy pulsed once. "Hah. We can handle them." The dewdrop shook a miniature fist in the direction of the gang.

I ached for his confidence.

The trunk of the SUV opened. The vehicle shook as

something lumbered out of it. He was at least a foot taller than me and double my mass. He looked like he could have been a stand-in for any brutish, ugly thug in television. His lips peeled back to reveal stained and chipped teeth. I had a feeling if I were any closer I would smell candy.

A trio of pops cracked behind me. I turned to see the rail thin homeless man slip between Cassie and me.

He craned his neck to the side and released a stiff grunt. "The big one's mine." I stepped back as he shed most of his clothes. "Catch." He yanked his scarf free and sent it towards me in a single smooth motion. Glamour faded, and I stared at a muscle-bound troll with a Mohawk. His hair flopped a bit as he moved forward.

The Night Runners bristled and exchanged glances. Lean muscles flexed and tensed within their clothing. Their blades angled up as their grips tightened. The bald-headed lump of grotesque muscle rolled his shoulders. A bearish burble left his throat as he moved to meet our newfound friend. His crude features melted as if they were painted with watercolors. It was like staring at mirror images.

Both trolls were near identical in size and appearance. Laden in generous heapings of muscle, wobbling Mohawks, and rudimentary tattoos representing a sun. They owed fealty to the Dawn Lady. Same tribe, same loyalties. Although I suspected the latter was no longer true. This was personal.

Our elven ambushers picked up on that as well. They wisely stepped aside. Both trolls paused for a split second. It felt like an invisible crackle of electricity leapt between them. They inclined heads in a form of mutual respect. It was short-lived.

They covered the distance between them in a three steps and locked arms. It was a contest of strength. Their fingers dug into each other's biceps and they twisted. Neither lost their balance. It was like watching two expert judokas trying to throw one another. One slip was all it would take.

Burning yellow eyes turned towards the three of us.

They narrowed and hardened as two of the Night Runners stepped forwards.

I looked to Cassie out of the corner of my eyes. “Ready?”

“No.” She shook once but settled herself and braced for what was coming.

Izzy threw his head back and released a peal of maniacal laughter. “Let them come.” He roared again as his body shook in the throes of adrenaline-fueled excitement.

The dewdrop booted Barnabus. Green light streaked towards the closest of the Night Runners. Izzy hurtled by, latching onto a piece of fabric causing the assailant to stagger and fight for balance. They flailed and swatted at the diminutive nuisance. It was rather comical. The remaining Night Runners leapt towards Cassie and me.

The comedy could have lasted a bit longer in my opinion.

I drew my saber and reeled back as three assassins sent their blades into a flurry. Dumb luck and my fumbling caused most of the blades to sail harmlessly by. My wrist throbbed as two daggers struck my sword in succession.

Cassie fared better, relying solely on Tatiana’s shield. The best offense is a good defense. Two Night Runners bore down on her, although with different intent. They hammered the shield as if trying to bury Cassie beneath their blows. Fatigue lined her face. They wanted her alive. I wouldn’t warrant such consideration.

My foot caught against the raised portion of the sidewalk and I fell. The closest of the Night Runners capitalized on my mistake. Her slender body snapped closer to follow me to the ground. I released my sword and reached out for her. My fingers closed around a bit of her outfit and I pulled. Her eyes widened under the off balance acceleration. My back sank into the snow and the Night Runner collided with me. They leaned back and adjusted their grip on the daggers. I held onto their clothes and snapped forward. My vision spun as our heads met. I lashed out blindly, clawing for her face.

The Night Runner tumbled back. The swath of clothing around her face hung in my grip. Her eyes flickered through a series of expressions that could have killed. She flicked her white hair out of her eyes as her lips peeled back. Her fingers flexed like she aimed to gut me with them. She lunged. I rolled as she landed in the snow and twisted. My elbow crashed into her back. The elf released a pained *oomph* as the second Night Runner inched closer with caution. The third stayed back and surveyed the scene, their eyes trained on everything around us.

Someone screamed. I turned and saw Cassie succumb to the weight of two elves as they tackled her to the ground. She struggled and spat. There was a grunt as one of the pair caught a rogue fist. The Night Runner growled, her hands moving to pin Cassie's wrists.

A bellow echoed in the air. Everyone stopped to look. One of the trolls was airborne, sailing towards me. The three Night Runners beside me scattered. It was a good idea. My palms slipped against compressed snow as I scrabbled for a hold to claw my way up and out of the spot. I got to my feet and struggled through the snow. The sound of air being let out of a large bag filled my ears as the troll landed a foot behind me. Snow went everywhere, the ground shook, and pavement cracked.

The standing troll gave me a toothy grin before enfolding his fist within the other. Knuckles cracked. The Night Runner furthest from me turned and lowered the garment obscuring his face. He bared his teeth in a challenging hiss. The troll took two steps and splayed his hand wide. The Night Runner slashed at it. Whatever alloy the blade was made out of, it wasn't steel or iron.

Shame.

The weapon cut deep into the flesh of the troll's forearm. If it was painful, the troll showed no sign of it. His fingers came down around the crown of the elf's skull. His features furrowed in exertion as his fingers went tight and he lifted. The Night Runner left the ground. He kicked his legs and pummeled the troll's arms. It was useless. His skin cracked and split before the sickening sound of crumbling bones graced our ears. The elf's screams buried all other noises. I shut my eyes as it fell silent. Seconds passed before I opened them again.

What was left of the Night Runner lay in a heap on the street, its blood bringing color to the snow. The two elves closest to me tensed and cast wary looks between myself and the troll. Snow shifted and purple limbs moved on the ground. The fallen troll grunted as it rose. It shook its head, giving itself a solid smack of its palm to help clear any lingering cobwebs.

Any sudden movements might have triggered the troll to turn its attention to me. I remained still, going so far as to hold my breath. It may have seemed an extreme measure, but in the moment, nothing seemed too ridiculous if it meant surviving. The troll righted itself and quivered as its fists clenched. It turned and stormed towards its counterpart. The elves not busying themselves with Cassie joined it. Three against one—not very sporting.

I felt I needed to even the odds. I ran for my saber, recovered it, and rushed towards Cassie. One of the two elves restraining her saw me. They pushed away from her and sprang to their feet. Blades whistled as they were unsheathed. The Night Runner leapt once and sank their weight. My first swing was too high, passing a foot over their head. We exchanged clumsy strikes as the snow hampered our movements.

All my years of combat taught me one thing. There is no such thing as fighting dirty when it comes down to it.

I stomped my foot deep into the snow. A blade arced towards me. I twisted without moving my feet and leaned back. The sword sailed by, and I recovered as the elf did. She took a step to close the distance. I made my move. I kicked hard, sending snow into her face. She sputtered and waved a hand as if it would help. Two short steps brought me close enough. Using both hands, I brought my saber down like a club across her body. The blade cracked into her collarbone and bit deep. I twisted and dragged it across her torso. She didn't have time to scream. The steel did its job.

Her eyes went wide as her skin crackled. Steam billowed from a gash across her midsection. She crumpled seconds later, her body still steaming. The Night Runner atop Cassie shivered and leapt back as if burned. She looked around wildly for help.

She wasn't going to find any. Cassie rolled and got to her feet as I rushed the Night Runner. I was too slow. Something twirled by like a black pinwheel. A Night Runner's body cartwheeled through the air. I stopped short as the other elf turned in time to see their comrade's body crash into them. It was a bone-jarring impact that drove both of them to the ground. I stared for a second that stretched too long. Their bodies were still.

I shook my head and ran to Cassie. She shuddered as she propped herself up on Tatiana's shield. The sword shook in her hand. I grabbed her by the crook of her arm.

"Come on." I gave her a tug.

Metal groaned and screeched nearby. We whipped around to see a Night Runner bounce off the hood of the SUV. A meaty fist hammered into the body and sent it back onto the vehicle. The hood caved in around the elf's body, and the Range Rover shook. One of the trolls barreled into the other, pushing him into the passenger side of the vehicle. The doors shied away from the troll with the sound of failing metal. Windows screamed as they turned to chips. He shook his head, and brought his arms down against the forearms pinning him to the body of the SUV. The other troll's grip faltered and our "friend" seized the moment. He grabbed the troll's hip and neck and shifted his weight.

They traded places. The other troll smashed into the already damaged portion of the vehicle. It rocked further, almost tipping to its side. A flare of green light pulled my attention to a spot several feet away from the trolls. Izzy streaked and strobed like a violent pinball. He struck the last Night Runner with his fists, probably causing more irritation than pain. With quick maneuvering I credited more to the Unifly than him, they landed on the bridge of the elf's nose.

Izzy leapt and clung to an eyelid like it was the only purchase he could find. He pulled.

The Night Runner stumbled and screamed. They lashed out to grab Izzy and presumably crush him. The little dewdrop didn't like the idea. He jumped towards the hand in excitement, teeth gleaming. Izzy grappled his way onto the Night Runner's forefinger. The elf howled and shook his hand, trying to dislodge the tiny fae biting his finger. Izzy was relentless, shaking his head as he dragged his teeth across the digit. The elf swatted at the dewdrop. Izzy released his hold but not in time. The back of the Night Runner's free hand caught him and sent him sprawling through the air.

"Izzy!" Cassie ran to catch him.

I followed by her side, eyeing the Night Runner. We traded glances before their gaze fell to their finger and then back to us. They turned, opened a Way, and left.

Smart.

Monstrous breaths of exertion made Cassie and I get out of the way of the two trolls. With a sweep of his leg and a push of his body, the homeless troll sent the other beast into the air and through the Way. The opening snapped shut. I wondered about the fate of the Night Runner on the other side.

Trolls are hefty creatures.

"Let that be a lesson learned, fiends!" Izzy burst forth from the snow, shaking himself off with his declaration. He dusted his hands as if he had done a great share of the fighting.

Something brayed, and a stone-sized bump appeared in the snow. Barnabus popped out, eyed Izzy, and snorted in something that sounded like disdain.

Izzy shook his head and held up a placating hand. "It was very much so a good idea at the time."

Barnabus huffed and looked away.

I had no idea of how to intervene in a micro-faerie spat. Instead, I turned to Cassie and looked her over. No visible injuries. Good. But sometimes it's the things that you can't see that hurt more. If left unattended, they fester.

"Are you alright?"

She rubbed her hands from her waist down to her thighs and patted herself. "Yeah, bit sore." Her voice faltered. Cassie's eyes flickered from me to the damaged SUV, to the troll, and finally to the ground.

I didn't know if putting a hand on her shoulder would be the right thing after a fight. I felt the simple gesture couldn't hurt. I let my hand rest between her neck and shoulder. "What's wrong? Talk to me."

She sniffed twice and rubbed her reddened nose. The cold was getting to her. My own cheeks and nose felt tight and distant. I'm sure they were just as red. I moved my hand to her back and gave her a nudge.

"Come on." I led the way towards the SUV.

"What are you doing?"

I brought her around to the driver's side and opened the door. "Get in and hop over."

Cassie eyed me and then the damaged door on that side. "Uh? Okay…" She did as I asked though.

I followed her inside, settling myself into the driver's seat. I made a silent prayer and reached for the keys. With a twist and a grumble, the Range Rover shuddered into life. A green light pulsed outside the window, followed by a small *thump*.

"Oy, Beanpole! Are you going to leave your guard out in this infernal cold?"

I was tempted—sorely so. I sighed and depressed the window button just enough so Izzy and his mount could squeeze themselves inside. With my other hand, I turned the heaters on full, both seat and vents.

Cassie shivered and moved her hands closer to the currents of warm air. "Thanks."

I nodded and honked the horn. It came out lower and stretched, like it was strained. I honked again. Our friend got the message.

Knuckles rapped on the rear door like heavy bits of hail. The back door opened, and the troll contorted himself to squeeze into the trunk. The SUV juddered as he struggled to find a comfortable position. He settled on tucking his knees to his chest and hugging them tight. It didn't look comfortable.

He grunted once to get my attention. "I didn't think you would bring me along."

I shrugged. It was true he helped us, but I knew he had his own motives as well. Motives that could change in an instant and put us in danger. But until then he could be useful.

"We could use the muscle." I gave him a thin smile.

His lips went as thin as mine. He wasn't a fool. He knew what I meant. He was welcome so long as he remained an ally, not a threat. "Fair enough. You square what you need to; I square what I need to. Mutually beneficial, huh?"

"Yes." I put the Range Rover in reverse and gave it just enough gas to rock back a foot. Another press of the pedal was enough for the vehicle to lurch back without slipping. I reached over to get Cassie's attention. "So what's wrong?"

She looked out the window before turning to me. "These freaks won't let up. How far are these monsters willing to go?"

"All the way. Far past the point of necessity, redemption—even sanity. They're monsters. That's what makes them so scary." I felt an intense pressure on the back of my neck.

I turned to find the troll staring at me. His eyes weighed me and my words. I waited for him to say something.

He waved a hand over his face. "Your kind has its fair share."

He wasn't wrong. I changed the subject. "That's what makes us different than them—better." Cassie looked at me with longing, waiting for an answer that would help her process. "That we're not willing to cross some lines. That we're willing to fight and die for them. That's why we're going to stick together and solve this. And we can be just as tenacious."

"Thanks."

"Of course." I accelerated just enough to ease forward without slipping.

"Sorry to break up your mortal back-patting, but—" The troll pointed out the rear window. A pair of SUVS identical to the one we were in lumbered down the road towards us. "Speaking of monsters—"

I put the car into drive. "Here they come."

Chapter Thirty-Four

The car slipped, polishing the snow into a tight pack beneath the wheels.

Great. Already off to a bad start.

It was fortunate this wasn't a race. Snow-ridden roads were not the place for a high-speed pursuit. They would keep us in view, tailing us until the opportune moment. I decided not to give them one.

The car groaned and ambled forward at a leisured pace. I eyed the rearview mirror. It wasn't an encouraging sight. The two Range Rovers were closing the distance. Reckless move.

"Uh, John? Far be it from me to tell you how to do things..."

"I'm sensing a 'but.'" I glanced at her before returning to the view ahead.

"*But* they're getting closer. I don't want to go another few rounds with a bunch of pissed off fae."

"Neither do I." The corner of the street came up. I let off the gas and let the car's momentum carry it onto the next street.

"You slowed down to take a turn?" I could hear the judgment in her voice.

"I have to agree with the little girl." The troll shifted uncomfortably in the back while rumbling.

"There aren't many things I hate in life—backseat drivers are among the few I do." I growled as the car swerved. I reined the steering back under control and straightened it out. "Trust me, I know what I'm doing."

"And what's that?" The troll moved and shifted the balance of the car noticeably.

"Sit down!" I lost my patience and slowed our speed.

The troll obeyed. "I took us out of their line of sight for a moment."

Cassie stared at me but said nothing after my outburst.

I answered the question I knew she had on her mind. "I needed a moment to think." She didn't respond but quirked a brow. I smiled. "I'm taking us to the best form of transportation this state has."

Cassie's eyes lit up.

I slowed the Range Rover to a halt as the light turned an angry shade of red.

Cassie bit her lip and shot me a nervous look.

"Trust me." I nodded out her window to a railing near a descending flight of stairs.

She inclined her head and thumbed the door locks. They snapped up with an automatic click.

I eyed her. "Ready?"

Cassie turned her head towards the stairs and leaned into the door. "Yes."

"Ahem, excuse me." Izzy zipped between Cassie and me. "Have humans suddenly developed the ability to communicate without words?"

I shook my head.

"Then would you be awfully kind as to explain what is happening…" He broke off to inhale. "And why you stopped the car?" His scream shook Barnabus' mane.

"What the green speck said," rumbled the troll.

Izzy spun about and glowered at him. He reconsidered any further action the next second.

I pointed to Izzy and Cassie. "You two are going to get out of the car when I say and run over there." I gestured towards the stairs.

The troll chuckled. "I get it."

Izzy's features scrunched. "I don't."

"You don't have to, just run." The two SUVs were halfway down the street now. I put the transmission into reverse. "Go!"

Cassie flung the door open and jumped from the car. She landed with a crunch and ran as best she could. Izzy streaked after her.

I put an arm on Cassie's seat as I turned to regard the troll. "I'm going to need your help."

He shook his head.

I waited until the cars slowed. If I was right, they would stop, exit, then surround us. I didn't intend to go quietly. I gave the pedal a gentle push. The car inched back. I gave it another and held. The vehicle grumbled once before composite plastics and metals crunched and cracked. I depressed the pedal further.

The first of the two vehicles slipped back against our push. The street light flashed green.

Good idea.

I put the car into drive and went forward several feet. The doors opened in the SUV behind us. I put the car back into reverse and hit the pedal. The second collision drove their vehicle into its tag-along.

"Get out!" I opened the door and followed Cassie's lead. I was around the hood when I heard the horrendous sound of wrenching metal and materials fail. The rear of the Range Rover flew towards the pursuing vehicle. It struck the windshield, shattering it. I couldn't imagine what was going through the minds of the occupants. The troll eased out and snorted once. I waved at him. "Come on."

He shook his head in defiance. "Go!"

His legs bent as he lowered himself and placed his hands below the bumper of the first car. Muscles flexed, and he grunted in exertion. He snapped his body straight, and over two tons of European engineering went airborne. The car tumbled back and landed on the final vehicle.

If anyone inside screamed, I hadn't heard them. Both vehicles looked like plastic toys after being stepped on by a rather heavy adult. I couldn't speak about those within.

The troll turned back to me. "Why are you standing there?"

I blinked, and my mouth worked without sound. I turned and ran to the railing, grabbing it as I slipped and slid on the first stair. My balance returned, and I gingerly made my way down to the dark tiled floor below.

Thin bars of light crept up pillars of blue metal. A black sign ran between two with a street name written in white. I smiled when I saw it.

Church Avenue, Brooklyn. I thought back to the blonde man we met. Cassie pulled me from the reverie.

"Hey, where to?"

I shook my head and faced her. A green light pulsed a foot above her. "Izzy, could you be a little less obvious?"

The fae eyed me like I was an idiot.

A dark-skinned woman in a saddle coat walked by. She paid no attention to the pair of us, but looked at the spot where Izzy radiated emerald light. She blinked and then shook her head. "There's always something up with these lights."

Cassie and I stared as she moved off. We turned our attention to Izzy.

The dewdrop shrugged. "Glamour and humans are the best at being oblivious."

We frowned at the little faerie. I nodded to a machine ahead. Cassie followed as I made my way over to it. My fingers were stiff and ached. I reached into my coat and fumbled for my wallet. I thumbed it open and breathed a sigh of relief. It was a good thing fae didn't go for petty things like cash and credit cards. I handed Cassie some bills.

"Not much of a fare." She gave me a furtive look but fed the money into the machine.

"It's not much of a trip. We're staying in Brooklyn, but we need to get off the streets. The metro is always reliable here. We'll be closer together, and I don't know if faeries understand how the system works." I gave her a lopsided grin.

"We have a pretty good idea."

I turned to the source of the voice. A homeless man in tattered clothes with a scarf around his neck. I grinned. "Glad you could make it."

The troll ignored me and eyed Izzy. His face broke into a toothy smile. "My glamour's better than yours."

Izzy bristled. "Because I am a big faerie, I will take the high ground and refrain from commenting on your overwhelming—and rather nauseating—aroma."

The troll's chest shook as he chortled. "Whatever you say, pipsqueak."

Izzy snapped. He booted Barnabus and released a shrill war cry. "Why, you—"

I lunged, swinging in blind hope. My fingers closed around the pair with just enough strength to restrain them without harm. Dark pine light strobed. "Izzy, calm down!" My hands shook like I was holding onto a piece of a storm.

"Brrsle, furfle, grumpf!"

I'm not an expert on faerie speech, but it didn't sound like Izzy was calming down.

"Izzy?" No response. I shook my hands like I was rattling a pair of dice. Green light flashed. "This isn't the time or place."

"Unhand me…with both hands…." His voice came out muffled.

I didn't oblige. The last thing we needed was Izzy starting a fight he couldn't finish. Especially in a metro station.

A moment of silence passed. Seafoam light bled out from between my fingers. "Please?"

I blinked and released my grip.

The faerie shot up from my palm and surveyed us. His gaze settled on the troll and he exhaled. "I have decided to be the voice of reason and calm. Fighting you would be pointless. Besides, nothing is sadder than a crying troll with a bloody nose."

The troll growled.

Izzy zipped behind me.

I sighed. With a shake of my head I moved towards Cassie. I went through the motions of procuring my own ticket and then eyed the troll.

He gave me a lopsided grin and rolled his hand with a flourish. A thin card materialized between his first two fingers. "I've been riding these for a long time, boy-o. You can't expect someone like me to always be traveling through the Ways." He rolled his eyes before giving Cassie an oblique stare. "Like some people."

Cassie answered back with a glare and sniff.

I glossed over the quick exchange between them and stared at the slip. My thoughts wandered. A short metro ride and we would be able to walk to what would, hopefully, be answers. If I was wrong about the power chasing after Cassie, I didn't know what to do. If I was right, I still didn't know what to do.

My right hand twitched, and I swallowed the urge to crumple my ticket. I left in silence, heading towards the turnstiles.

The trio fell into step behind me as I inserted my slip into the machine. It ejected on the other side with an automated *fwlip*. I snatched it up, pushed my way through the metal bars and found a nearby bench. Cassie joined me a second later with the troll following a pace behind. He looked at the small space beside us then stared at me.

I shrugged. "You'll have to settle for the floor, or stand."

To add insult to injury, a streak of green snapped past him and landed on the remaining space. Izzy dismounted and sat cross-legged. Barnabus shook his head and paced in a lazy circle atop the bench. Izzy's arms wound tight across his chest, and his lips turned up into a smug smile. I felt like I was in charge of a paranormal children's nursery.

The troll shook his head and turned to watch the rails as if the rest of us no longer existed.

"So, this club we're going to—it's safe?"

I exhaled through my nose. That wasn't an easy question to answer. "Yes, and no. It belongs to someone who has no allegiance to the fae or any other party in the Neravene. It's certainly not neutral but it might be the next best thing. The proprietor doesn't tolerate fights or other agendas. It's as safe as we can hope for now."

Cassie's mouth twitched. "What agenda do they have?"

"Their own."

"That's not comforting."

"It's not, but I'm not taking us there to be comfortable. I'm taking us there for answers, and—maybe—some help."

She glanced to Izzy, the troll, and then me. Cassie pulled her knees to her chest and hugged them. "Is it weird that I'm afraid to think we need *more* help than this?"

I shook my head. "Everyone needs help, that much is a given. It's not written how much help a person will need in their life. It changes with time and during certain moments in one's life. But it's always there if you need it, you just have to ask."

She smiled. "Well, John, I think I really need your help."

"You've got it. You've had it. I don't see that changing any time soon."

"Thanks."

Rattling metal and a rush of wind caroled down the tunnel towards us. Dimmed light came into view in the form of flaxen yellow beams. Machinery screamed and warbled as the train slowed. It shuddered to halt and jerked as if it didn't like the idea of stopping. The doors opened with an automatic hiss, and a handful of people exited in a colorful blur.

I scanned the top of the train's marquee. It was the right train. "Let's go."

I pushed myself off the bench and took three long strides to enter. Cassie matched me step for step and entered beside me, nearly shoving me into the doorframe. I glared at her. She gave me a sheepish smile as an apology. The troll stepped in next, surveying seats before settling on one a row away from ours. Izzy flew in as the doors closed.

Someone gasped. I looked to the source. She couldn't have been more than eight. Ringlets of dark hair fell behind her, standing out against the pastel green of her frock. Her eyes went wide as her mouth hung open. She stared at Izzy and pointed.

Her mother looked at her, then followed her finger to the spot where Izzy hovered. She squinted and shook her head. "What are you looking at, Sweet Pea?"

The girl jabbed her finger towards Izzy and bounced in her seat. The mother sighed, letting her head fall back against the window as she closed her eyes.

I pointed to Izzy, drawing the girl's attention. Her mouth opened further as she exhaled. "Ssshh." I pressed a finger to my lips and winked.

She mimicked my gesture and smiled.

Izzy perched his Unifly atop the railing in front of our seats. He stroked the back of Barnabus' head and turned to me. "As your guide and protection in accordance with the will of The Queen of Darkest Faerie, I must say I have concerns about this…" He broke off and pursed his lips as he searched for the word. "This contraption."

The train shook violently as it lurched forward.

Izzy's eyes ballooned and he snapped his head from side to side. "Those concerns have grown exponentially. This is wholly unnatural!"

I stared at him. "Izzy, I am on a train with a dewdrop, a troll, and a young girl who can open Ways as she sees fits. All of this is unnatural."

He wasn't deterred. "And you are one of the Timeless—a cranky old man who isn't that old at all! That…is unnatural."

"You're not wrong." The train rattled along, and our troll company let out a lengthy yawn. I cleared my throat to get his attention. He opened a lazy eye and stared in silence. "Thank you for..." I tilted my head in the direction we left from.

He nodded but said nothing.

"I haven't gotten your name."

"No." A crack left his neck as he bent it to the right. "You haven't."

A second of silence passed between us.

"I don't suppose it would be too much to ask?"

The troll leaned forward, propping his elbows on his thighs. He cradled his head in his hands and gave me a crooked smile. "How about 'Uncle,' since I'm looking out for you?"

"That's not a name."

"Then how is Bob?"

I blinked. "As in…"

His smile grew.

I don't appreciate smartasses.

Cassie let out a yawn of her own and stretched. "I don't mind it. Bob the Troll isn't the worst name."

Bob's lips spread from a smile into something smug. He twined his fingers together and leaned back to rest against his hands.

Cassie licked her lips, and her mouth twitched like she had something to say.

I glanced at her but said nothing. Sometimes it's better to let someone come forth and say what they need of their own accord.

"Um…Bob?"

He didn't open his eyes. "Hrm?"

"Mind if I ask you something?"

"You just did." He blew twice through his nose like it was clogged and then shifted in his seat.

"Ugh, something about what's going on."

Bob exhaled through his nose again but remained quiet.

"Why aren't you after me? I know what you said earlier, but wouldn't it be easier to take me and be done?"

"Young Princess of Soda, I don't think it's wise to give the troll ideas. They're not very good at coming up with their own. I prefer it that way." Izzy shot a nervous look towards Bob.

The troll had the grace to keep calm. "I think I'll eat you last, dewdrop."

Izzy's eyes ballooned and he released a shrill, *"Meep."*

Cassie waited patiently for her answer.

Metal shuddered and the panels of the train quivered from a nasty jostle.

Bob rolled his neck again. He grunted as he snapped it to the left and shrugged his shoulders. He was certainly taking his time. "If I wanted easy, I wouldn't be involved in this. I would be sitting on the street making a pretty penny—literally—from strangers. Life isn't about the easy thing, kiddo. It's about the worthwhile ones. And what's in it for me is worthwhile."

"Power." Cassie made a face like she'd swallowed something bitter. She wasn't fond of the word.

Neither was I. It takes a great many things to acquire power. More often than not, they're not good.

"It's the most important currency in this world, remember that." Bob opened a single eye to give her a knowing look. Satisfied he had made his point, he took a breath and shut his eye.

I counted to thirty in my head before leaning over and cupping a hand over my mouth. "He's wrong. Power isn't a currency, and it's not as important as you think. It's changeable. It moves from being to being, and it corrupts them. In my experience, the things with the most power change. They become something else."

Cassie looked like she didn't want to hear the answer, but she asked anyway. "And what's that?"

"Scary. Insatiable. They want more. That's the trick about power. It's never enough, will never be enough. There's always more out there. You can't trade something like that. You loan it in the hope it will come back to you greater. You make deals, compromises. It's a dangerous game, and when you lose, you lose big."

"Power isn't everything." Cassie's eyes lost focus for a moment, but there was a deeper thought running behind them.

"No, no it isn't. Power has a price—everything does. In the end, that price isn't always worth paying. And remember this: what has a price, clearly costs." I put the weight of steel and stone into those words.

Cassie said nothing, but I could see I made the impression I wanted. I had already compromised myself in dealing with Nox. I couldn't let Cassie do the same.

The rattling of the train slowed, as did the blur of old stone and metal works. I glanced at the orange dotted marquee above.

"This is us." I grabbed onto the railing to heave myself up.

Bob was already on his feet, balancing perfectly during the shaky deceleration without aid. Izzy doubled over, and his arms imitated frantic windmills as he avoided toppling over. Barnabus snorted and took to the air with ease. Izzy glowered and leapt after his mount, flailing as he tried to grab the saddle. He succeeded with his second attempt.

The train stopped.

Izzy let out a sigh of relief. "Blasted thing."

I kept from laughing. Izzy was a small thing with a great deal of pride. I didn't want to hurt it any further.

"Would you mind taking the lead?" I arched a brow at Bob and tilted my head towards the door.

"Sure." He exited the car. I followed with Cassie and Izzy to either side of me. Bob turned his head a fraction, so I could see the corners of his eye. "Didn't like the idea of me being behind you, where you couldn't see, did you?"

He was quick. I had to give him that much. "No, I didn't. Keep moving."

If he took umbrage at my tone, he didn't show it. We followed him up the stairs in silence.

Brooklyn greeted us again as only it could. Graffiti told stories on a wall, in the shape of angry and sickly faces. It was broken by a sneaker advertisement in shocking pink. The street art made its way to nearby poles with green paint chipped by age and weather.

Cassie eyed the street and walls before turning to me. "Pretty…"

"To some." I shrugged. "It has character."

Iridescent flickering pulled my gaze to a doorway directly across the street. Neon bands arced atop a metal door of baby blue. A shop window to its left was hidden beneath a cage of steel bars. Orange letters glowed within a small circle, letting passersby know the liquor store was still open. It was always open.

We were in the right place.

"There." I pointed to a metal railing much like the one

lining the metro stairs. It stood a few feet off the entrance to the liquor store.

"The club you brought us to is below a liquor store?" Cassie didn't sound pleased. I couldn't blame her.

"Can you think of a better place for one?" I didn't wait for her response as I left the sidewalk.

Cassie and the others raced to follow me as it became apparent I wasn't going to stop for them. A dulled blade of cold cut through the inside of my palm as I grabbed the railing to descend. Metal was always unforgiving. Doubly so in the cold. I clung to it regardless as I took the first step down. My foot fought for purchase as the snow had been packed down tight by previous footsteps.

It must be busy. Of course, it's always busy.

Through more luck than careful footwork, I made my way to a door of unpainted steel. Intricate carvings festooned every inch of it, as if a mad artist had been given permission to take a chisel and nail to it. The only reason they appeared smooth was because of time. I was only able to make out half a dozen of the symbols. That left a hundred-plus unaccounted for.

Wards. Magical writing and symbols imbued with the power to serve any number of purposes. In this case, security. The steel door was just a precaution. Nothing would get through this door if they weren't intended to. At least not by force. I chose a subtler option.

I knocked.

Cassie yelped several stairs behind me. I didn't look back.

"This place, huh? Smart move, kid." Bob's voice held a note of approval.

My mouth twitched in response to him calling me a child, but I resisted.

There was no answer at the door. The base of my fist hammered into it several times.

"I heard you the first time!" The voice sounded like it belonged to several men speaking at the same time. I knew better, but that didn't change its odd, deep resonance. The metal view slit opened. A pair of rust-colored eyes stared at me. They broke contact and moved to look past me. "How many?"

I thought about the question. Cassie wouldn't be safe inside, but considering how brazen the fae were becoming, she wouldn't be safe on the streets either. I sighed and held up four fingers.

The eyes blinked. "Four?" I watched as they moved from person to person, making a mental tally. "Can you count?"

I bit my tongue before asking if he could.

"Five!" Izzy landed on my shoulder. He hooked a thumb to his nose. "Four." Then he inverted his thumb, pointing down to Barnabus. "Five."

"So, three," said the voice behind the door. "Animals don't count."

Izzy sniffed and puffed his chest.

I fought not to laugh. "What about the dewdrop?"

"Like I said. You here for the club, or something else?"

"Grey."

The eyes stared at me with such unnerving focus that for a moment I thought they were made of wax. "Why?"

"I need answers." I did. So did Cassie.

"Busy. Need a better reason than you need answers."

I leaned forward so only he could hear me and whispered my name.

The metal viewing panel snapped shut.

Cassie nudged me aside to take a place next to me. "That didn't go well," she said. "What'd you tell 'em?"

"My name."

She laughed. "Some names close doors I guess."

There was a heavy click and the door cracked open just enough to notice it was no longer shut.

I smiled. "And some names open them." The door opened fully and I extended my arm to the side to block anyone from entering before me. "Age before beauty." Cassie snorted as I walked through.

A single light behind a carnation-colored shade fought

to illuminate the darkened hall. It was losing. The red-tinted light made me aware of how dark the area was. I squinted and focused. Steady, deep breaths came from my left side. I turned.

"You going to come in or what?" said the being that opened the door.

I couldn't make him out even though he was likely a foot away from me.

"You know the way, Hawthorne. Move."

I gnashed my teeth and moved further in. I made sure I was still within range to view the door as Cassie entered. Izzy stuck close to her. Bob paused at the door and sniffed. He cast a wary eye before taking a cautious step.

The figure in the shadows rumbled once. "Troll."

Bob froze just a step past the door. "I know that smell."

"Make no trouble here. This is neutral ground."

Almost neutral. I didn't voice that aloud.

A visible lump formed in Bob's throat. The muscles in his neck tensed and the only noticeable movement was his chest rising. It looked like his glamour was going to falter. It wouldn't have mattered if it did, but I had never seen a troll intimidated like that.

I held up a hand, hoping the hidden figure could see it. "He won't make trouble. None of us will."

The doorman didn't reply.

Cassie put her hands on Bob's shoulders and gave him a gentle nudge. "Come on, you'll be fine. Just ignore Spookula over here…there?" Cassie swiveled to try and pinpoint the source of the voice. She shook her head and waved a hand to summon Izzy. "Hey, Glow Bright, think you can shed a little light?"

Izzy didn't buck at her request. He zoomed past Bob and emitted slow pulses of green light.

Cassie laughed and raced to keep in Izzy's light. "In brightest day, in darkest night, let this tiny faerie be my light!"

I groaned. Izzy's last pulse flooded the entrance to the hall in his green glow. I peered at the spot near the door. It was empty. I exhaled and surveyed as much as I could.

Nothing. The doorman was elusive as ever, and just as keen at remaining unseen. As long as we behaved, we wouldn't need to worry about his presence.

I led the way down the end of the hall to another flight of narrow stairs. More red lights hung above. They cast an eerie glow on the gray stone walls.

"Not much on decorating the club, are they?" said Cassie.

"This isn't the club. Besides, we're heading for the lounge."

"Fancy…"

Bob and Izzy kept quiet during our exchange.

Dust and small particulates fell from the roof and bounced off my coat and head. The walls shook just enough to be noticed. A deep percussive throb emanated from ahead. The path before us split off. Double doors in front of us, and one last staircase to the right.

"The stairs." As I approached, the throbbing grew. It was like a colossal heart beat on the other side of the double doors. Cassie looked at them with a bit of longing. "We can hit the club *after* we get answers."

Cassie smiled.

We hit the last stair and pushed through the final door.

The lounge may have been located under a rundown liquor store in Brooklyn, but it looked like it was pulled from the finest of places in Upper Manhattan. State of the art. Comprised of cool steels, brushed aluminum and frosted glass. The lounge sported designer love seats fashioned from expensive leather. All of it was lit with purple-blue undertones.

Cassie whistled. Bob did as well. Izzy ceased flashing and blinked several times.

I left them in their stupor and headed towards the bar. I rapped my knuckles on the glass-topped wooden counter.

"You can pour your own bloody drink, Jonathan Hawthorne." Her voice cut through the mild clamor in the lounge. Some of the occupants gasped when she said my name.

The Timeless have a reputation. Some more than others.

The bartender made her way over to me. Her hair was pulled into a tight blonde tail that bobbed when she moved. She was dressed in a plain gray shirt and matching jeans, which she filled with an athlete's figure. Functional clothing. She pushed a whiskey bottle and empty glass towards me.

I arched a brow.

The corners of her mouth pulled into a slight smile. Her eyes looked mesmerizing under the blue tinge of the lights. Like dried mint blended with worn sapphires. "Are you still not drinking in public?"

I nodded.

She laughed through her nose and reached below the counter. The shift in her posture caused the lights to glint off something on her waist. The hilt of a sword that could have been lifted from a French renaissance exhibit. It wasn't uncalled for in this bar.

She caught me eyeing the blade as she put a green glass bottle on the counter. "It's for those who let their hands get away from themselves—or the ones who skip the tip." She patted the sword and gave me a smile I wagered was sharper than the blade.

I eyed the bottle of sparkling water. "I don't have any cash left."

She rolled her eyes as if it were irrelevant and undid the top. With a quick turn of her wrist, she sent the bottle into a twirl and upended it. The carbonated contents filled the glass and crackled.

"Thank you, Eleanor." I bowed my head a shade before picking up the glass. "I'm assuming he's in there?" I gestured to the lone door on the other side of the lounge.

She nodded.

I downed the contents of the glass in a single gulp. I wasn't here to savor drinks. I was here for answers. "Then I guess I'll have to get him to come out and socialize."

Eleanor eyed me askance. She pulled out a whiskey glass

and cleaned its inside, still giving me that look.

A perfume made of pure, revolting sugar irritated my nose. I followed Eleanor's gaze as she looked past my shoulder.

The muscles in my back shook like the surface of a disturbed pond. A second later, they turned to set concrete. I refused to turn. I didn't want them to know I was intimidated. "Can I help you?" I kept my gaze fixed on Eleanor. In truth, it wasn't a hard thing to do.

Five rods of steel sank into the soft meat around my collarbone. The troll squeezed, and I winced. His lips were close enough to brush against my ear. I shut my eyes and resisted shivering.

"Big price on your head."

Another wave of noxiously sweet breath wafted past me. I fought the urge to retch.

"Define big. Troll's aren't adept at math from my experience." I grinned. My smile slipped in an instant. My elbows slammed onto the countertop, holding me up.

I glared at Eleanor as she busied herself with cleaning a pilsner glass. My free hand crept into my jacket and closed around a simple shaft. Eleanor caught the motion and shook her head. I grimaced and endured the pain.

The troll pulled on my shoulder, spinning me around. He thrust his palm into my chest as I completed the turn. My lower back slammed into the edge of the counter.

He was big, even under his glamour. I didn't know if that was by design or not. His fleshy lips peeled back, and he gave me a smile suited for a gingivitis commercial.

My grip tightened within my coat. If he noticed, he didn't seem to care. I looked past him to Bob. He held Cassie tight, restraining her thrashing. He knew the rules. Izzy sat atop Barnabus, watching with mild interest. I let my body loosen and played along. The newcomer would learn his lesson soon enough.

He let go of my shoulder and jabbed a grotesquely thick finger at my chest. "Big price is big."

How eloquently put.

His brown eyes glimmered with greed, and his smile scrunched the fatty mass of his dark face. He was built like a cross between a professional strongman and a basketball player. He had the height and mass to cause anyone to think twice about fighting him. Even beneath the checkered plaid coat and workman's jeans, I could see his muscles straining to burst free.

I arched a brow. "And you'll be collecting this price I assume."

His bowler cap nearly slipped off his head as he nodded. One his large hands plunked onto the counter. The trunk-like arm kept me from moving out of his way and to the side. He was smarter than he looked. My eyes bulged as his fingers took hold of my throat.

Cassie swore and kicked harder. Izzy flashed once. Eleanor sighed.

The troll leered, and malice danced in his eyes. "Still big price if you die. Easier."

The easy way never pays.

I gripped tighter and wrenched my hand from my coat. My fist slammed on top of the troll's free hand resting on the counter.

Glass shattered, and a dull *thunk* followed. The troll released his grip on my throat and screamed. He pawed at the handle of my dagger. The blade pinned his hand to ebony wood. The troll howled as the metal wreaked havoc on his body. Dark veins pulsed in the limb like they were under the strain of bursting. His skin flecked and peeled like it was made of dried leaves. He swept blindly at me with his free hand.

I lurched to the side as his fingernails almost grazed my forehead. "You made a big mistake starting trouble here."

His eyes were lined with red and glistened with moisture. His nostrils flared as he ripped his hand from the counter, taking a chunk of wood with it. It wasn't a pretty sight. The remains of his hand dripped gore onto the floor.

He snarled, and a mixture of saliva and bile dribbled from his lips. "Only mistake...not killing you." He lumbered forward, his glamour dissipating. The troll was the same type as Bob, minus the hair styling and apparel choices.

"No." I pointed to the door at the end of the lounge.

Fog seeped through the bottom and side of the door. "That's your mistake."

The door opened.

Roiling fog swept across the floor like a blanket of gaseous gray waves. It stopped an inch from our feet, bowing back as if it struck an invisible wall. The fog held the troll's attention. The man at the head of it held mine.

Men embody many things. Courage. Fear. Power. Few men represent all those things and more. He did.

He was a walking grayscale from head to toe. His tailored suit was the color of slate and likely cost the same as several months' rent in a studio apartment. He ran a sun-bronzed hand through his hair. It was fine steel and iron in color. He stared at the troll and me.

I looked away. His eyes were the sort of a gray you find on an early winter morning. A cold and unsettling color of emptiness.

I sucked in a breath. "Father Grey."

The troll's eyes widened in recognition of the name. He backpedaled. His hand continued to crumble as lines raced over his arm. Sometimes it's not great to be the big bad faerie.

Father Grey approached in an unnatural silence. His designer shoes were the color of concrete and failed to make a sound against the club floor. He lifted a cigar to his mouth and inhaled. His eyes shut, and twin plumes of smoke left his nostrils as he exhaled.

"Nobody fights in here." His eyes opened and flashed like polished steel. "My establishment is *neutral*." His voice was a river of smoke over polished stones.

He stopped at the troll's chest, close enough to brush the tip of his cigar against the monster's body. Father Grey exhaled another cloud of smoke through his mouth. He pinched the cigar between his thumb and index finger.

The troll recoiled from the simple action.

Father Grey reached out as if he had all the time in the world. He touched the tip of the cigar to the troll's chest. Burning skin and hair tickled my nose. The troll turned and ran. He didn't get far.

Cassie flailed and lashed out with a kick as the troll passed.

She missed, but it's the thought that counts.

The troll collapsed against the door frame, clinging to it for support. A gray cancer spread from the center of his chest. His skin bubbled and cascaded like it was made of falling ash. It spread in seconds, enveloping his body.

Bob released Cassie and rushed to the fallen troll's side. He took a firm grip on the troll's good wrist and sank his teeth into the meat below the elbow. Bob wrenched. The limb tore free.

And the troll crumbled to ash.

Silence filled the room. It was broken by Bob munching thoughtfully on the end of the torn arm.

Father Grey puffed on the cigar and turned his head to Eleanor. "Do you mind getting someone to clean that up?"

She sighed and brushed her hands against her pants.

Grey turned to the rest of the crowd and waved a hand. "Play nice."

They returned to their conversations. A few patrons shot nervous glances his way. I couldn't blame them. My heart quickened a few beats at his display.

He gestured to a roundtable of black steel and glass.

I followed him as he took a seat and eased myself onto a stool opposite him. Cassie eyed the table, Father Grey, and then me. I nudged a stool with the tip of my foot and gestured for her to sit. She gave him one last look of apprehension before taking her seat. Steel scraped against the floor as she scooted the stool closer to my side and out of arm's reach of Father Grey.

Her caution was smart, and yet it made my chest feel like a brittle plate of ice. Cassie didn't need to be thinking of every unknown as a possible threat.

Izzy swooped onto Cassie's shoulder, and her posture

loosened. I gave silent thanks for the faerie's calming effect on her.

We all turned to the troll in the room.

Bob's lips spread into a macabre grin. Strands of flesh and sinew were lodged between some of his teeth. Troll blood stained much of his mouth. He waved the severed limb, and I found myself needing another drink. "Count me out of…" Bob moved his index finger in a lazy circle as he pointed to the table.

Cassie and I stared at him. Father Grey and Izzy could not have cared less.

Bob's mouth closed around the torn arm. He shook his head like a dog chewing on tough meat. A chunk came free and he wolfed it down.

Cassie pressed a hand to her stomach. "Oh, hell, no."

"I told you I was helping you for my own reasons." Bob gave the limb a shake. "This is one of them. I got what I came for."

Both of Cassie's eyebrows shot up. "A snack?"

Bob's grin grew. "A promotion."

Clever troll. "You couldn't kill him on your own, could you?" I leaned forward, waiting for his answer.

"No. I couldn't make it look like an accident either." He looked to Father Grey and inclined his head. Father Grey ignored him.

Heated gravel filled Cassie's voice. "You used us."

The troll rolled his shoulders like it was irrelevant. "I told you why I was sticking with you. And I told you what's important. Power." The word reverberated through the lounge. He turned, waving the mangled limb as he made his way up the stairs.

The muscles in Cassie's neck strained like she was about to retch. "He ate the arm!"

"Trolls are cannibalistic. It's another way to prove who's the strongest within their tribes. It's how they move up the ladder as it were. The bigger, tougher trolls kill off whoever is above them in rank. Then they eat them. It's effective."

Cassie shuddered then blinked. "Wait, so that's a

souvenir—proof?"

I nodded.

She swallowed.

Father Grey cleared his throat and adjusted his spruce gray tie. "Hawthorne." He gave me a level look.

"Desmond." I matched his look.

His lips tightened. The micro-gesture didn't go unnoticed by me. People don't call Father Grey by his first name. Smart ones at least. I had his attention. Maybe dangerously so, but I had it.

He motioned to Eleanor with two fingers and tapped them to the table. She nodded without a word. Desmond leaned back like the stools had an invisible backrest. "What brings you here?"

I opened my mouth.

He cut me off with a wave of his hand. "Let me rephrase that, Hawthorne. What can I do to get rid of you and not get involved in your mess? I don't take sides. Remember that."

"I know. I'm not asking you to. I have only one question."

Father Grey arched a brow.

The muscles in my hands ached as I balled my fists. My voice was raw enough to strip the steel table bare. "Where is Toshiro Nakamura?"

Chapter Thirty-Five

Cassie sucked in a breath.

Father Grey's face put professional poker players to shame. "Beg your pardon?"

I squinted as I fought the urge to grind my teeth. "Where is he?"

His eyes narrowed in equal parts suspicion and anger. "Why?" He rolled the cigar between his teeth and took a puff.

The pressure in my hands built. It felt like the bones would crumble from the force. "Because he's the bastard that endangered a young girl. He's the one who sent trolls after us. He's the one that ransacked my home!"

Cassie's mouth went slack. Her eyes widened as her face paled. She tried to say something, her mouth working soundlessly. In the end, she simply swallowed.

Father Grey inhaled and waited.

I didn't know if I counted the passing seconds or my escalating heartbeat.

Tendrils of smoke wafted from the corners of his mouth, like he was bleeding smoke. He leaned forward, resting his chin on his elbows. His eyes hardened and scanned my face. "And you know this how?"

"You think I'm lying?"

He leaned back and kept his face neutral. "I've known Toshiro for a long time, Hawthorne."

"I know. After all, you recruited him, Desmond."

Cassie did a double take between Father Grey and me.

He gave me a smile like a paper cut in stone. "He's a good knight."

"*Was*." I stressed the word. He needed to know Toshiro could no longer be trusted.

His lips pressed tight, and he shot a glance toward Eleanor. I followed it. She wore the same expression. The Order of the Gray didn't take well to the idea that one of their oldest members had gone rogue.

I quelled his doubts. "Someone has been tracking us." I pointed between Cassie and me. "Toshiro."

Eleanor placed a whiskey glass on the table and passed it to Father Grey. Its clear contents sloshed around, licking the lip of the glass as the fluid tried to spill over. It looked like paint thinner. He muttered a thanks to Eleanor and motioned for her to leave. She didn't. Anything concerning another member of her order was something she wanted to be present for.

Order of the Gray and Timeless had that in common—we stuck by and up for our own as best we could.

Father Grey pulled the cigar from his mouth with two fingers and took a sip of liquor. Glass clinked with enough force to crack as he placed the beverage down harder than necessary. The cigar slipped back between his teeth.

"That stuff will kill you, ya know?" Cassie let out a weak chuckle.

His gaze drifted towards her as if he just noticed her presence and wasn't terribly impressed. "So will your abilities, young miss."

Cassie inhaled sharply.

I bit my tongue.

"You've—the both of you—traveled dangerous Ways to get here." He puffed on his cigar. Eleanor loomed behind, impassive. "You're right, of course. Toshiro was following you." He leaned forward. "I ordered him to. That was his task, to bring you in. We all have our jobs, don't we? Among the Ageless, yours is to acquire knowledge and pass it to us. *My* order acts on that information to keep the balance." His eyes flashed. "You upset that balance. Toshiro was to bring you in for trial."

I ground my teeth and resisted the temptation to snatch his drink for a swig myself. "Was he supposed to do that by using thaumaturgy?"

Father Grey froze. The glass was an inch from his lips. The surface of his drink quaked in his grip. The cigar wobbled in his mouth. Eleanor's face shifted to a cold, unreadable mask.

Cassie leaned over to me. "John, isn't that the thing you said the trolls did?"

Her question grabbed everyone's attention.

Eleanor and Desmond spoke in unison. "Trolls?"

I nodded.

"What do *they*"—Eleanor's face contorted as she said the word—"have to do with Toshiro?"

"He's been using them to do his dirty work." I pointed to Cassie. "He set them after her." My voice could have sanded stone to dust. "He sent them after a young woman who, by all rights, should be living a normal life—free of all this!"

Glass shattered, but not a drop of blood fell from Father Grey's hand. He crushed the cigar and pulled out the few shards of glass buried in his other hand. "Prove it." His tone matched mine.

"I'm hoping you could."

He and Eleanor exchanged a quick glance.

I pressed on. "He saved me from a troll, but afterward he pinned me against a wall at sword point."

Their expressions told me they thought that was perfectly in line with Toshiro's character. Perhaps it was. But not all of it.

"He nicked me with his sword, enough to draw blood." I gestured to the nearly healed patch of skin on my neck.

Father Grey waved his hand for me to continue.

"Not too long after that, my home…" I broke off as every inch of my upper body ached and throbbed like it was expanding and shrinking at the same time. "My home was broken into by trolls."

Eleanor stepped forward and opened her mouth to speak. I didn't let her.

"I know what you're thinking," I said. "They could have followed my scent, trailed us back. They couldn't have. But for the argument's sake, let's say they did. Why then did they have a vial of my blood and hair?"

Father Grey was as readable as fog. But Eleanor swallowed. I had found a thread. I just needed to pull on it.

"You don't expect me to believe that trolls are smart enough, practiced enough, to perform thaumaturgy?"

No answer, which was an answer in and of itself.

"Someone helped them. Or rather, they were helping someone. After that point, he found me again in a matter of minutes after tumbling through another Way to where the Ageless Court held my trial. No one could have known where we were going or how we planned to get there."

Something hot and ugly flared to life in both Grey's and Eleanor's eyes.

"Everyone out—bar's closed." Father Grey's voice cut through the background clamor.

Nobody argued. Every occupant got to their feet and left without a word.

I didn't speak until the room cleared. "Can you guess my next question?" I waited to see if either of them would respond. They didn't. "Does Toshiro know how to perform thaumaturgy?"

To his credit, Father Grey didn't hesitate. "Yes." He looked at the flecks of glass on the table and sounded like he would rather swallow them than give the answer he had.

Eleanor swore and her hand went to her sword. She blinked, realizing what she was doing. Her hand fell from it, but the muscles in her arm twitched as if to protest. She had too much control to let her emotions get the better of her, but it was close.

Friendships are powerful things. And they only grow in power over time. All of the Ageless, regardless of affiliation, have formed bonds over the countless years. Betrayal cuts deep, and the older the sword, the deeper it cuts.

Toshiro was thousands of years old. Many of his order were just as old, if not more so. To have him be a turncoat after so long…

All too recently, I thought Quentin had betrayed me. I

knew what Eleanor was going through. It felt like my brain had frozen and was thawed by a blowtorch. A mixture of numbing cold that blotted thought and searing heat that fed the worst of your emotions.

When Desmond spoke, it sounded like the cigar and shards of glass were lodged in his throat. "What else do you have to back your claim?"

I couldn't look him in the eyes, so I turned to Cassie. She stared at the table like it was the most important thing at that moment. I didn't know what she was thinking. I wished I did. It would make it easier to find the right words to say to her. She had gotten her answer. She had a name and face to put to the power behind her problems and struggles of late.

And she knew that I had known—known and hadn't told her. I didn't want to damn Toshiro until I was certain, but I could've shared my suspicions at least. I didn't know what to say to her. My hand twitched, and I reached to touch her shoulder.

Cassie flinched, and I pulled my hand back. "I'm sorry, Cassie. I'm sorry for not telling you."

"What other proof do you have, Hawthorne?" Eleanor's hand was back on her sword, her knuckles white.

"Do I need any more?"

Neither Grey nor Eleanor answered.

"I spoke with the Faerie Queens—two of them at least." I watched both of them for a reaction.

Grey closed his eyes and took a breath. "Which two?"

"Does it matter?"

He said nothing.

Desmond deserved some form of answer. I exhaled and leaned forward, twiddling my thumbs. "I spoke with the Queen of Darkest Faerie—"

"Under which mantle?" His voice shook and he was halfway across the table, his hands gripping the sides of it tight.

"Nox."

His grip loosened, and the strength left his arms as he

breathed out. Father Grey slipped back onto his stool. "And she confirmed Toshiro's involvement?"

I eyed him and arched a brow. "She's a Faerie Queen. She wasn't so direct."

He waved his hand for me to continue.

"Nox did, however, point me in the right direction."

He opened his eyes. They were a swirl of lost grays, like morning fog. "And that direction was Toshiro?"

"Yes. Do you know what Cassie can do?"

She looked at me when I said her name, then slowly turned to Father Grey.

He nodded. "Word spreads quick."

"And you know what someone could use her abilities for?" I didn't give him time to respond. "Upsetting the balance—all of it. Whose task is it to keep that balance?" I stared hard at Eleanor and Father Grey. "And yet, nothing has been done. No one in your order has done a thing to stop Cassie."

My shin throbbed and I winced. Cassie glared at me, wearing a lopsided frown. "Can you not encourage people to come after me?"

I held up a hand as way of apology, hoping she wouldn't kick me again. "My point is...why haven't any of you become involved?"

They had no answer.

"But Toshiro did. Who better to break the balance than someone who's kept it for countless centuries? Who else would know how best to upset it?"

"But...why, John?" Cassie looked at me with a longing for an answer I couldn't give. God, I wish I could have.

I turned to Father Grey. "Why, Desmond? That's the one thing I can't understand."

He and Eleanor exchanged glances. A heavy mask fell over both their faces. There was a weight in their eyes I couldn't quite put my finger on. It was something like wet lead, heavy and bringing moisture to their lids. Eleanor brushed the back of her arm against her face.

Desmond rubbed his hand across his cheeks and

mouth. "Do you know how many members there are in my order?"

I shook my head.

"Less than a dozen—all charged with acting on information from the Timeless. All of them tasked with fighting and doing things in the name of balance for thousands of years. You've fought in wars. You know what kinds of decisions have to be made, the things that have to be done."

"What decisions, John?" asked Cassie.

I swallowed. "The sort where you would let a murderer go because it served to keep the larger balance. The sort where you would kill an innocent person to preserve that same balance. The sort where it's okay to let half the world burn just to save the other half." My jaw clenched until the muscles grew weary from the effort.

She looked at us in disbelief. "That's not balance. That's craziness. It's unfair!"

I gave her a knowing look. "Life isn't fair, Cassie."

"Don't I know it."

"The men and women serving with me have had to make those choices and worse...all to keep this world—and the ones beside ours—safe. That's not an easy thing. Those choices add up. Everything is cumulative. Toshiro has been my best blade, judge, and the scales of balance through periods of time now counted as distant history. He has made decisions that don't just haunt a man, they claw at him, strip him bare of skin and sinew. They're memories and things that gnaw you to the bone, Hawthorne." Grey's stare grew distant. He was watching something past us or, not there at all. I had seen that look in soldiers before.

My chest and mouth went tight. "That's it? It's that simple? Toshiro is old, and his demons are getting the better of him? His judgment is no longer balanced? I refuse to accept that as the reason for this!" I waved a hand across the table, nearly clipping Grey across the nose with the back of my fingers. "He's after *her* because he's losing his hold? It *can't* be that simple. It can't be."

Father Grey looked at me like he was staring at a particularly frustrating riddle. "Why not? You have lived long enough to know that many times it's the simplest things—reasons—that cause so many of the world's problems. That not everything is as complicated as we would like them to be. That sometimes people just break." He looked away, the distant look returning to his eyes.

I didn't know the exact thoughts running through his mind, but I imagined he was thinking about Toshiro. Grey realized Toshiro was broken. That didn't sit well with him.

Clearing my throat used up what little moisture was left. "And how broken does someone have to be to want to deal with the Former?"

The room was quiet enough to hear the faint trickle of water running through the building's plumbing.

Father Grey turned his thousand-yard stare toward me. Wisps of smoke rose from the table. The cigar wasn't lit. Tendrils danced out of the pores in his hands. They licked their way into air before dissipating.

"Which one?"

I told him the terrifying truth. "I don't know."

He didn't accept my answer. "Which one, Hawthorne?"

I repeated myself.

Grey sighed and brought a palm to his face, grinding it against one of his eyes. "Eleanor, I'm going to need another drink."

"Yeah, Elle, me too." Cassie gave her a weak smile.

To her credit, Eleanor reacted better than I could have imagined to Cassie. "I think we all could."

I nodded in agreement as she headed toward the bar.

"And sometimes the simple things are not so simple..." Father Grey sounded like he was speaking more to himself than us. He looked me in the eyes and I shifted uncomfortably. "There's nothing that's entirely black and white in this world—in any of them. Even among the simple things, they're endless shades of gray. Little variations that have to be considered and walked through with the utmost of care. And when you get to the end of those roads, you don't always find the answer you're happy with, or one at all. Do you understand, Hawthorne?"

I did, but I remained silent.

"How do you know he plans to let one out?"

I shook my head. "I don't, but..."

"Nox?"

I nodded.

Cassie looked at the pair of us and settled her gaze on me. "Let one of who out of what?"

I told her everything. Izzy flashed through a variety of bright and irritated greens.

"Oh...oh, damn." Cassie's color paled and she licked her lips. "I think math's about to be useful, because I'm about to raise the level of drinks I'm going to need."

Fortunately for her, Eleanor delivered. She plunked down a tray of eight glasses. A variety of amber and clear liquors sat atop. We reached out and grabbed one each.

Father Grey held up a glass and led the toast. "To the simple things."

"The simple things," the rest of us intoned in unison.

We tipped the glasses back and welcomed the drink. I shut my eyes and inhaled, savoring the subtle notes of cinnamon and vanilla as the alcohol brought warmth to the back of my throat.

Grey's glass clinked against the table. "The simple things are the reason there are so few of us, you know? Like I said before, the job gets to us—*all* of us. It's the accumulation of the simple, little things that break us in the end. I only wish I knew which crack was the one that broke him." He downed the rest of his drink.

Eleanor put a hand on his shoulder and took a gulp from her own glass. "So do I, Desmond. Maybe we could have done something."

He took her hand and gave it a squeeze. "I don't think we could have. We're all just strings in the end, pulled tight and waiting to snap. He was frayed long ago. Now he's just snapped." Father Grey stared hard and knowingly at me. "You can't trust anyone that lives that long."

I didn't say anything but his words struck me across the temple like a hammer. What did that mean for the rest of his order? What did it mean for the Timeless? For Quentin? For me?

Will we all end up like that?

I buried the questions. They wouldn't help.

"So," Grey said, pulling me from my reverie, "the Former?"

"It's a possibility, and the most likely one. Toshiro can open any number of Ways on his own. Most skilled beings can. What would be the point of trying to kidnap Cassie when you can already go most places? She was clearly never in any mortal danger."

She coughed and gave me a sideways glance. "Excuse me? For the record, there were plenty of moments I was in mortal danger. We all were." She twirled a finger through the air. "Not to mention, we sort of still are. I mean an ancient samurai with thousand's of years of issues wants to use me to open up a doorway to let out some cosmological being of disaster and destruction. Yeah, pretty sure the 'mortal danger' thing hasn't passed yet."

Father Grey reached for another glass and swallowed half its contents. He released a satisfied exhale. "You're right, Cassie—may I call you Cassie?"

She squirmed like someone had dumped ice water down her back when he said her name, but nodded.

"The danger isn't over, but it could be." He placed his hands on the table and pushed himself up. "I think I should give Toshiro a call."

Footsteps came from the stairs. We turned to the source.

"No need, Desmond," said Toshiro.

Chapter Thirty-Six

My stool clattered to the floor. I took a step back, brushing my coat aside as my hand plunged into it. In one smooth motion, I drew my pistol and squeezed.

Click.

Reason left me and I squeezed again. *Click. Click. Click.*

Gray robes fluttered as Toshiro crossed the distance between us in an instant. I interlocked my fingers and brought both hands down to the spot I anticipated he would be. His knees bent as my fists hammered down on the base of his neck. The pommel of his sword connected with my solar plexus. I doubled over, grabbing hold of his clothing as the air left my lungs. My grip faltered, and I dug my fingers into the meat of one of his arms.

Cassie snarled and drew her sword, casting it into a broad arc. Steel flashed towards Toshiro's shoulder, only to clang as it met resistance. Eleanor's blade locked itself against Cassie's.

Cassie blinked, her lips peeled back. "What the hell?"

Toshiro shook his body, twisting at the waist in an effort to shake me. I held on. He grimaced and pushed forward. I didn't anticipate the shift in force. I stumbled back before he turned sharply. My body snapped forward. He used my momentum to guide me with the added effort of his hand bearing down on my shoulder.

It felt like I had taken an uppercut from a baseball bat. Electrostatic bursts of pain shot up from the base of my chin and settled in my eyes. It was like a fireworks display had erupted in flares of white and red.

My mind tumbled through a bog of muddled thoughts, and my fingers were slow to respond. A static tingle danced over my extremities. I winced and focused my thoughts.

"Why, Eleanor?"

She let out a grunt of exertion and shoved Cassie back. Eleanor turned her head enough to glance at me out of the corner of her eyes. Her attention never wavered from Cassie though. "We deserve to hear his side of things. *I*...need to hear his side." She looked to Father Grey who sat motionless until that moment.

He nodded atop clasped hands. "As do I. I owe him that much."

"Well, we sure as hell don't!" Cassie bristled and her sword twitched in her grip.

Eleanor didn't miss it. Her posture tensed, but she kept a portion of her attention on me.

I struggled but Toshiro's fingers dug into the area below my collarbone. My motions stopped. "He attacked me—"

"In self-defense," countered Eleanor. "You drew your gun."

"Whose side are you on?" Cassie looked at Eleanor in bewilderment.

Eleanor's mouth went tight. "We're neutral. We're *supposed* to be neutral. Isn't that right, Toshiro?"

"Hai, which is why I am doing what I am." Toshiro eased the pressure on my body. In a single movement, he released his hold and bounded to his feet several steps away. He drew his sword in a fluid, practiced moment and leveled it at me.

I growled and pushed myself to my feet. I retrieved my fallen pistol and stowed it, lowering my hand until it rested atop my sword. My fingers drummed against the hilt. The urge to unsheathe it was difficult to resist.

Father Grey picked up on my intention. "Give him a chance to explain, Hawthorne."

I scowled. "Of course, but can I ask one thing?" I arched a brow and eyed Toshiro.

He inclined his head slightly.

"How did you find us?" My hand tightened on the sword.

Toshiro reached into his robes and withdrew a cloth.

There was a palm-length smear of red.

I touched two fingers to my brow, where Toshiro had struck me with his sheath and split the skin. He had offered me a cloth to clean it. I knew better now. "Thaumaturgy."

"Hai."

Eleanor's body shook. Her skin flushed a shade. "So, Hawthorne was telling the truth?" There was a quiet edge to her voice.

Father Grey intervened. He stepped into the space between all of us with his arms stretched out. "Hawthorne was telling part of the truth. Let's hear the rest before we jump to conclusions. We don't act on half-truths; we act on fact."

"Will you though?" Cassie scowled. "He's your buddy after all, and you weren't too thrilled about the idea of him being a traitor before. What are you going to do when you find out we're right?"

"*If* you happen to be right. Don't equate what-ifs with what is. That's how misinformation is created. And misinformation breeds trouble." Grey kept his eyes trained on Toshiro. "So, *friend*, is she right? Are you a traitor?"

The sword shook slightly in Toshiro's grip. He wasn't the sort of man to let a question like that shake him. His eye's glistened with a light sheen. A drop of moisture welled on his lid and rolled down his cheek. "It is not as simple as that, Desmond."

"It never is." Father Grey's gaze fell to the floor for a moment.

"No, it isn't."

"So, Toshiro, what is the truth?"

"Your truth, or mine?" Toshiro shut his eyes for a moment.

"The only one that matters." Grey's voice hardened in concert with his posture.

"Traitor to you and the order—yes. Not to what it stands for, what it really stands for, what it *should* stand for." Toshiro's body quivered like an animal about to attack.

Father Grey arched a brow and eyed him askance. "And

what does that mean?"

"It means that we are *not* judges. It means that we should have no right to take lives. We…I…have taken the lives of young men and women with dreams they will never see, and why? Balance." He spat the word like a curse. "Balance—one word used to justify controlled chaos. Killing the good, sparing the bad to preserve something that I have still not seen. Where is the balance, Desmond?"

Father Grey licked his lips and looked to Eleanor. She mirrored his look. It was an expression of pale stone. Neither said a word.

Toshiro went through a series of light breaths. It was a calming exercise. His body stilled seconds later. He stared at each of us in turn, his eyes weighted by something I'd seen in only a handful of people.

Conviction.

Belief is a power of its own. A dangerous one, at times. Men have convinced themselves of terrible truths throughout history and acted upon them. It has never ended well. Even belief has its costs—all power does. But it's a power that can turn you blind to horrible things when you believe you're doing them for the right reasons.

So what are Toshiro's?

Toshiro moved his arm in a semicircle, leveling the tip of his blade at each of our faces. "Look at this world, Desmond. A world where man is preoccupied with television, celebrity gossip, and greed. A world of self-obsession and blind eyes. There is no room left for truth or anything else. Where is the balance? I cannot see it. People die in droves—good people. The bad prosper. Misdeeds are rewarded, truth and honor…punished. I served to fix those things." He lowered his gaze to the floor, and I could see and feel the weight he carried. "I failed—we all did."

"It's not that simple, and you know that." Father Grey took a step toward Toshiro, his hand outstretched.

Toshiro gritted his teeth. "Nothing in this world is plain, hai. That is no excuse, not for the things we've done. The things I've done. I joined to save lives, not take them. I was supposed to be a shepherd, not a reaper."

"You knew what you were getting into when you joined. We all did." Grey's voice cracked. "This was never about fairness or being easy, Toshiro. It was about making the hard decisions no one else would—or could. It was about buying our tickets to hell so no one else would have to. You know this. You knew it then as well. Don't make a bad decision now." He took another step and kept his hand up, reaching for Toshiro.

"I have made too many bad decisions, Desmond. Now, I am trying to make the right one. The only one of any consequence." Toshiro gripped his sword a little tighter.

My blade slid a couple of inches out of its sheath. "By releasing one of the Former?" I exerted a hint of pressure with my thumb against the pommel of my saber. The blade slipped another inch forward. I wanted to be able to draw it quick enough to advance on Toshiro if it came to it.

"Hai."

Father Grey lowered his hand to his side and exhaled. His shoulders sank. He didn't doubt the truth any longer. "Which one?"

"The only one that can undo all we have done. The one that brings true balance. It has gone by many names. The First. The Formless One. Strife. Disorder. Bringer of Turmoil. Chaos."

Father Grey blurred into action the instant Toshiro finished. I didn't see where the slender knife came from; it seemed to materialize from nowhere. Desmond Grey moved with the speed of someone twenty years younger, with the conditioning and coordination that could only come from decades of practice.

Toshiro was quicker, but it didn't help. Father Grey's arm lashed out with serpentine speed. The old samurai bobbed and swatted the switchblade but couldn't break Grey's grip on the weapon. Both of them took a step back, appraising the other—waiting.

There was an opening. I took it. I jumped toward Toshiro, drawing my saber and twisting my body. The aged sword hissed through the air. Toshiro bobbed and sank to the side as my sword parted strands of his hair. The rogue knight snapped his foot out. Fire enveloped my knee, and it buckled. I collapsed to one leg, swiping blindly with my sword. It cut through clean air.

Desmond capitalized on my interruption. He rushed Toshiro with a burst of speed that could have matched a large cat. Toshiro was caught off guard and pulled his arms in tight. Father Grey moved past the blade's point of effectiveness and wrapped his hands around Toshiro's collar. The larger man hefted the Japanese swordsman and grunted. With a twist, he sent Toshiro airborne.

Tiling and walling crunched. The samurai's body bounced forward from the impact and he fell to all fours. Flecks of eggplant-colored drywall rained onto his back. He shook his head and grunted. His reprieve was short lived.

Eleanor snapped out of her reverie and let loose a bloodcurdling scream. She leapt into the air, taking her sword in both hands. The weapon sailed toward Toshiro's neck.

"No!" Father Grey stepped between the pair and caught her blow. He shoved Eleanor back a step. "I need to look him in eyes." He booted Toshiro in the collarbone, causing the fallen knight to grunt and grab the area. With a callous swipe of his foot, Father Grey sent Toshiro's sword skittering across the floor. One of his hands locked around Toshiro's throat, the other digging into the knight's hair. He brought the Japanese warrior to his feet and pinned him against the wall. "Look at me."

Toshiro met Grey's eyes. "Look then. See."

Eleanor's breathing quickened. Her chest heaved and her sword hand quivered. "Get whatever answers you need, Desmond. I'm going to carve his eyes out after this."

The Order of the Gray does not take well to traitors. It's a lifelong commitment. There are only two ways to leave. Death in duty, or death by accident. Accidents rarely befall their members.

I had the feeling that Toshiro would find himself in one

pretty soon however. At least if Eleanor could manage it.

Toshiro sighed and turned his head enough to look at Eleanor. "There will be no 'after this' I am afraid."

Father Grey grabbed Toshiro's lower jaw. He forced his head back to stare at him. "You seem to be under the notion that *I'll let* you go. That's not how this works. *You* work for *me*. This nonsense about the Former is at an end. Whatever demons you have—fine—I'll help you through those. But this"—he broke off and waved his knife at Cassie—"is over."

"It was over long ago, friend." Toshiro's voice softened. It pained him to admit that he still thought of Desmond as a friend. Maybe it would have been easier if he weren't.

Cassie came to my side with Izzy and Barnabus still perched on her shoulder. Her face was a reddened mask—tight, angry. Her hands shook, but she held Tatiana's sword firmly. Her eyes narrowed. The fiery opals danced with violent heat. Her hand stilled, followed by her breathing. I knew what she was thinking.

I placed a hand on her shoulder. She flinched in response and turned to face me. There was a wild light in her eyes. Her mouth twisted into a sneer. "You know what this bastard's put me through."

I inclined my head. "I know."

The sword shook again in her grip. She pointed toward Father Grey and Toshiro. "He roped you into this too. He…" Her face reddened further. "He set those freakish trolls after us. He whooped your ass in that alley, after his buddy pummeled you. He lied to you. He almost got you killed a crap load of times. Dammit, John, he ruined my life!" Tears trickled down her cheeks.

I gave her shoulder a squeeze. "I know, Cassie. Believe me, I know. But you can't do this. I won't let you."

She sniffed and glared at me. "It feels right."

Toshiro, Father Grey, and Eleanor stared at the young woman.

"It feels right *now*. What about later?" I moved slowly in front of her. I wanted to keep Toshiro out of her vision for a while. She wasn't thinking clearly, and if I didn't do something, she would act on those thoughts—those impulses. That wouldn't end well for her. Not in the long term.

"What about it?" She leaned to look past me.

I moved in concert with her, obstructing her view. "I can't let *you* kill him."

She arched a brow in defiance but her eyes told me what I needed. She was second-guessing herself. The grip on her sword loosened.

"I'm not saying he doesn't deserve to die." I stopped and exhaled. My fingernails dug into my palm. I pinched the bridge of my nose and shut my eyes for a moment, breathing deep. "Cassie, I'm resisting the urge to kill him myself."

Father Grey and Eleanor gave me cold looks.

I answered in kind. He may have betrayed them, but he came after me and my friends—the only family I had. I've tried to learn to be a forgiving man through my years. I haven't learned it well. There are some things you can't forgive.

"And what happens if you kill him?" She gave me an oblique stare.

"I live with it, like everything else. It won't be easy. It won't be the first time. I don't want that for you." I looked away for a brief spell.

"Even if I want it?" she said.

"Sometimes we don't get the things we want in life, and that can be a blessing. Don't trade what you want in the long term for what you want now, Cassie. Don't ever do that."

She blinked away the tears and sniffed once. "I don't know what that is though."

I stepped forward and placed my other hand atop her sword. "He's not worth it, not for what it will cost you." I placed gentle pressure on the blade, hoping she would feel it. "Remember, everything has a price, but not every price is worth paying."

"A lesson I learned too late," said Toshiro.

I eyed him over my shoulder before turning back to Cassie. The blade was close to slicing the tips of my fingers as I pressed a bit more. She lowered the sword and I breathed in relief. "Killing can turn into a slope. If you do it enough, the lines start to blur."

"Hai, but she deserves this." Toshiro's statement sent a chilled slurry through my veins.

I swallowed the bubble of fury building in my throat. Some of it escaped when I opened my mouth. "No, she deserves better."

Toshiro struggled to nod in Father Grey's grip. "Which is why in exchange for aiding me, I offer her my life. Once my task is complete—balance restored—she can find her own balance." His voice never shook.

I crossed the distance between us in a fraction of a second. Toshiro's head snapped to the side and a wet sound filled my ears. I shook my hand to ease the throbbing in my knuckles. The tip of my sword found itself hovering above his heart. A simple step forward was all it would take. "You don't get to offer her a choice—especially one like that."

"Why not? What better choice is there for her?" He spat a glob of saliva and blood to the side. "I have taken too many of the wrong lives in the belief I was making a stable world. It is not so." He turned his gaze to Cassie. "Do you know what it is like...taking a life?" He didn't wait for her to answer. "It is like watching a screen of flashing images flicker into reels of black. A body is left behind, but there is nothing. No light in the eyes. Emptiness. It is watching dreams you know nothing of...die. A history you know nothing of...with no future. I have done all those things for a belief. That belief was wrong. I know it. I have found a new one. I will see it done. And my penance will be giving up my own life. I am not deluded in this." The stare he gave Cassie showed he had doubts about that. He intended to die, and wanted Cassie to help him do it.

She simply needed to help him. Just one deed. Let loose a force that predated the primordial and could destroy the world. I didn't honestly know how he believed she would take the deal.

Father Grey had heard enough. His fingers dug deeper into Toshiro's throat. "Your plan is done—over. You're not getting the girl. I don't know what you hoped to accomplish by coming here, but you won't be leaving." Father Grey's face flickered through a series of emotions.

For a brief second, I saw the same look I had worn when watching a comrade fall beside me on the battlefield. It faded and was replaced by a look of cold granite. He loosened his hold on Toshiro's throat. Grey freed his other arm from pinning the samurai. There was a metallic *snickt* as the switchblade flicked within his hand.

Toshiro's face shook, and he gasped for breath. "I hoped to get closer to the girl." He struggled but did not beat against Grey's arms. "And to you."

"Desmond!" Eleanor rushed toward the gray-clad man with one arm outstretched, the other snapping toward the fallen knight.

Father Grey twisted, sending the switchblade on a path to Toshiro's throat. The old warrior moved faster. Toshiro brought his arms over his head, sending them crashing down hard. They collided with Father Grey's wrists, stopping the blade strike and breaking his hold. The Japanese knight fell to a crouch.

Eleanor's blade sank into the wall where his head had been. Toshiro lashed out with his palm, impacting the inside of her calf and ruining her balance. Father Grey recovered and jabbed at Toshiro, using his free hand like a flat club.

Toshiro moved into the blow and reached into his robes.

I joined the fray after my brain had finished processing the blisteringly frantic chain of events. Snarling, I brought the pommel of my saber down like a hammer. Toshiro pivoted and withdrew a slender weapon resembling a diminutive katana. I stumbled as my blow carried me past him.

He thrust his arm and buried the tanto in Father Grey's abdomen and turned sharply. The blade dragged across his stomach for the length of a dollar bill. Toshiro planted the sole of his foot against his former leader's pelvis and pushed.

Desmond Grey reeled, pressing a hand to his side. He collapsed to a knee, but there was no torrent of red staining his hand. Tendrils of smoke billowed from the wound and through the space between his fingers.

Eleanor shrieked as an animalistic light filled her eyes. Her sword went through dizzying patterns, forcing Toshiro to give up ground.

Cassie echoed Eleanor's cry and followed a few paces behind her. Izzy took Barnabus to the air, and I raced to Desmond's side.

"Desmond—Father Grey—what..." I trailed off when he groaned and pulled his hand away.

Streams of smoke swum through the air around the gash. They wound their way around the injury and through the skin like they were thread guided by an invisible needle. The opening knitted shut.

My left bicep throbbed as Father Grey's fingers dug in. He hauled himself to his feet and stumbled against me.

I caught him and eyed him warily. "What are you?"

"Tired, old, and in need of a drink." He sounded like he had coughed up raw sewage. Desmond put more weight on me and I struggled to keep my balance.

A panicked shriek came from the far side of the room.

I turned and watched as Toshiro drove the women back. It was an odd contest. Both women assailed him with swords. Cassie lagged steps behind Eleanor's practiced footwork. She made up for it with enthusiasm. There was only so far that would take her however.

Toshiro used their lack of coordination against them. His small blade darted in and out, stabbing like a chisel-tipped hornet. Eleanor backpedaled, leaving Cassie exposed. Cassie snarled and swung, devoting more energy than finesse to her strikes. It was enough to keep her from being stabbed, but not enough to best Toshiro.

I eased Father Grey into a seat and muttered a weak

thanks. Fine cracks ran through one of his hands and across his cheeks. The skin of both areas looked like it had received a dusting of ash. I stared at him.

He gave me a grim smile as his eyes fluttered in fatigue. I left him there.

A viridian light pulsed in the air above the fight. Izzy's face furrowed in concentration. I could picture his mind calculating the perfect moment to contribute to the fight. I decided to make things easier for him.

The inside of my chest rattled as I let loose a cavernous roar. The trio paused their fight and turned to the source. I jumped into the space between all three of them and swung my blade across my waist.

Toshiro hissed and leapt back before lunging forward with a thrust.

I used my reach to my advantage. My grip shifted and I held the blade as he did, stepping toward him. He broke his attack and sidestepped. His palm brushed against the hilt of my weapon, diverting its momentum. I compensated for the shift in direction but didn't anticipate the next blow.

A softball-sized explosion filled my ribs. Toshiro repeated the blow within a second. I groaned and snapped an elbow in his direction. I glanced his hip, but it was enough to cause him to lose balance.

The little faerie saw his opportunity. He threw his head back, screaming to the point where I worried about his tonsils. An electric current of green shot toward Toshiro.

The knight blinked and swiveled to pinpoint the source of the noise. He brandished his Japanese dagger at the little fae. Izzy wasn't deterred. The faerie bypassed the attack effortlessly.

"Feel my sting, rapscallion!" Izzy dismounted Barnabus and twirled in a display of aerial acrobatics that could put many circus performers to shame. He landed on Toshiro's chest, bounced and grabbed hold of the man's nose. The fae's face broke into a feral grin before he opened his mouth.

Toshiro growled and brought a hand to his face. Izzy

acted fast. The faerie sank his teeth into the samurai's nose. Toshiro howled and dropped the tanto. He clapped his hands over his nose.

Green light strobed. Toshiro blinked and opened his hands. Izzy was gone.

The faerie tumbled through the air before grabbing onto the knight's lower lip. His weight caused the soft tissue to sink and Toshiro's head to move in sync to prevent further pain. The knight winced, reaching for the fae. Izzy released his hold and let out a shrill whistle. The Unifly followed its rider's descent, moving into position. Izzy caught hold of it and managed to mount.

Toshiro slapped a hand at the fleeing nuisance but struck empty air. Eleanor swung overhead; Cassie jabbed at the knight's thigh. Toshiro pinned himself to the wall. Cassie's blade passed through empty air, but Eleanor adjusted her weapon's path. The tip of the sword clanged against the wall and dragged against it. Scarlet beads leapt into the air as Toshiro rolled away from Eleanor's strike. He clutched the side of his arm and squeezed the wound.

I lunged, driving my sword toward the center of his mass like a spear. The knight moved a shade slower than before. Four of his fingers struck the flat of my blade, pushing it down before he snapped his hand forward. My sword impacted the wall at an odd angle, scraping against it. Toshiro's hand struck my chest in a knife-edge-like blow. I sputtered and clubbed him with my free hand. The blow staggered the knight.

The three of us set on him. Cassie twisted, sending her blade in a horizontal arc. Eleanor thrust, and I brought my sword down like I was splitting wood.

Toshiro had more experience than the lot of us, and it showed. The former knight screamed and clamped a hand to his left eye. He stumbled back. Crimson jelly coated his hand. We had attacked him with three blades and he walked away with a single cut from Cassie's. A normal man would have been dead several times over.

His lips peeled into a sneer and he howled something

incoherent. Blood poured from a ragged gash over his eye. The remnants of his eyelids welded themselves shut and twitched without pause.

The room smelled of cotton candy.

I watched Eleanor's eyes go wide as she turned. Time slowed as she completed her roundabout. A hand the size of a dinner plate glanced the front half of her face. Eleanor took to the air like a rag doll caught in a storm. She tumbled and struck a dark sofa, upending it. Her body slumped to the floor where it stilled.

"Eleanor!" I ran toward her, but the troll positioned its bulk between us.

My movement ground to a halt and I shuffled awkwardly. The beast leaned toward me and snapped what few teeth it had. I lurched to the side and swung off balance. My blade struck one of its misshapen molars, eliciting a sound like cracking bone. A portion of the tooth broke away and crumbled into bits as it fell.

The troll's head shook, and it bellowed once more. It rubbed a hand across its mouth while swinging its free limb toward me. I took two steps back and lunged in a riposte. The tip of my blade had blunted from striking the wall earlier. It didn't matter. I didn't need it to be sharp. I needed its metal. My saber shot toward the creature's massive belly.

The beast was quicker than I anticipated. It inhaled and sucked in its mass. The troll's stomach caved in as it shambled to its side. I overextended, and my momentum carried me into open space. The troll seized the opportunity and lashed out with an open hand.

Cassie's arms wrapped tight around me, driving me away from the blow. Father Grey's lounge flipped sideways and half of my upper body cried out. I collided with the floor. Cassie's arms were still around me. The troll's hand sailed harmlessly above. I muttered a quick thanks to Cassie and rolled her off me.

A pair of black boots came into view on the stairs. My heartbeat accelerated to a pace that could not have been healthy, nor maintained for too long. I took in everything I could in the fleeting seconds where I wasn't in danger.

The troll was in the midst of recovering from its missed swipe. Toshiro composed himself less than six feet away, his hand glued to his marred eye. The owner of the black boots came into full view.

They could have passed for the Grim Reaper. The entirety of their body was masked by a cloak and cowl that was clearly tattered by design and not wear. It was likely part of a costume at one point. Black mesh obscured their face. The hidden figure brandished a misshapen length of chitinous material. It looked as if bits of it were forcibly removed to give it a jagged form.

"Cassie, get Eleanor!" I spread my legs and adopted a wide stance. My fingers drummed my sword as I gripped it tight in both hands. I exhaled once to steel myself.

Toshiro, a troll, and whatever the hell—or Neravene—that thing is. Simple—simple.

I took a breath and screamed. Neither the troll nor the cloaked figure was phased. I felt it best to let my sword do the talking. I took one step and brought the blade up and over my shoulder and across my body. The damaged tip grazed the troll's collar, making its way to its hip. Its skin didn't break, but it was enough contact with steel for the desired effect.

A narrow band of fire flared into existence across the creature like a burning sash. The troll's eyes reddened and went wide as it beat its body furiously. It was a pointless exercise. Violent silvery-white flames licked their way over the troll's fingers.

One down.

The dark fiend let out a dry screech that sounded like every bit of tissue from its vocal chords to its tonsils tore to accomplish the task. It leapt at me with insect-like speed. The chitin-formed weapon clinked once against my sword but didn't crack. A clear jelly-like fluid clung to the area where our blades locked.

Poison?

I adjusted the angle of my weapon and bore down with

more strength.

The troll flailed on instinct, its thick limbs coming close to impacting both me and my opponent.

I glanced past the hooded creature's shoulder and saw a trio of similarly dressed figures walking down the stairs. I swallowed and applied more pressure to our contest of strength. The creature's knees bowed. I broke our lock and snapped my head forward. Something gave way under the black mesh with a *crunch*. I recoiled but not before getting a whiff of an odor like wet, spoiled meat.

The figure shook its head and grabbed a fistful of the cowl. It wrenched the entire outfit off, revealing pale skin that had never seen sunlight. Its face was a horrid mix between a Night Runner and a deep-sea fish. Thin, gaunt with oversized slender teeth protruding past its lips. Amethyst blood oozed from its broken nose.

I addressed Toshiro without taking my eyes off the creature. "You're working with dumnen?" I didn't hide the contempt in my voice.

He scowled. "A necessary evil."

At least he wasn't deluding himself about their nature.

The haunting creature was dressed in patchwork leathers belonging to various creatures I would never be able to identify. Its oversized, bulbous eyes narrowed in anger. The cloudy green organs were filled with hate.

I looked at my sword in uncertainty. Dumnen were a distant cousin to Night Runners. Distant enough that a Night Runner would kill over being mentioned in the same breath. Dumnen were bastardizations of elven blood and culture. Creatures driven into the darkest parts and realms of the Neravene. Bred for untold ages in darkness and adapting to the environment. They were just as cold and unforgiving as the hellholes they came from. And because of that, they were so far removed from the creatures I was accustomed to that I wasn't sure if steel would do anything.

It was in my best interest to find out however. I slashed at its face. The creature slapped its crude weapon against mine without a hint of finesse. My arms shook from the effort. They were stronger and scrappier than I imagined. I heaved and pushed forward. We broke contact once again.

The dumnen staggered back a step. It hooted something incomprehensible to its companions. It never finished its sentence.

The troll bellowed and sent the back of its fist toward us. I let the strength leave my body and crumpled to the floor. The dumnen wasn't a quick thinker it seemed. There was a sound like a particularly large beetle being stepped on. The creature's body broke through enough of the wall to remain partially lodged in it. Its friends released a chorus of echoing screeches.

They were drowned out by a single, resolute voice of smoke and iron. "Get the hell out of my bar!"

I turned as Father Grey lobbed bottles of alcohol into the air with incredulous accuracy. The first smashed against the wall nearest the troll as it lumbered by. Enough of the flammable contents made their way onto the still burning troll's body. The flames spreading over its mass burst to life with renewed vigor. It was fully engulfed within seconds.

The second bottle tumbled and landed at the base of the stairs. The third crashed against the doorframe. The fourth struck the skull of an unfortunate dumnen, causing it to teeter as it likely wondered what had just happened to its world.

Father Grey. My intestines knotted and felt like they were filled with cold rocks.

Cassie's head popped from the door Father Grey had come from earlier. "John, get your ass in here!"

I hadn't seen her make her way there. I heeded her advice without a second thought, sprinting as hard as I could. As I passed Father Grey, I cast a quick look over my shoulder.

The proprietor of the club reached into his suit and withdrew a book of matches the size of a deck of playing cards. He flicked his wrist and they opened. A match the length and nearly the thickness of my pinky appeared in his hand.

I made it to the door and barreled my way in. I gave Desmond Grey one last look as he flicked the match.

There was a horrendous keen that could have belonged only to a mythological beast.

I slammed the door and bolted it shut, leaving Father Grey to face the impossible odds alone.

Chapter Thirty-Seven

The door shook as if it were trying to break free of its hinges. A superheated roar screamed on the other side. I stepped away as the metal door's color shifted like a prism. Desert heat came off it in waves. I turned to find Cassie kneeling over a dazed Eleanor.

The pair were huddled against the side of a heavy ebony desk. Eleanor breathed in shallow, ragged gasps. Her lips were split at one end and caked in crusting blood. She gave me an unsteady stare. I replied with a weak smile. Cassie cradled her and whispered something to keep her attention. She was smart, keeping Eleanor from drifting into unconsciousness.

I summed up the sparse room in the hopes of finding something to aid us. Bleak did not do the place justice. It consisted of the sole desk, an equally expensive looking office chair to accompany it, and the two objects atop it. An antiquated scale made from an unknown blackened material sat next to a stone bowl filled with two unlit incense. Not much décor for the leader of a powerful order of knights.

I cast an eye to the door. Its color warped from a rainbow-like hue to a metallic blue before returning to normal. "Stay with Eleanor." I gave Cassie a knowing look and reached for the door handle.

I paused a few inches from touching it, closing my eyes as I felt for radiating heat. There wasn't a hint of heat at all. It was like the door had never been subjected to severe temperatures. I winced in anticipation and grabbed the handle. A slender beam of coolness passed over my palm. I pushed the door open.

Cassie sputtered behind me.

A corona of white-blue flame surrounded a naked

Father Grey. The same fire ebbed and waned across the walls and floor of the lounge. There wasn't a trace of the dumnen or troll.

I gingerly took a step outside the confines of Father Grey's office and threw an arm up to shield my eyes. My skin broke out in sweat. It felt like it was being pulled tight as I navigated the fire-filled room. I made my way to a spot three feet from Desmond, just outside the crown of fire that seemed to emanate from him.

The bare man turned and flashed me a crooked, tired grin. "You look terrible."

I eyed him from head to toe and arched a brow. "You look like naked shit."

He hooked a thumb to the fire around us. "Hot naked shit."

I snorted, then sobered up. "Is it over?"

Father Grey shook the oversized matchbox. "Wyvern's breath on a stick. Costly—worth every bit."

I let out a long low whistle. "Where did you get the matches?"

He tapped his first two fingers against the box like it was a little drum. "An alchemist in Virginia."

Quentin mentioned something like that earlier. I was going to have to look into that.

Something else crossed my mind. I gave him an oblique stare. "How did you survive the explosion?" I waved a hand around the burning lounge.

He grinned. Fine strands of smoke spilled from between his lips before disappearing.

Another mystery.

I took a deep breath and released it, relishing the calming exercise. It was taken from me the next instant. A shadow stirred within the fire. The flames waned, allowing me to see the figure before they snapped into clarity.

My hand shot toward Father Grey. I banished the fiery ring around him from my mind. I couldn't hesitate. "Down!" I collided with him, driving him back several feet. The shadow burst forth from the fire.

Toshiro let loose a mangled snarl, slashing at me with a sliver of metal. My arms waved as I struggled to regain my lost balance. His aggressive drive and jabs pushed me back, foot after foot. I hissed as I came close to brushing against a patch of the alchemical fire. There was a lull in the barrage of frenzied attacks, giving me a moment to regard Toshiro.

His wounded eye and the surrounding area were matted in a combination of soot and grime. His other half did not fare better. It looked like he had been gripped by a hand of acid. The skin was discolored and covered in weeping red sores. Chunks were blackened, severely burned. It was a gruesome sight, but nothing short of a miracle for being the only price for surviving the explosion.

"Toshiro." My body heaved, and I fumbled for my sword. "Stop."

He gave me a glare hotter than the fire around us.

"Look what it's cost you." I pointed to his face, then to Father Grey. "It's cost you your friends, their trust in you, and your body."

His voice came out like broken bits of burning charcoal. "A small price to pay."

I held my sword in both hands and bent my arms. "Small prices yield small rewards. You get what you pay for, Toshiro."

Father Grey roared and rushed the burned knight. Toshiro's speed did not seem affected by his condition. He moved with fluid grace and pushed the larger man back. I moved to bury my sword in the area where the collarbone meets the neck.

Toshiro flicked his wrist. A mixture of powdered glass and shreds of flaming clothing flew at my face. I shut my eyes in defense. My thigh quivered and burned as a finger-length piece of metal pierced it. I screamed and swatted Toshiro with the flat of my sword. He endured the blow and hooked his foot against the inside of my knee. The limb had little strength after having the metal file jammed into it. I crumpled to the ground.

I lay there, blinking, as Toshiro stepped past me. The

mad knight approached Father Grey with the confidence of a predator hunting wounded prey.

"You have used much of your power, and yet you refused to bring some of it to bear." The knight grimaced and ducked the haymaker thrown by his once boss. He connected with a short jab to Father Grey's ribs. He followed suit with a second before bringing stiffened fingers to the man's throat. Father Grey sputtered and gagged. Toshiro yanked him by the hair. "I cannot kill you, but I can stop you." He removed another metal shiv from his robes and slammed it up and at an angle between Desmond's ribs.

The heart. A fraction of the file protruded from Father Grey's ribs. Toshiro followed the reeling man and pivoted. He planted his feet, twisting at the hips. His palm struck the base of the file.

Father Grey howled as the slender weapon buried itself fully inside him. His legs quaked. Desmond Grey collapsed to the ground like a building with a weak foundation. A hand still pressed tightly to his ribs. His chest was still, as was the rest of him. He was done.

It wasn't enough for the rogue knight.

With nothing left but stone and metal to burn, the flames dwindled.

It wasn't the case for the fire inside Toshiro however. He knelt over his fallen leader, cradling one side of Father Grey's head. "When you wake, you will find a world I have brought balance to. Then, you can answer for your greatest sin." He lifted and shook Father Grey's head before letting it hit the floor.

I wanted to tell him that dead men don't wake. I wanted to know Desmond's greatest sin. And I wanted to bury the shard of metal in my leg in Toshiro's throat. One out of three wasn't so bad.

My fingers wrapped around the metal. I licked my lips before pressing them tight together, hoping they would muffle what was to come. All it took was a sharp tug. The beam of pain made its way from my leg to my throat as a scream. I grappled with the blood-slick piece of metal and channeled my scream into the throw. It tumbled towards Toshiro.

His hand snapped out like it was guided by an elastic cord. He batted the file away with contempt.

I heaved and caught my breath. The simple action was taxing. "You murdered him."

Toshiro kept his stare on Father Grey. "He was dead a long time ago—I simply nailed the coffin shut."

I squeezed my eyes shut and blinded myself to the pain. The muscle in my wounded leg shook. My elbows supported me as I pushed against the floor with my body. An acute point of pressure flared within my quivering leg. I shut it away, hefting my blade. The ligaments throughout my body trembled in fatigue, feeling stretched and weary. The sword trembled in my grip. I swallowed the pain, pushing it into the pit of my stomach where it became something else.

Anger. It throbbed in my gut like a second heart. I let it drive another charge against the fallen knight.

The distance closed, and my sword sank towards him. He moved, his palm colliding with the underside of my chin. My blade met resistance, but I couldn't make out what had stopped it. White spots sparked across my vision. It felt like a large stone hammered into my wound. Red replaced the white spots and my leg buckled. The same stone struck my skull and beat the red out of it. All that remained were sporadic flashes, each accompanied by a head jarring impact.

"You should have laid down to die a long time ago. You are a glutton for punishment."

Blood leapt from my lips in weak spurts. "Perseverance is the key to success."

He answered with another punch that rocked my head. Toshiro used his position above me to his advantage. He put his weight into every punch as I lay on the floor and absorbed them.

"Leave him alone!" Cassie's voice shook, but I could hear the undercurrent of steel in it.

My eyes fluttered opened. Toshiro stood over me, his chest heaving in effort. My head lolled to the side, and it took me a moment to register what was wrong with his left arm. Most of it below the elbow was missing. The saber had struck the bone in his forearm, paring flesh and sinew. And he still managed to pummel me to the ground.

Cassie stepped closer. She held her sword firm. It never shook.

I tried to smile, but my face refused to move. I was proud of her.

"Back the fuck off...or I'll give you a Viking colonoscopy!" She accentuated her point with a wave of Tatiana's sword. "If that wasn't clear, I meant I'm going to jam this sword up your ass."

Violent coughs wracked my chest and throat. The laughter didn't help. I leaned to my side and spat another mouthful of blood.

My gut filled with fire ants as Toshiro planted his foot into it.

"Leave him alone!" Cassie bristled and took another step forward.

Toshiro nudged me onto my back and bent to retrieve something. A Civil War saber.

I killed a man to take it. Was it fair that I would be killed by it? I didn't think so. Maybe that made me a hypocrite. Or maybe it just meant I was human.

Toshiro came into a new clarity to me in that moment. I understood him. I knew why he was doing everything that he was. It didn't make it right, but it made it clear. And it made me sick.

He was human, like me. We were never meant to live immune to time. It caught up with him. It broke him. Another one of life's little ironies. Only this one had come back to kill me.

The fallen knight reversed his grip on my sword. Its tip hovered a hand length from my right eye.

Cassie sucked in a breath. "Wait."

Toshiro did. His face had lost much of its color. The blood loss, pain, and fatigue took their toll. He wouldn't last much longer.

"Don't kill him. You can't."

Toshiro remained silent.

"If you do, I'll kill you." Cassie kept the blade level. Her voice was filled with molten metal. She meant it.

"Death cures the fear of itself." Toshiro raised the sword.

"I'll come with you. Shit, stop, just stop. I'll come with you—I swear."

Toshiro stared at me for a moment that couldn't have been longer than the time it took to inhale. But it felt like counting all the breaths I had ever taken. He turned his gaze to Cassie. "Toss your sword aside."

Metal on stone clattered to my right. A deeper variation of the noise followed. The sword and shield.

Dammit. I couldn't let this happen.

The traitorous knight pointed my sword at Cassie. "Come here."

She didn't answer, but the growing sound of her footsteps let me know her decision.

I reached up and brushed my hand against Toshiro's leg. His clothing rustled. I grabbed him tight around the ankle. "Don't do this—"

My ribs throbbed as Toshiro pulled his foot back.

"You said you'd leave him alone!" Cassie stopped and eyed her fallen sword. She was reconsidering.

Good. I hoped she'd go as far as picking it back up and running the bastard through.

"I will kill him if need be—then take you. I kept my word. He is not dead."

Cassie sighed and conceded. She approached Toshiro, stopping a shade outside his reach. Something moved under her hoodie. It looked like she had stowed a football under her clothing.

It hurt too much to smile when I realized what was transpiring. *That's where the little pest went.*

Toshiro held out a hand. "Come."

Cassie hesitated and looked down at her stomach.

The saber leapt to the spot she stared at. Toshiro's voice

dropped to a dangerous whisper. "Remove the sweatshirt."

"Uh, kind of a perv move there." She gave him a weak smile. "You're going to ask a lady to take off her clothes?"

"It is one article. Remove it."

Cassie scowled and pulled her arms into the sleeves. She paused and folded her arms over her stomach. "Now!"

Green light flooded my vision as Cassie's hoodie flopped over Toshiro's face. Izzy and Barnabus flew towards the knight, releasing a mangled chorus of noises. "Eee-argle-bahooo!"

Toshiro slapped the sweatshirt aside and whipped the sword through the air. Izzy pulled Barnabus into a turn, narrowly avoiding the blade. Cassie lowered her posture and rushed the knight with her arms outstretched. She wrapped them around his waist. Her momentum drove him back a foot. Cassie cried out and sank to her knees as the pommel of my sword crashed into her back.

"You—" Izzy was cut short.

Toshiro dropped the sword, and retrieved the fallen hoodie in a fluid motion. He ensconced the faerie and Unifly within the sweatshirt. Izzy and Barnabus thrashed inside. The makeshift sack struck the tiled floor, silencing the diminutive pair.

Toshiro released his hold and grabbed Cassie by the back of her hair.

"John!" She landed blows against his sternum and remaining arm. Toshiro gritted through them.

My body felt like lit kindling.

He yanked hard, striking an open hand blow against her skull. Cassie went limp in his grasp.

The kindling broke. My hands wrapped around Toshiro's ankle, and I rolled. My shoulder barreled into the side of his knee, toppling him. I rode the momentum until I was atop him. His head thudded against the floor. I reintroduced it to the tiles as I put my weight into a haymaker. My fingers fumbled for a hold on his face as I clawed at him.

Toshiro snarled and scissored his legs around my arm.

His heel struck my forehead and chin in quick succession. I lost my hold. My vision turned hazy. Toshiro ignored me and stumbled over to Cassie. He grunted as he hauled her to her feet, draping one of her arms over his shoulder.

Blinking did nothing to clear my distorted view. I inhaled and turned to my side, hoping that any movement would galvanize my mind and body to further action. I was wrong to hope.

"Help me." Toshiro's voice was sandpaper over rough wood. Dull thuds emanated from the staircase.

Two dumnen came into view. The pair were mirror images of the dumnen from earlier. They moved to his side, helping to steady him.

"Take the girl." Toshiro shifted his weight and pushed Cassie towards one of the cloaked monsters. "Do not let any harm befall her."

I ground my teeth. Fine thing to say considering he was the chief cause behind Cassie's situation and injuries. My head buzzed like damaged speakers. The static coursed through my skull and eyes. I shook them clear and pressed a palm to the side of my face. Toshiro and the dumnen limped up the stairs, paying me no mind.

They would regret that.

I rolled to my side, using an elbow to prop myself up. My joints creaked as I pushed and came to my feet. Wet, sputtering coughs came from behind me. I groaned and managed to ignore the pain in my neck enough to glance at the source.

Izzy's chest heaved and he coughed again. His lower lip was coated in blood a color somewhere between cherry and eggplant. Barnabus brayed and nudged the dewdrop.

I scuttled on all fours to his side. It felt like cold chains were pulling my body back as I reached for the faerie. I inhaled and hesitated, deciding to nudge him with the tip of my index finger. My gentle touch rocked his body. "Izzy, can you hear me?"

A pained groan left his lips. He blinked several times, staring like he was trying to put together a difficult jigsaw puzzle. "Yes. You, the bells, Cassie—I hear you all."

I shut my eyes as a hot needle of pain lanced behind them. "The bells—Cassie?"

Izzy placed a hand to his stomach and the heel of his other palm to his forehead. He rose and winced. "I believe that is what mortals call it—'having your bell rung'?"

I snorted and regretted it instantly. It felt like metal rods were lodged in my nostrils and expanding. I rubbed the bridge of my nose, wincing as I did. "Yes, Izzy, you've had your bell rung. So did I. Forget about that for now."

His focus seemed to clear and he eyed me.

I swallowed. "He has her, Izzy." I pressed the back of my hand to my mouth as my chest shook. The coughs racked my body and lungs. "Toshiro's taken Cassie."

Izzy stared like he was seeing for the first time. He nodded slowly. "Right. After them then."

"Are you up to it?" I cast a quick glance towards the stairs. Toshiro was gone. It hadn't been long. If we moved now, we had a chance.

Izzy's face hardened and he gave me a look that answered my question. "I will have to be." He grabbed hold of Barnabus and hauled himself up. The dewdrop mounted his Unifly and booted his sides twice.

Barnabus took to the air. The creature's eyes blinked rapidly before settling. The Unifly hadn't endured the beating any better. Despite its injuries, the little creature took to the air and zoomed up the stairs.

My hands shook as they closed around the hilt of my saber. I planted its tip against the floor, using it as a prop to steady myself. The muscles in my legs felt like hot batter. They shook and burned as I got to my feet. I drowned the pain and fatigue in something else—anger. I ground my teeth and stole a quick breath before hobbling after Izzy.

The dewdrop hovered at the top of the stairs. He jabbed a finger to the doorway we had passed earlier. "Through there!" He dug his heels into Barnabus and charged the door. The faerie didn't have the mass or strength to force it open. Izzy pushed it open regardless. It shut a second later.

I blinked, worried that what I saw was the result of head trauma. Each step jarred my body as I raced up the stairs. At the top, I stopped and placed my hand against the door. A gentle thrum emanated from it like it was buzzing with energy. I pushed it open.

Acoustic waves bombarded me with concussive force. I raised a hand to shield my eyes. An onslaught of prismatic colors strobed and swept over the club in pulsing beams. Father Grey certainly knew how to give people a lively time.

An emerald light stood out against the light show. It flashed steadily against the discordant techno patterns. The faerie hung a dozen feet over the energetic crowd. His light blinked as if signaling me. If he was shouting, I couldn't hear it.

I pushed my way through the nearest group. It was like navigating through a live battle. The same intensity filled the air. I slipped through a pair of women caught in what looked like a possessed dance.

Toshiro knew what he was doing. It wasn't going to be easy to track him through a sea of club-goers. I shoved my way through a trio of dancers and glanced at Izzy.

The faerie's head was on a swivel. He stopped, staring at a spot just over my shoulder.

I turned on instinct. The black cloaked figure trailed six feet behind me. Izzy had great eyes. I took advantage of the interweaving crowd and slipped between a small bunch of people. Flashing chemical lights adorned their bodies as they spun and twisted to create intricate patterns with them. If the lights didn't disorient the following dumnen, the sheer number of shifting people would.

I moved further into the group and cast a look over my shoulder. The dumnen followed with less grace. It forced clubbers aside, earning itself heated glares.

I exited the crowd, increasing my pace as I circled around behind the creature. It paused in the middle of the living light shows. The creature's body visibly stiffened within the dark garments. Its head turned slowly, scanning the crowd for me. I raced forward. A crowd member crashed to the floor as I barreled through. I paid them no mind. My heel plowed into the spot just above the dumnen's calf. It sank to a knee. I didn't slow my momentum. Seizing its head, I drove its skull into the base of a nearby stage. A hollow drum of protest echoed from the collision.

I looked at the surrounding clubbers. Few paid any mind to the scuffle. The rest dismissed it and resumed their activities. I searched for Izzy's light. The faerie had moved another twenty feet away from his previous position. I ran.

I gained new appreciation for people who navigated the club scene without incurring crippling injuries. Izzy streaked further ahead and I followed, taking care not to knock anyone else over. The dewdrop stopped above and bobbed like a radioactive buoy. I waited.

He put his hands to his mouth and shouted something. It was pointless with the deafening thunderclaps of music and bass. Izzy jabbed a finger to spot ahead of me.

I followed his gesture and gave silent thanks I had stopped moving when I did. Another dumnen waited like a statue hewn from charcoal. Its gaze fixed on a pair of metal double doors the color of fire engines.

A small, battered man pushed the doors open. Two dumnen followed, supporting the limp form of a young woman.

Toshiro. Cassie.

The tremoring music enveloped my insides. My heart and blood felt like they were beating in sync with it. I grabbed the nearest man by his shoulder, twisting and sending him sprawling out of the way. Three long steps closed the distance between the dumnen and me. I never gave it the chance to turn around.

My fingers dug into the meat around the creature's windpipe as I wrenched back on it. The saber ran through the small of its back with ease. I drove the blade forward until the hilt pressed against the monster's back. All it took was a twist of my wrist to tear the sword free, cutting a path through the dumnen's torso.

People screamed. I ignored them. Placing the high-pitched noises in the background. I clawed at the front of a man's mesh shirt, grabbing a fistful and hauling him out of my way. Between the sword, blood, and my snarl, most people cleared a path for me. I raced towards the doors. Izzy remained in the air, an emerald beacon amidst the kaleidoscope of electronic colors.

I reached the doors and plowed through. Winter embraced me in a chilling hug. I ignored it and focused on the four figures in the middle of the street. The two dumnen placed themselves between Toshiro and me. My lips peeled back and I let loose a snarl that would've been heard even in the club. I charged.

The closest of the two fiends moved to intercept. It withdrew a crude hatchet from its cloak. The dumnen matched my earlier snarl and swung.

I brought my other hand to the hilt of my saber, putting as much force as I could behind the blow. The length of my saber decided the fight as soon as it started. A dry keen left the dumnen's mouth as it gripped its weapon hand below the wrist. Its hand and hatchet tumbled before settling in the snow. I took a step, twisting and driving the saber between the dumnen's parted lips. A hand's length of the blade protruded from the back of its skull. I wrenched the blade free, shaking the gore clean from it.

The remaining dumnen hesitated.

Cassie took advantage of the momentary lull. She sprang into action, snapping her head at Toshiro. Cartilage broke with a sound like wet twigs snapping. She pushed herself free from his grip as he brought a hand to his broken nose. Blood made its way through the space between his fingers and onto the back of his hand.

Toshiro released an animalistic growl and swept a hand at her. Red beads fell from his hand and nose, marring a patch of clean snow.

I used the distraction to advance on the remaining dumnen. It was more aware than I had imagined. The creature backpedaled before turning its back to me. I ran after it, aiming to skewer it through its back.

The dumnen was quick to flank Cassie and prevent her from fleeing Toshiro. She was caught in a triangle between us. I couldn't advance without putting her at further risk of being set upon by the other two.

I inhaled and raised my sword over my head to draw attention. "Toshiro, stop!"

To his credit, he froze. It didn't stop him from giving me a look that implied I was mad.

I had to be if I was trying to appeal to his better nature. From where I stood, he had none left. But it was worth a shot for Cassie's safety. I waved a hand back to the club. "Look at everything that's happened. When is it going to be enough?"

"When it is over." He didn't look like he had much strength left. What remained filled his eyes. It was like staring at dying coals and cooling metal. "She is coming with me."

"Like hell I am!" Cassie gave him a glare that could have turned steel molten.

I smiled. "What she said." I took a step forward.

Toshiro and the dumnen mimicked my movement. I ran my tongue against my teeth. The air felt like frozen glass. If I took another step, it would crack.

Cassie ran a hand through her hair. Several strands caught in her fingers. She brushed through it a few more times, letting the hairs fall to the ground. Cassie's opalescent eyes flared with a wild light that reminded me a feral animal. Her fingers raked through her hair again. Cassie was on edge, boxed in between us. She took a step towards me.

The simple action sent reverberations through the invisible glass around us. Everyone but Cassie tensed as she took another step.

I drummed my fingers against the side of my thigh. The small bones in my hand ached from the cold and force of which I gripped my sword.

Toshiro and the dumnen exchanged a quick glance.

The glass wall shattered. It was a mad haze of movement.

I leapt towards Cassie, swinging my blade to intercept Toshiro's rush. The dumnen pressed its opening, advancing to grab her. Without a break in momentum, I pivoted, sending the tip of my sword arcing by the dumnen's face. My strike came up short. The dumnen sank to its knees. It struck me full force below the waist. I crashed into the cushioning snow. My fingers clawed through the snow as I scrambled to my feet.

Cassie swore.

I turned and took a step before freezing. Toshiro and the dumnen fought to restrain Cassie, but she was in their grip.

She flailed and dragged her nails across Toshiro's scalp. I couldn't tell if she had drawn blood, but threads of hair fell free. With a violent twist, she managed to lash out and catch the dumnen under the chin with an impressive kick. The monster struck her with the back of its hand. Ruby drops welled on her lips. She pressed them tight, forcing blood to pool before she spat at the creature's feet. Cassie opened her mouth to snarl something no doubt witty and defiant.

Toshiro dug his fingers into the area around her windpipe, cutting her off. He produced another sliver of metal and pressed it against her neck. "Enough."

"You won't kill her." I took a step.

Another drop of blood formed on her throat. Toshiro raised a brow and shot me a challenging glare.

"You need her." I held back the urge to advance another step.

"I do. I also need to live to carry out my plans. Between the girl's life and mine, I know which I will choose to save, and which to discard."

A cord of beaded ice formed around my throat preventing me from speaking. My breathing intensified. I swallowed the ice and took another step. "You're a coward."

The words had quite the effect. Something ugly and hot flashed through his eyes. Toshiro's hands tensed on the metal spike. I could see him restraining the desire to puncture Cassie's throat in retaliation.

"It's okay, John." Her voice rattled me. There was something off. "Let him take me."

I felt like someone had taken a hammer to every disc in my spine.

"Just make me a promise..." Her eyes filled with a light like kindling bursting into a full fire. "Find me." She dropped her gaze to the snowy streets.

My eyes widened when I saw what she did. I licked my lips but couldn't bring myself to speak. Her words rooted me to the spot.

Toshiro used my deliberation to open a Way behind him. It wasn't a gleaming silver ribbon like before. The Way resembled a ragged tear in clothing with frayed threads flitting and ready to come undone.

Cassie gave me a final look. "Let him take me."

I did.

Toshiro and the dumnen wasted no time dragging her into to the Way. The magical door shut. Cassie was gone. I let them take her.

God forgive me.

Chapter Thirty-Eight

There's a certain rush that goes through your body after a fight and chase. It's like popping the cork of a champagne bottle only to upend all its contents. There's a bubbling expulsion of energy. Then everything spills to the floor.

I fell to my knees, staring at the spot where Cassie had vanished. The silence didn't last. Izzy buzzed and flashed like a viridian taser.

"You let him take her?" There was an accusatory tone to his voice. But he wasn't wrong. I did. His voice increased to a shrill horn. "You let him take her!"

"Yes." I got to my feet but refused to meet the faerie's eyes.

"Why? You could have—"

"Could have what, Izzy? You saw the situation as well as I did. I have a promise to keep." I walked a few paces to where Cassie had run her hands through her hair.

"And what promise is that?" His voice carried an edge like a piece of broken glass.

"To find her and bring her back."

"How do you plan on doing that?"

I knelt and plucked red hairs from the snow. "I don't. Cassie did the planning for me." I held the hairs up for Izzy to see.

His eyes widened when he caught onto Cassie's idea.

I cut a swath of material from my coat, winding the hairs into a neat coil and stuffing them into it. The leather folded with ease, and I stowed it in my pocket. "Izzy, fetch me something like a cup—an open container."

"What?"

"Now."

He didn't respond but zoomed off.

I scanned the ground, and a fierce grin crossed my face when I found Toshiro's hair. My sword snipped another piece from my coat and I repeated the process to store the strands safely.

"Hey!"

I turned to the source of the commotion. He couldn't have been out of college yet. Youthful, slender, and in need of a shave. The young man was dressed in the sort of loose clothing you'd expect in winter but not without making it clear he was proud of his university's sports team. An angry flash of green emanated from the ends of his hands.

Izzy was engaged in a fierce contest of strength with the youth. He tugged on the lip of a red plastic cup.

The young man's eyes were close to dancing in circles. He gazed at the cup like it was possessed. "The hell?" He struggled to pull it back. "Ow!" His grip faltered and he shook his hand, looking at his reddened finger in astonishment.

The youth squinted at the air in front of him as if the answer would suddenly materialize. He looked around until he caught me staring. His face flushed and he walked off at a brisk pace.

It was a rather embarrassing situation from his perspective.

Izzy flitted back towards me, carrying the red cup by its lip. Liquid the color of pale wheat sloshed over the edge. Barnabus stopped near my shoulder and Izzy presented me with the cup. "Will this do?"

"Yes, but not as it is." I got to my feet and moved to where Cassie stood when the Way had opened. A splotch of red, a bit bigger than a quarter, stood out against the blanket of white. I reached out blindly for the cup. "I need to empty and clean it so it doesn't change the nature of blood."

"Aye!" Izzy nudged Barnabus into descending.

The Unifly touched the ground, and Izzy released his hold on the cup. It fell flat, nestling into the snow with another slosh of ale over the side. Izzy dismounted and brought his face to the cup's lip. He leaned over and inhaled.

"Izzy—no!" I snapped a hand out to grab the cup and upend its contents. My fingers closed around it, and I flipped it over in a single motion. Not a drop fell onto the snow. I blinked, eyeing the inside of the cup. Empty. I looked at Izzy.

His stomach was distended like he had swallowed a ping-pong ball. He patted and rubbed it with satisfaction. A split second later, it shrank in size until it reached its normal proportions.

I stared in silence. First he'd managed to open a door that weighed infinitely more than his own self. Now he'd downed enough beer to give something his size alcohol poisoning.

Izzy belched and released a content sigh.

"Are you okay?" My fingers twitched as I controlled the urge to reach out and touch him.

"Heeek!" The dewdrop's body shook violently as he brought a hand to his mouth to stifle the hiccup. "Blackh! That was most foul." He eyed me like I was a lunatic. "You mortals subject others to this for torture, yes?"

I shook my head. "Recreation."

Izzy blinked. "Your species is most strange."

I had to agree. I refrained from telling him that his was equally as baffling. "Thank you for emptying the cup."

He bowed his head.

The snow bit at my exposed fingers as I scooped up a lump and ran it against the insides of the cup. I dumped it out and repeated the process a few times before drying it with my coat. Satisfied that I had removed any lingering traces of alcohol, I carefully dragged the lip against the blood spot. The red patch of snow slipped into the cup. I prayed the water content wouldn't be enough to distort the blood's attunement to Cassie.

"Excellent, we should have enough to find her, John."

I gave him a curt nod. "We should."

Izzy wobbled in place. His eyes looked like they were ready to perform cartwheels. "So..." He stretched his arms in front of him and fought to steady of himself. "Which one of you Johns will do the finding?"

I blinked. "How many of me do you see right now?"

"That is a rather stupid question. Two, of course!"

My ribs shook, and the rest of my body followed. I tried to swallow my laughter. The dewdrop was drunk.

"Izzy, please focus." I couldn't tell if I was keeping a straight face or not. "We need to find Cassie."

"Right!" He bobbed his head and his eyes widened as he pressed a hand to one temple. Izzy realized the sudden movement was a bad idea. "I believe that is your job, biggun. Have you always been that big? I don't think you have—"

"Izzy!" I raised a hand to shut him up. "I can't perform thaumaturgy."

His eyes grew larger. "Oh, John, I'm most sorry to say this but...I see a mighty flaw in your plan." He pointed an unsteady finger at me. "Perhaps the other John knows how..."

I exhaled through my nose. "Maybe it's best if you stay here and out of sight. Glamour yourself."

He stamped a foot and gave me a resolute look. "Where you go—heeek—I go!"

Without another word, I got to my feet, taking care to cover the mouth of the cup with my hand. I headed towards the flight of stairs we first used to enter Father Grey's establishment. The club didn't seem the best place to be at the moment. Most people weren't welcome after running their sword through the back of a monster. A part of me wondered what Grey's employees were doing to cover it up.

I descended the stone stairs and rapped my fist against the door. The viewing slit remained shut. I banged the base of my fist into the door again. It opened.

The hall was dark, but it wasn't empty. I could feel waves of cold hatred wash over me. Frigid pine needles pricked my skin. I swallowed and held up a calming hand to reassure Grey's bouncer that I wasn't a threat.

A rumble associated with minor earthquakes vibrated from the entirety of the hall.

"I need his help, please?" I took a step and crossed through the doorway without invitation. No dark horror rushed to toss me out, or worse. I took another step.

The rumble intensified. "You brought trouble here," said the bouncer.

"Trouble that belonged to Grey's entourage."

A moment of silence passed between us. Maybe I shouldn't have talked back to it.

"True." The cold prickling receded followed by some of the darkness. It didn't do much for the hall's brightness, but the dim lighting was visible. "Enter."

Permission. Wonderful. A part of me felt it would have been better to be denied entry.

"Heeek!" Izzy's light came in an unstable burst like that of a high-speed camera flash. "We have a perilous problem!"

A ball of iron chain links formed in my gut. "What, Izzy?"

"I cannot see!"

I turned and watched the little faerie squint as he leaned forward on his Unifly.

"Your vision is a side effect of being drunk. I don't see how it is a big problem either."

He scoffed and made a raucous nasal noise I thought incapable for something so small. "Obviously you don't. You are far too big to comprehend the problem. If I cannot see, who will lead us? Heek!"

I buried my face in the palm of my hand. "Izzy, you are not in charge in any way whatsoever." My pace increased in the hope the dewdrop would be left behind. It was the best course of action given his condition. An inebriated faerie with a Napoleon Complex wasn't going to be much help.

The Unifly kept pace, keeping his faerie master a foot behind me.

I walked faster and kept on alert for Father Grey's bouncer. The last thing I needed was for him to have a change of heart. Darkness and dim lighting bled together into an illusion, making the hall look far longer than it was. I lost myself in it until I reached the doorway to the lounge.

"Heek!"

A heavy sigh left me as I entered. The lounge was devoid of furniture. All that remained was the bar counter sans the alcohol. Tiles shone with the look of a fresh scrubbing and polish. I focused on the metal door to his office. "You cleaned this place up fast."

"Good help—hard workers."

I looked over my shoulder to the source of the voice. Father Grey cleaned up as well and as fast as his establishment. It was almost like he hadn't been caught in the fire. He was back in a perfect match for the suit from earlier. In fact, it looked as if he had never left it. There was only one thing letting me know something was off. His face carried a gray tinge, like the surface of his skin was a thin film stretched over stone.

"You don't look well, Desmond."

He grunted and pulled a gray handkerchief from his pocket to dab his brow with. "It's going around. What do you want? You've done a fine job of wrecking my establishment—both here and upstairs."

I refrained from reminding him that was Toshiro's doing. "I'm sorry."

Father Grey eyed me askance. "No, you're not. What do you want, Hawthorne?"

"Toshiro's not the only one who can perform thaumaturgy." I gave him a level-eyed stare.

He met my stare, giving me a look like frozen concrete. His voice matched. "No, he isn't."

I fished out the patches of leather containing the hairs and presented him with the plastic cup.

He took them from me without a word, heading over to the bar counter. Father Grey laid the items over the countertop. His lip furled under his teeth as he thumbed one of the folded leather pieces open.

"How did you get these?" He pinched and held Cassie's hair up for me to see. Grey repeated the process with Toshiro's hair in his other hand.

"I didn't. She did."

He smiled and gave me a curt nod. "Smart girl."

"She is. Now help me find her."

"One condition, Hawthorne." Father Grey gave me a look that said this was more than just a simple request.

I arched a brow and waited.

"Don't bring Toshiro back alive." His eyes flashed with a heat that I had to look away from.

"I don't plan to, believe me." My knuckles cracked as I made a fist.

Father Grey nodded and ducked behind the counter. He reappeared holding a vial. Crimson fluid clung to its edges.

Blood.

He gave the vial a little shake. "I make sure to keep a sample of all my knights."

"For moments like this?" The words left my mouth before I had given them proper thought.

His fingers curled around the vial. I thought it would crush from his grip. "Yes." His mouth was tight.

There was a flaw with his plan however. "If your knights know you have this—"

"My knights are old enough that something as trivial as taking a blood sample will be forgotten over their lifetime. It's one of the first things I do."

I didn't care so long as Toshiro hadn't taken precautions to circumvent the method. "Find them."

"I will. Wait here." He turned, taking the materials back to his office. The door shut with a somber note.

I stood in silence, ignoring the irritating strobes of green light reflecting off the glass counter. "You took your time getting here, Izzy."

"Barnabus lost his way." The Unifly huffed and snorted in what sounded like a rebuke. "Did so! You, lousy lout. How is this—hurp—my fault?"

My temples felt like a vice-grip around my forehead. I rubbed a hand against them, hoping to relieve the pressure. The door to Father Grey's office opened.

Each hand held strands of hair pinched together between his first two fingers and thumbs. Individual hairs clung together like an invisible glue held them. I was able to discern why seconds later. Father Grey stopped just outside my reach, holding up the sets of hair. The strands were coated in blood. It wasn't hard to guess whose.

Izzy hiccupped and eyed the macabre tracking devices dubiously. "That hardly looks sanitary." His stomach made a sound like a sink regurgitating murky water. He clasped his belly as his face flushed.

I ignored him and plucked the hairs from Desmond. Smooth plastic slid against my thumbs. Black fishing line bound the hairs together. A gentle tug came from their base and the hairs moved. I looked up from them to Father Grey.

He gave me a thin smile.

"And that's the easy part, right?" I arched a brow.

"It is. You'll have to go through some interesting Ways to find them. It won't be easy. It won't be safe."

"I didn't think it would be." I held Cassie's hairs a bit higher. "How do I follow them to, or through, a certain Way."

"You don't."

I blinked, holding back a snarl. "What?"

"This isn't something you want to do alone—or can."

He was right. I looked over my shoulder to Izzy then back at Grey. "He's in no shape to help."

"I wasn't talk about the piddling faerie, Hawthorne. You need real help."

Izzy managed to straighten up and bristle. He shot Father Grey a look that could have been fearsome if it weren't for Izzy's size.

"Is this the part where you offer me some of your knights?"

"No, believe me, I wish I could but..." He looked to the door at the end of his lounge.

"You want to keep Toshiro's betrayal quiet—between you and Eleanor. Typical. How is she?"

"Resting. Angry, but resting. She will be fine."

The answer was good enough for me.

"I don't suppose you have something else to help me

besides these?" I shook both sets of hairs.

"I do."

"What's that?"

"A Way." He turned and moved his hand before I could react. Cassie may have had a miraculous ability, but Grey had untold years of practice and finesse. He opened the doorway with a gentle wave of his hand.

I shut my eyes. The Way ripped the air aside as a gaping mouth of fire peeled into the lounge. I squinted, peering through an opening I made with my fingers. Waves of fire rolled out from the sides of black space. They bowed and crashed against an invisible barrier. Torrents of smoke billowed around the ends like gaseous cushion. It didn't look like an inviting Way.

The flames pulled at my eyes, begging me to walk through them. I swallowed and tore myself away from them. "I thought people couldn't open Ways here?" My heel struck the tile as I stamped the ground.

Desmond Grey's lips split into a smile suited to a reptile. It was cold, thin, and left me wondering at his intent. "They can't." He arched an expectant brow. "Well?"

I took a step and hesitated. "Where does it lead?"

"Where you need to go."

Fair enough. I touched two fingers to my forehead and gave Desmond Grey a salute. "Take care of Izzy for me."

The faerie flashed and nudged Barnabus into flight. "Wait!"

I jumped and let the fire engulf me.

Chapter Thirty-Nine

My knees absorbed a soft impact as I landed in snow. The cold seeped through tissue and into my bones, numbing me to most of my pain.

I was in the middle of a familiar street, one Cassie and I had landed on earlier. The Ways needed some adjustment. Opening to a spot dead center on a street was not safe.

I plowed through the snow and onto the sidewalk, stowing my saber. Powdered blue shutters blocked the view inside the bakery's windows. I stopped outside the door, my knuckles an inch from rapping against it on instinct. They never made contact. I froze. Trolls had smashed the door the last time I had seen it. A steel door, a color somewhere between black and navy blue, blocked the way.

I never thought my home would need something like that. Steel would bar the way to many things from the Neravene. But a gentle touch always goes a long way. I knocked. The simple action caused me to wince as the cold metal sent an unforgiving jolt through my battered knuckles. Metal slid against metal—the sound of a chain being undone. An unlocking bolt followed.

The door opened and Tatiana stood there. There was a moment where nothing happened but registering each other's appearance. Her arms wrapped around me and squeezed tight. My ribs and spine protested.

Tatiana was strong. Baking wasn't an easy profession, neither was centuries of warfare and monster slaying. Thankfully, she released her hold.

I breathed through my mouth and caught my breath. "Nice to see you too."

She gave me a smile that faded as she looked past me. "Where is Cassie?"

I broke contact with her gaze.

"Come inside. Tell me what happened—everything." Her fingers closed around my collar and she yanked me through the doorway. Tatiana's iron grip moved to my shoulder as she spun me around. "Tsk. Look at you. What's happened? Where have you been? Where is my stuff? Talk!"

My eyes were close to spinning under the rapid-fire barrage of questions. With two long breaths, I cleared my head and told her everything.

She spat and said something in a language I didn't understand. It didn't take much guesswork to figure it was a curse. "Toshiro. I always hated him," she said.

"I know. Your instincts were right."

Tatiana looked at me over her shoulder and gave me a lopsided grin. "They're always right."

They were in my experience. I didn't agree aloud however. Doing so would set a dangerous precedent.

She beckoned me with a hand. "Come, Quentin and George are waiting."

"Quentin?" I followed her, taking a quick look around the bakery. She had done a wonderful job restoring the place.

"He figured you would return here eventually." Tatiana stopped outside the elevator. "We need to prepare if you plan to take Cassie back by force."

"Toshiro hasn't left any other options. And *we?*"

A pale golden eyebrow arched. She shot me a look that made me reconsider what I said.

"Of course, we. All of us."

Tatiana flashed me a glare. "Don't be a smartass."

I bit my tongue.

She pulled the gate open and stepped onto the platform, giving me an impatient look. I moved to her side and shut the gate. Tatiana pulled the lever. The lift shuddered and we descended.

My eyes were fixed on the wall. It was like a scrolling marquee of brick and mortar.

"John, how are you taking this?" Her hand fell on my

shoulder and squeezed.

I flinched from the question and sudden contact. "I let him take her, Tat. I let him."

She squeezed harder. "We will get her back."

My throat dried and speaking was an effort. "How do you know? I don't want to fail her again."

"Look at me, John."

I did. Her eyes made cold steel seem soft and warm by comparison.

"We will get her back." Tatiana's eyes flashed.

I believed her. My fingers wrapped around hers, and I pulled her hand down. "Thanks, Tat." I gripped her hand tighter for a moment.

We let go at the same time. The only sound remaining was the shaking of antiquated machinery. The lift shook as it came to a halt. I pulled the gate aside and stepped out first.

George sat opposite Quentin at a small table of cherry wood. They passed a bottle between each other, pouring caramel colored liquid from it. Neither of them seemed to register the elevator.

I cleared my throat and raised a brow.

Quentin downed the contents of the glass in a single swig. "'Bout time, kid." He squinted and leaned to look past me. "Where's the smartass? I liked her."

George took a slower, more refined sip from his glass before giving it a little swirl. "She had spunk. Good girl."

I told them what I had told Tatiana.

Quentin exhaled through his nose and eyed the bottle. He gave it a little shake. "I'm going to need more of this. Poor kid, rough deal."

George raised a glass. "When do we leave?"

I bit my lip and turned to Tatiana. She gave me a look that advised me not to argue. "As fast as we can." I held up both sets of hairs. Everyone's attention honed in on the strands.

Quentin nodded. George mirrored the action. Both men slammed their glasses down at the same moment. It was a tad eerie.

I tuned the world out and walked towards the door at the end of the room. Nobody followed me. I was glad for that. My hand closed around the doorknob tighter than necessary. I held it for a moment, glad to be able to grip something without worrying about how hard I squeezed. Metal dug into my palm. My knuckles turned white before I opened the door. I shut the door behind me as calmly as possible.

My movement through the endless hall was mechanical. Doors passed without properly registering in my head. I came to a stop outside one I had shown to Cassie. It was an automatic process. I stowed the hairs and pushed the door open to step inside.

Clothing hung off racks around me. I was blind to it all. My insides shook like they were expanding fast. There was one outlet for the pressure—my mouth. I opened it and screamed. My hands wrapped around a rack, and I yanked hard. It clattered against another. I tore my coat from my body and flung it against the wall. My shirt followed. I stood there, seething.

I didn't know how long passed before my breathing slowed. That needed letting out, but it didn't do me any good. I took control and reached down, grabbing a white shirt. The toppled rack consisted of jackets. Each was a duplicate of the one I had been wearing. I pulled one from the rack, deforming the coat hanger in the process. The trench coat hugged my body with a comforting weight.

I exited the room, letting the door drift shut on its own. One thing remained. I crossed the hall to the door opposite. It wasn't a room I was fond of entering, but Cassie was counting on me. The door opened to a room borne of requirement.

A wooden rack ran against one wall. I reached out and pulled an 1892 Winchester rifle from it. I worked the lever and heard a satisfying *click*. A metal box sat at my feet. I sank to a knee and opened it. Brown leather was the first thing I saw. The bandolier felt good in my hands, but not the memories it dredged up. I buried them and slung the leather around my body. My hand dove into the box. Rounds filled my palm, and I systematically loaded the rifle, taking the time to slip a dozen through the bandolier's loop.

I got to my feet and reached blindly towards the nearest wall. Cool metal brushed against my fingers. I pulled the .38 Special from the wall mounting and went back to my knees to repeat the process of finding its ammunition. Loading the pistol was a cold, empty process. I filled the remaining loops on the bandolier and exhaled.

There was a knock on the door. I ignored it and ran my thumb and forefinger against the pistol. The knock came again. "Yeah?"

"John..." Tatiana stopped.

While waiting for her to continue, I grabbed a holster of burgundy leather. The revolver slipped into it while I undid my belt.

"We're ready."

The two words had a great amount of weight behind them. I deafened myself to them as I pushed the belt through a loop and secured the holster to my hip. The rifle followed as I slung it over my shoulder. "Are you, Tatiana?"

She didn't respond.

"Last time you were in a fight...it didn't go well."

Tatiana snorted. "The trolls were nothing."

"That's not the fight I was talking about."

Something in her voice changed. It grew hollow and distant. "I know. Death and rebirth is part of my kind's fate."

It was true, but that didn't mean I had to like it. "Your memories follow that cycle too. I don't like that."

She ignored me this time.

I cleared my throat and pulled the door open. A sleeveless tunic of chainmail hung over a flannel shirt. She wore a pair of loose-fitting sweat pants held up by a drawstring. Her hands held a sword and shield pair identical to what she had given Cassie. Tatiana was a woman that favored practicality to appearance.

She looked me over and quirked a smile. "Nothing

bulletproof?"

I eyed her back and arched a brow. "I could ask you the same."

"Toshiro doesn't believe in firearms. Neither do I." She waved a hand to her chainmail and shield. "We're traditionalists."

I waggled the Winchester. "I'm not."

Her smile grew. "Heathen."

I snorted and moved out of the room.

"John, you don't have a way to find them, do you? Thaumaturgy won't be enough, not at this distance."

"You're right." I broke eye contact and looked down the hall. "I have a door for that." I flashed her a grin that she didn't return.

The door at the end of the hall opened. George entered, followed shortly afterwards by Quentin. The former hadn't changed his attire from earlier. He carried a canvas tool bag which I presumed was filled with medical supplies. It suited George. I didn't see a weapon however.

I arched a brow and nodded at the bag.

"Someone needs to make sure you don't fall to pieces. Besides, looks to me like you've already started." George pointed to my leg. The wound had ceased bleeding but it was still obvious. "Miracle it hasn't been infected. Speaking of which—you get that mess sorted out?"

"I did." I conveniently left out the cost at which it came.

He grunted. "If I had any control over you, I'd make you sit this one out."

I gave him a look to let him know that wasn't happening. Pain flared through my leg, and Tatiana's arms came under mine to keep me from toppling. I glowered at George. "Why did you do that?"

He pulled his foot back and hefted the bag. "I was making a point. Shut up and let me dress that."

I did. The process was quick and efficient. George didn't bother going the extra distance to heal it his special way.

Quentin watched from the back. One of his hands

rested on the pommel of his sword. Like Tatiana, he had chosen to forgo modern weaponry. He caught me staring and gave me a look.

I shot it back and shared it with the other two. "I'm surrounded by antiques. I finally understand what it feels like to be Cassie—ergnh!" I winced as George's fingers dug into the tissue around my wound.

"Sorry, I'm old, fingers slipped." His face was neutral, but a light danced in his eyes.

"Of course." I pulled away from him and Tatiana. "Let's go. Cassie is counting on us."

They fell into step behind me as I led them down the hall. Doors blended in a dervish of varying colors like a children's box of crayons. I had spent a long time coding them to ensure I would never open the wrong door without a good reason. In my home, that could cause a disaster.

I stopped outside a door painted a garish red that suited expensive sports cars. "Here we are."

Quentin huffed and pointed at the chains before it. "It's padlocked."

"It is."

He gave me a sideways look. "Do I want to know why?"

"It's a door to a Way."

The hall grew quiet to the point where I could hear air passing through it.

"Which Way, kid?"

"The kind that leads anywhere—once." My statement was proof that silence could indeed grow quieter.

Quentin buried a cough in his fist and eyed me over the top of it. "I believe I once told you building a home here was a bad idea." He arched a brow.

"You did."

He sighed. "Kids."

I ignored him and frowned at the padlock. "I know I have a key for this somewhere."

Tatiana shouldered me aside. She took the chain links between her fingers and pulled. They came apart like pieces of wet paper. Link after link dropped to the floor until only the padlock remained. She let it fall with a heavy thud. The entire display was unnecessary. Tatiana could've broken the chain and left it at that. She looked over her shoulder and smiled.

"Show off."

Her smile grew.

I nudged my way between her and the door. "Everyone ready?"

A chorus of mixed answers came from behind me.

My hand shook as it fell on the knob. Tatiana placed hers over mine. The shaking stopped. I gave her a look and twisted. The door opened. Everyone sucked in a breath.

The room was the vastness of space and all its possible colors encapsulated. Gaseous formations of stardust hung at a distance that gave the illusion I could reach out and touch them.

Quentin swallowed and prodded me with an elbow. "I'm starting to think you're a tad touched, kid."

I rapped my knuckles against the side of my skull. "Here goes nothing." I picked the hairs out of my pockets and held them up to the Way. The ends swayed gently towards the expanse. The pull lasted a second before they fell back towards me. *Come on.* An invisible leash tugged on them once again. A few hairs broke free, tumbling from sight. The pull grew stronger. Strands bent until they were completely horizontal.

Quentin let out a long, low whistle.

George coughed.

Tatiana tensed and gave me an uncertain look. "How do we know this will take us where we want?"

"We don't." I nodded to the strands of hairs. "But these..." I broke off as the Way shifted. It morphed into a mural painted with gradations of white. The painting was alive. Colors swam and bled together, separating on occasion. "But...I have a feeling."

"Oh, great, you have a feeling." Tatiana looked like she was ready to hit me.

I put a reassuring hand on her shoulder and pushed Tatiana through.

Quentin swore.

I dove in after her.

***

For a moment, I believed I was still in the Way. I squinted against the white light. The ground was dusted in several inches of snow that brushed over my shoes with every gentle passing of wind. Cherry blossoms stood in full bloom despite the winter. The occasional petals broke free and tumbled towards us.

"It's beautiful." Tatiana smiled.

"It is." I tried to match her expression before my head snapped to the side. Heat enveloped my cheek, made worse by the harsh bite of the cold. I rubbed the spot where she had slapped me. "That was for pushing you through the Way?"

She turned to look to the distance. "That was for pushing me through the Way."

I followed her gaze to a house that looked plucked from a shogun out of the movies. It was an elaborate estate that conjured up everything one could dream about nineteenth century samurais. I held up both sets of hairs. They lurched towards the home with a violent snap that nearly pulled them from my fingers.

Tatiana watched the reaction. "We found Toshiro."

"And Cassie." My jaw tightened and I fought to keep from balling my fists around the hairs.

Something crunched in the snow behind us. "Impressive place."

"We're not here to admire his home, Quentin." My vision narrowed and I set off.

A winding path was the only way ahead. Shaped stones raced along both sides of the path. They blurred as I picked up my pace. I ignored the fire building in my legs. As far as landscapes went, it was sparse. Toshiro hadn't done much to liven it up. He wouldn't have to worry about it soon.

The wind picked up, howling like it was being funneled

through large pipes. It wasn't loud enough to mask a sound like wooden chimes. The clattering grew closer.

I turned as a shower of snow kicked into my face. A shadow was buried within it. The hairs slipped from my grip. I fell to my side, shouldered the Winchester and squeezed. The round struck with a crack like it had impacted something hard and brittle. A shape tumbled into the snow.

I scrambled to my feet and leveled the rifle again. A dumnen lay on the ground, clad in pieces of chitinous material that looked like they had come from an insect carapace. It chest expanded and fell. It was still alive. I aimed to change that. I squeezed the trigger again. The second round broke through the armor and buried itself in the creature. Its movements stopped.

I sank to my haunches and recovered the two sets of hairs. Losing them this close to finding Cassie wasn't an option. I placed them back in my pocket.

Tatiana came into view. She looked down to the dumnen, then me. An eyebrow arched. "This is what happens when you run off."

"I'm fine." My voice came out as cold and rough as the snow and stones around me. "Keep moving, I'm sure there's more of these things around."

Something hardened in her eyes. "I hope so." She drew her sword and sent the blade crashing into her shield. She repeated the drumming.

I glared.

"It will be easier to deal with them before dealing with Toshiro."

"And alert him to our presence."

She eyed the fallen dumnen, then my rifle, before raising her eyes to meet mine.

I raised my hands to concede the point.

Quentin came up behind Tatiana followed by George. My mentor and friend gave Tatiana a disapproving look. "Is there a reason—a particularly good one, mind you—for that racket?"

Tatiana's mouth spread into a feral grin. Sword clanged

against the shield once again.

Quentin shook his head.

George ignored the scene and kept his eyes on our surroundings. He was the smart one. His face wrinkled and he sniffed the air. "Something smells like shit. Sweet shit."

My eyes widened. "Trolls. Where?"

George sniffed again and swiveled his head. "Everywhere."

Pillars of glamour collapsed on cue. A horde of blubber and muscle stood to one side of us. Trolls snarled, bristling in anticipation. An equally large number of dumnen stood to the other side.

Quentin looked both ways without turning his head. His hand went to his sword. "What's that about a rock and a hard place?"

"Do the rocks smell like sugary crap, and does the hard place look like scrawny elven bastards?" George smirked at Quentin as he buried his hand into his bag.

"We will cut through them all the same." Tatiana flourished her sword and her smile grew.

There are a great deal of things we don't get to choose in life. Many things are decided for us. Our friends are among the few things we do have say in. Mine are clearly insane. I chose them well.

Nobody moved. We might have been the targets, but trolls and dumnen don't hold much love for each other. I could almost feel their hatred for one another. It was like a web of quivering cable waiting to go taut around us. Not the place I wanted to be.

Quentin moved to my side, placing a hand on my shoulder. He pulled his blade an inch out of the sheath. The cables grew tighter as the monsters tensed. He surveyed them without turning. "I don't suppose you would let us pass without trying to kill us?" He gave them a lopsided grin.

I wish he hadn't. Trolls lumbered towards us, weapons raised high, bellowing. A wave of armored dumnen sent snow flying as they rushed us. It's never a good idea to let yourself remain between the rock and the hard place. We split.

I ran ahead, breaking free from the center. One particular troll seemed to have access to a treadmill because it outpaced the rest of its group. It raised its cudgel to hammer me like a nail. I didn't bother raising the rifle to the proper height, instead firing from my waist. At this distance, I could hardly miss. The weapon kicked and cracked loose the round. It struck the troll's bare belly, burying itself in the generous amount of mass.

The creature staggered back and fell to a knee. Its grubby hand went to the wound. It blinked in confusion. I didn't let it finish its thoughts. The next round struck the creature's skull. It fell flat in the snow. I chanced a look to my side.

Tatiana released a primal scream and rushed to meet a trio of trolls running in a tight group. Her momentum slowed six feet from the group. She came to a jarring halt and jumped back. The closest of the trolls held a small tree stripped of branches. The creature's crude weapon sailed harmlessly through the space she had stood in. It stumbled from the missed blow, struggling to lash out with the awkward weapon. Its friends bustled past in a bid to claim the kill.

Trolls aren't bright.

Tatiana dove to the ground and pressed herself flat. The first troll's backswing caught its companion to its right. The heavy blow sent the other troll off balance and limping to the side. She snapped a kick that connected with the third troll's groin. The creature's eyes shut, and it stumbled into the middle troll, grasping it for support. Tatiana arched her back and flipped to her feet in an impressive display of athleticism and flexibility. Her sword flashed against the middle troll's throat.

The troll, still grabbing its genitals, swiped a hand at her. She twisted her wrist and sent the blade clean through its fingers. The troll yanked what remained of its hand back and howled. Without losing her momentum, she jumped towards the troll struck by its companion. Her sword went over her head like a metal spike she planned to drive into the ground by sheer force alone. She buried the sword in its broad back. With a violent twist, she pulled it free and turned her focus to the maimed member of the trio.

The monster kicked its way back through the snow, a hand still pressed to its groin. Its other hand sizzled as flesh burned from a sightless flame. Nordic steel didn't agree with trolls.

Another troll caught up from the pack, coming to her side. Its hands were encased in some form of faerie metal substitute. The troll interlocked its fingers, intending to club her with nothing more than its armored hands. Tatiana never broke eye contact with the injured troll on the ground. She whipped her shield arm out, striking the new troll against its chest. The steel scalded its skin and left welts. She turned and drove her sword through its ribs.

I picked off the fallen troll with another shot.

She glanced over her shoulder and gave me a heated glare.

I shrugged and pointed to the closing crowd of trolls.

Tatiana turned away and rushed to meet them.

I chambered the next round and was turning when something hit me with the force of a small car. My feet left the ground and I landed a few yards away, rolling twice through the snow. Numbness crept over my extremities and my fingers felt too distant to respond. The impact drove a cloud of haze over my eyes and the surrounding white didn't help. I fumbled with the rifle, trying to aim at the recovering dumnen. The creature had plowed into me like a battering ram and followed me to the ground. Its shell-like armor clattered as it shuffled. The dumnen was quicker in getting to its senses and feet than I was. It jumped.

My fingers were sluggish, but I had better control of them. I slipped them into place and fought to steady the gun. A blur of red leather barreled into the monster, driving it back to the ground. I shook my head clear and scrambled to my feet.

Quentin peeled himself from the chitin-clad dumnen. He wrapped both hands around the hilt of an unadorned rapier. It was a sword favoring simple function of form. He held the blade horizontal and put his weight behind it as he pressed its edge against the dumnen's throat. It didn't require much effort to slit the creature's neck.

"Thanks." I planted the rifle stock into the ground and braced against it.

"Not out of the fire—" Quentin took a series of quick steps back, poking with his rapier at arm's length.

A troll tiptoed awkwardly at the end of it. It was a precarious situation for both of them. If Quentin overreached or, left an opening, the troll would advance. If the troll wasn't careful it would be skewered. A third danger presented itself.

Another dumnen closed in on Quentin's back. The creature was bare, save for ragged bits of leather and cloth hanging off its rail-thin body. Each hand held onto a hatchet with a head of poorly sharpened stone. They weren't much, but they could get the job done.

I was still on my knees and didn't have the time to fire a proper shot. I fired anyways. The round hit half a hand above the dumnen's knee. The creature's momentum was cut from underneath it.

Quentin reacted on instinct. He pulled back from the troll and managed to brush a hand against the falling dumnen to push it. The creature stumbled into the troll's path.

Wrong place. Wrong time.

The troll batted the dumnen aside with contempt. It was an action that didn't go unnoticed by the other dumnen. The troll should have left it at that. It lost all thought about Quentin as its eyes widened and nostrils flared. The troll's breathing quickened and it snarled at the fallen dumnen. It seemed irritated that a hatchet-wielding creature had gotten in its way. The troll changed direction and stomped over to the dumnen. It drove a meaty fist into the creature's body. The troll screamed at the broken dumnen and repeated the process several times.

Irritated may have been an understatement.

For a moment, the only sound was the wind. Everything stopped. Everyone went quiet. Whatever fragile alliance Toshiro had created between the two groups shattered.

The troll looked up and across the field to the group of dumnen, realizing what it had done. Instead of making an apology, the troll did what its kind did best. It gripped the dumnen's mangled leg and tossed its remains across the field. The broken body crunched upon landing, folding over itself.

I'm sure it seemed like a diplomatic gesture in the troll's mind.

The two groups lost interest in our rescue band. They locked eyes and unleashed a torrent of incoherent noises.

Quentin traded looks with me and nodded towards Toshiro's estate.

Both bands of creatures exploded into action.

I ran after Quentin as he raced ahead and onto the path, making for the home. "George, Tatiana!" I never slowed my pace as I raised a hand to wave and get their attention.

Turning to spare a look wasn't an option. I had no idea if they had heard me or seen the wave. My patched leg twinged from the effort and strain it had endured. Fortunately, I faltered a step.

A dumnen ran through the gap between Quentin and me. It paid me no notice as it sprinted towards an oncoming troll. Another dumnen rushed through a second later. It paused after making it two feet past me.

I didn't wait to see why it stopped. I moved up the path, trying to close the distance between Quentin and myself. The dumnen released a shrill cry and leapt after me. One of my legs almost went out from under me as I adjusted to combat the creature. I maintained my balance on the snowy ground and flipped the rifle around. My arms worked like pistons, driving the rifle butt forward. It cracked into the dumnen's face, clearly breaking its nose. I hammered the rifle into it again. The dumnen dropped. I reversed the weapon and fired to ensure it stayed down.

George came up the path, still dozens of feet away. I took the small blessing though. Another of my friends was in sight and safe. Finger-length needles fanned out in his hand. His acupuncture tools. I didn't see the reason or practical application.

A troll caught sight of George and lumbered his way. The beast held a limp, armored dumnen in his hands, using it like an organic flail. It picked up speed and waved the armored body like a child with an exciting toy. George didn't have time for it. He flicked his hand like he was throwing darts. Two needles left his grip. They imbedded themselves a foot apart. One dug into the troll trachea, the other buried itself into its solar plexus.

I took aim at the troll and fired. A plume of snow rose where the bullet struck empty ground. The troll's momentum slowed. It staggered until coming to a standstill before George. The monster heaved in place like it was struggling to breathe. I squinted and noticed the surface of its throat and chest peeled away. What tissue remained quickly blackened. I unloaded a succession of shots into the troll's side. The impact toppled the monster, driving it into the snow.

George turned and gave me a curt wave, cut short by a pair of battered dumnen. Their armor was cracked and missing in some places. They looked like they'd gotten into it with a troll and won—barely.

The duo advanced on George faster than he could react, seizing his arms and bearing him to the ground. All three trashed against one another. The two dumnen fought to hold George down while trying to take the kill for themselves. George flailed and sent a knee crashing into the hips of one of the monsters.

I took aim with the Winchester before catching a sharp breath. If I missed, I could hit George. If I did nothing, the dumnen would kill him. I chose what seemed like the lesser of two evils. My breath froze in my lungs and my heart thrummed louder. I counted the beats, waiting for the split second between them. My finger applied a hint of pressure to the trigger. The split second came. I fired.

There was a horrible crack like lightning striking a dead tree. The broad of the dumnen's back exploded as armor shattered like a brittle clay. It collapsed against George, a bit of its body pushed against its companion.

George wasted no time. He shifted his weight, rolling out from underneath the dead dumnen. His free arm snaked over and buried a trio of needles in the other creature's face. The dumnen shrieked and pulled itself away from him. It hands went to its eyes and mouth, shaking through the pain.

I loosed a round into its chest. My hands went to the sides of my mouth. "George!"

He turned his attention back to me.

"Tatiana?"

He shrugged and shook his head, running to the path and up towards me.

The battle continued on all sides. Trolls, dumnen, and the occasional outliers that broke free to come after us. I spun and raced up the hill, hoping Quentin and Tatiana were fine. Japanese doors greeted me atop the hill. Quentin stood to the side, a dumnen and troll lay at his feet.

I slowed and rubbed my sore leg. "Where's Tat?"

"I don't know, kid."

An Amazonian scream tore through the air.

We turned to face a troll that had come up the hill at an angle obscured by a row of trees. It stiffened and arched its back, eyes wide and unfocused. A grunt of exertion came from behind it. There was a wet tearing sound as blood sailed over the creature's shoulder and onto the snow before it. The troll fell to its knees.

Tatiana stood over it. Blood marred her clothes, and none of it seemed to be hers. A few flecks and drops made their way to her chin and cheeks. She flipped the sword in her grip and buried it in the base of the troll's skull. She wrenched it free with a single, controlled pull.

Quentin put a hand to the side of his mouth and eyed me. "Anyone tell you that your girl has anger issues?"

I remained silent. Tatiana had excellent hearing.

She shook the gore clean from her sword before wiping it against her shirt. "Where's George?" She cast a look around the area.

George appeared over the last steps. His chest moved with no signs of physical exertion. He breathed like he had just woken from a nap.

Tatiana's body was the same.

I bit my lip and swallowed a curse about non-humans. "Come on." My fingers slid against the side of the door, and I pulled. We stepped inside and looked around the room. It had oiled wooden floors and nothing else but more doors.

"Bit of a maze in here, isn't it?" Quentin leaned forward and peered through an open doorway.

The rifle's strap tugged against my collar as I let it fall against my stomach. I pulled the hairs from my pockets and held them up. Both sets leapt toward the room in front of us. They quivered in my grip, going so far as to split and fray. Loose strands peeled away and fell to the floor. The hairs were coming apart from the force of their own shaking. All eyes turned to it and narrowed.

Tatiana's grip tightened on her sword.

George fanned another set of needles through his fingers.

Quentin let the rapier hang at his side, nonchalant about the endeavor.

The hairs fell from my grip as I drew my pistol. I reached out and wrenched on the door, sending it crashing open to its side. "Hold on, Cassie."

Wood and screen doors vanished. A hall of cold stone replaced them. It was a place built for giants; the ceiling was high enough to accommodate an air hangar. The walls near the end of the hall recessed where beams of moonlight shone through. A stone table sat at the end. A young woman, with red hair that clearly came from a bottle, lay atop it. Her clothing was torn and shredded. I could see her muscles quiver and contract without pause. Chains arced over her body like steel serpents pinning her to the stone.

"Cassie!" My feet pounded against the stone as I ran as hard as I could. She didn't turn or seem to register my scream. "Cassie!" The distance closed. Several dozen feet and I would be able to save my friend. "Cassie!" She remained oblivious.

"She cannot hear you, Hawthorne."

I ground to a halt.

Smoke and shadows swirled into a dervish near one of the far recesses.

Toshiro stepped out from a nook in the wall. He was clad in his full knight ensemble. His gray cloak was fastened around his neck. Its material didn't appear in its solid state. It looked to be made of morning fog and condensation, flowing out behind him. He had the cowl drawn up to hide his marred face. His robes were pristine and clean. One of his hands rested on his sword as he positioned himself in front of the table.

"What did you do to her?" Any louder and my voice could have cracked stone. It reverberated through the hall.

He waved a dismissive hand. "Her mind is elsewhere—between here and nowhere. She cannot hear you."

My jaw clenched to the point of locking. The pressure grew to the point I felt I would crack enamel. I relaxed and stared at Toshiro. "Let her go."

He chuckled from within the cowl. "Are you going to offer me another chance to walk away? Will we talk now? You will fail her again."

Toshiro was right. "Fuck talking!" I clasped both hands to my pistol, tucking my arms to my chest before extending. I squeezed. Thunder cracked through the hall, giving the impression it could shake loose stone from the foundations. My eardrums lurched inside their cavities.

Toshiro crashed against the lip of the stone table. He slumped against it, both hands gripping it tight for support.

I fired again, and watched his body snap like it was suffering from a violent spasm.

His body fell until the back of his head leaned against the table for support.

My eyes went back to Cassie and her condition. I let my gaze sink to Toshiro's fallen form. I squeezed the trigger until the action seared into my mind. Thunder returned and filled the hall until the storm passed. At some point, my finger did nothing but elicit hollow clicks. A hand fell on my shoulder and pulled me from the maelstrom in my mind.

"John, stop." Tatiana moved in my field of vision. Her free hand went to one of my wrists. She applied gentle weight, easing me down.

I lowered the gun.

Her fingers dug into my shoulder without pain. "It's not him." She gave me a little shake. "It's not him."

I followed her gaze to the table. A curtain of air fell from around Toshiro's form. Ashen skin and hair appeared ghostly under the moon's light. Golden eyes lost their luster and stared at me like hollow lenses.

"A Night Runner." I shook my head and rubbed a hand against my face. "Another pawn."

"I'm sorry. I know how bad you want to stop him..." She stopped and gave me a pained look. "Don't let yourself go into that place. It's one step down a long staircase, John. That first step is easy. After that, you'll fall the rest of the way. It's how men become like *him*."

Her words made it feel like the cold chains holding Cassie slid through my veins, making their way to my heart.

"It was never easy. It was the hardest thing I had to learn." Toshiro's voice came from the recess the Night Runner had appeared from. His armor looked to be authentic, pulled from one of the eras when samurai fought one another at the behest of their feudal lords. It was the color of dried blood, and each visible piece had its collection of nicks and dings. His face was clear and unmasked underneath the horned helm.

I noticed his other arm seemed functional. It was a neat trick, considering I had severed it. *What in the world and Neravene did that cost him?* I had done something much like that in dealing with Nox. Toshiro made a deal with someone, and it could come back to haunt us all.

Quentin sucked in a breath. "What in the world happened to your face, Toshi?"

The samurai growled and pulled a demonic mask from his side, fastening it to obscure his face. He pulled a shorter variant of his katana from a scabbard on his waist and pointed it at me.

My friend and mentor turned his head slightly towards me, raising a brow. "You did that?"

"Not alone."

Quentin let out a low whistle and faced Toshiro. "Good job, kid. It's an improvement, Toshi. Now, if you don't terribly mind, move aside, sprat." He motioned with his hand like he was shooing a fly.

The samurai bristled in his armor. His gaze narrowed on Quentin. "I have never been fond of killing—never. Your death will be the exception."

Quentin bowed with a flourish of his hands.

I took a step closer and holstered my pistol. I wasn't going to bother appealing to the lunatic. "Toshiro, you're going to die. Step aside, and I'll make it clean."

He laughed.

"Look around you. Your army is fighting itself. Did you really expect dumnen and trolls to put their loyalty to you above themselves and their greed? What did you convince them with? Money? Power?"

"Both—a hollow promise. They're weak. Cruel things manipulated by simple desires."

"Don't let them hear you say that. They don't know what you're really planning, do they?"

He shook his head.

"How did you convince Night Runners to help you?"

"There is still quite a large bounty on young Winters." He pointed to me. "Not to mention a great deal for your death, Hawthorne."

"They're going to be wiped out—we all will. No one is going to be around to collect those bounties."

"Hai, that is the plan. A new beginning without us—without the corruptible and broken. A fairer world."

I looked to the ground for a moment. "Oh, you idiot. There's no such thing as a fair world; there never was, and that's not its point. It has always been about just doing better. Picking up the broken pieces wherever we can and leaving something better behind. I don't know if it will ever become a fair place, but it will become a better one. It has always been on that road—improving slowly. We just can't see it!"

"My way will be fair, balanced—clean."

"And how many more pawns will you have to throw away to make that happen?"

He took a step back as my words rocked him.

"People and things aren't pawns, Toshiro. And in your fair world, remember this, everyone is a king when there is no one left to pawn. In my years of living, I've learned one thing: kings, more often than not, cause a great deal of harm. It's when men and women think themselves greater than others—untouchable—that we have a lot of problems. People like you. You don't get to make that sort of decision!"

"The decision was made for me by others." The heat raised in his voice. "And as for pawns..." He threw his arm to the side, cutting through the air.

The far walls of the hall sounded the way oceans would if filled with stoppers, and all of them had been pulled. Vortexes of marbled white and gray appeared. Four Ways.

As if one wasn't enough trouble these days.

Night Runners spilled out from each Way, filling the hall and stacking the odds vastly in Toshiro's favor.

Tatiana's head rocked like it was on a string that was suddenly jerked. She gave me a look that caused me to recoil. Her sockets deepened and darkened around her lids like bruising. Tatiana's skin thinned and appeared too tight for her face. Her lips paled as she grew gaunter. She turned her gaze to Toshiro and held it for a moment.

The Night Runners exchanged worried glances and moved themselves from Toshiro's space like a sea being parted.

Tatiana exhaled then inhaled like she was starved for breath.

I grabbed her tight and helped steady her. "Are you okay?"

"I'm fine..." She broke off and gave Toshiro a heated glare. "He won't be though."

"Is that *you* saying that, or did your *other half* make that choice?"

She gave me a smile that would have made any hungry wolf proud. "Both."

I matched her smile. "Works for me." My smile twisted and turned into something darker when I stared at Toshiro. "Hear that? You're already finished. It's been decided."

He roared and drew his other sword. "You think one of *his* little birds frightens me? I will break the chooser and her predictions." Toshiro slashed the air with his katana. "Kill them all!"

Chapter Forty

Waves of Night Runners charged, ready to break ashore. It's never great being the shore.

The four of us backpedaled to put a bit more distance between us and the approaching horde. They drew closer. Stone shook and shuddered from their weight and screams. It was a primordial thing that caused my blood to throb.

Fabric and wood splintered and tore behind us. Trolls and dumnen stormed the room, caught in their own fury. It became a battle on all sides.

I raised my rifle and unloaded a triplicate of shots. Three Night Runners tumbled like a rug had been pulled from under their feet.

Tatiana screamed and leapt from the group. Her sword arced towards a dumnen's collarbone. She used her blade like a club, beating against the armor until it gave and her sword buried deep in the meat of its torso. The heel of her foot impacted the dumnen's chest and drove its body to the ground. She recovered, springing back as she whipped her blade in a horizontal slash. Its tip clipped the unprotected edge of another dumnen's wrist.

The creature pulled back and wailed.

Tatiana moved to silence the screams. She sank her weight as she closed the distance. Her legs straightened as she drove the sword from her waist into the dumnen's belly. The weapon's point cut through the monster's spine and came out its back. She didn't take any chances. Tatiana pulled the blade free and swung with a double-handed grip. The sword passed through the dumnen's neck. She released a triumphant scream and banged her sword to the shield. It roused us and drew the attention of every creature near her.

Quentin stood locked at the edge of an invisible triangle

consisting of himself, a Night Runner, and troll. He rolled his wrist and sent his rapier into a circular pattern. With a feigned lunge, he sent the troll stumbling back in caution. It collided with another Night Runner. The troll's bulk knocked the elf to the ground. It pounded a fist into the ground and snarled. The Night Runner whirled around and pointed a finger at the troll. It shouted something in a foreign tongue.

A handful of Night Runners disengaged their fights and swarmed the troll. Skin, sinew, and gore filled the air. The troll's mutilated husk crashed to the floor.

The Night Runner eyeing Quentin attacked. It flourished a pair of curved blades in a dizzying pattern. Quentin's eyes lit in amusement and stepped back, pointing the tip of his rapier over the Night Runner's shoulder.

"You should pay attention behind you." Quentin moved out of the line of fire.

I emptied what remained of the Winchester's ammunition. Each shot cracked into the elf's back until the only movement from the creature came from the rounds' impacts.

Quentin didn't have time to reply with thanks. He was swept into a fight with four dumnen trying to circle him. A pair of Night Runners dove into the fray.

George yelled, drawing my attention as my fingers fumbled to pull bullets free from my bandolier and load the rifle. His back was against a stone wall. All that kept a pair of trolls from flattening him against it was the needles he brandished. If he took a second to throw any of them, the trolls would move in and use their bulk and momentum to crush him. It was a suicidal situation for all parties. One wrong move, and all three could die.

Two out of three deaths were acceptable to me. The round slipped into the rifle, and I worked the lever. A pair of arms wrapped around my waist, twisting until I followed their owner to the ground. The Night Runner scrambled to right herself atop me. She brandished a pair of curved daggers with jagged teeth. Her legs pressed tight against my ribs as she straddled me. If the daggers didn't kill me, the pressure would injure my sides. I floundered and batted her weapons with the rifle. It wasn't ideal, but it worked. The rifle's size and density helped fend off the blades.

Time seemed to stretch as I took in the mayhem around me. *This is what Toshiro wanted?*

Three fronts of pressure brought me back to reality. My sides ached, and the Night Runner bore down on me with her daggers. The rifle was the only thing staving off the daggers from slicing my throat. A fire built in my arms and shoulders. I grunted and demanded increased effort from them. I upset the Night Runner's balance with a sudden exertion of force. She leaned back, creating enough space for me to aim the rifle at her, albeit poorly. Accuracy hardly mattered given the distance.

The rifle bucked against my chest as it discharged. Her head snapped back like she had received an uppercut from a troll. The Night Runner fell back and over my legs. My feet kicked against the floor as I dug my heels in to push me away from the scene. George was still pinned in place by the two trolls flanking him. I rolled to my belly and fired.

The round hurtled past them striking stone. Both trolls blinked and swatted the air like they were fending off unseen insects. George took the moment to rush the gap between them. His arms blurred as he buried several needles into the sides of both trolls. They flailed in agony. Their hands went to their hips and froze an inch from the needles. They twitched in a mixture of pain and the uncertainty in removing the needles at the cost of touching steel. George paid them no mind, moving towards another group of mixed fiends.

The scene around me was like being caught in a tornado of furious limbs, and weapons.

I tuned it out, searching for the eye of the storm. A flash of red peeked from the swaths of other colors. Toshiro hadn't moved since the fight broke out. He stood like a lone sentry, guarding the table and Cassie. I got to my feet, taking hold of the rifle by its barrel as I did. A dumnen staggered by and paid me no heed. Its head wrenched to the side with a vicious crack as I sent the butt of the rifle against it like a club. I brought the end of the rifle down on its skull. Wood and chitin crashed, shattering as they met.

My feet left the ground as something took hold of the Winchester's butt and pulled. A troll had seized its end and snatched the weapon from me. With little effort, it succeeded in crushing the back end of the rifle. It tossed it aside with contempt and advanced on me. I didn't have time for this. A Night Runner was pressed back by a feral assault from a dumnen ahead. I reached out and grabbed the elf by its shoulders and pulled. I took its place as it stumbled into the path of the troll.

The dumnen paused, taken aback by the sudden switch. I didn't give it a chance to resituate itself. The heel of my palm rocketed into its chin, forcing it to take several steps back. I extended my arm like a stiff rod and carried my momentum forward. It struck the dumnen around its throat, toppling it flat to the ground. Slowing my pace wasn't an option. I tucked low as I approached an unaware Night Runner. I sprung to full height at the last moment, driving my shoulder and weight into the elf's side. It spiraled out of control and to the ground.

My lungs felt tight and compressed the harder I worked to close the distance between Toshiro and me. The battle was like watching swarms of warring hornet hives. I picked my way through them until I broke free of the largest concentration of creatures.

Toshiro stood as the definition of calm.

I tore the pistol free of its holster and pointed it at his head. Before he had any chance to react, I squeezed. *Click.*

He didn't move. "Is that all?"

"Is that all?" I echoed. "Look around you. This is chaos! This is what you wanted?"

Toshiro shook his head like I didn't understand. "No, not wanted—*needed.* Sometimes a thing becomes so corrupted—so filled with rot—it must be burned away. There are times when we need to start over. It is not so different now."

How broken does someone have to be to see the word like that?

He walked away from me, circling the table until he stopped at the other end. One of his hands fell to Cassie's cheek and made its way to her chin.

Every ligament in my body went tight. "Don't touch her!"

Toshiro lifted his gaze. His eyes widened slightly before returning to normal. He pulled his hand from her face.

I calmed. It was short-lived.

His hand blurred across her face, splitting her lip as it passed by.

Something ingrained in me took hold. I pulled a round from the bandolier as I opened the cylinder. It was a smooth and quick process of loading the round. I snapped the cylinder shut with a snap of my wrist and fired at Toshiro.

Cassie screamed as she woke.

The bullet became a miniature crater in the stone walls.

Toshiro had already crossed the table and planted a boot to my sternum.

Electric whips lashed the small of my back as I hit the floor. Toshiro gave me no reprieve. He advanced in a flurry of Japanese metal. Luck won over technique. I adjusted myself and surged forward, taking him by the ankle and bringing him down with me.

Falling hurts. It's exponentially worse for the man in armor. A pained gasp left his mouth as his body compressed under the weight of his gear and the impact. I was over him the second it happened. The pistol rolled over the single finger through the trigger guard. I bludgeoned it against Toshiro's helm, adding new dings to those already there. His eyes lost their focus, and his hand batted against my coat without control. I lurched forward as his fingers clung to the bandolier, pulling it tight. He was reacting with no forethought as another pistol blow landed against his helm.

I yelped and tumbled back as steel flashed towards my midsection. Leather frayed and tore. The bandolier left my body, curling like a dying snake on Toshiro's chest. He brushed it aside and screamed a command. A handful of Night Runners broke from their frenzied battle and roused to his cry.

One lunged at me like it was aiming to claw the meat from my bones with nothing but its fingers. It pushed me until my back was against the stone table. The side of my pistol pressed against its cheek. My other hand went around the back of its head, grabbing it firm by the hair. I held the American steel to the Night Runners face and ground it against its eye.

The scream drowned out most of the nearby sounds.

I pushed it back with a callous shove of my hand and gave Cassie a quick look. She was conscious and staring at me without saying a word. My fingers closed around one of the chains holding her in place. I shook it. "I'll get you out of there, I promise!"

She nodded before her eyes went wide. "John!"

A ray of heat went through my sides and erupted from my back. I looked down to Toshiro's katana. Crimson splotched against the inside of my shirt and coat. My core grew cold.

Chapter Forty-One

"John!" Cassie's scream warbled through my ears like it was coming from under water.

I slumped against the table, my arm resting on the stone for support.

The Night Runners moved towards me in unison.

"Wait!" Toshiro held out an arm to stop them. They listened.

My body shook uncontrollably. It hurt to laugh, and my eyes shut as I did. The pain grew despite how hard I worked to push it away. "You're offering me mercy, now?"

"Possibly." Toshiro released his grip on the sword and walked to my shoulder as if I weren't a threat.

I looked back to the sword. He had a point, one I wished wasn't literally running through me at the moment. My strength slipped and hot coals filled my muscles. Holding onto the table was getting difficult.

Toshiro put an armored hand on my shoulder. He pulled his faceplate away and looked to Cassie. "You can save him."

There was a noise like someone racking their throat. I couldn't turn my head to see. A glob of blood infused spit smacked against Toshiro's chest.

The samurai frowned.

I smiled. Even chained, Cassie giving him hell.

Toshiro's hand fell from my shoulder to the sword. The pressure that came with the simple gesture caused my injury to scream. It was one that made its way out through my mouth. He waved a hand to me. "You can stop his suffering."

I don't know how I managed it—my body and thoughts grew distant—but I summoned the strength regardless.

"Don't...listen to him, Cassie."

Toshiro flashed me a cold glare. His arm twitched. I could see him resisting the urge to pummel me.

Good. If I pushed him to that point, any chance he had of manipulating Cassie would fail.

"You know what he wants. He's going to kill us all." It was hard infusing my words with any heat. What little I had left was leaving my body.

Toshiro ignored me, focusing solely on Cassie. "*I* do not want to kill anyone. What happens next is up to you, young one. It is not written anywhere that you and your friends have to die. The world will have a new beginning, but that takes time. It will not be over in an instant. You will have months, maybe years to spend with your loved ones. There is the possibility you will endure what will come and survive. Is that not better than dying now—here?" He waved a hand to the carnage around us.

The Night Runners exchanged quizzical glances. One of them stepped forward. "What are you talking about?"

Toshiro spun. His armored hand struck the elf across the cheek. It staggered back into the grips of its allies. They bared their teeth at Toshiro. The knight was undeterred by the threat. "It is of no consequence to you. You want the girl and the bounty on them. You shall have it all...*after* I am done with my work."

The room—the sounds and voices, my own warmth—all of it was slipping away fast. My arm quaked and I could no longer sustain the effort of holding myself up. Stone slid from my grip and I crumpled to the floor, using what energy I had left to avoid bashing the tip of the sword against the stone table. It would have pushed the blade from my body. I couldn't risk that. It was the only thing slowing the blood loss.

Toshiro watched me fall with an empty expression. "It seems Odin's chooser was wrong about who would fall."

Salt and iron ran over my tongue and against my teeth. I could feel blood staining the inside of my mouth. My lips spread as I gave him a macabre smile. "I've lived a long time. During all of it, Tatiana hasn't once been wrong about that sort of thing."

Something cold and pallid flashed through his face as he looked away. He leaned against the table, pushing his face closer to Cassie. "Jonathan Hawthorne does not have long."

Cassie laughed. It was a hard and dry thing that sounded like gravel in a rock tumbler. "I haven't known him that long, but it seems like he never has long for a guy who doesn't age. He's getting hurt and almost always dying." She laughed until it shook her body. Metal chinked as her contortions strained the chains. "But here he is, trying to help me. He found me, like he promised."

Something surged through me. It was like a carbonated cold drink. Snapping and fizzing its way through my veins. It renewed me. She was right. I did promise to find her, and I delivered. I just had a few more to fulfill. Kill Toshiro, and bring my friend back. And I was going to.

There was still hope. There always is. That is something to never forget.

The fight raged on in front of me. Tatiana refused to yield, screaming in defiance with every swing of her sword. Everything fell before her or stopped at her shield.

Quentin carved through faerie creatures in the definition of grit and grace. His rapier never failed to find its mark. It was like watching a serpent made of quicksilver. A hypnotic thing to watch.

George was a firecracker. Small, explosive and—at times—unpredictable. He was a doctor first, out of his element in this sort of fight. My diminutive friend didn't let that stop him.

None of them let anything stop them.

I had no right to do anything less.

My hand slapped blindly against stone, trying to find the table's lip. I brushed against it and gripped hard. My nostrils tickled from the cold air rushing through them as I took two breaths. I hauled, pulling my skewered-self up. Cassie's eyes were level with mine. I looked directly into them. "Cassie..." The muscles in my throat seized and burned for a moment.

I fought through it. "Look around you. We're all here fighting for you. We are going to bring you back. Don't...don't let him get what he wants."

The side of my head felt like a brick had crashed into it. Endless camera flashes strobed through my eyes as I toppled to my side. There was a scrape of metal against stone.

"Enough." Toshiro's voice cut through my muddled mind. He dragged a portion of his shortened blade over the edge of the stone table, letting its tip hit Cassie's chains. "If you are resolved to not help me, then I will kill Jonathan Hawthorne. I will kill the rest of your friends. I will continue until everyone you know and have ever loved is buried or dust. And then when you have no more tears and no love left, you will open the Way, Cassidy Winters. Decide."

Decisions are such a simple thing at first. It's just a choice. One out of many possibilities at times. A choice that can have an infinite and untold number of outcomes farther down the road. It's impossible to know all that can stem from one decision. We take choices for granted in life. Toshiro had forgotten that somewhere along the line, and fallen into a pattern of picking the wrong ones. Cassie would choose right.

"The Dark Side always makes those promises, then they screw you and blow up Alderaan. Bite me!"

I didn't understand most of what she said, but I got the gist of it. I smiled and let my head rest against the floor.

Toshiro didn't let me enjoy the moment.

An acute line of pressure made itself known against a part of my neck below my jawline. Toshiro's other sword.

"He dies." There was no threat in his voice, only fact.

I didn't bother swallowing. What little breath I had leaked through my nostrils, and I let my eyes shut. I was not one for going quietly into the night, but we had won. Toshiro could kill me. Cassie still wouldn't give him what he wanted. The pressure vanished as he pulled the blade away for the plunge.

"Despite everything, Hawthorne, I will still make this

quick—clean."

I almost laughed. He still wanted to cling onto some idea that he had honor—integrity—left. I couldn't see any from where I lay.

He thrust the sword.

"Wait!" Her words cut sharper than anything Toshiro held that moment. I heard it in her voice. She had given up. "I'll open your Way, you douche-strudel." A faint breath left her mouth before it was choked off. "I'm sorry, John."

Hearing my friend's voice crack was worse than feeling the sword through my side. People often focus on the physical pains in life. They're more direct and sudden, but that doesn't mean they are always the worst. Human beings have the remarkable gift of tenacity. The ability to shove aside their discomfort and agony for the sake of others due to pure will. It's harder when that pain is on the inside. When you're breaking from within, everything on the outside seems to find its way in easier.

My fatigue doubled like I had undergone everything of late with a heavy rucksack on my back. The sword passing through my ribs didn't just make itself known; it was like an air raid siren. It drowned out all other noise and drew my mind and body's attention to itself. All I could do was work to steady my hands and bring them to my wound to press tight.

Clarity returned, and I wasn't happy for it. My friend had lost her resolve. Toshiro had won, and I didn't want to see it. True to his word, the samurai didn't put his other blade through my gullet. He laid it flat against the stone and leaned over Cassie. "Open the Way—now."

The fight raged on around me. How much longer till we lost to the overwhelming odds and chaos? This had gone on long enough. My left hand twitched. It took all my effort to bring it to my waist and pull on my saber. The blade inched up. It wasn't a full draw, but it was a start.

"I don't know how. Opening a Way has always been instinct to me."

"I will tell you. Close your eyes and listen well. Imagine

what I tell you. Feel it, let it overwhelm you. Become lost in it. Picture the streets of Times Square when Jonathan Hawthorne entered your life. Imagine being chased through the roads no matter the time of day, morning and night, no reprieve. You do not know rest, and your head is swarmed with thoughts you cannot focus on. Imagine days of running through worlds and places you know nothing of. Think of the monsters that crossed your path, each so close to taking your life. How long did you go without meals at a time? Remember all of the questions you had with no answers. That is chaos."

I wasn't going to let him do this to her. Blood spilled past my lips despite how hard I clamped my teeth together. It did little to mask the pain. My fingers slipped, slick red and struggling to hold my saber and scabbard. I fumbled regardless. The blade inched further.

"Remember all you have gone through and suffered to arrive at this point. Think of the battle right now, fae creatures and mortal. What of the entire world and all the needless death, misery, and trauma that fills it? That is chaos, but the wrong sort. It is made by man, and poorly so. Think of how your life was snatched away from you. Remember being chased from home and having to leave those you love out of fear."

My hands slid from my weapon and slapped against my thighs. Cassie had told one person her full story. That person wasn't Toshiro. I stifled a cough and turned as far as I could to face him. "How..." I broke off as the buried cough resurfaced. "How did you know her story about leaving home, Toshiro?"

Toshiro's body went rigid. He shot me a glare, but there was something else in the back of his eyes—fear.

"Cassie, I think you have an important question to ask him."

Her chains jangled and she let out a grunt. "Toshi, how long have you been after me?"

He didn't answer.

"How long have you been watching me?"

The samurai took a step back. His fingers tightened on his short sword.

I had a good idea where he wanted to plant the weapon. I slid a foot away.

Cassie's voice dropped to a dangerous whisper. "Have you been after me from the beginning? Did you chase me from my home?"

I smiled and waited for his answer.

"It was necessary." He looked away as if the action could deny all that he had done. It was hard to believe there was enough of his old self left to feel shame.

"Why? For what? All of this to drive me here?"

Toshiro blurred forward, grabbing her by the hair and pulling hard.

I squirmed and put both my hands to my sword. My body arched as I used the motion to pull the blade free.

"I needed you here for this!" He thrust a hand towards the carnage behind him. "Turmoil needed to happen to generate chaos in your life and as many others as possible. Chaos begets chaos."

"So that's it, huh? I never had a chance? You've been planning this, playing me from the beginning. My life's been pushed and pulled by you? You set us all up!"

"Hai."

No, no, no. Come on, Cassie, don't let him push you. She was cracking, and Toshiro forced every bit of doubt he could through those breaks.

"From the moment your gift manifested, your purpose—your life—has been controlled to lead to this singular outcome. Now, fulfill it. Open the Way. Know that you never had a chance, that this was always meant to happen. Your choices were and are irrelevant. Realize this. Open the Way. Your friends failed you, but you do not have to fail them. Open. The. Way!"

This wasn't supposed to happen. Toshiro had wormed his way inside her mind and twisted everything that had happened. He made her believe that she didn't have a choice. I was going to remind her that she did and always would.

My saber came free and I hauled myself to my feet. I let loose a bloodcurdling scream. Crimson jelly flooded over my lips as I twisted, sending heated rods of metal through my insides. My wound flared as the sword found its way through a gap in Toshiro's armor.

He screamed and pulled himself away, taking my sword with him. The blade was lodged in his bicep.

The effort sapped my reserves, and I collapsed. On instinct, an arm went out, coming to rest on the table and support me. I looked Cassie in the eyes.

"John, I don't know what to do. He's right." Lines of moisture ran down her cheeks.

"No, no he's not! We don't deserve this. You don't! Especially here, in the darkness, in a situation like this. But we are, you are, and it's okay."

She swallowed and held her stare. I was shaking her, but she wasn't fully convinced. Not yet.

"It's like the faerie tales of old. They're dark, they're scary, and we're in one right now. And you know what, Cassie? It's okay. Most of us don't want to know how those stories end because we know deep down, in the old stories, they end badly. But that's not true, not anymore. This is our story, and stories can, and have been retold over and over until they have become something else. They can change into brighter things. It all comes down to choice and belief. Do you believe that you really had no choice? Or that we got here, no matter how bad it is, on our own? That no matter how bad it looks, we can still find a way out? This is our chance, Cassie, your chance. Change it. Make it something better. Do something!"

And she did.

Toshiro recovered and snarled as he pulled my sword free. Cassie acted before he could charge.

"You want chaos? Here you go!" Cassie's eyes snapped shut, and the walls tore as Ways opened.

Stone warped and twisted as sections of the walls appeared to pull away from us. The walls sank like they were made from wet clay and could no longer support themselves. Gray stone bled like garnet syrup as the Ways formed. The wall behind Cassie split with a primordial sound that signaled volcanic eruptions. The Ways melded into one, running the span of the entire back wall.

I looked into the Way and wanted to recoil. My hair blew back and the surface of my skin pricked from a torrent of blistering heat. The light that followed wasn't any kinder. It was like looking at a sea painted in hellish oranges and reds. My vision cleared, and I was able to make out something through the veneer of fire.

A field of sand the color of old brick. Tattered and torn banners hung off nearly splintered poles. An untold number of bodies, dressed in clothing that could have represented people from all ages, littered the ground. The fire flashed, banishing the glimpse into the world behind it.

Cassie did a marvelous job. It certainly looked like chaos. It also looked like somewhere else.

Toshiro's eyes fixed on the Way. His mouth worked soundlessly. He blinked several times before whipping to face Cassie. "That is not the Way! What is this?"

It looked like hell. A lopsided smile crossed my face. I promised to send him there. *Thank you, Cassie.*

"Where you belong, you douche-strudel!"

Tiles cracked along the floor. The world shuddered as if it were in discomfort. Dust leapt into the air and filled the room with small clouds of particulate matter. Every single being's eyes were locked on the Way. The shaking intensified. Air rushed past us from the opening to the room. It buffeted us with hurricane level winds, rushing into the fiery maw.

Cassie's chains rattled and wrenched on the stone table. Bits of rock cracked from the force with which the Way inhaled. Toshiro's boots scraped and slid against the tile.

The vacuum-like force doubled and my body lurched. I used the upheaval and momentum to barrel into Toshiro. The knight left his feet and tumbled into the air.

He released both swords, letting his blade spiral into

oblivion as he grabbed hold of Cassie's chains. The samurai hung in the air, struggling to maintain a hold against the Way's hunger.

I followed his example, snatching the edge of my saber's hilt as it tried to sail away. My free hand looped through another of Cassie's chains. I sheltered the lower half of my body behind the stone table, using its mass and immovable bulk to protect me from the vacuum.

A few Night Runners were not so fortunate. They released a triplicate of echoing screams as they took to the air and sailed into the Way. The winds increased. It was almost unbearable this close to the opening. It grew worse.

The sword running through my ribs tugged free without restraint or mercy. I doubled over. My scream was drowned out by the sound of the Way's vacuum. "This is what you wanted, Toshiro. What's wrong? Is this not enough for you? You wanted the world to start over, you thought it was wrong—broken—but it's not! You are. Just you." I groaned and gritted through the pain. My feet scrabbled against the floor.

"That's the problem, Toshiro. You've been viewing the world through a broken lens. It doesn't need to start over, but you do." I looked past him to the Way before glaring hard into his eyes. "And it looks like you're going to have a lot of time to do it."

His eyes widened, and he cast a frightened look over his shoulder. Countless creatures flew by, vanishing from sight. He blinked before turning away from the fires. "Hawthorne, you have done things like I have. How much suffering and chaos caused by man's hands did you witness in your wars? There is a way to make it stop. You have endured much of what I have. We are the same!"

"No, no we're not." I looked into the Way before meeting his gaze. My eyes and jaw hardened. "When you look into the abyss, it looks back at you. The difference between you and me is that when it looked at you, you blinked." I strained my body, reaching closer to him as I cast the saber into a final arc. It went through the unprotected region of his wrist.

Toshiro screamed as his hold on the chain no longer existed. He tumbled back into the Way, disappearing.

"Cassie, shut it! Shut it now!"

The roar of fire ceased. Wind no longer blasted us as the vacuum followed. The Way collapsed in on itself and everything stilled within the great hall. I looked over my shoulder to the remaining mix of faerie creatures. "There's nothing left for you here. Leave."

Nobody moved.

"Cassie, open the Way again. Get rid of the stragglers."

Every being scrambled into action. Groups popped open their own miniature Ways to return to wherever they called home.

I scanned the room for my friends. They were nowhere to be seen. My weight grew too much for my failing body to support. The strength in my knees fled and I fell against the table. I pushed my hands to my side, pressing with all my might. The muscles around my eyes quivered from the effort and pain. Another scream left my lungs.

"John!" George ran towards me, his figure blurring. A canvas bag slapped against his legs as he did. Two more people trailed behind him. Tatiana's clothes were matted with blood and torn like she had tumbled through thorny brambles. Quentin had not a scratch nor a drop of blood on him.

Of course...

The back of my throat stung, and I gargled to collect the fluid. I strained and spat a handful of blood tinged with spit. "You made it?"

George wasted no time. He skidded to a halt, dropped to his knees and snapped open his bag. "Yes—move your hands—we took cover in the nooks and recesses—shit you made a mess of yourself—now pull your hands away!" His mouth moved as fast as his hands, without pause. He snatched a parabola-shaped piece of rubber out from the bag.

"What's—" I flailed as he shoved the piece into my

mouth.

"It will muffle the scream, and keep you from biting off your own tongue. Bite down."

I did.

George's hands pressed against my wound. I wish that's all they did. His thumbs dug into the tissue, pushing against the sides.

My head went back and my eyes shut. I followed his advice and ground into the accommodating rubber. The heat of lounging under a summer day's sun radiated within the injury. My insides felt like they were tightening. The constricting tissue made my eyes come close to somersaulting in their sockets. The muscles in my throat bulged, and my feet beat an erratic percussion against the floor.

George pulled his thumbs free and turned me to my side. His hands smacked into the front and back of my wound. A fibrous material clung to my skin.

I muffled another scream.

"You need to stop getting hurt like this." George leaned back and dragged a bloody hand across his lips. "I've healed most of the damage. You're lucky; sword ran through nothing important, just flesh and muscle. The dressings will hold the skin together, won't be long till it's back to normal. But John..." He broke off and sucked on the back of his blood-coated thumb. "You're making it hard to keep my nature at bay. This much blood? This much chi? I'm having a hard time not wanting to take more for what I'm expending. Manipulating life force isn't easy."

I let my mouth fall open. Red syrup trailed from my lips and clung to the rubber piece as it fell. "Thank you, George." I exhaled and relaxed. "Tat, do you mind?" I nodded to the chains pinning Cassie in place.

She bobbed her head and moved past me. Tatiana pulled the chains from the stone like a gardener ripping weeds. The chains clattered to the floor and Tatiana reached out to scoop up Cassie. She was brushed away.

I groaned and used the table to pull myself up. My eyes

met Cassie's and I smiled. "How are you?"

"Scared." Her eyes stared at the ceiling but she wasn't looking at the stone. They were unfocused—lost in thought. Grime and tears stained her face. "Is it over?"

I nodded. "It is."

"I don't know what to do now. Where do I go? John, what do I do?"

I offered her my hand and smiled. "You're going to take my hand, Cassie."

Her fingers folded within mine and she pulled.

I hauled her into my arms, wrapping them around her. "Let's take you home."

She looked up at me. "What if I don't want to go back? Not there?"

"Well, I know another place where you're always welcome. A crazy home beneath a bakery with a hall of endless doors."

Cassie smiled. "Sounds perfect."

I removed my jacket, placing it around her shoulders. "Do you think you can open one last Way to take us home?"

Her grin widened. "I think I can manage that." She lifted her hand and motioned with it. A Way of warm, sunny yellow ebbed into life. Cassie moved ahead, leading the way before Quentin placed a hand on my shoulder to stop me.

"I need a minute with John." He nodded to everyone else and then to the Way. "You lot can go on."

Tatiana and George followed the suggestion and disappeared into the Way. Cassie lingered at its edge, watching the pair of us.

Quentin gave her a reassuring smile before leading me further away. "You did a good job. Much of it was a crock of shit, but...you came out fine."

I blinked from the half compliment. "Thank you?"

"Don't thank me yet, kid. Remember, the Ageless Court put you on probation until this was sorted. It is. They're going to want a recounting."

He was right. I looked past his shoulder to Cassie.

Quentin gave my shoulder a quick squeeze. "Don't worry, I'll feed them something good. They'll hear the truth, the best of it anyways. You'll come out of this fine. But..." He followed my gaze to Cassie before meeting my eyes again. "Word about her is going to spread further now. Everything that happened here—you can be sure every realm in the Neravene is going to know soon, if they didn't already. It's not over for the girl."

My jaw tightened. "I'll look after her."

"For how long? She could be in danger for a while."

I turned away from him and looked down the hall. Toshiro's plans had ended, but there was an endless world of worlds out there. Many of its lords and ladies could drum up plans for a girl who could circumvent the Ways and their rules. My work would be cut out for me. I grinned more for myself than anything. "I have all the time in the world."

"You do. But does she?"

I blinked and turned. Quentin was gone. Cassie hooked a thumb to the Way. I shook my head and tried to keep my grin from widening. "Always has to have the last word." I walked over to Cassie and put an arm around her. "Come on, let's go home."

"Home, and food. I'm freaking starving."

I snorted and nodded as I ushered her towards the Way. Quentin's words echoed through my mind before we stepped through. He was right. It wasn't over for Cassie. Not yet.

About The Author

R.R. Virdi is the Dragon Award-nominated author of The Grave Report. He spends his time at his home in Falls Church, Virginia, chasing after his dog, tinkering on cars, and building gaming computers. There are rare moments when he is caught writing or wandering in public in nothing but a robe and fuzzy teal slippers. No one knows why.

To find out more about him, go visit the following links.

Website: http://rrvirdi.com/

Twitter: @rrvirdi

Facebook: R.R. Virdi

If you enjoyed the novel, please consider leaving a review. They help the author.

www.ingramcontent.com/pod-product-compliance
Lightning Source LLC
Chambersburg PA
CBHW030551310726
48979CB00011B/2107/J

* 9 7 8 0 9 9 8 1 0 4 9 2 8 *